A Very Marietta Christmas

Jane Porter
Megan Crane
Roxanne Snopek

TULE
PUBLISHING

Contents

The Kidnapped Christmas Bride

A Taming of the Sheenans Story

Jane Porter

Chapter One

I T WAS QUIET in the truck.

The kind of quiet that made Trey know trouble was brewing. And if anyone knew trouble, it was he, Trey Sheenan, voted least likely to succeed (at anything legal, moral, or responsible) his senior year at Marietta High.

At eighteen, he'd been proud of his reputation. It'd been hard earned, with rides in the back of sheriffs' cars, visits to court, trips to juvenile hall, and later, extended stays at Montana's delightful Pine Hills, where bad boys were sent to be sorted out. *Reformed.*

It hadn't worked.

Trey Sheenan was so bad there was no sorting him out. Maybe back then he hadn't wanted to be sorted out, and so he'd continued his wild ways, elevating trouble to an art form, growing from a hot-headed teenager with zero self-control, to a hot-headed man with questionable self-control.

Now at thirty-six, after four years in Montana's correctional system, he was tired of trouble and sick of his reputation.

Just hours ago he'd been paroled, a whole year early. It'd come as a shock when the warden came to him early this morning, letting him know that he was being released today. Trey knew his brothers had been working on getting him released early for good behavior, as Trey had become a model inmate (at least after the first year), and the back bone of the prison system's successful MCE Ranch, but he'd never imagined he'd be out now. In time for Christmas.

It gave him pause. Made him hope. Fueled his resolve to sort things out with McKenna.

He missed her and his boy TJ so much that he felt dead inside. But now he was out, coming home. Finally he had the opportunity to make things right.

"It was sure good to see you step outside those gates," Troy said, breaking the silence.

Trey nodded, remembering the moment he'd spotted Troy standing outside the prison entrance in front of his big black SUV. He'd nearly smiled. And then when Troy clapped him in a big hard bear hug, Trey's eyes had stung.

It'd been a long time since he'd been hugged by anyone. A long time since he'd felt like anything, or anyone.

Prison had done the trick, breaking him down, hollowing him out, teaching him humility and gratitude.

Humility and gratitude, along with loneliness, shame and pain.

His dad had died while he was at Deer Lodge, last March. He hadn't been allowed to attend the funeral. Talk about pain.

He shifted ever so slightly in the passenger seat and flexed his right foot to ease the tension building inside of him, aware that Troy might not actually be looking at him, but he was keeping him in his peripheral vision. Smart. You didn't let a Sheenan out of your sight. Especially not Trey the Dangerous. Trey the Destroyer. Hadn't he even tattooed that on the inside of his bicep on his nineteenth birthday? What a joke he'd been.

What an ass he'd become.

"Should hit Bozeman in thirty minutes or so," Troy said.

Trey said nothing.

"Want to stop for anything? Need anything?"

Trey shook his head. Silence descended. Troy ran a hand over his jaw. It really was too quiet in the truck, what with the volume down on the Sirius radio station, muffling the country songs, making the lyrics an annoying mumbo jumbo, so that the only other sound was the salted asphalt of I-90 beneath the tires, and the windshield wiper blades swishing back and forth, resolutely batting away the falling snow.

He itched to lean forward and turn up the radio volume, but it wasn't his truck and he didn't want to be demanding. He needed to prove to his family and community that he wasn't the hot-head Sheenan that intimidated and destroyed, but a man who protected. He was ready to show everyone who he really was. A solid, responsible man, a *good man*, who was committed to making things right.

And the first person he had to see was McKenna. He was dying to see her, and TJ. It'd been a long time since he'd seen either of them. Two years and a month almost to the day. It had been Thanksgiving weekend the last time he saw TJ, his son. The boy was three. McKenna had been so very silent and sad, sad in a different way than he'd seen before. He hadn't realized that would be their last visit. He hadn't realized she'd decided then that she was through…

He winced at the hot lance of pain shooting through him.

It'd taken him a long time to process that she wasn't coming back. In the beginning of his incarceration, she came every two weeks with the baby. And then gradually she came once a month and then every five to six weeks until that last trip for Thanksgiving when she never returned again.

He'd about lost his mind at Deer Lodge. He'd died in ways you couldn't explain.

She wouldn't write him back. She wouldn't visit. She just…cut him out.

That was when he truly suffered. That was when prison became a living hell. He was trapped. Hostage. He couldn't do anything about it but write and write and write…

He must have made a sound because Troy suddenly looked at him, brow creased. "You doing okay?"

Trey clamped his jaw tight and shoved all the worry and fear deep down into that tough hard heart of his and snapped the lid, locking it, containing it.

He wouldn't let guilt and anxiety get the best of him.

He'd sort it out. Make it work. There was only one girl for him, one family, and that was McKenna and TJ.

But he had put her through hell. He was the first to admit that he'd done her wrong. She didn't deserve any of the pain and heartache he'd given her… the trouble he'd dished out in spades.

So he had one task: fix the mess he'd made of their lives.

Tonight, tomorrow, sometime this week after he'd cleaned up and calmed himself down, he was going to go to her and apologize for his stupid asinine immature self and beg her forgiveness and show her he was different. *Changed.*

She'd see that he'd finally grown up, and he was ready to be the husband she deserved. Ready to be the father TJ needed and a real family at last.

A wedding, a honeymoon, more kids, the whole bit. He couldn't wait, either.

"Worried about going home?" Troy asked, breaking the silence.

"No," Trey said roughly, his voice a deep, raw rasp. He winced at the sound of it, but what did you expect? He hadn't talked much the past four years. He'd never been a big communicator to start with, but prison just put the silent in him.

"Home for Christmas," Troy said.

"Yeah." And it would be nice. He'd missed the ranch. Marietta. Everyone.

But mostly he'd missed McKenna and his boy.

Just thinking about her and TJ made his gut burn, and his bones ache. Their memory was a pain that never went away.

He dug the heel of his foot into the floor and pressed his shoulder blades against the seat back, pinning himself to the black leather.

Warden and his officers might think it was their excellent corrections program that had turned him around, but it wasn't the work program, or the ranch, or the counseling. It was losing McKenna.

They'd been together for years, since high school. Well, they'd been together off and on for years, but in the months—or years—they were off, there had never been another woman he'd loved. Sure, he'd screwed a few. He was a Sheenan and Sheenans weren't saints, but he'd never cheated on her when they were together.

He'd rather cut his dick off than betray his woman that way.

And then his conscience scraped and whispered, just like the windshield wiper blades working the glass.

You betrayed her in other ways, though.

The drinking. The fighting. The small bar fights. The big bar fights.

And finally, the afternoon at the Wolf Den that changed everything…

"You've been home for a few days now?" Trey asked his twin, wanting to find out about McKenna and not sure how because Troy hadn't brought her up, nor had he mentioned TJ, and Troy always talked about the five year old, wanting to keep Trey in the loop.

"A week."

"What's it like without Dad around?"

"Quiet." Troy hesitated. "It's just Dillon there at the ranch, you know. I'm still dividing my time between San Francisco and Marietta, and when I am here, I'm usually at The Graff."

"Things still good with your little librarian?"

"Yeah."

"Wedding date set?"

"We're talking February, maybe around Valentine's Day since we were paired up for that ball. But things are kind of hairy at work and I'm honestly not sure a February wedding would be the best thing."

"How hairy is hairy?"

"Got hit with a big lawsuit. It should sort out but its damned expensive and time consuming until then."

"Then wait till it's settled to marry. No sense being all stressed out over a wedding."

"I agree." Troy tapped his hand on the steering wheel and then exhaled. "There are some other things going on, too. Family things." He shot a quick glance in Trey's direction. "Dad was a real bastard when it came to Mom."

"That's not news."

"He had an affair with Bev Carrigan. A *long* affair."

Trey said nothing.

Troy increased the speed on the windshield wipers. "Mom probably knew. Or found out."

Trey had heard enough. He'd only just been out a couple hours. He wasn't ready for family conflict and drama. "They're all gone now, and the past is the past. Maybe it's time to let sleeping dogs lie."

"Except they're not all gone, and it's not just the past." Troy flexed his hands against the steering wheel again. "Because there is something else going on—"

"Another affair?"

"No, but with Callan." Troy shot him a swift glance, brow creased. "When her dad passed, he didn't leave the place to her. Or any of them."

"*What?*"

"There's some talk in town—just gossip at this point—that maybe he wasn't their biological father—"

"Bullshit."

"Well, why didn't he leave the Carrigan ranch to his kids?"

"I don't know. But Callan must have been pretty broken up. She loves that place."

Troy was silent a moment. "I think Dillon knows something, too, but he's not saying."

"Those two friends again?"

"More friendly than friends. While you were gone they became drinking buddies. Every Friday night you can find them at Grey's, playing pool and shooting the shit." Troy's lips curved. "Dillon practically lives at Grey's on the weekends."

"He's not driving back to the ranch drunk, is he?"

"Usually he finds a warm bed in town, along with an even warmer woman."

"Our Dillon is a player."

"He's certainly enjoying being a bachelor."

"No little Sheenans on the way?"

"None that I've heard about." Troy leaned forward, turned up the music and then halfway through the Martina McBride Christmas song turned it back down. "There's something else I've got to tell you."

Trey glanced warily at his brother. "Brock got cancer?"

"Um, no. Thank God." He sighed. "But it's not going to make you happy."

Trey stiffened. "No?"

"It's McKenna."

Trey held his breath.

"I didn't know how to tell you, or when to tell you, but seeing as you're out today, now, you're going to need to know." Troy's eyes narrowed and his jaw tightened. "McKenna is getting married tomorrow."

They drove another mile in deafening silence, snow pelting the car and windshield. Trey stared out the window blindly, seeing nothing of the Tobacco Root Mountains and Three Forks before them. Instead he fought wave after wave of nausea. McKenna getting married….McKenna marrying tomorrow…

Unthinkable. Impossible.

His stomach rolled and heaved. He gave his head a sharp shake. This couldn't be happening. He couldn't lose her now, not after waiting four years to make things right.

"Hey, Troy. Pull over." Trey's deep voice dropped, cracked. "I'm going to be sick."

Chapter Two

THESE WEREN'T BUTTERFLIES McKenna was feeling. They were giant wildebeests swarming with flies. So no, she wasn't nervous. She was *terrified*.

Not terrified of marrying Lawrence, but terrified that if she didn't marry him, the rest of her life would be just as hard as it'd been the first thirty-three years.

She was ready to lose the Douglas off her name. Ready to no longer be that tragic McKenna Douglas who'd lost five of her immediate family members as a not-quite-fourteen year old in the Douglas Home Invasion Tragedy nineteen years ago. People spoke of it like that, in newspaper headlines.

She was ready to stop being the brave girl folks hovered over, worrying about, petting, protecting to the point that McKenna couldn't show fear or anxiety or everyone would hover more and worry more and suffocate her with the worrying that changed nothing, and the hovering that made it impossible to breathe. The only one who never hovered and worried was Trey and she'd loved him for it.

And hated him.

But that was neither here nor there. He was the past and

today she was stepping into a bright new future as Mrs. McKenna Joplin, Lawrence Joplin's wife.

She was more than ready to relinquish the title of 'devoted single mom'. Of course she was devoted, she was a mother. And yes, like all moms, she tried to be a great mom, but she was ready for a partnership, ready for a daddy for her boy, and a warm, kind loving husband to help carry the burden…emotionally, physically, financially.

Lawrence would be a great partner, friend, and father for TJ, and just minutes from now she'd be walking down the aisle, joining Lawrence at the altar. But my God, the butterflies…

The wildebeests…

They were bad. She was shaking. She was this close to throwing up.

From joy, not nerves.

And okay, maybe a little bit of nerves and exhaustion thrown in there, too, as TJ had spent the last week sick with a virulent flu and she'd been up with him, night after night, fussing over his temperature, holding him as he heaved into the toilet, measuring out thimblefuls of fever reducer and pain killer since his five year old body ached and ached so that her normally busy and bright boy was a whimpering tangle of arms and legs against her.

She loved that boy to distraction. Some said she loved him too much. But how could you ever love a child too much? Children needed love…tons and tons of love. And fortunately, TJ was better—bouncing back the way five year olds do—and at this very moment, tearing away with her brothers in the groom's dressing room. Even better, she hadn't come down sick, herself, so everything was good.

Everything was fantastic.

Which was why her eyes burned a bit, and her heart thudded. The only thing that could make today perfect was if her mom and dad could have been here, and Grace, Gordon, and Ty...

There were days where she didn't think about them, those who died at the house that day, and then there were days she couldn't forget them. Today was one of them. But then, it was natural for a bride to wish her mom was there to help her dress, and her dad was there to walk her down the aisle...

She blinked hard, quickly, holding back the emotion even as the door to St. Jame's bridal dressing room opened, and the delicate light bright strains of Vivaldi reached McKenna, the organist continuing to make her way through the prelude play list, and then the heavy oak door closed behind Paige Joffe, silencing the music.

"The church is full," Paige said, hands on her hips. "The flower girls are in place. The bouquets are in the foyer. All we need is you."

McKenna nodded and reached up to wipe beneath her eyes to make sure they were dry. "I'm ready."

But Paige heard the wobble in McKenna's voice and was immediately at her side, ruby red bridesmaid dress swishing. "What's wrong, Kenna?"

McKenna shook her head, forcing a smile. "Nothing. Absolutely nothing!"

"You're sure?"

"Yes."

"You're not getting cold feet, are you?"

"No!" McKenna's voice rose, horrified. She didn't have cold feet. Her nerves weren't cold feet. Her nerves were an accumulation of emotion. Fear, hope, love, loss, longing.

But was there a bride who didn't feel emotional? Was it such a bad thing to be a tiny bit apprehensive? She wasn't a twenty-two year old virgin. She was a mother, and it'd been just her and TJ for years. Now she was moving her boy into a new home, another man's home. Thank goodness Lawrence wasn't like those testosterone driven alpha males who were all weird and territorial about raising another man's child. He wanted to be a good stepfather. He wanted to do scouting with TJ and teach him to fish and how to throw a ball.

Not that Lawrence could actually throw a football. Or catch a pop up ball. But her brothers could teach TJ those things. Her brothers were tough and testosterone-fueled. What TJ needed was Lawrence's quiet strength. His calm, his self-control.

So, no, Lawrence Joplin wasn't a he-man, cowboy, athlete, bar room brawler. But he was invested in the community, and constantly giving back, which made him the right example for TJ Sheenan. The right example for a little boy who was growing up with his biological dad in jail.

"You look beyond beautiful," Paige said, giving McKenna's silk train a shake to make sure it didn't wrinkle. "Simply gorgeous," she added, adjusting the long veil to float above the gleaming white silk.

McKenna looked at her reflection in the antechamber's oval mirror, thinking she'd taken so many photographs of brides in this very spot, doing one last make up check before leaving the dressing room for the church. It was a bit surreal being the bride herself today, and not the photographer. She was far more comfortable being in the background than in the starring role.

Paige kept up a steady stream of chatter to try to distract McKenna. "TJ looked adorable. I love tuxedos on little boys, so cute." Paige had been McKenna's best friend for the past two years, from practically the moment she arrived in Marietta with her two young children in tow.

"I hope he's behaving," McKenna answered.

Paige grinned. "He's trying his best."

McKenna smiled ruefully. "Are my brothers losing their minds?"

"Not too badly. And your brothers seem up for the challenge."

"I think they wish he had more Douglas in him and less Sheenan."

"But you love that little boy because he's all Sheenan." Paige leaned in and gave McKenna a warm hug. "Now don't be sad," she added, her voice dropping. "This is a happy day. You're marrying your best friend. Lawrence is as steady as a rock. You know he'll always be there to take care of you."

Paige was right. Lawrence was exactly that—steady and reliable. A tad conservative, too, but she'd learned the hard way that conservative was better than crazy-ass wild. "I just hope that he'll always be as patient with TJ as he is now, because a spirited five year old is one thing, but a sassy or sarcastic thirteen year old is another."

"You'll just have to work hard to make sure TJ doesn't get sassy or sarcastic—"

"If he's anything like his dad, he's not going to be a saint, and you to have admit, he's the spitting image of Trey."

"I haven't actually met Trey, but I know Troy, and yes, TJ is a miniature of his uncle Troy."

"If only he acted like Troy…instead he's wild. Wild like Trey."

"Wild and adorable," Paige retorted. "The cutest kindergarten kid ever, with an incredible sense of humor."

McKenna smiled a watery smile. "He does have a good sense of humor."

"Yes. He's hilarious. And he just needs a good kind father figure, a father who is there." Paige hesitated, picking her words carefully. "Is this about…Trey?"

"No!" McKenna shook her head. "*No.*"

"You're sure? Because it's not too late—"

"I'm sure." McKenna's voice hardened. "Absolutely sure. At least, with regards to him. He had his chance. He had dozens of chances. He's not an option. At all. In any way."

Paige reached for the box of tissues and pulled two soft sheets. "Look up," she said, before dabbing beneath McKenna's eyes. "I know you two had a stormy relationship, but he is TJ's dad."

"Then he should have acted like TJ's dad. He should have been careful. He should have been responsible. He should have put his family first."

The door to the dressing room opened, organ music swelled in the background, and Rory Douglas, McKenna's oldest brother, stuck his head inside the dressing room. "I think they're ready for you, Kenna," he said.

And just like that, the butterflies were back. McKenna placed a hand across her stomach, calming the flutter followed by a wave of nausea. Coffee with weak toast probably wasn't the breakfast of champions. "How's TJ?"

"Looking sharp." Rory crossed the floor, caught her in a quick hug. "And you, Kenna, you're one hell of a beautiful bride. Mom and Dad would be so proud of you."

And just like that, the tears were back, and the knot of hot emotion. She clung to her handsome big brother, fingers digging into his arms, needing the support. "I miss them," she whispered against his chest. "I miss them so much, Rory."

"I know, kiddo. I know." His voice dropped low, his tone husky. "But I'm sure they are here with us today. I'm sure they're looking down on you, as proud as anything."

"You think so?"

"Yeah, Kenna, I do." He stepped back and kissed her on her forehead. "Now no more tears. You don't want to mess up all that make up." He glanced at Paige who was picking up McKenna's heavy train. "Does this mean we're ready?"

McKenna smiled through her tears. "I think so."

"Then I'll round up TJ and meet you in the vestibule."

Chapter Three

TREY SAT IN his truck in front of Marietta's St. James Church watching the second hand on his watch, aware of every passing minute.

Two minutes after four o'clock.

Three minutes after four o'clock.

If the four o'clock candlelight wedding had started on time, McKenna would already be down the aisle, at the front of the church, getting ready to say I Do in front of Marietta's most respectable citizens.

It would be a beautiful ceremony. The bridesmaids would probably be wearing red. It was a Christmas wedding after all.

Four minutes after four o'clock.

If he was going to do this, it had to be now, before she'd said her vows.

He grimaced, aware that his appearance would be problematic. McKenna was not going to be happy to see him. No one was going to be pleased by his appearance…not even Troy, who was sitting inside with his librarian girlfriend.

Common sense and decency forbad him from interrupting McKenna's wedding.

But Trey apparently had neither.

He glanced down at his watch. Five minutes after four o'clock.

If he was going to do this, he had to do it.

He drew a deep breath, feeling the snug blazer pull across his shoulders. The jacket was too tight. The trousers a little too fitted. It wasn't his suit. It was Troy's, and if the hand sewn label inside the jacket was any indication, very expensive.

He didn't have to dress up today. One didn't need to be in formal wear to interrupt a wedding, but he wanted to be respectful. This was McKenna's big day. So he'd borrowed his brother's suit, and paired it with a black dress shirt, but had passed on the tie—he wasn't a tie guy. He was wearing black boots with the suit because those were the only dress shoes he owned, but he did feel a bit like Johnny Cash, The Man in Black.

Today the black shirt wasn't a fashion statement.

Today he'd dressed for a funeral. McKenna marrying Lawrence was an end...the death of a dream. But he wasn't going into the church to fight, or to protest. He just wanted to speak to McKenna, to make sure she'd recognize his rights as TJ's father. Because he could maybe—just maybe—accept losing McKenna, but he couldn't wrap his head around losing TJ.

TJ was his boy. His son. His flesh and blood.

He loved that boy, too. Fiercely. Completely.

But that didn't matter in a court of law. Not when McKenna had sole custody, just as she'd had sole custody from the beginning, and let's face it, no judge would ever take him from his mother, not when the mother was as good as McKenna, and the father as rotten as Trey Sheenan. Or so said Judge McCorkle when he gave McKenna sole custody all those years ago.

Six minutes after four o'clock.

He hadn't slept last night. Couldn't sleep after failing to find McKenna earlier in the evening. And even though Troy and Dillon had warned him off, Trey had gone looking for her. He had to. He had to talk to her—not just about her choosing Lawrence, but about TJ, and what would happen to TJ once she married another man. So after showering and changing at the ranch house yesterday afternoon, he'd grabbed the keys to his truck—which still ran thanks to his brothers taking care of it—and headed back to Marietta to try to find McKenna.

He'd searched for her without success. She and TJ no longer lived in the old apartment complex, the one by the Catholic church. Part of him was glad—it was a crappy neighborhood—but he didn't know where they'd gone and the few folks he asked either didn't know or weren't about to tell him.

But she had to be somewhere. She was getting married the next afternoon, which meant there had to be a rehearsal dinner someplace that night in Marietta. Maybe at Beck's, or one of the other nice new restaurants that had opened in the last few years, or at the Graff, not that he could see any sign of McKenna or a wedding party there.

It was possible they were doing a BBQ dinner at one of the fancy barns, or even hosting the dinner in Livingston or Bozeman.

Trey had been sure Troy knew, and Dillon, too. But they weren't talking.

In the end, Trey had gone to bed at midnight and spent most of the night lying on his back staring up at the beamed ceiling of his bedroom, trying to imagine the future without McKenna and TJ, aware that he'd be lucky to see his son a couple days a month.

Trey, who had a cast iron stomach and nerves of steel, had thrown up again in the middle of the night.

If only he'd been able to talk to her.

If only he'd been able to have a chance to plead his case, asking her to consider joint custody, asking her to promise more visitation time…

She needed to know how much TJ meant to him.

He glanced out the window, up at the sky. The sun was dropping, shifting, soon to disappear behind the mountains, leaving Marietta in darkness. He looked from the sky to his watch. Eight minutes after four.

If he didn't do something soon, it'd be too late.

If he hoped to state his case, it had to be now.

But he dreaded what was to come. He dreaded making her unhappy. She wouldn't appreciate him interrupting the wedding, creating drama. Even he could see the pattern there. Trey = Chaos. Trey = Shame.

But he wasn't doing this because he wanted to embarrass her. He was doing what he had to do to protect his rights as a father, even if he was only allowed to be that father on a part-time basis.

It was now or never. And God help him, but he couldn't handle forever without his boy, so it looked like the time was now.

Trey shook down his sleeve, covering the watch, and opened the truck door.

Things were going to get interesting fast.

McKENNA STOOD AT the back of the church, trembling in her high heels, praying no one knew she was about to wobble her way to the altar. This was supposed to be a slow and stately procession down the aisle, but she didn't feel stately at the moment, not with her legs shaking and her knees knocking.

It was the blasted Wedding March that made her shake. Those loud, bright chords so familiar to all. The entire congregation had risen to their feet at the first one, heads swiveling to the back, one hundred and fifty pairs of eyes fixing on her.

She'd smiled to hide her terror.

She wasn't an exhibitionist. She'd never liked being the center of attention. This was definitely a lot of attention.

Rory covered her fingers where they rested in the crook of his arm and gave an encouraging squeeze. "Buck up," he said with his deep, low-pitched voice. "You got this."

She flashed him a smile, a real smile, some of her tension easing. "This is crazy," she whispered. "So many people."

"All here for you, darlin'."

And then they were walking, and she wobbled in her heels, but not as badly as she'd feared. She pulled her shoulders back with every step, standing taller, her attention on Lawrence and TJ where they stood together at the front of the church.

TJ was wriggling away from Lawrence, trying to escape.

Lawrence's hand rested on TJ's shoulder, trying to keep him in place.

In a flash, McKenna saw the future, realizing that this was how it'd always be. They were so different, those two. TJ would always pull one way and Lawrence would pull the other. She'd have to be careful not to get caught in the middle. She'd have to learn to be neutral so that she didn't put herself in the middle.

And then she was there, with Lawrence and TJ and all the groomsmen before the altar, the dark wood pews filled with family and friends behind her.

The music died.

The priest spoke a few words and Rory placed her hand into

Lawrence's and stepped away.

Rory stepping away was significant. She was leaving the Douglas family to start a new life as a Joplin. Her chest squeezed with a rush of emotion. Her life was changing. Everything was changing. She was glad. But it was also somewhat overwhelming—

"Wait. Stop." A deep voice rang out from the back of the church. "I'd like a word with McKenna."

She knew that voice.

But he couldn't be here. He couldn't be. He was in jail.

Wasn't he?

Heart thudding, she pulled her hand from Lawrence's to turn around, aware that the church had gone strangely quiet. No music. No voices. Nothing but Trey in the middle of the red carpeted aisle, and candles flickering on the lip of each of the stained glass windows.

Dark handsome Trey, still so tall and lean and intimidating even in an expensive black suit and black dress shirt.

For a moment she couldn't breathe. For a moment she just looked at him, gaze locking with his.

Trey.

Here.

Now.

For a moment all she could do was drink him in as the past fell away and the future disappeared and there was nothing but now. And he looked more beautiful now than ever before. Her beautiful Trey.

Her beautiful destructive Trey.

He'd had this effect on her from the very beginning…such a fierce, visceral reaction. A recognition so deep that she couldn't remember a time when he hadn't felt devastatingly important. Just one look into his eyes and she felt connected, connected deep, all the way through her heart and tissue and bones.

No one had ever understood her love, or attraction. Friends had rolled their eyes when she said she felt connected to his soul…

It wasn't normal, they said. Wasn't healthy.

But that was how it had always been with them.

Deep and fierce…a love that was all consuming. A love that was endless.

"Momma." TJ was suddenly there at her side, his small fingers snaking into her left hand as she clutched her bouquet in the right. "Is that…is that—"

"Hello, Tiger." Trey's deep voice seemed to rumble from his chest. The corners of his mouth lifted but his expression looked pained.

Haunted.

"Daddy?" TJ whispered.

McKenna's eyes burned. Her pulse continued to race. "This isn't the time, Trey," she said quietly, and yet in the hush of the church, her voice carried, clear, loud.

"If you'll excuse us—"

"I need five minutes."

Rory was on his feet. "You don't have five minutes."

Quinn rose, tall and broad, next to Rory. "Think you need to see yourself out, Sheenan."

Trey didn't even glance at her brothers. His gaze rested squarely on McKenna and TJ. "Five minutes," he repeated.

"I don't want this to be ugly," Rory said, leaving the pew, moving towards McKenna.

She lifted a hand to stop him. She had to control this. Her brothers would just make it worse. "TJ's waited a long time to see you," she said, voice husky. "Protect him now."

Trey winced and glanced down at TJ, a shadow crossing his

features. She saw pain in his eyes, regret, too, and she had to steel herself against the wave of emotion slamming into her, because Trey had made a lot of mistakes in his life but he had always adored his baby boy. He had always been so patient and sweet with TJ.

"Can we just step out and speak for a moment?" Trey asked, looking back up at her, looking straight into her eyes.

She started to shake her head. She started to tell him no but she could feel his anguish and his love for TJ, and it made her eyes burn and her throat swell closed.

She should hate him for what he'd put them through, but she couldn't hate him. Couldn't hate him when her little boy looked just like him, and walked like him, and talked like him. TJ was Trey in miniature…

She glanced at Lawrence, who'd come from the front of the church to stand behind her, somber and protective. "I'll be back in just a minute," she said crisply, before squaring her shoulders and marching back down the aisle, head high, refusing to make eye contact with any of the guests who'd been breathlessly observing the drama unfolding.

OUTSIDE AS MCKENNA faced him, Trey could tell she was fighting mad, her green eyes flashing, her high cheekbones a vivid pink.

She'd always been beautiful, but with her dark red hair swept up and covered by the tiara and veil, leaving her neck and shoulders bare, she looked ethereal and fragile, almost too delicate for the white silk wedding gown with the fitted bodice and full tulle skirt.

"You're thin," he said, frowning at her.

"I've always been," she retorted, shivering at a gust of icy wind. "And what are you doing here? I'd think this would be the last place you'd want to be."

He peeled his suit jacket off and moved to drape it around her shoulders but she took a swift step back. "No, thank you," she said shortly.

"It's thirty one degrees. I can't have you freezing."

"I won't be out here long enough to freeze." Her chin lifted. She stared him down. "Why are you here? What do you want?"

"You," he said bluntly.

"Too late."

"And my son."

"I've never kept him from you."

"Not true. You stopped bringing him to see me, and wouldn't let my brothers bring him for a visit."

"The prison visits were giving him nightmares."

"Seeing me scared him?"

"Leaving you each visit destroyed him." Her lips pressed thin. Her eyes shone emerald, the black mascara on her lashes wet. "He needed to be protected. He needed to be a child….innocent, free, happy."

"And so you stopped coming."

"I gave TJ his childhood back."

Her gaze locked with his, fierce and defiant, and as much as he hated what she was saying, he respected her position. "You should have told me that," he said. "At least I would have known what was happening and why."

Her shoulders hunched against another gust of icy wind. "I asked your brothers to explain."

He glanced up at the darkening sky. There were no clouds, and no snow in the forecast. "My brothers know better than to get involved when it comes to you and me." He thrust his jacket at her again. "Please put it on."

"I have to go inside. Lawrence is waiting."

"And TJ? TJ is still my son?"

"Of course he's your son."

"And you'll let him come see me on weekends…stay with me on the ranch?"

"Well, eventually, maybe—I mean—he's just five, Trey."

"I know. I've missed out on four of his five years. I don't want to miss anymore—" he broke off as the church doors crashed open and TJ bolted outside.

"Mom! Momma!" he cried, racing towards McKenna with Lawrence hot on his heels.

"Stop, TJ," Lawrence said sharply, racing after the boy. "Stop! TJ, listen to me."

But TJ wasn't listening and he didn't stop until he'd flung himself against McKenna, his arms wrapping tight around her waist. "I wanted to see Dad," he said, pressing his face to her tummy. "But Lawrence wouldn't let me."

"Come back inside with me, TJ," Lawrence said, putting his hands on TJ's shoulders. "It's cold out here and your mother needs to talk."

TJ shrugged a shoulder, shaking the hand off. "She's talking to my daddy."

Lawrence's jaw tightened in exasperation. "Come inside, son."

TJ squirmed away, glancing shyly at Trey. "I want my daddy. My real daddy. *Him*."

TJ'S INNOCENT WORDS made McKenna go hot then cold. Lawrence must be beside himself. She was beside herself. Nothing was going today as she'd expected.

"I'm sorry," she said to Lawrence.

He just shook his head, uncomfortable, and probably offended.

She swallowed hard, confused and conflicted. She should reprimand TJ for being rude to Lawrence, but how could she get angry with TJ when he was staring up at Trey in shock and awe?

"Give us a minute, hon," she said softly to Lawrence, reaching out to take his hand. She gave his cold fingers a squeeze, hoping he wouldn't feel rejected. "Let TJ have a minute with his dad."

But Lawrence wasn't in a mood to be placated. He was annoyed, embarrassed, and yes, deeply offended. "His *dad*?" he echoed, angry and surprised. "Since when has Trey Sheenan acted like a dad? Since when—"

"*Lawrence*," she choked on his name, cutting him short, squeezing his hand again, expression pleading. She couldn't do this now, couldn't fight with Lawrence, not on their wedding day. But she also had to be sensitive to TJ's feelings, and for that matter, she wouldn't shame Trey in front of his son. "I know this is hard, but let me handle this. It won't take long. I promise."

Lawrence pulled his hand from hers. "Everybody is wondering what's going on out here. Everyone is worried about you, McKenna."

"They don't need to be worried. Everything's fine," she answered.

"If everything was fine, you'd be in the church, McKenna, not out here with your—" Lawrence shot Trey a caustic glance, "*ex.*"

The doors of the church swung open again. "You okay, honey?" Aunt Karen called to her.

McKenna looked up and Aunt Karen, Rory, Quinn, Paige, and Troy Sheenan had all crowded into the doorway. Paige looked anxious, Aunt Karen indignant, Troy troubled, and her brothers ticked off.

"I'm fine," she answered, checking her irritation. "We're almost through here and I just need everyone to go back inside and let me finish speaking with Trey—"

"And leave you alone with that convict?" Aunt Karen demanded. "I don't think so!"

Trey shot McKenna's aunt an incredulous look. "You think I'd hurt my girl?"

Lawrence stiffened. "She's not your girl anymore, Mr. *Sheenan.* She's my wife—"

"Not yet your wife," Trey corrected, "still just a bride."

"If you'd let us finish the ceremony, she'd be my wife."

Trey's dark head dipped, conceding the point. "True."

Aunt Karen wagged her finger at Trey. "Why aren't you in jail?"

"Got out early," Trey answered, smiling faintly. "Good behavior."

"Hah!" Karen snorted. "Don't believe that for a second. You probably broke out. They're probably looking for you now."

His lips curved higher. "With guns and dogs."

"I knew it!"

"It's good to see you, too, Karen."

"Ha!"

Lawrence shifted his weight, arms folding across his chest. "Karen's right. What do you want?"

Trey's smile faded. "Nothing from you."

"Then perhaps you'd be kind enough to go? As you might have noticed, we're getting married today, and it's a day we've looked forward to for a very long time."

"I respect that, sir, I do," Trey answered. "And it looks like a lovely wedding. The candlelit church is a very nice touch. But I've waited two years to see my boy, and I'd like just a few minutes with his mother to sort out our son's future."

"Sorry to be the bearer of bad news, but nobody's going to be able to sort out TJ's future today." Lawrence managed an apologetic shrug. "And certainly not now, in this courtyard, when we have guests waiting inside."

"I hate to inconvenience your guests," Trey retorted. "But if I could just speak to McKenna without the aunts and brothers and onlookers, we could be done in just a few minutes."

Lawrence turned red. "And what's so important that it has to interrupt *my* wedding? This is *my* wedding, *sir*. I think you forget yourself."

Trey didn't move, but McKenna felt him tense, energy shifting, muscles coiling. "This isn't about me, Larry, this is about my son, and I'm sorry you've got to cool your heels, wait five minutes for my girl to become your wife, but I need to know he's going to be okay—"

"Okay? TJ has it made. He's going to have the best of everything with me—"

"But he won't have me," Trey shot back.

Lawrence looked smug. "Exactly."

"No more," McKenna choked, stepping between them, arms extended, a referee in the ring. "I can't do this. I won't do this. Not today." She looked at Lawrence, tears in her eyes. "Don't provoke him," she whispered. "Please don't make this worse than it is." Then she looked to Trey. "And you, stop throwing your weight around. You've been gone four years. You don't get to waltz in and demand your parental rights. If those rights were so important to you, you wouldn't have thrown us away in the first place!"

Both men stared at her, expressions grim.

"You are not dogs," she added, "and TJ is not a bone. Respect me, if you can't respect each other!"

Lawrence stepped close to mutter, "It's only difficult because you're letting him be difficult, McKenna."

She lifted a brow. "He's TJ's dad."

"Only in name. You and I both know he's never tried to act like a father—"

"I'm not going to argue about this now. And I refuse to embarrass TJ, or Trey. This isn't the time."

"But you'll embarrass me?"

"No!" She winced at the gust of frigid air, goose bumps peppering her arms. "I thought you of all people would understand how important this moment is for TJ, and how important it is that we protect his feelings—"

"He should know the truth about his dad. He should know Sheenan is no good, and has a criminal record a mile long—"

"That's not true. The only time he's ever been in trouble was for fighting," she protested through chattering teeth. She was cold all the way through. "Now, I'm freezing, and I'm sure you're freezing and we both would love to be inside and getting married. So let me send Trey on his way, and you go tell our guests that I'm coming, and we'll still have our wedding day, okay?"

Seconds ticked by. Lawrence ground his teeth together, then shook his head. "I don't like this."

"I know. I don't either. But he'll be gone soon and everything will be fine. I promise."

Lawrence stalked off, and ushered the gawkers in the doorway back inside.

McKenna waited for the tall wooden doors to close before turning to Trey, who'd wrapped TJ in his suit jacket.

"Your timing sucks," she said bluntly.

His broad shoulders shifted. "I tried to find you last night. I didn't want to do this today."

"When did you get out?"

"Yesterday."

For a moment there was just silence, and the cold air whistling through the valley. McKenna was so chilled now she wasn't sure she'd ever feel warm again. "Who told you?"

"Troy. Just before we reached Marietta." He exhaled. "I wished you'd told me. A letter…just a few lines…"

She said nothing. He was right. It would have been the right thing to tell him. The decent thing. But her relationship with Trey wasn't easy. Her feelings weren't simple, nor easily managed, at least, not when it came to him. The only way she'd been able to move on was to do it full stop. Cold turkey.

It'd hurt like hell. She'd suffered, especially as each of his frantic letters arrived, but she'd reached the end of her rope. She had nothing left. Not for him, or them. She barely could keep it together for TJ, and that was the only thing that kept her from falling apart completely.

TJ needed one whole, healthy, available parent.

He needed her to be the whole, healthy, available parent. He depended on her for everything.

And so she stopped reading Trey's letters. She took down Trey's photos. She boxed up his extra jackets and boots and things he'd left at the apartment and dropped them off at the Graff Hotel, leaving them for Troy to deal with.

And gradually TJ stopped asked about his dad. They stopped discussing Trey. There was no mention of a dad, or a dad in prison. It was almost as if Trey had never been in the picture.

But seeing TJ and Trey together in the courtyard, McKenna knew she'd gotten it all wrong. TJ hadn't forgotten his father. It might have been two years since he last saw his dad, but TJ knew exactly who he was, and where he'd been, and from the wondrous look in his blue eyes, it wasn't going to be easy peeling TJ out of Trey's arms."

"TJ, honey," she said. "We need to go back inside. We still have the wedding and the party after—"

"Is Dad coming?" TJ asked hopefully.

"No, honey."

"Why not?"

"Because he's not…invited." Her stomach felt heavy, as if she'd swallowed a rock.

TJ wrapped his arm around Trey's neck. "Can I invite him?"

"No, babe. But you'll see him again…" Her voice faded. She struggled to smile, her eyes hot and gritty. It hurt to look at TJ and Trey together. "Soon."

"When?"

She blinked, clearing her vision. "After Christmas, after we get back from Disney World."

"Can Daddy come?"

"No."

"Why not?"

"It's…a honeymoon."

"But—"

"TJ, no." Her voice cracked. "Now say goodbye and don't be sad, because you'll see your dad in early January."

"Your mom's right," Trey said gruffly, putting TJ down. "No need to be sad. I'll be here when you get back."

TJ clung to Trey's fingers. "How long will you be here?"

"Forever," Trey answered.

TJ frowned. "You're not going back to jail?"

"No."

"What about the dogs? Will they get you?"

Trey crouched down and stared TJ in the eyes. "That was a joke. Your great aunt Karen was being funny. There are no dogs. No one is coming to get me." He clapped his hand on TJ's shoulder. "I'm home, son. For good."

"You're going to live with us?"

"With you and Mom and Lawrence? No, bud. I'll be at the ranch. Grandpa's ranch. You know, where Uncle Dillon lives."

"TJ doesn't go out there much," McKenna said quietly, uncomfortably.

Trey glanced at her for a split second, expression inscrutable, before returning his attention to TJ. "You'll live with your mom and Lawrence, but you'll see me. Evenings and week-ends…whenever we can work it out."

TJ frowned. "But why do we have to live with Lawrence if you're not in jail anymore?"

"Because your mom loves Lawrence."

"But you're my dad."

"Yes, and I'll still be your dad, even when—" Trey broke off, took a deep breath, finishing, "—they're married."

"I don't know why they have to be married if you're here."

Trey clasped TJ's face in his hands and pressed a swift kiss to his forehead. "When you're grown up, you'll understand." He stood, and looked at McKenna. "I'm going to want to see him, Mac," he said roughly, using his nickname for her. "I need you to promise me that you won't keep us apart."

"I'd never do that."

"Or let Lawrence keep TJ away," he added.

"He wouldn't do that, either."

Trey's laugh was low and mocking. "I don't believe that for a second, and neither should you. I want a promise. A cross your heart promise."

A cross your heart promise. That was the promise they used to make to each other…

Cross my heart, I promise to always love you…

Cross my heart, I promise to one day marry you…

Cross my heart, we'll raise our baby together…

She swallowed hard. "I promise. Cross my heart."

He nodded, apparently satisfied. "Now go inside before the two of you freeze to death." And then he was off, walking to his truck at the curb, his black dress shirt billowing from an icy blast of wind.

TREY WAS HALFWAY down the front steps when TJ let out a shriek and came running after him, his shoes ringing on the pavement. "Daddy, wait! Wait!"

"Stop, TJ!" McKenna's voice rose, short, sharp, firm.

"Daddy, don't go!"

Trey kept walking. He couldn't stop. Couldn't turn around. Couldn't look at his son or see his face, or those bright blue eyes. Couldn't let himself remember how good it felt to hold TJ in his arms, his son safe warm and good and still so very innocent.

TJ's innocence mattered. He was just a little boy. He deserved good things, and good people. He deserved to be protected. Which was why Trey had worried all these years, worried that while he was in prison McKenna and TJ were vulnerable. He'd worried about their safety, and their financial security. He'd worried that without him there to protect them, something horrible might happen, just as it had happened on the Douglas ranch when McKenna was just a thirrteen year old girl.

Trey shuddered at the curb's edge, his heart and mind in conflict.

McKenna needed Trey to walk away now. But did TJ?

Would leaving now be the right thing for his son?

He hesitated on the curb, hearing TJ's fast light steps behind him. The boy was running, his breathing ragged.

It tore at him, wounding him.

His boy running after him, wanting him, and he just leaving...

"TJ!" McKenna shouted again, louder, more frantic.

Teeth grinding tight, Trey stepped off the curb and into the street. He had to honor McKenna's wishes. He had to respect her. He had to be a man of integrity—

"*Dad!*"

TJ's panicked scream filled the air as Trey opened the truck door and climbed inside the cab even as he wondered how did a man live like this? Survive a life like this? He felt cursed. Broken. He loved McKenna and TJ but it didn't matter. He'd screwed up. Messed up. And he was always going to pay...

"Daddy!" TJ's voice rose higher. "*Wait! Wait for me!*"

Trey had just put the keys in the ignition but now he froze, shoulders hunching.

Wait.

Wait for me.

But that was all Trey had done, the past four years. Wait, and wait, and wait.

The pain roared through him, hot, blistering. This was hell….pure hell…

And then suddenly TJ was there, climbing into the truck, his arms wrapping around Trey's neck.

"Don't go," TJ begged, voice trembling, "not without me."

Prison was bad, Trey thought, heart on fire, but this was so much worse.

This…there were no words for this…

Trey held TJ tight, breathing in his son's warmth and sweetness, aware that TJ belonged with his mom. By law, TJ belonged to his mom. There was nothing he could do at this point. Nothing he could do but reassure TJ that he loved him, and would always love him. "I can't take you now, son," he murmured, "but one day it'll be different. One day we will be together and do fun stuff together. Hiking and fishing and camping. Sports, too—"

"Not one day. Now," TJ said, arms squeezing tighter.

"I can't," Trey said.

"Why not?" TJ pulled his head back to look at Trey.

McKenna was there now, in the street, shivering, teeth chattering. "TJ, get out of the truck right now. I've tried to be patient. I've tried to be understanding, but I can't do it anymore. You can't do this now. We have everybody waiting. Lawrence is waiting—"

"I don't care!" TJ shouted at her. "I don't like Lawrence. I don't want Lawrence. I want my dad. He's my real dad."

McKenna paled. Her gaze lifted. She stared into Trey's eyes. "Trey, tell him he has to come with me. Make him listen to you. I'm sure he'll listen to you. Tell him he has no choice."

McKenna's eyes were a brilliant green, shimmering with emotion. She was angry and scared and he understood, he did. But at the same time, she had no idea what he'd been through, living without TJ these past four years. She had no idea what it was like to love someone so much and then be completely cut out...

Trey held her gaze, his voice soft. "Why doesn't he have a choice?"

Her lips quivered. She pressed down, thinning them. "He's five. He doesn't know what's true, or right, or real—"

Trey's brows flattened. "Real? Am I not real? Is my love not real? Am I not here, fighting for him, fighting for a chance to be his father?"

"That's not what I mean!"

"What do you mean?"

"He just...He just..." she took a quick breath, shivered, arms crossing over her chest, "doesn't *know*."

"Know what?"

She shrugged helplessly. "*You.*"

"Then maybe it's time he does."

Chapter Five

MCKENNA SUPPRESSED A shiver as Trey's dark head jerked up, his narrowed gaze locking with hers. For a split second she could see his shock. She'd hurt him. But in the next moment, the surprise disappeared, replaced by fury.

Mistake, she thought, inhaling sharply, she'd make a big mistake. Perhaps even a critical error.

You didn't really want to make Trey angry. Not truly angry.

When pushed too far, Trey didn't bend or yield. He didn't compromise, nor was he a man of words.

Trey Sheenan was a man of action, and she could see from his hard, shuttered gaze that he was done talking. Done playing nice. Trey had tried diplomacy and he was reverting to what he did best: taking control.

Fighting.

And this time he was fighting her.

McKenna's heart pounded. Her legs shook. She took a step toward him. "No, Trey, no," she choked, seeing him place TJ in the middle of the truck's bench seat. "Don't do this."

He clicked the seatbelt around the child's waist and then turned the key in the ignition. The big truck roared to life. He had to raise his voice to be heard over the powerful engine. "I won't have him thinking I don't love him, Mac. I won't have him believing I don't care—"

"But this isn't the way, Trey. This isn't the answer."

His brow creased, his jaw thickening. "He thinks I don't love him. He thinks I don't want him. Nothing could be further from the truth."

"Take him out of the truck."

"And put him on the curb and drive away like he isn't my whole world? Like he's not the most important thing in my life?" He drew a swift, shallow breath. "TJ's the only reason I survived in that place. He's the only reason I'm still here." His deep voice dropped as he spit the words at her, each syllable sharp and rough. "He's five and I've only had one Christmas with him and I want more. I want more with my son. And I deserve at least one Christmas with him before he becomes part of your new family with this other man."

"TJ will always be your son, Trey."

"Then you shouldn't mind him spending one Christmas with me." He slammed his door closed and shifted gears.

She pounded on his door. "You're not taking him! You're not—" She broke off as he swung the door back open. She fell back a step, tripping over the hem of her gown. "You can't, Trey. It's wrong. It's illegal. You'll be charged with kidnapping!"

"I've been charged with worse," he retorted grimly.

She shook her head frantically. "But not this, Trey."

"I don't want my son to grow up without me."

"You can't just take him from me."

"Fine. Then you can come with us, too." And with stunning ease, he stood up, picked her off the ground and dropped her onto the truck seat, next to TJ. "Buckle up, darlin'. We're heading out of town."

Trey had done a lot of stupid things in his life, but this might just be the stupidest.

But had no choice. He had to do something. He couldn't just stay there on Church Street fighting with McKenna in front of TJ and St. James.

She wasn't fighting fair. Women never fought fair. They argued. They yelled. They cried. They used torrents of words, endless words, words that drowned a man in sound and nonsensical emotion.

He'd tossed her into the truck because he wanted TJ, and he knew very well he couldn't take TJ from his mom, not on Christmas.

What kind of man would he be to separate a mother and young child on Christmas?

So he was bringing her along. Letting her come. He was being generous and thoughtful.

Magnanimous.

Not that she'd see it that way.

Nor would her groom, who they'd just left in the church with the guests and her brothers and his brother and good old Aunt Karen…

Aunt Karen would be the one to call the sheriffs. Aunt Karen would be delighted to hear he'd been arrested. *Again.*

Something hard and sharp turned in his gut. Regret filled him.

He'd just screwed up badly, hadn't he? She sat beside him, a blur of white in his peripheral vision and didn't say a word, but he didn't need her to. He knew it. He knew what he'd done.

He flipped on the truck lights as he approached Highway 89, steering with a tight knuckled grip that made his hands ache.

It was dark out. The wind whistled and howled.

He fiddled with the truck heater, the truck interior almost as chilly as the frigid temperature outside. But the biting cold was nothing compared to the ice in his heart.

He'd made a terrible mistake just now.

What was he thinking? Taking TJ, and McKenna, too?

What kind of madness had taken over him back there at St. James?

Merging onto the highway, easing into the traffic, he kept his gaze fixed on the road, while McKenna's silence felt as huge as her gown.

He'd thought he'd finally grown up. He'd thought he'd changed. He was wrong. He was still stupid and impulsive, and what he was doing now, heading north on 89 with TJ and McKenna, was illegal. McKenna was right. This *was* kidnapping.

He'd only been out of jail one day and he'd already broken the conditions of his parole.

Trey exhaled in a low, slow rush, sickened, aware that he'd just proven Judge McCorkle and Karen Welsh and all the other skeptics that they were correct: he was a loser. A bad seed.

Leopards didn't change their spots.

It didn't matter now that he'd left Deer Lodge determined to make amends and be the stand up father TJ deserved. Good intentions were just that—intentions. What mattered was actions. And just look at his actions…

McKenna's stillness only made his regret worse.

He glanced at her from the corner of his eye. She was rigid, staring out the window, her expression one of shock. And horror.

He'd failed her, *again*. Ruined one of the most important days in her life.

Damn all.

But TJ was oblivious to the tension. He'd buckled his seatbelt as they'd pulled away from the curb and now he was sitting tall, trying to see over the dash, curious about where they were going, but not afraid. From his bright eyes he looked excited. This to him was a great adventure.

McKenna must have her hands full with him. TJ didn't just look like a Sheenan, he seemed to have inherited the Trey-Sheenan-Chaos DNA.

Not good. For McKenna, Marietta, or TJ himself.

Trey struggled to think of something he could say to her. He wanted to apologize, and yet at the same time he knew that if he was truly sorry, he'd turn around right now and take her back. Take them both back.

Taking them back now, before they traveled any further, would at least allow her to salvage today…marry and have her party and cake and dancing.

But he wasn't that sorry.

He didn't want her to marry Lawrence. He understood why she wanted to get married, why she wanted stability, but Lawrence…? *Really*?

McKenna deserved a real man. A strong man who'd love her deeply, passionately for all of his life.

The way he loved her.

The way he'd always love her.

He glanced at her again, the deepening twilight swallowing her profile. "McKenna—"

"Don't say it."

"I'm—"

"You're not. And I don't believe it. I know you." Her voice was hoarse and it shook, trembling with emotion. "I once thought you were a dream, but I was wrong. You're not a dream. You're a nightmare, a never ending nightmare—" She broke off, shook her head, turned her face away, her white veil gleaming in the lavender-purple light.

He winced.

He deserved it, though.

"An Enderman," TJ said brightly, breaking the silence. "You're an Enderman, Dad."

Trey glanced at him. "A what?"

"An Enderman," TJ repeated. "An evil guy from Mine Craft. He's all black kind of, like you."

"What's Mine Craft?"

"My favorite game. But I can only play on the weekends when I don't have school and Mom lets me use her iPad."

"Is there a good guy in Mine Craft?"

"Yeah, Steve. But I like Endermen better. They're crazy. They're also called Henchmen and they kill things—" he broke off, looked at Trey. "Not real things. It's just a game. I promise."

Trey wasn't sure he liked being compared to a bad guy, and was pretty certain the comparison wasn't lost on McKenna, either.

McKENNA DIDN'T KNOW if she should laugh or cry. Only TJ would think it was cool that his dad was a bad guy.

A henchman.

Only TJ would love an Enderman over Steve, the Mine Craft protagonist.

Only TJ would enjoy the drama and be excited about a road trip with his man-in-black, bad guy father.

But she wasn't TJ. She wasn't a wild, reckless Sheenan. She was a Douglas. She tried hard to be good, and thoughtful. *Kind.*

And yet, being kind today ruined everything.

At the church, she'd wanted to be kind and protect Trey's feelings. She'd tried to save him from being embarrassed in front of his son. What a tactical error that had been, because in trying to protect Trey's feelings, she'd lost control of the situation, giving Trey the upper hand.

And he hadn't worried about her feelings. He hadn't worried about doing the good thing, the kind thing. No, he'd swooped in, and taken advantage of the upper hand. He'd exploited her weakness.

But then, when had Trey had ever tried to be kind?

She bit down into her lower lip, trying to hold in all the angry words, not wanting to escalate things further, not wanting to get hysterical when TJ was caught in the middle.

TJ.

She glanced down at him and he was smiling, blissfully oblivious to the angry currents, or maybe being a Sheenan, he just didn't mind them. Maybe being a Sheenan, he enjoyed the tension and fighting.

It boggled her mind that her son, the child she'd raised single handedly for the past four years, was his father in miniature.

How was that right?

How was that fair?

But then of course, life wasn't fair. She'd learned that in 8th grade when she'd kissed her family goodbye and hopped into seventeen year old Rory's truck so he could drive her to Jessica's for a sleep over.

Her parents and three youngest siblings were slain within a half hour of her leaving. Fifteen year old Quinn—the only one at the house who survived—had been bludgeoned like the others, and left to die.

Quinn wasn't supposed to survive. It was a miracle he had.

But that night changed everything. That night taught her that life was short, and fate was capricious, and there was only now. There was only the present. You couldn't go back. You couldn't live in the future. Instead there was today, and today was too important to waste with anger, hatred, or regret.

Far better to live fully. Far better to love completely. Far better to forgive and forget and count one's blessings.

This was the philosophy that had allowed her to love Trey all these years.

Forgiving, forgetting. Counting one's blessings.

But after fifteen years of forgiving and forgetting she was tapped out. Her patience and her emotional reserves were gone. She had nothing left to give Trey. Nothing left at all, she repeated, watching the purple sky darken until the truck's head beams were just pale circles of light piercing the night.

Unable to bite her tongue a moment longer, McKenna blurted, "This is crazy, Trey."

He didn't even hesitate. "Yeah."

She heard the disappointment in his voice and it made her ache, and the fact that she could still care about his feelings just made her angrier.

She shouldn't care for him. She shouldn't care at all. He deserved what he got. He did.

He did.

She swallowed hard, fighting the lump in her throat. "So what *are* you doing?"

This time he took a moment to answer. His big shoulders shifted. "Buying time to be with my son."

"Wrong way to go about it."

He laughed low, the sound mocking. "When have I ever gone about anything the right way?"

"It's one thing at eighteen, Trey, another at thirty-something!"

"Yeah. I know." He shot her a swift glance, his profile hard in the dim light of the dash. "On the bright side, at least I'm giving you the chance to reconsider your decisions, and maybe you'll come to your senses and realize that Lawrence isn't the right guy—"

"And you are?"

"No. Not saying that. Couldn't say that, especially not now, after doing this, but there has to be someone else in Marietta for you. Marrying Lawrence would be a mistake, and you know it."

"Falling in love with you was the mistake!"

"Probably, so let me do you a favor. Help you out before you compound your mistakes. You don't want Lawrence. He won't make you happy. You and TJ both deserve better."

"How can you say that? You don't even know him!"

"I might not win any debate competitions, but I'm a pretty good judge of character."

"Huh!"

"And Lawrence is weak. He has no back bone."

"You think he should have wrestled you to the ground?"

"I think he needs to be a better role model for TJ."

"*What?*" She shot TJ a swift glance and saw from his expression he was listening. She dropped her voice, trying to sound less agitated and confrontational. "He's a perfect role model for TJ. He doesn't drink or speed or stay out late or fight—"

"He probably pays all his taxes on time, too."

"Yes, he does. And he donates money to lots of local charities."

"What a great guy. Next thing you'll tell me he volunteers to serve up meals at a homeless shelter on Thanksgiving morning."

"He has in Bozeman, yes."

"Wow, Mac. You lucked out. Larry Boy's a real Prince

Charming."

"Yes. He is. And his name is Lawrence, not Larry, so knock off the attitude, turn this truck around now, and take us back. I love him—"

"*Please.*"

"You're so childish."

"I'm not saying you need to love me, but honestly Mac, he's too soft for you. And TJ will run all over him. Lawrence won't have a clue how to manage our son."

She looked away, staring pointedly out the window, even as his words ate at her, making her feel raw.

Trey was saying all the things she secretly worried about. Could Lawrence handle TJ? And maybe Lawrence could manage TJ now, but what about when TJ was ten? Thirteen? Seventeen?

What then?

But she wouldn't let Trey know she was afraid, wouldn't give him the satisfaction.

Instead she had to get through to him. She had to talk sense into him, make him understand that this—what he was doing— was going to backfire in a horrible way.

"Just take us back," she said, voice low. "It's not too late to turn the truck around and take us back. I won't press charges. I just want—"

"*No.*" Trey's hands tightened on the steering wheel, his broad knuckles shining white against his olive skin. "No," he repeated more quietly. "I can't. I want a chance to get to know my son first."

"Just because I'm getting married doesn't mean you're losing your son—"

"That's not true. You have custody. Full custody—"

"You weren't around for shared custody, buddy."

"I get that. But I also know how this will work. You marry

Larry and TJ will live with you and Larry, and Larry will become the Dad. I'll be that guy who sends lame gifts on birthdays and Christmas."

"Then don't send lame gifts."

Trey shot her a narrowed glance. "In the old days I would have laughed."

"Yeah. 'Cause in the old days it would have been funny." Her throat ached and her eyes burned. "But this isn't funny, Trey. What you are doing isn't funny. It's illegal. You're breaking the law. You'll be going back to jail for a long *long* time—"

"Yeah, I pretty much figured that out."

"So turn around!" she begged, heartsick.

"Darlin', I'm already screwed. Everybody in that church knows what happened. I've no doubt in my mind that Larry or one of your brothers has alerted the police. It's not a question of if I'm going back to prison, it's just a matter of when. So, since I'm going back behind bars for another couple of years, I want a Christmas to remember. A Christmas when we were almost a happy family."

"*Trey.*"

"I understand you don't love me. I won't ask you to love me. But I will ask you to let me be my son's dad for a few days. That's all I want."

She looked at him for a long minute, taking in his hard beautiful profile, a profile that glowed in the light of the dash.

He was bad….he was trouble…and yet whenever she'd needed him, he'd been there. When she'd been terrified of the dark, scared of the bad buys, scared that she'd be attacked and murdered, he'd held her and protected her, vowing to keep her safe.

And he didn't just do things like that for her. When Neve

Shepherd had disappeared in the river after the 1996 prom, he and Troy had driven their pickup back and forth along the river bank with Trey at the wheel, shining their headlights in the water for an hour, trying to find her. Trey had driven with huge skill. He hadn't wanted to give up. He'd hated that neither he nor anyone else had managed to save her.

As long as he lived, he'd promised McKenna, no one would hurt her.

As long as he lived, he'd vowed over and over, she'd be fine.

And she'd believed him.

She'd felt so safe with him...

McKenna turned her head away and stared out the window again, unable to see anything through the hot tears blurring her vision.

She'd once loved him so much. He'd been her everything.

McKenna blinked back the tears. "I hate you," she whispered. "I hate you, Trey Sheenan."

He was silent a long moment and then he sighed. "As you should."

Chapter Six

T HEY DROVE THROUGH Livingston, and continued north for nearly another hour, the highway a dark ribbon beneath the rising moon. TJ broke the silence to ask if he could play a game on McKenna's phone.

"I don't have my phone, TJ," she answered.

"It's not in your purse?"

"I don't have my purse." She shot Trey a glance. "I don't have anything but what I'm wearing."

TJ was silent a moment, processing, and then he looked at Trey. "Do you have games on your phone?" he asked hopefully.

Trey grimaced. "I don't have a phone."

TJ's brow creased. "*Here?*"

"At all." He looked down at TJ. "You can't have one where I was."

"Ah." TJ pursed his lips and thought about this for a few seconds. "But you're out now. Don't you want one?"

"Yes. I just haven't had time to get one."

"Didn't you have one from before?"

"I did. But it's old now. Technology changed while I was away."

TJ nodded. "There's a new iPhone out now, you know. Mom wouldn't get it though. She said her old one still works. But I'd like one—"

"How do you know all this?"

"Commercials. TV." TJ shrugged nonchalantly. "And from Mom and Lawrence talking. He wanted to get Mom a new phone but she said no."

Trey glanced down at TJ again. "Are all five year olds as smart as you?"

TJ thought about it a minute then shrugged. "Some. Some aren't." He thought about it some more. "Lawrence thinks I'm too smart. He says I'm going to end up just like you."

McKenna winced, even as Trey exhaled hard.

That couldn't have felt good to hear, she thought. But what did he expect? He'd never been Marietta's model citizen, but going to prison and leaving her alone with a baby certainly hadn't endeared him to the community.

"I hope you don't end up like me," Trey said after a long pause, his voice pitched low and heavy. "I want you to be better. I want you to be successful. Be a good man. Be strong and smart. Do good in school. Be the man your mother is raising you to be. Make her proud, TJ. Make her happy."

FOR THE NEXT thirty minutes no one said much of anything, but after a while, TJ got restless and he shifted on the seat, drawing his legs up and then down, leaning first against McKenna and then on Trey.

"I'm hungry," he said grumpily. "And I have to go to the bathroom."

"Me, too," McKenna agreed, thinking that if they stopped

she could use a phone and call Lawrence and let him know what was happening. She didn't want him calling the sheriff or the police. The last thing TJ needed was to see his father arrested in front of him.

"We are almost to White Sulphur Springs," Trey said. "There's a little diner just a mile or so from here. Nothing fancy, but food's warm and the floor's clean."

"Do they have chicken?" TJ asked.

"Yes," Trey answered.

"And buttered noodles?"

"I'm sure they do."

"Good. Let's go there."

The diner's parking lot was empty except for a couple of pick ups and a lone big rig parked in a far corner of the lot.

A few evergreens hugged the broken asphalt, and years of snow and ice and heavy trucks had pitted the parking lot's surface.

Climbing from the truck, McKenna's heels caught in the cracks and ruts, making her stumble.

Trey scooped up TJ who was still wearing Trey's suit coat, and came to her side. "TJ, what if we give your mom the coat? She's not wearing much and it's cold out."

"No, thank you, I'm fine," she answered crisply. "Let's just get inside. It'll be warm there."

"So stubborn," he muttered, putting his hand at her elbow to help guide her across the icy parking lot, but she wasn't having that, either, and tugged her arm free.

"I'm not an old lady, Trey. I can manage."

But this time he ignored her, and took her arm again. "It's dark and slippery and you're wearing high heels and right now I don't feel like rushing you to a hospital should you fall and break something."

"I'm not going to fall and break something!"

"And I'm not going to argue." His fingers closed around her elbow. "Let's just get inside."

IN THE DINER bathroom, a shivering McKenna shut the stall door behind TJ and turned around to face the mirror. She blinked when she caught sight of her reflection.

Oh.

Oh. *Wow.*

She knew she was in white, knew she'd been driving for an hour and a half in her dress and pearls and veil with the sparkling tiara. But she'd forgotten the impact of so much white, had forgotten she looked so very...bridal.

TJ emerged from the bathroom stall, struggling to close the zipper on the little black trousers that matched his tuxedo jacket. "Can't get it," he said, frowning.

"Let me," she answered, crouching in front of him, and fastening the snap at the waist band and then pulling the fabric taut and away from him, not wanting to catch his boxers or boy parts in the zipper. She'd done that once, when he was two. She'd never forget it, either, and ever since always zipped him up oh so carefully. "There. All boy junk safe and sound."

TJ grinned, a lopsided grin that was so Trey it made her heart ache. "You're crazy, Mom."

"I know." She chucked him gently under the chin and stood up. "Wash your hands while I use the restroom. Use plenty of soap and water, okay?"

"Okay."

In the narrow stall it took some maneuvering to get the full skirt and tulle petticoats up, and the silky fabric and train out of the toilet, but she managed without damaging the dress too much, although the hem was dirty in places, probably from the walk across the parking lot caked with packed dirty snow and salted ice.

She'd woken up feeling emotional this morning. She'd felt jittery at the church, and worried about everything going well, but it had never crossed her mind, that this was how today would go…

Practically kidnapped at the altar by Trey.

TJ was waiting for her by the sink, his brow wrinkled and expression brooding.

"What's wrong?" she asked him. "You okay?"

"*No.*"

"Want to talk about it?"

"Lawrence said after you marry him I have to call him Dad. But I don't want to. He's not my dad."

"He's going to be your step-dad. That means you're lucky. You get two dads—"

"He's not my dad," he stubbornly repeated.

"I think you're being a little mean to him because your real dad's home, but that's not fair to Lawrence who has always been really good to you."

"Because he likes you."

"Lawrence likes you, too."

"Not that much."

"Oh, TJ, that's not true. He cares a lot about you!"

"Then why does he smile weird when he talks to me? Like he's got to poop and doesn't want anyone to know it."

"Trey James!"

"It's true."

"You are being ridiculous!" She turned to the paper towel dispenser and took a paper towel to dry her hands. "And rude."

She shot him a disapproving glance. "I won't tolerate you being rude to him, either. He hasn't done anything to deserve disrespect." She held his gaze. "You know what disrespect means, don't you?"

He hung his head. "Yes."

"You're to be polite, and kind. You're to listen and follow the rules. Understand?"

He hung his head lower. "Yes."

She threw away the towel. "Now let's go have dinner and I'm going to call Lawrence and Aunt Karen and let everyone know we're fine. Lawrence will come for us and we'll go back to Marietta and tomorrow everything will be normal again."

She started for the door but TJ hung back. McKenna glanced over her shoulder. He was still standing there, small and dejected. She suppressed a sigh. What was the matter now? "TJ?"

He looked up at her, worried. "Are they going to arrest him? The police? Are they going to take my dad?"

Her chest squeezed. She felt a flutter of panic. "I don't know—" she broke off, grimaced. "Maybe."

His eyes filled with tears. "Will they handcuff him, like they do on TV?"

Her heart fell. "I hope not."

"'Cause he's bad?"

A lump filled her throat. Her eyes felt gritty. "He's not *bad*...not really."

"I heard you say that he's going back to jail and he'll be there forever."

Of course TJ was listening to everything. TJ was her little silent sponge. "I don't know what's going to happen to your daddy, but let's not talk this way. It makes me sad."

"But you hate him. I heard you say that in the truck. Two times."

"I shouldn't have said it. It wasn't nice of me. It wasn't kind."

"But you do hate him."

"TJ, he's your daddy. He loves you a lot. And we're here right now because he loves you so much, so let's go have dinner with him and not worry so much, okay?"

He stared at her a long time, expression brooding.

"TJ?" she prompted.

"I just don't understand," he said.

"Understand what?"

"If he loves me so much, why do you hate him?"

"It's complicated." She hesitated. "And I don't hate him."

"Then why did you say it? It was mean. It hurt his feelings."

They exited the bathroom to find Trey was waiting for them by the hostess stand, a red flannel shirt bundled under his arm. "I remembered I had this tucked behind the seat. It's been sitting there for a long time, but it should keep you warm." Trey gave the large cherry red flannel shirt a shake, and held it out to her.

She opened her mouth to say she was fine, but she wasn't fine. She was cold and tired and sad, worried about Lawrence and TJ and how everything had changed so fast that she couldn't get her head around it.

Right now she should be at the wedding reception at the Graff, finishing dinner, or perhaps having the first dance. Instead she was here, at a rustic diner outside White Sulphur Springs, a town with a population of less than a thousand.

She was definitely over dressed and over exposed for a Montana diner that was pretty much in the middle of nowhere.

"I'll take the shirt, even if dusty." She slipped the soft flannel over her shoulders, pushing her arms through the sleeves, buttoning the front and tying the long shirt tails around her waist to keep her warmer. And she was warmer, and she did feel better. "Thank you."

"By the way," Trey said, "there is only one waitress on tonight and the regular cook didn't show so service will be slow and the meal questionable."

"Do you want to go somewhere else?" she asked.

"I was wondering about that."

"I just want to eat now," TJ said. "I'm hungry."

McKenna glanced around the mostly empty restaurant. Just a half dozen tables were filled. It couldn't be that much of a wait here. And then she spotted the phone by the cash register. She could call from that. As soon as they ordered, she'd ask if she could borrow it. Lawrence and her family must be frantic. She didn't want them sending out search parties. "Let's just stay."

The waitress, an older woman in a red checked apron, emerged from the kitchen's swinging doors, flushed but smiling. "Sorry to keep you waiting. A bit hectic in the kitchen but everything is good. Homestyle cooking at its finest."

McKenna smiled. "Sounds great."

"And it looks like congratulations are in order," the waitress added. "We don't get many wedding parties here. You all look so nice." But she frowned for a moment at the ill-fitting red flannel shirt. Reaching for menus from the hostess stand, she chucked TJ under the chin. "Especially you, little fellow. You look very sharp."

"My mom was going to marry Lawrence but then my dad came so now we're here."

"Sounds like a great day," she answered, obviously not understanding anything TJ was saying.

McKenna managed a faint, weak smile. "It's certainly been a day of surprises."

The waitress grinned back. "Aren't those the best kind?"

TREY TOOK A seat on one side of the burgundy booth tucked along the wall, and McKenna and TJ sat on the other. Trey barely glanced at the plastic coated menu but TJ wanted to have all his options read to him, even though McKenna knew he'd order chicken and buttered noodles.

The waitress returned a few minutes later with glasses of water and to take their order. Trey wanted a steak sandwich and TJ chose his chicken and buttered noodles. McKenna was more stressed than hungry and asked about the diner's soup.

"It's vegetable beef," the waitress answered. "It's from yesterday but it's good. I had some earlier."

"I'll have a cup of that," McKenna said, closing her menu. "And coffee, please."

The waitress put away her notepad. "Cream with that?"

"No, thank you."

"Is the coffee fresh?" Trey asked.

"Brewing a new pot now."

"I'll have a cup, too," he said.

"Two coffees coming up," the waitress said. "And what about the little guy? Milk, chocolate milk, juice?"

"Milk," McKenna answered. "Thank you."

The waitress headed to the kitchen and McKenna glanced to the register and phone. She needed to call. She should do it soon.

As if reading her mind, Trey said, "You need to call. Everybody's going to be worried."

McKenna nodded. "Yeah."

"I'm sure the waitress will let you."

McKenna nodded again. She was dreading the call. It wouldn't be easy. Nothing about this was easy.

Trey was studying her face. "What's wrong?"

She shrugged. "It's going to get messy. Fast."

"It's already messy," he answered.

"Yeah, but—" she broke off as the waitress returned with their coffees and the milk for TJ.

"Anything else?" the waitress asked.

"Would it be all right to use the phone?" Trey asked. "It's a call to Marietta."

"Sure thing, hon. You know where the phone is? On the counter, up front? Help yourself. Just dial normally."

"Thanks."

The waitress moved on and McKenna looked at Trey. "You didn't have to do that. I could have handled it myself."

"Just trying to help you."

"Mr. Helpful, that's you."

His blue eyes sparked, lips curving slightly. "I can be good."

"Mmm."

"I was instrumental in making Deer Lodge's ranch program successful."

"You've always been a good rancher. That was never the problem."

"I always loved you, and TJ."

"Your love wasn't the problem, either." She sipped her coffee. It was surprisingly strong and hot. She sipped again. "I think you know what the problem was."

"You've always known who I am. I've never hidden it from you."

"It's one thing to fight at seventeen, and another when you're a thirty-one year old man with a fiancée and a baby."

"Who did you kill?" TJ blurted.

"Who told you he killed someone?" McKenna demanded.

"Lawrence." TJ shrugged. "He said he wasn't supposed to

say anything, and so I shouldn't say anything to you 'cause it'd upset you." He looked across the table at Trey. "Did you really kill someone?"

"Yes," Trey said bluntly. "I did. I didn't mean to kill him though. We got into a fight in a bar."

TJ clasped his milk, more intrigued than scared. "How you'd do it?"

Trey held his gaze. "I punched him."

"You punched him to *death*?"

"No. I hit him three times. On the third punch he went backward, hit his head on the edge of a table. He died a couple of days later."

"The police arrested you?"

Trey nodded. "There was a trial, and two days before your first birthday I was sentenced to five years in jail."

"What's jail like?"

"Bad. You don't want to ever go there."

"I used to go there. That's what Mom said."

"Yeah, but it's not a place for kids. It's not a place you want to visit again." Trey looked up at McKenna. "I didn't know why you stopped coming to see me, but I do now. And you were right. It wasn't the place for him." He hesitated. "Or you."

McKenna struggled to speak around the lump in her throat. "I should have explained it to you. I should have told you—" she broke off and bit down into her lip. "It's been such a mess, hasn't it?"

Trey grimaced. "Still is."

"Yeah." She glanced toward the phone, knowing she needed to make the call, knowing that the moment she made the call everything would change. Again.

"What are you worried about?" Trey asked, still able to read her so well.

Aware that TJ was listening intently, she picked her words with care. "I'm concerned Lawrence will have made some calls."

"I'm sure he has," Trey said bluntly. "If the situation was reversed, I would have."

"I don't think more...messy...is good for...anyone." She glanced at TJ who was toying with his milk glass but his dark head was bent, and she knew he was taking it all in. "And I definitely don't think it's good for him."

TJ glanced up, and looked from her to Trey before returning his attention to the glass.

"So what do you want to do?" Trey asked her, leaning against the burgundy vinyl, by all appearances comfortable and relaxed. But appearances were deceptive. This was Trey's best defensive position. He was always relaxed before a fight.

She clasped her coffee mug between her hands, warming them. "Avoid unnecessary drama."

"How do we do that?"

She shot TJ another quick glance. "We have dinner. You go. I call. We wait for Lawrence to come."

"I just leave you here?"

TJ's shoulders hunched up. Her own insides churned. It took her a moment to reply. "I don't know who will show up. I don't know how all the pieces will come together. I do think it'll be less—tense—if it's just me and TJ here."

Trey's jaw tightened. He looked away, out the front window onto the dark, mostly empty parking lot.

He didn't like the plan. He was wrestling with himself. It wasn't his nature to walk away from those he loved. If left to him, he'd rather stay and get handcuffed and hauled away, than to drive away, leaving them behind.

She nearly reached out to touch him but remembered herself at the last second. "I know you don't want to," she said quietly, fingers curling into her palm. "But it's better. Better for him."

Trey glanced at TJ, and TJ looked up at that moment, to meet Trey's gaze.

Two Sheenans, cut from the very same fabric.

Her jaw ached and her eyes burned. She wished she could protect them both, but that was impossible. So she had to do the next best thing, protect their relationship. They loved each other. They needed each other. And they hadn't had enough time with each other.

"I'll go home and smooth things over," she added. "We'll let things settled down and then with a little luck and maybe some finessing, we can get you two together for Christmas, for a bit—"

"What is a bit? An hour? Two?" He shook his head. "That's not Christmas."

"It's better than the alternative."

"But is this the future? That I'll have to learn to be grateful for an hour with my son on Christmas?"

"I hope not."

"Me, too."

They both watched TJ who was frowning into his milk, his forehead furrowed.

Trey shifted then abruptly said, "I'll leave as soon as we're done eating."

She nodded, grateful. "Will you head to the Sheenan ranch?"

"I don't know. Depends on how things work out."

"I'm not pressing charges. Nobody will come after you—"

"That's not the point. I just can't be there without you and TJ. There's nothing for me in Marietta if I don't have you."

"You've got your family—"

"*You* and TJ are my family. You're the ones I love. Without you, there's no point in sticking around—"

"Can I go wash my hands?" TJ asked, interrupting, showing them his palms. "They're sticky."

"I'll take you," McKenna said, sliding out from the bench.

"I can do it myself," TJ answered, climbing from the booth. "I'm in Kindergarten now."

She smiled a little. "Okay, but hurry. Dinner will be here soon."

Chapter Seven

TREY WATCHED MCKENNA'S gaze follow TJ across the diner, her expression troubled.

"You're a good mom," Trey said quietly. "He's so lucky to have you."

She looked at him, tears in her eyes. "He's missed you. So much."

"He's a sweet little boy. Smart, too."

"You're smart. Very smart. You just never liked following the rules."

"True."

"TJ doesn't, either."

"That could be problematic."

"It already is." She struggled to smile. "I worry about him. I worry that no one will understand him. I worry that people will judge him…much the way they've judged you." Her voice broke and she looked away, swiftly wiping tears from beneath her eyes.

"It's going to be okay, Mac."

She looked at him, eyes wet. "Will it?" she asked hopefully.

Her make up had begun to fade and her high cheekbones jutted, her skin pale, gleaming like porcelain.

She looked younger without the blush and lipstick. More like his McKenna, the one he'd met his senior year at Marietta High when she was just a wide-eyed freshman, and the baby sister to Rory and Quinn.

It was impossible not to notice McKenna when school started in September. She was on the Frosh-Soph cheer squad and wore the short uniform red and white skirts every Friday, game day, and with her long bare legs and dark red hair spilling all the way down her back, she looked like a siren, and yet she was only fifteen years old.

He did his best to avoid her. He didn't want to be attracted to her. He didn't date freshman. He didn't even like dating sophomores. But every now and then he'd find her looking at him, and she looked at him in a way no one else ever did.

She looked at him as if she could see him, see who he was, not who he pretended to be.

She looked at him as if he was good. Maybe even wonderful.

It made him feel funny, and his chest would get heavy and tight, and he became protective of her, not just because she was that Douglas girl, and not because she was impossibly pretty, but because she made him believe that maybe he was worth something. That maybe even though he was brash and reckless and in and out of trouble, that there was something still decent in him. Something real that had value.

And so he went out of his way to avoid her, not wanting to be tempted, because he was already far too tempted.

He stopped glancing her way when he knew she was around. He refused to meet her gaze. He wouldn't get to know her.

He didn't want to disappoint her, and it was inevitable he'd let her down. In his eighteen years, he'd disappointed everybody else.

But McKenna didn't take the hint. She didn't go away. She

shadowed him as they took the same path to their respective fourth period classes. She stared at him as he hung out with the other seniors during lunch. She'd stand with her books on the sidewalk bordering the school parking lot waiting for her ride, and yet he sensed she wasn't as much waiting to be picked up, as waiting to watch him walk by.

From all accounts she was a nice girl, and a smart girl, taking honors courses and getting straight A's.

Why was she so interested in him?

He'd thought initially it might be the good girl-bad boy opposites attract thing, but she wasn't one of those sheltered good girls. She wasn't naïve. A year or so earlier she'd had her world blown wide open with the horrific home invasion on the Douglas Ranch and she was still coming to terms with the unthinkable tragedy.

You'd think she'd want to stay away from trouble.

You'd think she'd feel safer with the nice guys that hit the Honor Roll.

She was the one that approached him between classes, the day before the two week Christmas break. She was selling Christmas ornaments—flat brass angels—as part of a choir fundraiser and she wondered if he wanted to buy one.

Or several.

She was happy to sell him a dozen.

It was for a good cause.

He'd watched her face while she talked, fascinated by the curve of her lips and the glint of laughter in her wide, cat eyes. She was pretty at a distance, but stunning up close, her face all elegant lines and planes—cheekbone, jaw, nose, lips. But it was her eyes, jade green with flecks of sapphire and gold, that made it impossible to look away.

So he didn't.

He cornered her against the gym wall and stared into her eyes. "And what would I do with a dozen angels, little girl?" he asked, his voice low, husky. Dangerous.

He saw the flicker in her eyes and the tip of her tongue dart to wet her upper lip. He couldn't tell if she was afraid or intrigued.

"Give them as gifts," she answered coolly. "Your mother and girlfriend might like one."

"I don't have a girlfriend."

"Well, your mother."

"So that's one. What about the other eleven?"

"You could hang them in your truck, put them in your room, string a few over your bed." Her long black lashes blinked, her expression innocent. "Might help keep you out of trouble."

She knew his reputation, then.

And she wasn't afraid.

"I see you watching me," he said.

"How is that possible?" she asked, arching a brow. "You never look at me."

He looked from the winged brow to the full curve of her lips. His body hardened. Damn, she was hot.

And she was also fifteen. Only fifteen.

"How much are the ornaments?" he asked gruffly.

"Fifteen each, or two for twenty-five."

"And if I buy twelve?"

"I'll buy the popcorn when you take me to the movies this weekend." She smiled up at him, eyes dancing. "There are lots of really good movies out right now, and I'm free Friday and Saturday—"

"I'm not a big movie guy."

"Then we can skip the movie, and just go park."

She hadn't really just said that, had she? For a split second he couldn't breathe. "You're *fifteen*," he said, voice strangled.

"I'm not asking to have your baby."

"Good. Because you're not going to have my baby." He stared at her, baffled, fascinated, outraged. And wildly turned on. "You're out of control."

"I'm not, actually. I don't mess around. I've never even been kissed." She took a quick breath, her smile unsteady, her confidence flagging. "But I'd like to kiss you."

"McKenna Douglas," he growled.

"So you do know who I am."

"Of course I know who you are. I know which classes you have. I know what you eat for lunch. And I could probably tell you what you wore every day this week."

Her lips parted, then closed. Pink stormed her cheeks. "Really?" she squeaked.

And it was that breathy little squeak that did him in.

She was gorgeous and sweet and smart and far too good for him. But he needed her. He needed someone good like McKenna to believe him in.

He bought the brass angels, a whole dozen, and he gave one to his mother for Christmas and hung the other eleven from his truck, his room, the mirror in the bathroom, and yes, on fishing wire over his bed.

Trey shifted in the diner booth and looked past McKenna's shoulder towards the bathroom. "Maybe I should check on him."

He rose without waiting for her to respond.

MCKENNA SAGGED AS Trey left the booth, his long strides carrying him across the diner floor.

For the past two years she'd known that TJ was looking more and more like his father, but she'd forgotten the details. She'd forgotten the way Trey made a room feel small and other people boring. She'd forgotten Trey's height and his sheer physicality. He was stronger than other men, more charismatic, too. But his nearness was wreaking havoc on her nerves. She felt tangled up in emotions she didn't want, and couldn't handle.

For two years she'd worked to forget him.

For two years she'd pretended he didn't exist.

But he did exist. He was here. And already he was changing everything.

Trey wasn't gone long. In fact, he seemed to walk into the men's bathroom and out again. He opened the women's door, stuck his head inside and then he was walking back to the table. "He's not there," Trey said bluntly.

She was on her feet. "*What?*"

He peeled money from his wallet and dropped the bills on the table. "We've got to go find him."

CARS AND TRUCKS whizzed by on the highway, headlights blindingly bright. The sky was clear and the moon shone white, no clouds to diminish the brightness. McKenna was grateful for the moonlight as she and Trey traveled the perimeter of the parking lot, searching for TJ, calling his name.

She was shivering from the cold, her tulle and silk skirts tangling between her legs, but there was no way she'd go inside until TJ was found.

Cupping her hands to her mouth, she shouted his name, telling herself not to panic, telling herself he was here some-where. He hadn't been gone long. There was no way he could have gone far.

Trey reached for her hand, taking it in the dark. "We'll find him, Mac."

His fingers curled around hers, his hand warm and hard, the skin callused on his palm.

She felt Trey's heat as his fingers laced with hers. His touch was meant to be comforting and yet she felt only electricity, as if he'd plugged her into something live and potent.

Just like it used to be.

But no, it wasn't like it used to be. It'd never be that way again.

"I think I see him," Trey said, releasing her hand and taking off at a run, darting across the highway to the other side of the road.

She watched him duck behind a cluster of garbage cans and come up with a little boy.

TJ.

Her heart lurched with relief. Thank God. Trey had found him.

INSIDE THE DINER, Trey put TJ down and McKenna didn't know if she should hug her son or shake him.

"What were you thinking?" she cried, crouching in front of TJ, holding him by the upper arms. "You could have been hurt out there, or killed! Why on earth would you do something like that?"

"I'm running away," he said hotly, totally unrepentant.

"Why?"

"'Cause you're making Dad go, and so I'm going, too—"

"I'm not making your dad go—"

"Yes, you are. I heard you. You said that he had to go so Lawrence can come get us and take us home, but I don't want to go with Lawrence. I don't like him. I'm not going to live with him."

"Oh, TJ—"

"I'm going with my dad," he interrupted fiercely. "You can go live with Lawrence."

"What about me? Won't you miss me?"

"No!"

"No? Why not?"

"Because you're sending him to jail!"

"I'm not."

"I heard you." His pressed his mouth shut in a mutinous line for a moment. "And if you send him to jail, I'm going with him, too."

Her heart fell and she sank back on her heels, full white skirts puffing around her like an airy cloud of meringue. "Oh, honey."

"I will," he insisted, arms crossing defiantly over his chest. "Where he goes, I go."

"They don't send little kids to jail." She folded her hands in her lap, studying his unhappy face. "Not even if they're bad. And you're not bad." She glanced past TJ to Trey who stood with his arms folded, too. Like father, like son. "Neither of you are bad," she said, holding Trey's gaze. "Sheenans aren't bad. A little hot-headed, yes, but bad….no."

TJ was still struggling to process everything. "So he didn't kidnap us?"

She leaned forward to kiss TJ's chilled cheek. "No, babe."

"And he's not in trouble."

"No."

"So he doesn't have to leave. He can stay with us and we can have Christmas together. Right?"

She struggled to smile. "How about we start with dinner first? And then we can talk about Christmas after."

WHILE TREY AND TJ finished their dinner, McKenna used the diner phone to call Lawrence.

He didn't pick up on his cell. She hung up without leaving a message and tried Paige, who didn't answer, either. McKenna wondered where everyone was, and what they were doing. She prayed no one was out searching for her and TJ.

Prayed that everyone was calm and pragmatic. But if she wanted everyone calm, then she needed to let people know what was going on. How could she do that, though, when even she didn't know what was happening?

"Hey Paige, it's McKenna," she said, getting Paige's voice mail. "I'm with TJ and Trey and we're fine. I'm calling from a restaurant phone, where we're having dinner. Trey and TJ are eating and talking and doing some bonding. Please tell everyone that we're all good and no one needs to worry. We'll be back soon and I'll explain everything then. Could you please let my brothers and Aunt Karen know I called? Love you. Bye,"

McKenna hung up, and taking a breath for courage, she dialed Lawrence's number again.

She really needed him to answer. She really needed to tell him what was happening. But once more she went to his voice mail, and this time she didn't hang up but listened to his entire greeting, which was very lengthy as he gave his office hours and address, but then the beep sounded and she had to speak.

"Hi, Lawrence, it's me. It's about six thirty or seven I think, and I'm outside White Sulphur Springs, calling from the restaurant phone. TJ and I are fine. I'm so sorry about this afternoon. . ." Her voice trailed off and for a moment she didn't know what to say.

It was ending, wasn't it?

She couldn't imagine how she and Lawrence would ever recover from this. And suddenly she wasn't sure she wanted them to recover.

Trey and Lawrence would never see eye to eye and she couldn't bear for TJ to grow up, caught in the middle. And he would be caught in the middle.

She'd be trapped, too.

McKenna tugged on the phone cord and drew a quick breath. "I won't be back for a few days, probably not until Christmas. TJ and Trey have really missed each other and need to spend some time together. I want them to have this time. You've always said TJ was too much like Trey, and now that I see them together, you're right. They are alike and they need each other…they need a chance to be a family together…"

Her voice trailed off as she struggled to think of a way to end the call. "I hate doing this over the phone. Hate doing this in a message, but I don't want you wondering and worrying about us so I just want you to know that we're okay, and safe. I hope you're okay, too."

"And I'm sorry," she added softly. "I'm sorry for disappointing you, but we're not the right family for you. We're not the ones who will make you happy. There's someone else for you, I'm sure of it. I hope one day you'll understand and hopefully forgive me."

She gently set the receiver down, ending the call.

For a long moment she just stared at the phone.

She'd just ended it with Lawrence. It was over. They were done.

Chapter Nine

FROM THEIR TABLE at the diner, Trey could see McKenna on the phone, but he couldn't hear what she was saying. She dialed three different times, and each call was short. From the brevity of the calls he suspected she was leaving messages. It'd be interesting to know who she'd called and what those messages were.

TJ's voice caught his attention. "What's that, son?"

"Why didn't you apologize?" TJ repeated. "If you didn't mean to kill that man. Why didn't you say it was an accident and you were sorry?"

Trey glanced from McKenna, who was heading back to their table, to TJ. "It doesn't work that way," he answered. "An apology doesn't change some things."

"But you didn't want to kill him."

"No."

"Did you want to hurt him?"

"No."

"What did you want to do then?"

He hesitated. "I wanted him to stop hurting someone else."

TJ put his fork down. "Who was he hurting?"

"We shouldn't talk about this."

"Why?"

"It's just going to upset your mom—"

"What will upset me?" McKenna asked, sitting down at the table and placing her crumpled veil on the seat between her and TJ.

Several long dark red tendrils had come loose from the elaborate twist at the back to frame her face. Trey wished she'd take the pins out of her hair and let it spill free. She had the most gorgeous hair. He couldn't understand why she'd ever put it up.

"Talking about the man he killed," TJ said bluntly. "He said it makes you sad if we talk about it around you."

"He's right." She looked baffled. "Why are we discussing this again?"

"TJ wanted to know why I didn't apologize, since it was an accident," Trey tried to sound just as matter of fact but he hated the subject. It was obviously a sensitive subject. Trey had spent a lot of time at Deer Lodge asking himself what he would do differently, if he had to do it over again. Ignore Bradley beating up his girlfriend? Walk out of the Wolf Den as if nothing bad was taking place?

Trey couldn't.

He'd never be able to stand by as a man used a woman as a punching bag. He'd never be able to allow a person to hurt an animal. He'd never let anyone abuse or threaten a kid.

It wasn't his nature. It wasn't acceptable to his own code of conduct.

Sure, when he was younger, he fought to fight. He'd liked fighting. He hadn't been afraid of taking a hit, either, because he realized physical pain was temporary. The real pain was the abuse that went on behind closed doors, the suffering of women in bad marriages, the agony of children raised by unstable parents.

Trey's dad had never hit his mom, but he didn't love her, and she'd suffered. She'd been a beautiful young woman when she married Bill Sheenan—and she'd given him five sons, one after the other, but his affections were elsewhere, with Bev Carrigan, and his mother had known.

She'd taken her life the summer after he and Troy had graduated from high school. Troy had been the one to find her. Their family had never been the same.

How could it be without their mother?

"None of it should have happened," Trey said flatly. "It's a day I will regret for the rest of my life."

"But why did you hit him?" TJ persisted.

Trey opened his mouth but no sound came out. How could he explain to a five year old that he'd seen a man using his girlfriend as a punching bag, so he'd intervened. The man, seriously inebriated, threw a punch at Trey, and Trey answered. A fight ensued and then Bradley lost his balance and went down.

If anyone else had stepped in that day, the outcome would have been different. Even the judge said as much. There might not have been an arrest, and there certainly wouldn't have been a five year prison sentence, but it was Trey Sheenan who'd interfered, and Trey had a long history of fighting in Crawford County, and Judge McCorkle wanted to make a point that he wouldn't tolerate thugs and petty criminals while he was on the bench.

McKenna sat forward. "Your dad went to jail because he tried to save a woman who was getting beat up by her boyfriend. Your dad didn't think it was right so he stepped in and there was a fight. Your dad is really strong, and a really good fighter, and he threw a hard punch which made the other guy fall, and when he fell he hit his head, and later died." She exhaled, face pale.

"He didn't mean for the other man to die. It was an accident, and he did apologize to the family, but it didn't matter. Someone had died."

TJ frowned. "But a man should not hit a woman."

"That's right," she agreed.

"So my dad's a good guy? A hero?"

She made a soft, inarticulate sound as she glanced at Trey. "I guess it depends on who you talk to."

Trey held her gaze a long moment before fishing out his wallet and peeling two twenties from the other bills and leaving them on the table. "Should we go?"

They left the diner and crossed the parking lot quickly to climb into Trey's truck to escape the cold. He started the truck and turned on the heater but it'd be a while before it put out hot air, and McKenna wrapped her arms around TJ to keep them warm.

He glanced at the shivering pair. It was damn cold. None of them had proper clothing for a Montana winter night. "What now?"

"What do you mean, what now?" McKenna answered, her gaze lifting to his, her winged eyebrows arching higher. "I thought you were the man with a plan. I thought you were determined to spend this Christmas with your son."

Her expression was mocking. She was throwing it down, daring him, challenging him, just as she had all those years ago when she was an innocent freshman and he the big bad high school senior.

Heat swept through him, blood surging through his veins, making him hot, and hard, filling him with longing for the life he'd had. The life he'd lost.

He missed her. He missed her body and her mind, her curves, her lips, her fire, her sweetness and that flash in her eyes.

She knew him so well.

"That hasn't changed," he said, his voice low and husky.

"Then give TJ a special Christmas. Give him a Christmas he'll never forget."

TREY DIDN'T TELL her where they were going. He just drove and she was fine relinquishing control and being the passenger, settling in while he took them wherever it was he wanted to take them.

As they headed west on Highway 12, she'd wondered if they were stopping in Helena, but he kept going, passing through Helena, and then north on 83. They'd been driving for three hours and TJ had crashed out a couple hours ago, leaning against McKenna.

It was getting late and they were traveling a mountain road but McKenna was relaxed. Trey was an exceptional driver and he might make her nervous in a bar, but he was good behind the wheel, and his truck was a four wheel drive vehicle with snow tires so if they hit snow or ice they'd be fine.

And she felt fine, now.

Mellow. Thoughtful. A little sad, but not heartbroken.

That told her something, didn't it?

Shouldn't she feel a *little* devastated?

Shouldn't she feel something besides…relieved?

"Cold?" Trey asked, glancing at her.

She shook her head, and wrapped her arm more securely around TJ's hip.

They drove another five minutes in silence.

She could tell Trey had something on his mind from the way he glanced at her every now and then but she didn't press him to speak, thinking no conversation was better than conflict and she was enjoying the quiet and the lack of tension and the big night sky which wrapped the truck.

Traveling together like this was both familiar and intimate. Trey on one side, she on the other with TJ in the center.

Trey cleared his throat. "Were you able to reach Lawrence?"

She shook her head. "Tried twice, got his voice mail each time. I left a message the second time."

He was silent for another minute, before shooting her a side glance. "What did you say in the message?"

"That you and TJ needed to catch up and I thought it was a good idea for you to spend Christmas together." She could tell he wanted to ask another question and so she headed him off, adding, "I also left a message for my friend Paige, letting her know everything was okay and that we were with you. I asked her to let my brothers and Aunt Karen know."

"Your family won't be happy."

"I don't know who will be more upset, my brothers or Aunt Karen."

"Your aunt's never liked me."

"She didn't dislike you until she found us naked together in my bedroom."

"I wasn't naked, and you had…a few things…on. Your blouse…your bra…" His voice trailed off and his lips curved in a rueful smile. "You know she wouldn't have come running if you hadn't been loud."

"Don't blame me! How was I to know how good it would feel? It's your fault for being so…talented…that way."

"We didn't see each other for a while after that."

"Two months I think, which was ridiculous because we'd been dating two years at that point. Did they honestly think you and I weren't going to try anything? That we weren't going to eventually mess around?"

The corner of his mouth quirked and they slipped back into silence, traveling another five miles with memories hanging over them.

She and Trey had grown up together. Hard to remember a time when they weren't together...

"I didn't think you wanted a big wedding," he said, a few minutes later, his attention on the road. "You'd always said that when we got married you just wanted immediate family, something small and intimate."

McKenna didn't immediately reply. She would have preferred a small wedding but Lawrence had wanted to invite all his clients and friends so the wedding grew from fifty to one hundred and then one hundred and fifty, and that was where she put her foot down. One hundred and fifty was plenty for a candle light wedding the last Saturday before Christmas.

"I think the wedding was for Lawrence and the community," she said after a moment. "There are many in Marietta who want closure for me...they want that happy ending."

"And a fancy wedding would give them closure?"

"I think people want me to be happy, and they hoped that by marrying Lawrence, TJ and I would have stability."

"Or maybe they were just glad that Lawrence would keep you away from me."

She started to protest but closed her mouth, swallowing the protest. He was right. He was not Marietta's favorite son.

"I never cared what people thought," she said softly, glancing at him, and taking in his profile with the jutting jaw and firm press of lips. He was leaner than she remembered, and yet bigger, harder. He was carrying a lot of muscle still, but he seemed to have virtually no body fat.

In the light of the truck dash, he glowed, rugged and Hollywood handsome. Black hair, long black lashes, piercing blue eyes, chiseled bone structure.

He'd always been good looking, but in his mid thirties he had a maturity that suited him.

The last vestiges of boy were gone. He was all man. A gorgeous, darkly beautiful man.

When he'd been sentenced to prison she'd thought her heart was permanently broken and so it'd been a surprise when she finally accepted Lawrence's invitation to dinner.

Maybe she was comfortable with Lawrence because he was nothing like Trey.

Lawrence wasn't sexy or sexual. He wasn't hard taut muscle. He wasn't a rancher or a cowboy. He couldn't rope a fence post, much less a steer. And no, he couldn't fix the engine of a car or deliver a calf. He couldn't drive in snow. He couldn't shoot, hunt, fish or build a proper fire.

But he was sweet, and thoughtful, gentle and kind. If he said he'd be there at seven, he always showed up…five minutes early. If she needed anything, he was there. He treated her like she was the best thing since sliced bread and it felt good to be important and valued.

It felt good to know he'd be there the next day, and the day after, and the day after that.

It felt good not to worry that he'd be out too late, drinking too much, getting heated, instigating fights.

It felt good to be with someone that folks didn't criticize.

"People really thought Lawrence would be a better husband and father than me?" Trey sounded incredulous. "A man who has so little backbone that he allows a five year old to walk all over him?"

"Well, TJ's not just any five year old. He is *your* five year old."

"My point exactly."

She chewed on her lip, thinking, remembering the fight, the trial, the sentence and then those two years she drove twice a month to see him, carting the baby, who was quickly growing into a spirited toddler.

TJ always cried during the drives to the prison, but he cried the most when they left Trey behind. He cried because he didn't know why he had to leave his daddy behind, again, and TJ's tears and grief had worn her down. TJ had been too young to feel so much anguish. He hadn't understood. She couldn't seem to make him understand. And what about when Trey was released?

Would he be there for them then? Did she believe deep down he'd ever be there for them?

She hadn't known anymore.

She hadn't trusted Trey anymore.

She'd come to see him as others saw him—a dominant male, fierce and physical—but a man who was in need of reason and self-control.

She'd finally heard what everyone said....that he was reactive, responding instinctively without regard to risks and consequence, and she'd seen that they were right. He refused to grow up, refused to control his temper, refuse to bend or yield which meant he could never be depended on.

She loved how beautiful he was, remembered how amazing it felt when they were together. Making love with Trey wasn't just sexual, it was emotional and spiritual....or at least it used to be before she was so angry with him. So frustrated and hurt.

And so she'd found the opposite of Trey in Lawrence Joplin, and when Lawrence proposed the third time, she put aside her reservations, telling herself that passion was less important than predictability, and accepted his marriage offer, determined that the future would be different from the past.

But now everything had changed again and instead of being teary and conflicted, she was…calm.

Relieved.

There was that word again. She almost felt a little guilty for feeling relieved that she wasn't marrying Lawrence. And now she wondered if that was why she had felt so many butterflies earlier, at the church. Had she been getting cold feet and she just wouldn't admit it? Had she not wanted to marry him but was too afraid of hurting his feelings to say something?

She hoped she wasn't that much of a coward. She'd been through too much in life to be a doormat…

But no, she wasn't a doormat. She'd stood up to Trey plenty of times, refusing to marry him until he got his act together and grew up and acted like a man.

She'd stood up to her family when they'd pressured her to stop seeing Trey.

She'd ignored the gossip in Marietta when she'd chosen to be a single mom rather than marry a man she didn't think was ready to settle down.

No, she wasn't a doormat. And she had a spine. But she also was tender hearted when it came to those she loved. And she loved Lawrence, but probably more as a friend than a lover and life partner.

Which was why it baffled her that Lawrence had taken it upon himself to tell TJ why his father was in prison. Lawrence had promised her he wouldn't say anything, agreeing to leave it to her so she could tell TJ when she thought the moment was right.

But Lawrence had broken that promise. Why?

And if he'd broken that promise to her, how much others had he not kept?

Chapter Ten

THEY ARRIVED AT Bigfork at a little after midnight, the high full moon reflecting white off Flathead Lake as they drove south fifteen miles on Highway 35 to the little town of Cherry Lake.

If they kept going another eighteen miles they'd come to Polson.

Trey's mom, Catherine Cray, had spent her early years outside Cherry Lake, a member of the Bitterroot Salish tribe that formed part of the Confederated Salish and Kootenai Tribes of the Flathead Nation.

All but the northern tip of Flathead Lake was part of the extensive Flathead Indian Reservation, and when Trey's mother's grandparents died, they left an old cabin on the lower slope of the Mission Mountains, and a couple acres of land to their daughter, hoping she'd return and raise her sons on the land of her ancestors.

Trey's father hadn't minded taking the boys to the cabin with its spectacular view of Flathead Lake for fishing trips, but he wasn't interested in his wife's native ancestry. She wasn't even half Salish and he wasn't about to raise his sons as native this, or that.

Trey hadn't been to the cabin in years, but until recently Cormac visited regularly, and apparently just this past summer Brock had brought Harley and the kids for a ten-day vacation, using the time to rebuild the old stone fireplace, install a new stove in the kitchen, and make a number of smaller repairs.

"Know where we're going now?" Trey asked McKenna as they drove past the turn-off to sleepy little Cherry Lake, a Flathead Lake town that came alive in summer with tourists and the colorful fresh fruit stands dotting the road selling crates of Lamberts, Rainier and Hardy Giant cherries.

"I had a suspicion when you took 83 north," McKenna answered, shifting TJ to free her arm, which had gone numb sometime in the last half hour. "When's the last time you were here?"

"It's been a long time, but you were here with me. It was a couple years before TJ was born."

"I remember," she said softly. They'd driven from Marietta for a long weekend at the cabin in late September. Most of the tourists were gone and the local kids were all in school. It jad felt like they had the lake and town to themselves. "We had fun."

He shot her a swift glance, expression somber. "We did," he agreed. "And we will again."

The last words were spoken so quietly she wasn't sure he'd even said them. She glanced at him but his attention was on the steep private road that wound back to the cabin.

THE KEYS TO the Cray cabin were right where they'd always been, tucked high up the hollowed leg of the wooden grizzly cub gracing the cabin's front porch. Trey unlocked the cabin's front door, flipped on the light switch and was gratified to see light flood the open main room, a combination of living room, dining room and small kitchen.

The one and a half story log cabin had been built in the late 1940's and had just the bare minimum in maintenance until Cormac started paying regular visits ten years ago. The cabin was still rustic, with stacked log walls and exposed trusses in the vaulted ceiling but everything looked clean and weather proofed.

Trey did a quick walk through, flipping on lights in the two downstairs bedrooms and turning on the heater. The windows in both bedrooms were original, and weren't double paned. Once the wooden shutters were removed, the bedrooms would be a lot colder. He hoped the big cedar chest in the master bedroom still held all the sheets, quilts and comforters. They were going to need to make up the beds and get extra blankets on them, too.

He returned to the truck where McKenna and TJ were waiting. "Got the heater on and the lights on," he said. "But we'll need to get the beds made up."

"If you've got clean sheets, I can do that," she said, shivering as she handed TJ over.

"The cedar chest should be full of them."

McKenna lifted her full skirts high as she followed Trey up the path to the cabin. Her heels weren't designed for hiking up a rutted dirt path. "I don't suppose there are any clothes here? I'm not going to want to put this dress back on tomorrow."

"I'm sure we can find something for the night, and then tomorrow we'll go shopping in Cherry Lake, and if Cherry Lake doesn't have it, Polson or Bigfork will."

MCKENNA QUICKLY MADE up both twin beds with sheets and blankets in the smaller bedroom, before taking a sleepy and disoriented TJ to the bathroom where she stripped off his pants, shoes and socks and then tucked him into one of the twin beds in his shirt.

Trey made up the queen size bed in the master bedroom while she put TJ to bed. She'd slept in the master bedroom the last time she was here. It seemed as if they'd spent most of their time at the cabin in bed.

But she wouldn't think about that. There was no point dwelling on the past. She hadn't agreed to let TJ spend Christmas with his dad so she and Trey could rekindle a romance. She wasn't interested in romance. She'd like to be friends with Trey, though. And she'd like to see TJ and Trey have the kind of father-son relationship they both craved.

MCKENNA COULD HEAR Trey moving around in the central room, bringing in firewood and stacking it next to the big stone fireplace.

She lay on her side in the narrow twin bed listening to him open and close doors and arrange the firewood.

It was strange lying here, listening to him work. It was one in the morning. Wasn't he tired?

Or was he out there working because he felt all wound up, too?

McKenna turned onto her back and stared at the ceiling. She wasn't sure how she felt, being back at the Cray cabin. This was a place shared by the five Sheenan brothers. They never invited outsiders. It was just for family. When Trey had brought her here that September, they were still newly engaged.

Now she was back and her emotions were all over the place.

It might not have been a good idea, coming here for Christmas.

But then, this Christmas wasn't about her, and what she wanted. This Christmas was about Trey and TJ. This Christmas was about them having a special holiday together.

Restless, she flipped her covers and quilt back, floorboards creaking beneath her bare feet as she went to his bed. Even though Trey had left the wooden blinds closed, slivers of moonlight slipped through the cracks and streaked the log frame.

TJ looked small in the twin bed, his cheek nestled deep into the down pillow, his hair dark on the crisp white pillowcase.

She leaned over and lightly kissed his warm cheek, before tugging the covers higher on his shoulder.

She loved him so much. From the beginning she'd tried to do everything right. She wanted him to have everything a little boy needed. Halloween costumes and Christmas traditions. Swim lessons, summer vacations, Saturday matinee movies.

But despite her best efforts, she hadn't been able to give TJ everything. He didn't have a daddy that was there, and it was the only thing he asked for.

Again and again and again.

A daddy to take him fishing. A daddy for cub scouting. A daddy for wrestling and hugging and loving.

A lump formed in her throat. She'd agreed to marry Lawrence for TJ's sake. It was a terrible thing to admit. She didn't need the company as much as TJ needed a father figure.

She'd thought Lawrence was the answer. At least, she'd hoped he was the answer. But Lawrence and TJ had never really clicked. She could admit that now. She could see that she'd tried to force them to like each other, planning activities to help them get along. She'd thought if she tried hard enough eventually they'd grow fond of each other but it hadn't happened. Lawrence, a forty-year old bachelor when he'd begun dating McKenna, couldn't relate to a headstrong little boy who wasn't interested in learning cribbage and chess. TJ wanted Lawrence to box and run and wrestle. He wanted physical activity not quiet games.

Lawrence criticized McKenna's parenting.

McKenna privately pleaded with TJ to do the activities Lawrence enjoyed so they could all be happy together.

The more pressure McKenna put on TJ to cooperate with Lawrence, the more resistant TJ became to all of Lawrence's suggestions. Lawrence thought it was a problem. But TJ wasn't a problem and he wasn't spoiled or a little monster. He was just himself...active, healthy, busy, smart.

McKenna loved his sense of humor. She loved his personality. She didn't want him to be anybody but himself.

The only times she and Lawrence argued was over how she was raising TJ.

Now, asleep, TJ looked impossibly angelic, and nothing like a little monster. She lightly placed one last kiss on his soft cheek. She could feel his warm breath as she straightened.

Her boy. And Trey's boy.

TJ's lashes fluttered. He opened his eyes and looked up at her. "Mommy, what are you doing?" he asked, his voice rough with sleep.

"Checking on you."

"Where are you sleeping?"

"In here, with you. Now go back to sleep."

"Good night, Mommy."

"Good night, sweet boy."

He closed his eyes and yawned. "I love you."

"I love you, too."

IT WAS LATE, after two in the morning, but Trey couldn't sleep in the big bed in the master bedroom.

He'd taken a hot shower after finishing stacking the firewood and laying a fire for the next morning. And he was physically tired but he couldn't clear his mind long enough to let him relax.

McKenna and TJ were here, under his roof.

It was incredible, so incredible he didn't know how to process it. This morning he'd woken up, sick that he'd lost McKenna, and desperate to make sure he didn't lose TJ, too.

It'd been an intense afternoon and everything that could have gone wrong…didn't.

By some miracle, McKenna and his son were here, with him. Not with Lawrence. By some miracle he had been given a chance…

It was time he redeemed himself.

And he would.

God…fate…whatever you called it… had given him this opportunity, and this time Trey wouldn't blow it.

He loved his family. He needed his family. And he was prepared to do whatever it took to prove that he was here for them, too.

EVEN THOUGH TREY had fallen asleep late, he was up early to turn up the heat and light the fire. He was lucky that there were clothes he could wear—jeans and t-shirts and flannel shirts, boots and a pair of running shoes, left by his brothers.

There was nothing for TJ to wear in any of the cabin closets but McKenna could maybe get away with a pair of sweat pants and a flannel shirt and the running shoes.

He left the clothes folded outside their bedroom door before grabbing his keys and driving into town to pick up coffee, eggs, bread, milk, butter, bacon and juice from the twenty-four hour convenience store attached to the gas station. He was just about to walk out when he spotted a couple bright red sweatshirts with the slogan Stay and Play at Cherry Lake folded up on a shelf with other souvenir items. The smallest size they had was a Youth Medium but Trey grabbed it, thinking it would at least give TJ something warm to wear.

Back at the cabin, he stoked the fire, added another log, and then made coffee in the old coffee machine he found in one of the kitchen cupboards.

He was busy frying bacon and whisking eggs when the bedroom door opened and McKenna appeared, still wearing the red flannel shirt from Trey's truck.

And from the looks of it, only wearing the red flannel shirt.

"Sleep okay?" Trey asked, whisking the eggs more vigorously, forcing himself to look away. She was almost too beautiful, her long hair loose and spilling over her shoulders, the soft flannel fabric outlining the swell of her breasts and the shirt hem reaching only to mid thigh, leaving her long shapely legs gloriously bare.

"Better than you, I think," she answered, smiling and crossing behind him to check the coffee. "Can I have a cup?"

"Please do."

"Have you had any yet?"

"No. It has only just finished brewing."

She opened the upper cabinet doors until she found two mugs and rinsed them out at the sink before filling them. The coffee was hot and she set a steaming cup at his elbow. "You don't know how much I wanted this," she said, circling her cup with her hands. "I don't do well without my coffee in the morning."

He smiled ruefully. "I remembered."

She leaned against the counter, watching him flip the sizzling bacon. "I thought I would be freezing this morning but you've made it toasty warm in here."

"Didn't want you and TJ cold."

"You've been up for a while, haven't you?"

"Hard to sleep with so much on my mind."

She sipped her coffee, and a long lock red hair fell forward. Carelessly she pushed it back, anchoring the curl behind an ear. "What's on your mind?"

He placed another skillet on the stove, turned on the burner, and added butter to the pan. "I want you and TJ happy," he said after a moment.

"TJ's happy."

He shot her a look over his shoulder. "I want you happy, too."

She didn't look at him. She stared at the pan, watching the butter melt. "We're here for TJ. This is about him."

"Not for me."

"Trey, it's important I be straight with you. I want to be fair to you. I'm not interested in romance, or a relationship with you. But I would like to be friends. Good friends. That way we can raise TJ amicably, without tension."

"I agree."

"But a romantic or sexual relationship would just complicate everything. You know it would. The sex thing always gets us in trouble."

He'd learned a lot living for the past four years with little personal space and zero privacy. He'd learned to check his emotions by removing himself from a situation. He did that now, aware that this wasn't about him, but her, and what she needed. McKenna needed to feel safe. She needed space. She needed time. No problem.

He nodded as he poured the beaten eggs into the skillet with the melted butter. "You're right," he said. "The sex was a problem."

Her jaw dropped ever so slightly. "You think so?"

"I do." He put the ceramic bowl in the sink and rinsed it out before reaching for one of the green checked dishtowels to dry his hands. "The problem is that the physical side of our relationship was too good. Making love felt so natural that I think we expected the rest of our relationship to be that way." He glanced at her. "Now, I don't regret the sex. It was hot. Pretty damn amazing. You know how much I love your body, but maybe the touching and kissing got in the way."

She blinked. "Wow. I'm….shocked. But in a good way."

"That's good." He smiled at her. "It's nice that we are on the same page."

She pushed her hand through her hair, shoving it back from her face, and he told himself he hadn't noticed the way her shirt cupped her breasts or lifted to reveal several inches of pale creamy skin high on her thigh.

They weren't lovers anymore. They were friends. Platonic friends. Platonic friends who didn't have fringe benefits. He'd make sure of that. And he'd be the best platonic friend she ever had. So good that she'd be the one to begging to get back into his bed.

He gestured to the pile of clothes still stacked outside her door. "I picked up a sweatshirt for TJ at the convenience store, and found some clothes that belong to one of my brothers that will get you covered and warm until we can go shopping after breakfast. Feel free to top off your coffee before you shower and dress. I'm sure you'll feel far more comfortable and less naked once you're out of that old shirt and dressed."

She stared at him a moment, and then nodded. "Sounds like a plan."

Chapter Eleven

I T WAS THE twenty-first of December, the last Sunday before Christmas, and Cherry Lake sparkled beneath the sunlit blue sky, Main Street picture book pretty with festive green boughs and red ribbons on the lights and carols playing from invisible speakers. The cafes and shops lining the street were perfectly festive, too, decorated with fragrant wreaths, frosted windows, and charming holiday displays.

But trying to find everything they needed in Cherry Lake took some creativity and visits to six different stores to purchase the necessary undergarments, outer garments, shoes and coats. In the past, Trey had dragged his feet on shopping trips, but his patience and good spirits this morning amazed McKenna. He carried all the bags, kept TJ entertained, and hummed along with the carols, reminding her that he had a gorgeous voice.

He was gorgeous, too, and she wasn't the only one who'd noticed. Women in the shops stared appreciatively, while others passing them on Main Street, cast swift, furtive second and third glances.

McKenna had forgotten what it felt like to be out with a man that drew tons of female admiration. Lawrence had been pleasant looking, attractive in that wholesome kind of way, but Trey was in a whole other league. Trey was darkly beautiful, sinfully beautiful, and she understood why women looked.

Men weren't that handsome in real life.

Men weren't that tall and muscular. They didn't have hair that thick and dark or eyes that brilliant a blue. Their cheekbones weren't that high or their jaws that chiseled. They didn't flash dimples when they laughed. Their laughter and voices didn't rumble in their chests. They simply weren't made so perfectly.

They weren't.

But Trey was. And his brother Troy. However, Troy wasn't Trey, and McKenna had only ever had eyes for Trey since seeing him at Marietta High, surrounded by a group of guys that looked like they were up to no good.

And they weren't. Trey's friends cut class, showed up drunk or stoned, and spent more time in the front office than in class.

McKenna shouldn't have been intrigued. She shouldn't have been attracted to someone so obviously bad.

But when Trey looked at her, his gaze would always soften, his expression gentling. It happened so quickly she didn't know if he was even conscious that his expression changed, and he didn't look at anyone else that way. She knew because she watched him. She watched him a lot, fascinated by the way he carried himself, and the way others whispered about him, saying he was dangerous, reckless, saying he didn't care about anybody, saying he would probably die young.

She didn't want him to die young. She wanted him to play it safer. She wanted him to look at her more. She loved seeing how his hard, handsome features transformed when he saw her…lips curving, blue eyes creasing.

He might not enjoy school, but he was smart, and tough,

and he made her feel safe.

He made her feel pretty, too.

And he might never ask her out, but she was his. They both knew it.

"What?" he asked, shooting her a quick glance, black eyebrows lifting.

"Nothing," she answered, amazed that seventeen years later she still felt so connected to him.

"You're smiling."

"You're humming," she said. "Christmas *carols*."

"I like Christmas carols."

"You're humming the sacred ones."

"I can't like songs with a little substance?"

His innocent expression, and his blue eyes, suddenly so guileless, made her laugh out loud. "I know you. I know who you are."

"And who am I, darlin'?"

She looked up into his eyes, and he let her look, inviting her in, and she could have stood there all day, feeling close to him, feeling connected.

Heart, mind, soul.

And then someone tried to get past and accidentally bumped into McKenna and McKenna tripped a bit over TJ and the spell was broken.

The old gentleman who bumped into her apologized and McKenna said no, it was her fault, and blushing, she felt like a fool.

She wasn't being smart.

She wasn't being careful.

Trey Sheenan might be gorgeous and charismatic but he wasn't good for her. He wasn't settled or stable. She couldn't let him back in, couldn't drop her defenses.

They could be friends. And friendly. But that was all.

No romance, no love, no sex, no happy ever after.

No happy ever after. It didn't exist. Not with him.

AFTER CLOTHES SHOPPING they stopped for lunch at one of the little cafes on Main Street. Trey asked TJ what he wanted for Christmas, and once TJ started in, he didn't stop. He hadn't seen Santa yet, and he hadn't sent him a letter but usually if he left him a note at Christmas Santa brought him what he wanted, although last year he wanted holsters and pistols and Santa didn't bring those. Santa never brought guns. Or any fighting things. TJ was disappointed that Santa wouldn't bring him fighting things when everyone else got them. Didn't Santa know he was a boy, not a girl?

McKenna could feel Trey's eyes on her now and then while TJ talked.

She told herself she didn't want to know what he was thinking. She told herself she was happy to keep distance between them. Distance was good. Distance was smart.

After lunch they stopped at the local grocery store and Trey thrust a wad of bills in her hand and told her to go get whatever she wanted while he and TJ went to the hardware store next door and picked up a few things for the cabin.

McKenna didn't want to be in the grocery store while Trey and TJ shopped at the hardware store. She liked being with them. She liked their energy and the way they talked and teased. It was boisterous and brash and fun. She'd forgotten how much fun Trey had always been. Trey had so much energy and good humor. He liked to laugh. He'd always loved to make her laugh, and now his focus was on TJ and TJ was eating it up.

It would be silly to be jealous of TJ. He was Trey's son. He deserved Trey's undivided attention. But she knew what it felt like to be the focus of Trey's attention. She knew how special she used to feel…

Cart full, she waited in line to check out and then pushed the cart outside, heading for Trey's truck.

Trey and TJ were already in the truck waiting for her, and Trey stepped out and immediately began loading up the back with the groceries.

"What did you buy?" she asked him, glancing at the dozen paper bags with the hardware logo on the front.

"Tools, nails, screws, light bulbs, wood glue, extension cords. How about you?"

"Steaks, potatoes, vegetables, peanut butter, flour, sugar, salt."

"Chocolate chips?" he asked hopefully. "Gingerbread mix?"

"You got a little sweet tooth, Sheenan?"

"Not usually, Mac. But for some reason when you're around, I do."

He'd said it quietly, casually, but the words wrapped around her heart and stole her breath.

It wasn't fair how much she'd missed this—*him*—these past few years. She'd missed the banter and the teasing and his sexy laugh and the way he used to kiss her so slow, kiss her until she was dizzy and mindless and so perfectly content, wanting nothing more than to share a life with him.

"I think that's it," she said breathlessly, placing the last bag in the back and straightening. "I'll just take the cart back—"

"I've got it. You get in with TJ."

"I can do it—"

"I've got it, Mac. Please get in. Get warm. Be safe."

BE SAFE.

Be safe.

The words played in her head during the ten minute drive from town to Cray Road and up the winding private road to the cabin.

Be safe, she heard as she unpacked the groceries.

Be safe, she heard as TJ and Trey disappeared up into the attic, with TJ giggling and whispering and Trey hushing him saying, *Sssh. You don't want to ruin the surprise.*

She couldn't figure out why those words were bothering her so much. Why should she mind him saying be safe? Why should that be a bad thing?

And then it hit her—he was the one who needed to be safe.

He was the one who took the chances.

He was the one who'd left her and TJ alone for four years because he was the one who wasn't safe.

If she wanted to be safe, then she needed Lawrence, or someone like Lawrence, in her life. She needed someone who sold insurance and didn't take risks. Someone who insisted on slow and safe. Someone who preferred predictable. Someone who avoided extremes and change and adrenalin and danger.

But when all was said and done, she hadn't really wanted Lawrence, or someone like Lawrence.

How was she to ever fall in love with anyone else when Trey still possessed her heart?

WHILE MCKENNA BAKED an easy pumpkin bread and made chewy molasses cookies, Trey and TJ worked outside putting something together. She heard hammering and sawing and the scrape of metal. She wondered if it was an old sled they'd found, but she didn't know what they'd do with a sled since there was no snow on the ground, and she would have gone outside to see what they were working on but she'd been given strict instructions to stay inside and be *surprised*.

And so she was baking, waiting to be surprised, and smiling whenever she heard TJ's high bright peal of laughter. He was so happy today. He was in his element helping Trey drag boxes from the attic, carrying paper bags of stuff from the truck, tramping in and out getting cups of hot cocoa for 'the men', making noise, creating chaos. Having fun.

Finally, the front door banged open again and TJ shouted for her to close her eyes and not peek.

"I'm making cookies," she shouted back. "I have to peek."

"Just keep your eyes closed two minutes," Trey answered.

And so she squeezed her eyes shut and propped her chin in her hands and waited. She knew what it was by the smell, even without the sound of branches brushing and scraping the front door.

A tree. They were bringing in a Christmas tree.

"Are you looking?" TJ asked.

"No." But her lips curved and she was smiling, happy for TJ. This was a special Christmas. This was exactly the kind of Christmas he needed.

Muffled voices and whispers and an ouch came from the main room.

"Okay," TJ said after a moment of some huffing and puffing. "Open your eyes!"

She opened her eyes and a tall douglas fir filled one corner of the living room. This was not a fat, full perfectly shaped tree from a Christmas tree farm, but an eight foot tree that had been cut from the Cray land, that had character along with gaps between some of the branches.

"What do you think, Mom?" TJ asked, beaming. "Pretty nice, huh?"

She nodded and smiled back. "One of the nicest trees I've ever seen."

The boxes TJ and Trey had brought down from the attic contained old strings of lights and dozens of vintage glass ornaments.

While the pumpkin bread cooled and the molasses cookies baked, McKenna helped Trey and TJ put lights on the tree—not the old ones from the attic, but the box of new lights Trey had bought today from the hardware store—and then used the new ornament hooks to hang the beautiful vintage ornaments on the tree, the tarnished glass balls a mix of silver, white, and gold, as well as some that were a soft rose and aqua blue. They glittered, sparkled and shone on the green branches of the fresh douglas fir.

After they were done, Trey turned off the living room lamps to admire their handiwork. Outside it was dusk and the lavender shadows pressed against the windows. Inside the fire burned and glowed and the tree gleamed with balls of color and the strings of white miniature lights.

"All we need are some stockings and Santa can come," Trey said.

"Santa will find us here?" TJ asked.

"Of course." Trey paused. "If you were a good boy. Were you a good boy this year?"

TJ was silent a long moment. "Most the time," he said finally, his voice uncertain. "Does that count?"

Trey laughed. "Absolutely." He glanced at McKenna, still grinning. "Don't you think, Mac?"

"Yes. When it comes to you two. It's got to. Otherwise, we'd never have Christmas or visits from Santa Claus."

LATE THAT NIGHT, after dinner and dishes, they sat in the living room admiring the tree, enjoying the fire. Trey told TJ stories about when he was a boy and how he and his brothers would go look for the perfect tree and how they'd always end up fighting and one or more would return home with a bloody nose, or worse.

TJ loved the stories, and he asked questions about who was stronger—Uncle Brock or Uncle Cormac, and who ran faster, Uncle Troy or Uncle Dillon, and McKenna sat curled up in one of the threadbare armchairs listening to Trey answer all of TJ's questions. He was so patient with his son, so incredibly sweet, and it moved her more than words could say.

Lawrence had tolerated TJ but he'd never loved him. He'd never enjoyed him. He'd never cared about the things that interested TJ...not the way Trey did.

And she got the feeling watching Trey with TJ that if he'd met her, and she'd been a single mom to TJ, Trey would have cared about her son. He would have tried to not merely parent him and keep him safe, but would have laughed and played. Trey would always engage and entertain. Trey would make a child's life...fun.

And fun mattered.

Happiness mattered.

Safety and stability was important, but what was a stable, safe life without humor and excitement and pleasure?

One of the reasons she'd loved Trey was that he'd always made her laugh. He'd made her giggle and smile and feel good.

Those things mattered.

Watching Trey and TJ together now she felt as if she could see Trey, truly see him, all the way through to his soul.

And no, his soul wasn't shiny and silver bright, but tarnished like the vintage balls on the tree, and perhaps even bruised and broken, marked with jagged cuts and welts and scars.

Yet for all those scars and dull marks, there was something so very beautiful in him. He was alive, and strong, and deep.

But then, wasn't that the appeal from the beginning. That he was flawed and real? That he was open and honest? *Human.*

He'd never tried to cover up his weaknesses. He'd never sugar-coated anything for anyone, and he certainly had never pretended to be a perfect man, one of those romance novel heroes….all good and pure, the idealized boyfriend every girl wanted.

No. He wasn't that great, stand up guy.

But it hadn't mattered. She'd loved him anyway, as even broken and flawed, he'd felt like hers.

She'd been the one to seduce him. She'd been the one to push his buttons, wanting him to treat her like a woman, not a girl. Wanting him to be hot and demanding, sensual and physical.

He'd wanted to marry her ever since he graduated from high school. He'd wanted to do the right thing by her, but she refused to marry him until he stopped fighting and drinking and driving and staying out late causing trouble with 'the boys'. She didn't like that he was one person with her, and then this street-tough alpha with everyone else. Why couldn't he be as kind and charming with everyone as he was with her? Why couldn't he try harder to fit in? Settle down? Be good?

They'd fought about his behavior for years…

Don't cause trouble. Don't stay out too late. Don't drink too much because you'll just end up doing something stupid...

But he liked who he was and he wasn't interested in changing. He enjoyed all the things she was afraid of...the fist fights, the late nights, the rowdy groups of guys he hung out with. He enjoyed being tough, strong, slightly dangerous.

"This is who I am," he'd told her more than once. "This is what I am."

"Someday something will happen," she'd answer. "Someday something beyond your control."

And then it had happened. The fight at the Wolf Den, with its disastrous results. Bradley Warner had died after falling and striking his head on the edge of the bar, and Trey was arrested and charged with manslaughter.

It didn't matter that Trey had intervened to protect Bradley's pregnant girlfriend from Bradley's fists. It didn't matter that witnesses said that Trey had only thrown a few punches and had never lost control. It didn't matter that Trey was supposed to be the good guy and Brad was the bad guy. Because Brad died and Trey was responsible and Trey had to pay.

There were consequences for fighting.

Consequences for not following rules.

Consequences for being tough and physical and fearless.

For the past two years McKenna had told herself that she was rejecting Trey because she didn't want TJ to grow up like him, but suddenly she knew she'd wronged them, both of them.

There was so much good in Trey, and so much good in TJ.

She couldn't reject one without rejecting the other and suddenly she wasn't so sure that being good, being safe, was the right answer.

She didn't want to be stupid and didn't want danger, but she wanted more than safe, wanted more than predictable.

She wanted teasing and smiles, love and laughter.

She wanted her heart back.

She wanted her life back.

She wanted Trey and TJ together.

With her.

Together a family with her.

But she was scared. She was scared that if she let down her guard, if she allowed Trey back in, something bad could happen—again—and she could lose him, and her heart, and her happiness all over. Again.

Chapter Twelve

McKENNA WOKE UP to the incessant trilling and drumming of a bird outside her cabin window. It had been going on and on and she'd tried to ignore it and fall back asleep but it wasn't happening, not while the bird kept thrumming and kuk-kuk-kuking outside the window.

Climbing from bed she went to the small window and pushed back the shutter. She shivered in her pajamas, which was really just a man's t-shirt, X-Large, and craned her head to try to find the offending bird. The sun was just starting to rise and she couldn't see a bird, but she could still hear it, *kuk-kuk-kuking*, over and over.

McKenna bumped into Trey in the hallway. He was fully dressed and she tugged the hem of the t-shirt down, trying to cover herself.

"You're up early," he said.

"What time is it?" she asked, thinking that the t-shirt had seemed perfectly roomy and modest last night but seemed to cover far less of her now.

"Not quite six."

"I didn't want to be awake this early," she answered, smothering a yawn. "But there is the most annoying bird outside—"

"Our resident woodpecker. I heard it, too."

"It's been making noise half the night."

"The pileated woodpeckers do. Our woods are full of them. They love the old growth trees."

"Great."

He must have noticed that she kept tugging on the hem of her t-shirt. "Aren't you wearing panties?"

"Yes. Why?"

"You're acting excessively virginal, Mac," he said, sounding amused.

"Be quiet. Go shave. Or better yet, be useful and make some coffee."

"I have, and it's waiting for you, Princess. Or was I supposed to bring it to you in bed?"

"*No.*" And yet the moment he said the word bed, her imagination sparked, creating all sorts of wanton images in her head. Images she didn't want or need. Because when it came to making love with Trey, reality was so much better than fantasy. He was that good. And he felt that good, and no, she'd never slept with any other man than Trey, so she didn't know if it'd be that good with someone else, but honestly, she hadn't wanted to find out.

Trey had been her only one.

Although once she married Lawrence, she would have obviously had to make love to him. She suppressed a faint shudder. She hadn't been looking forward to that.

Although she was pretty sure he had.

She crossed her arms over her chest, hiding her breasts. "Did any of your brothers ever leave a robe behind?"

"Nope, but I did find an old wool cardigan. It's huge, XXL, and rather moth eaten but it could be a robe on you."

"I'll take it. Thank you."

She was in the kitchen filling her cup when he returned with a grey, beige and cream knit sweater with an Indian motif.

"That's beautiful," she said, taking the wool sweater from him and examining the intricate Indian design.

"My great Grandmother Cray made it. My mother said she made hundreds of sweaters and blankets during her life to help pay bills. Cormac has been able to track down a few in antique stores and on eBay as her stitches and designs are different from the Coastal Salish, but this sweater has been in the family forever. It was probably made for one of my uncles, or even my great grandfather."

"It should be in a museum."

"No, it shouldn't. It was made for family, it should be worn by family."

"But I'm not—"

"Yes, you are. You're my family. You'll always be family to me."

She undid the sturdy buttons and slipped one arm in and then the other. The sweater was heavy and long, and a little bit itchy, but it was a Cray family heirloom, and she could feel the history in it, and the love.

Her eyes suddenly burned and she looked down, focusing on working the wood buttons through the holes. "Do you ever think about that side of your family?" she asked, voice husky. "Do you ever think that maybe the reason you felt like such an outsider in Marietta was because you take after the Crays? That maybe you were never meant to be cooped up in classrooms and offices but outside…free?"

He didn't immediately answer and she looked up, to find him staring hard at her, a strange expression on his face.

"What?" she whispered. "Was that a bad thing to say?"

"My mom used to say that," he said quietly. "She said that

Troy and I might be identical twins, but he'd inherited the Sheenan blood and I'd inherited the Crays." His mouth curved but the smile didn't reach his eyes. "Every time I got in trouble when I was little, every time my dad took the belt to me, or a switch, she would apologize to me, saying that we needed to forgive my father for not understanding who I was, and being unable to recognize my spirit."

His powerful shoulders shifted uncomfortably. "I didn't know what to think when I was younger. Dad didn't recognize Mom's Native American heritage. He didn't want a wife that was 'mixed', and forbad her from telling us stories about Indian folklore and customs. But now and then when I couldn't sleep, I'd go find her, and inevitably those were the nights my father was out and my mother would be awake, staring out the window, looking westward."

Trey glanced down at McKenna, expression pensive. "I didn't understand then how deeply lonely my mother was. She never talked about her loneliness but looking back, we all see it—her sons—and it's hard to realize how much she gave to us and how little she got back—"

"I don't think that's a fair assessment," McKenna interrupted-ed. "Children are not responsible for meeting their parents' needs."

"Maybe not when they are young, but by high school, I should have been more aware, more sensitive. Instead I was at my most rebellious."

"Because you were a teenager, filled with testosterone!"

He shrugged. "I wish you could have heard her stories. I wish I had recorded them or written them down because on those nights when my father was gone, she would talk about the Salish, the Kootenai and the Pend d'Oreille Tribes and how their beliefs about life were so different from the righteous Christians that only talked to God in Church. She said for the Flathead tribes, spirit was everywhere, and that all things were connected and to be respected, plants, rocks, animals, people. She said it was hard to find peace when one simply used things selfishly, and never gave back to the earth. She said the land wasn't there simply to be stripped, but to be protected. The trees and animals have a right to exist. Man is to recognize the spirit in each of them."

McKenna swallowed around the lump forming in her throat. "But you didn't need to record her stories to remember them. You've remembered."

"I miss her."

She went to him then, and wrapped her arms around his waist and held him, hugging him, knowing he needed to feel her—his mother's love—and if he couldn't have that, he could have her love.

Because she would always love him.

And she had always seen his spirit—and it was good. Yes, he had a wild streak, and he might not ever be completely tamed, but maybe that was who he was meant to be? Beautiful, fierce, and protective.

"She's still with you," McKenna whispered. "Especially here. I can feel her here."

Trey wrapped his arms around her and held her for a moment, before placing a kiss on the top of her head and breaking free.

"There is supposed to be a storm coming in tonight," he said gruffly. "I'm going to go have a look at the generator, make sure it's in working order." And then he was gone, disappearing quickly out the front door.

IT'D BEEN A dry and cold December in much of Montana, with freezing conditions but very little snow. It had snowed hard early in the month but whatever remained in the valleys was now compacted and brown.

With Christmas Eve just three days away, everyone was ready for fresh snow, saying it wouldn't be Christmas without a dusting of powdery white, but the storm coming was supposed to be a big one, with a foot or two of snow falling steadily throughout the night, making it difficult for the snowplows to keep up.

A foot of snow was a lot for Cherry Lake, and the record for heaviest snowfall in one day was sixteen inches back in December of 1929. No one wanted a foot of snow, not so close to Christmas when there was still so much shopping to do and last minute presents to mail.

Trey chopped more firewood and had the generator ready, then stood in the kitchen with McKenna making a list of emergency supplies, although neither of them were too worried, having grown up on isolated Paradise Valley ranches where winter storms routinely knocked out power, forcing families to adapt and make do.

McKenna wanted more milk and eggs, bread, lunchmeat and cheese along with tea, hot cocoa and ingredients for simple dinners for the next couple of nights.

Trey added candles, flashlights, and batteries. He glanced at the list and then to the living room where Trey was stretched out by the fire, staring at the tree. "What about stockings and presents for TJ?" he asked, dropping his voice. "We don't have anything for him, do we?"

"I have gifts for him in Marietta, not here," she said.

"But we're here...unless you're thinking you want to head back early?"

She glanced outside, at the sky, which was patchy with clouds. It didn't look bad now. "Try to beat it, you mean?"

"We wouldn't beat it. We'd be driving through it."

She wrinkled her nose. "But why do that? There's no reason to take extra risks when we could have a cozy Christmas here. We just need to do some shopping, pick up a few things so he has a stocking for Christmas morning and some gifts to open."

Trey nodded and McKenna checked her smile as Trey added, *Buy Toys and Wrapping Paper*, to the bottom of their list.

"I could even do some shopping if you wanted to take him to a matinee movie," she said. "I know there's a theatre showing kids movies in Bigfork. I could drop you two off at the movies and then shop and get all the errands done and then come back for you."

"Or we could divide the errands up and I go do some shopping for TJ now, and then come back and get you two, and then we all head to Bigfork." He looked at her, expression earnest. "It's not that I don't trust you to buy good things, but I really want to pick out something for him, some toys for him from me. Haven't been able to do that since he was born."

His words made her chest tighten and ache.

She loved how much he loved their son. "That's a great idea," she said. "You shop, I'll make him lunch, and that way when you return, we'll be ready to go."

TREY KNEW HE didn't have a lot of time to shop and it'd been years since he'd been able to buy gifts for TJ and McKenna. As he drove to Cherry Lake he tried to remember all the shops downtown, thinking there had to be a toy store somewhere. He couldn't recall seeing one, but that hadn't been their focus when they'd gone shopping yesterday.

And McKenna...what could he give her? What did she need?

She wasn't one of those women who loved fancy things. She didn't collect jewelry or like high fashion. She did enjoy art but a painting didn't seem like the right kind of gift after not giving her anything for a number of years.

It seemed as if everyone had come to town to finish shopping today. Town was crowded, and parking on Main Street non-existent. Trey parked a few blocks down, by the small post office, and walked back to the shops, sticking his head in any that looked kid-friendly.

Trey found red and green and cream knit stockings at one of the artsy stores. They had three left and he wanted to buy all three and hang them all from the stone fireplace but it seemed silly to buy himself a stocking. He was a man, he didn't need a stocking. But he wanted one for TJ and he'd love to fill one for McKenna even if it was just with tea and some jars of the local cherry flavored honey.

He ended up buying two and headed next door to the colorful candy shoppe that sold fresh saltwater taffy and homemade fudge. He bought taffy and a big lollipop for TJ's stocking and rich creamy blocks of marshmallow-studded fudge for Christmas Eve, hoping TJ liked marshmallows and fudge, unable to imagine a five year old that didn't. But it was an uncomfortable thing realizing he didn't know what his son liked. There were so many things Trey needed to discover and he looked forward to the day where he knew his son as well as McKenna...if not better.

The lady in the candy shoppe told Trey where to find a toy store and Trey headed there next. Again he wasn't sure what kinds of games and toys TJ liked, and felt hopelessly out of depth as he stared at the shelves filled with dolls and fairies, forest animals and farms, Lincoln Logs, puzzles, Duplo, Lego, robots, acrylic tubes and cylinders and other kinds of building blocks.

The sales clerk approached him. "Can I help you find something?"

Trey nodded, perplexed by all the choices. "I'm looking for something for my son," he said. "He's five."

"And what does he like to do?"

Trey rubbed the back of his neck. "I'm not sure."

"Does he have any favorite hobbies?"

"I uh…don't know."

The lady looked perplexed. "Is he into arts and crafts…?"

"I don't think so."

"Does he like costumes and to dress up?"

Trey frowned. "I don't think so. But I don't really know." He chafed at her baffled gaze. "I've been…gone," he said shortly. "I haven't seen him for years."

Her expression cleared. "You just got back from overseas. Bless you, dear, and thank you for your service to the country."

Trey felt sick. He wanted to correct her but couldn't bring himself to extend the conversation a moment longer than necessary. "Can you just show me the toys that are appropriate for five year old boys?"

"Of course. Right here." She led him down a few feet and tapped the shelf "These are all excellent choices. Legos, Ninja turtles, Power Rangers—they remain popular year after year—Transformers, Transformer dinosaurs or bots as some people call them." She pointed to another shelf. "Robots, Hot Wheels, army men—" she broke off to give him a warm smile. "—and then all the Nerf guns and mega blasters. Some parents are funny about giving toy guns but in my experience, most Montana boys love them. We are a hunting and fishing state!"

Trey thanked her for her help, ready to do make some decisions on his own but the sales woman seemed inclined to stay, and chat. "Now, I was one of those parents who didn't want to give toy guns," she said. "But my sons found a way to make guns anyway with their Tinker Toys and Lincoln Logs. Finally one day I thought enough, a boy is a boy, let him be a boy—"

"Thank you," Trey interrupted kindly, but firmly. "You have been so helpful. I'll bring my purchases up to the counter. Will you be the one at the register?"

"I will."

"Perfect. Then I can show you what I've picked out."

Trey was on his way to the truck, his arms filled with plastic bags and wrapped packages when he passed an artsy looking little shop named Montana Hearts that featured glazed mugs and pottery, sculpture and paintings and what looked like handmade jewelry.

It was the jewelry display in the window that caught his attention and made him stop, and then go inside.

"The necklace with the brass angel," he said. "Can I see that?"

"It looks like brass, doesn't it?" the young woman said, leaving the counter to head for the display. "But it's actually standard yellow gold with a pink gold overlay, kind of like Black Hills gold, but we can't call it that since it's not made in South Dakota." She reached into the display and lifted the necklace with the angel out. "I love this. It's so delicate and unusual. It reminds me of a Christmas ornament."

She placed the angel in his open palm and he studied the little angel's swirl of skirt and sweep of halo and wings. She looked so much like the brass angel ornaments he'd bought from McKenna her freshman year of high school. "She's pretty," he said.

"Handmade by a local artisan. We also have another one that's with the same angel, but she's more gold than pink and instead or a harp, she's holding a dark blue Montana sapphire. It's really gorgeous. It's probably my favorite thing we have in the shop."

"That's the one I want."

"It's rather pricey. It's real gold and a genuine sapphire—"

"That's fine. It's perfect. It's exactly what I've been looking for."

Chapter Thirteen

RETURNING TO THE cabin Trey tucked the bags and presents in the closet in the master bedroom and then helped TJ into his coat before doing up the zipper.

TJ ran outside to climb in the truck and Trey and McKenna followed more slowly.

"Looks like you had some success," she said.

Trey nodded. "It was hard at first. I wasn't sure what TJ would want but I ended up buying some Legos and then I spotted these sets of miniature tin soldiers at the antique store next door to the post office. There are actually two armies, one in red and one in blue. It's something I would have liked when I was a kid. It has cannons and guys with flags and guys on horses, too."

"I think he'll love it."

"Do you?" Trey looked uncertain. "I wasn't sure. So I also got him this Transformer dinosaur thing just in case."

"TJ is just so happy to have you here. The presents don't matter."

"It's Christmas, of course they matter."

"What about stocking stuffers? Find anything?"

"I found a stocking and picked up some little things—candy, silly putty and matchbox cars—but you might want to get a few things, too."

"Will do."

He hesitated on the bottom step. "Oh, and Mine Craft. I looked for them everywhere. Couldn't find anything and I'd really hoped to get him one of those Enderman guys."

"You're spoiling him. It's not necessary."

"I'm excited about Christmas."

She smiled. "I know. And so am I. It's going to be fun to watch him open his gifts together."

Trey gave his keys a jingle. "We still need wrapping paper, though. I forgot all about that."

"No worries. Anything else?"

"If you can find a Mine Craft Enderman… can you pick it up for me?"

Her smile grew. "Yes, I will, and don't worry, Henchman, it'll be from you."

IT BEGAN TO snow mid afternoon while McKenna was in the grocery store. She was heading for the check out when she saw the first fat flakes flutter down.

The clerk noticed the snow, too. "Supposed to be the biggest storm of the year. At least one foot tonight, maybe more."

"I heard it's unusual to get that much snow here at one time," McKenna said, taking another quick look over her shopping check list to make sure she hadn't forgotten anything.

"You're not from here?"

"From Marietta." She saw the clerk's puzzled expression. "Between Bozeman and West Yellowstone."

"You get some cold weather."

"We do," McKenna agreed.

"We get off easier, here, protected by the Mission Mountains, and then the lake itself keeps things warmer."

"Does it?" McKenna asked, helping bag up the groceries.

"It's our secret," the clerk answered with a wink. "We're far more temperate than the rest of the state. Great summers, mild winters, but don't tell anyone. We like our quiet little community."

The snow was falling thicker and faster as McKenna drove from the grocery store through downtown Bigfork, windshield wipes scraping back and forth to clear her vision. She scanned the storefronts, looking for a shop that might carry the Mine Craft toys for TJ. There was a toy shop a couple blocks from the movie theater. McKenna snagged a parking spot out front and headed into the store.

"Sold out of all the Mine Craft figurines we had, and didn't get any of the stuffed toys in this year," the teenage boy answered, "but we do have a youth backpack with a Creeper and a Zombie on it. How old is the kid?"

"Five," McKenna said.

"Would he like a backpack?" The teenager scratched the side of his nose. "Does anyone like backpacks? Hard to say. How much does he like Mine Craft?"

"A lot."

"Then he'll like it. I mean, the Zombie and Creeper are both green and the backpack is black. So that's kind of cool, you know?"

McKenna agreed and was at the counter paying for the backpack, keeping one eye on the snow outside which was coming down even faster now, when she spotted a green and white knit stocking hanging from the counter overflowing with packages of Moose poop (chocolate nuggets) and candy coal (licorice). Over the stocking hung a small sign, *For Those on Santa's Naughty List.*

McKenna smiled to herself. "Is this for sale?" she asked.

"Yep. Want it?"

"Yes." She plucked the stocking off the hook and handed it to him. "It's perfect."

THE THICK LACY flakes fell in heavy swirls as McKenna pulled up in front of the movie theater to pick Trey and TJ up. She slid all the way over on the bench seat so Trey could lift TJ into the truck for his middle spot.

"How are the roads?" Trey asked, climbing in and closing the door.

"Good. The snow is sticking but it's powdery so there is no problem." She buckled TJ's seat belt. "How was the movie?"

"Awesome," TJ said, "And we had popcorn and candy."

"Let me guess," she said. "Red Vines?"

"How did you know?"

"That's always been your daddy's favorite at the movies, and what we had when he and I went on dates back in high school."

"They had Red Vines all the way back then?"

She smiled and tweaked his nose. "It wasn't that long ago."

"Was I born then?"

"No."

"Then that was a long time ago."

IT CONTINUED TO snow steadily the rest of the afternoon, with the snow piling up outside on the wooden railing of the deck, burying the shrubs outside the cabin door. When they first arrived back at the cabin, Trey had made several trips outside to bring in enough firewood to see them through the night, and now they sat at the pine dining table playing Go Fish with an old deck of cards Trey had found in one of the kitchen drawers, while Christmas carols sounded on the little transistor radio.

Trey shuffled the cards at the end of the latest game. "Are we done?" he asked, stretching his legs under the table. "Everybody had enough?"

"No!" TJ cried, leaning on the table, reaching for his cup of spiced apple cider. "Let's keep playing."

McKenna glanced out the window. Dusk had fallen and it was quickly getting dark. "I need to start the spaghetti sauce soon or we won't eat dinner until late."

"But I'm not hungry yet," TJ said. "And this is fun."

McKenna made a soft sound that sounded an awful lot like a groan. He glanced at her, smiling. "Still having fun?"

She gave him a tortured smile and tugged on her ponytail, tightening the elastic band. "You know how much I love card games."

Trey laughed softly, enjoying himself, but then, honestly, this was a gift. When he'd learned that McKenna was getting married he'd gone through a hell all of his own and he'd never imagined then, waking up Saturday morning that he'd be here with Mac and TJ today.

This was his Christmas. This was the best gift ever. He honestly couldn't ask for more, and he wasn't ready to think beyond today…and maybe tomorrow.

He and McKenna hadn't talked about the future. As far as he knew, there was no future and maybe once upon a time that would have been hard for him to accept, but four years at Deer

Lodge had taught him patience, as well as acceptance.

He couldn't control everything. He couldn't please everyone. He might not be able to please anyone. The only thing he could do, was do his best.

He was trying his best now.

He was focusing on gratitude, too.

Life was short and unpredictable. Instead of going through life feeling entitled, he was going to count his blessings, every single one of them, and right now, his greatest blessings were sitting here at the table playing cards and sipping cider and making him feel like the luckiest man alive.

THE GROUND BEEF and tomato sauce and seasonings were simmering in a pot on the stove and McKenna stepped outside the toasty little kitchen to stand on the porch and watch the white flurries.

Twilight had given way to night. Snow piled high on the porch railing and buried the shrubs by the front of the cabin.

She left the porch and climbed down a step and then another, feeling the snowflakes land on her face and catch in her hair.

It was so quiet out, so blissfully still.

The fresh white snow transformed the landscape, hiding the barren spots, the rocks and dirt, coating weeds so that everything looked beautiful and new.

But wasn't that the magic of Christmas? Wasn't that what made this season so special? Birth, hope, new life…

She glanced over her shoulder back at the cabin and could see through the big picture window Trey and TJ at the table, building a house from the cards. Behind them the fire crackled in the stone hearth and the Christmas tree with the white lights and vintage ornaments cast a colorful glow.

From here on the porch, it looked like a scene from a movie…

If only life was as warm and sweet as a Hallmark movie…

She could use one of those happy endings. TJ, too.

Her eyes burned and she blinked, wanting so badly to give TJ the life she hadn't known. She wanted him to have happiness. She prayed he could grow up without the tragedies she'd experienced. She hoped he could grow from boy to man before he should ever have to suffer and grieve, as she'd suffered and grieved.

It was more than nineteen years since that terrible night when her family had been attacked. And still she couldn't think about it, couldn't picture it, dwell on it, remember in any detail at all how horrific it had been.

Just learning to live without them all had been hard enough. She didn't need to have the horrors burned into her mind.

Trey was such a big part of her healing.

Trey was the one that helped her start to feel safe. Secure.

He was her angel. Her tough, rebel angel.

No one else saw the side she did, but she knew something no one else did—he would protect her with his life.

He would die before he'd let anyone hurt her.

He was there to help her through.

And so when TJ had been conceived, it wasn't this terrible shame, but a gift, and a blessing. TJ was a testament to their love, and proof that good things did happen. Good things would continue to happen.

The cabin door opened and Trey stepped out, gently closing the door, but not shutting it all the way.

"You okay?" he asked, coming down the steps to stand next to her. The snow swirled around him, flakes drifting onto his hair.

She smiled up at him. "Yes."

"You just felt like taking in some snow?"

She crossed her arms over her chest, holding in the emotion. "This has been an amazing day. It's…perfect."

"We didn't really do anything."

"We didn't have to. Just being together made it perfect."

He reached out, and smoothed his hand over the top of her head, and then down the length of her ponytail. "I agree."

He was standing close, very close and she could feel his warmth and his strength. It would be so easy to just lean against him, to absorb his warmth and strength. He'd feel good. He'd feel right. He'd feel like love.

Like home.

She stared up at him, her gaze locking with his, her chest growing heavy, tight.

She wanted him to kiss her.

She wanted him to hold her.

She wanted him to be hers again.

But they'd been down this road before. It hadn't gone well. And the pain of living without Trey when things had gone wrong had been so extreme. The pain was excruciating. It was honestly more than she could bear.

So how did one make it work? How could she love him without constantly worrying, and fearing the worst?

He must have seen her fear and doubts because he clasped her face in his hands, lifting her face to his. His blue eyes "You don't have to know everything, babe. You don't have to solve all the problems of the world tonight. Just live. Just love. Just breathe."

And then his head dropped and his lips covered hers, his lips warm, his breath scented with cinnamon and cider. He kissed her lightly, gently, the pressure just enough to send shivers of pleasure racing up and down her spine.

She reached up, cupping his cheek, fingernails lightly playing against the rough bristles of his beard. He felt so good, his mouth knew hers and she did exactly what he said—she breathed him in, loving him.

It was impossible to be McKenna Douglas without loving Trey Sheenan.

He deepened the kiss, just enough to part her lips, the tip of his tongue tracing the softness of her lower lip and she tingled, growing hot, cold, feeling alive from the top of her head to her tippy toes.

She wanted to tell him she loved him. She wanted to tell him that she'd never stopped loving him but the words wouldn't come. She was still too afraid of giving him the power to break her heart.

Again.

"Hey, um, Mom." It was TJ in the doorway, and he'd stuck his head outside. "Your spaghetti sauce smells weird on the stove."

Chapter Fourteen

SOMETIME IN THE night it stopped snowing and when they all woke in the morning, the world was a sparkling landscape of frosty white beneath a brilliant blue sky.

TJ and Trey spent the morning sledding and building a snowman before coaxing McKenna out for a massive snowball fight.

It was, as TJ described it, the fight to end all fights, and they ran through the woods, down Cray Road, tramping through knee high powdery snow.

The air was cold and the chill stung McKenna's cheeks but it was also exhilarating racing around lobbing soft snowballs while ducking behind trees.

For a half hour the snowballs flew fast and furious with TJ and Trey joining forces to ambush McKenna. But then TJ changed teams and she and TJ launched a dozen snowballs at Trey, succeeding in getting several well placed ones in his face and collar.

TJ howled with laughter as Trey shook the snow out of his shirt, and then laughed again as Trey took McKenna down, turning her into a shrieking snow angel.

And then they were all snow angels, lying on their backs beneath the intensely blue sky, moving their arms and legs to create their angel wings.

Chilled from lying in the snow, TJ jumped up and raced to get the sled for one more trip down the hill and Trey gave McKenna a hand, pulling her up to her feet.

"When he stops moving, he's going to be soaked through and cold," McKenna said, watching TJ wrestle with the sled.

"He'll need a hot bath and dry clothes."

"Then lunch, and hopefully a nap."

Trey stretched. "A nap sounds good." He looked down at her and there was heat in his gaze. Desire, too.

She felt herself grow warm even as her heart began to thud, harder, faster.

Awareness licked at her veins, making her belly flip flop.

It would feel amazing to be with him, naked against him, his body filling hers. But the physical would cloud her judgment. The physical would make being rational impossible.

She took a steady step backwards, even as she hoped he'd close the distance and kiss her anyway.

Kiss her again, like he had last night...

Instead he took several steps back, also, and they were now standing a yard or two apart. As if strangers.

She didn't know why she felt a sudden urge to cry. She didn't know why everything about this moment suddenly felt so deeply unsatisfying.

"This is the Christmas I wanted," he said. "Thank you, Mac."

He sounded sincere but for some reason his sincerity just made her more upset. My pleasure," she said stiffly.

"I've loved every minute I've been able to spend with TJ."

She ground her teeth together. "You said you wanted

Christmas with your son. I'm glad you're getting it."

"Not just with him, with you, too."

"Right."

The edge of his mouth lifted. "I mean it."

"Sure. That's why you came to the church to sort out TJ's custody."

"You know it wasn't just about TJ. I was there for you, too."

Her chin jerked up. "It didn't seem that way."

"You were in a wedding gown, marrying someone else. I couldn't exactly storm the church and take you prisoner. There were a hundred and fifty people watching. I had to be careful. Discrete."

She exhaled hard. "You might want to stop talking. Now you're just making me mad."

"Why? Because I've finally grown up enough to realize that what I want and need might not be what you want and need?"

"I'm not sure what you're saying."

He clapped his black gloves, knocking off excess snow. "Let's not do this now."

Her heart felt as if he was about to leap out of her chest. "Do what?"

"Have this conversation. We've had a really fun day, and it's been an incredible Christmas so far—"

"We absolutely do need to have this conversation now. This," she said, jabbing her mitten finger downward, "is exactly what we need to discuss." She stared him in the eye, fierce and furious. And scared. Terribly, terribly scared. "Are you saying you don't want me?"

"That's not what I'm saying."

"Then what *are* you saying?"

"I'm saying…." He drew a breath and yet his expression was firm, and totally unapologetic. "TJ needs us together. *I'd* like us together. But I'm not sure if *us* being together is the best thing for *you*."

She dragged air into her lungs, hating the bittersweet pain that filled her heart. She focused on the wet sheen of icicles lining the edge of the cabin roof to keep from crying or getting even more emotional. "I don't believe you."

His shoulders shifted. "I love you enough to want what's best for you. I'm not sure I'm the best for you."

"Why? What's changed?"

"I have. I know why I love you, and I know what I want for you, and that's for you to be happy. And peaceful. I make you happy some of the time, but together, darlin', we're not peaceful. I don't make you calm and easy. With me, you worry. But I don't want my girl scared and worrying. That's not good for you, not good for us, and not good for our son."

She couldn't believe what she was hearing. And yet, hadn't she just wondered if she could love him? If she could trust him not to hurt her? Not to break her heart again? Did she feel confident in them...or him? "I don't know why you're doing this now."

"I want to protect you."

"Protect me? Or, do you mean, protect yourself? Because my gut is saying you're the coward. My gut is saying you don't want to do the hard work required to make us succeed. My gut thinks you've decided to give up...take the easy way out. That's what I think!"

He gazed at her a long time, eyes flashing fire, but he waited to speak until his tone was calm. Controlled. "I haven't given up on us—I will never give up on us—but we have to be honest and do what is best for each other. Loving me is hard on you, Mac. Loving me hurts you, honey. It took me a long time to get it. Took me those four years in prison to understand what it means to hurt for someone, and baby, I hurt for you. And I hurt for hurting you and I can't ever cause you pain like that again. I couldn't live with myself if I did that."

She turned away to look toward the dark blue lake with its perimeter of snow frosted trees. It was so pretty...so romantic...and yet there was nothing pretty or romantic about what Trey was saying. "You're killing me," she whispered, reaching up to tug her knit cap down. "You give me hope and then you just take it all away."

"I'm not trying to hurt you. I'm trying to protect you from future pain—"

"The future isn't here! There's nothing here but you and me and TJ. So Sheenan, don't you dare say you're being practical and honest and all mature, because guess what? You're not that practical and mature. You came to my wedding Saturday, you interrupted the service, you took TJ and then you grabbed me, stealing us from the church. You kidnapped me on my wedding day. And you didn't turn around, you didn't go back, and you didn't feel remorse. You dragged us to a diner for a wedding night dinner and somehow between Marietta and White Sulphur Springs you captured TJ's heart, and melted mine, and sorry, but you can't act all good and chivalrous now, because it's too late! You're not this great guy. You're not selfless and you're not altruistic and your love is demanding and fierce and you do want me. You still want me, you bastard, and don't you ever say you don't!"

She shoved her mitten across her face, wiping her eyes, swiping at her nose. "Don't you ever," she repeated thickly. "Because it's not fair. Not when we both know what we've always known—we were made for each other. We are meant to be together. And that's why we have a son together. He's not an accident. We are not an accident. And I'm tired of living like we—this—us—is just one colossal mistake!"

She marched back to the cabin, desperate to get inside before TJ saw her cry.

Damn him.

Damn Trey.

He was the worst, most awful man in the world.

And if he was her angel, he was a fallen angel and it'd fallen on her to save his ass.

❦

TREY SAT IN one of the chairs by the fire, cleaning the snowshoes he'd found in the shed. The wood frames still looked good but the rawhide lacings were worn and needed attention. It seemed that mice had gotten to the leather and he made a note to order new lacings once he returned to Marietta. In the meantime, he carefully rubbed the ash frames dry, grateful to have something to occupy his hands and attention.

Dinner had been on the quiet side, at least between himself and McKenna. TJ had talked up a storm and hadn't seem to notice, and once the dishes were done, McKenna curled up with TJ on the little couch, making up stories and asking TJ what he thought Santa Claus was doing right now.

She was still mad at him, still not talking to him, while showering TJ with hugs and kisses.

He didn't mind McKenna showering TJ with love. McKenna should be an affectionate Mom. She should tell stories and play and be fun.

But Trey was having a hard time being shut out from the fun. He struggled with McKenna punishing him for being a *bad* guy, when in this instance, he was the *good* guy.

He hadn't spent four years missing her and picturing a

future with her, a future that hopefully included more children and family trips and holidays and traditions, to let go so easily. It was a life he wanted with every bit of his being…but it had to be right. For both of them. Otherwise it wasn't the family life either of them desired.

He didn't want a resentful or anxious wife. He didn't want to be the source of someone's anger, or worry.

He was who he was, and he was trying damn hard to do things better, but he'd never do everything perfectly. He'd make mistakes. He'd be impulsive, using his heart before his head. But that was who he was. He wasn't Troy. Or Brock. Dillon or Cormac. He was himself.

Not bad.

Just not perfect.

Which was why he was trying to think of *her*, and what *she* needed. McKenna had been through a lot in her life. They never talked about what happened at the Douglas Ranch that one night, but he'd read about it in the papers. The murders had been discussed in agonizing detail around town. Trey's dad had been one of the first responders on the scene, as the Sheenan ranch lay close to the Douglas property, but he wouldn't talk about what he'd seen at the Douglas ranch, other than the thing he'd said when he came home: *it was the worst, most violent scene imaginable, and if God had any mercy at all, he'd let that one poor boy survive.*

Trey glanced up from the snowshoes to McKenna, watching her whisper something playful into TJ's ear and making TJ giggle.

She deserved to be happy.

They all deserved to be happy.

Which didn't mean he was walking away from her, or giving up on her, or giving up on them.

It just meant they had to be mature, and patient. They had to talk, and listen, and get a hell of a lot better at communicating.

They nailed some parts of it. They were experts at hot sex. But now they needed to get good at the other things, working together to make sure their relationship would last. He wanted what his parents didn't have. A happy marriage.

A true partnership.

And you only got that with respect, trust, faith, forgiveness.

McKenna had forgotten that when Trey was hurt he grew quiet. She'd forgotten that he wasn't loud and out of control, but silent and thoughtful. Reserved.

He was certainly reserved now. He'd shut down, retreating to a chair in the corner where he sat doing manly chores and repairs, like weatherproof the old wooden snowshoes.

She wasn't trying to ignore him, but she wasn't going to struggle to fill the silence with meaningless small talk, either.

However, once TJ fell asleep on her lap, worn out from sledding and snowball fights and tramping around in the snow, the living room, silent except for the crackle and pop of the fire, felt uncomfortable.

Tomorrow was Christmas Eve. This wasn't how she wanted Christmas to be.

She didn't even know what had happened outside, earlier. Everything just seemed to shift and tilt and go wildly wrong.

She felt an ache as she watched Trey work, his dark head bent.

She wanted things different. She wanted them better. She wanted more with Trey, not less.

Not this.

Silence and anger and hurt.

Suddenly his head lifted and he looked up at her, his brow furrowed, expression shuttered. "If I didn't want what was best for you, Mac, I'd be no man at all."

"But who are you to decide what's best for me?" she retorted defiantly. "Who are you to tell me what I need?"

"I know what you need. I've known you too long not to know. And for the record, I never said we're finished, never said we're through, because God as my witness, I will never ever walk away from you. I will always want you. I will always love you. And we might fight, and we might disagree, but that doesn't mean I'm abandoning you. You're my girl. But I've got to do right by you."

"Then love me."

"I do."

"And don't say we can't make it work—"

"Never said that."

"And don't imply that you're the wrong guy, or that there might be a better guy. Whether there is, or isn't, is a moot point, because I want you. I choose you." She drew an unsteady breath. "I love you."

There was just silence for a moment, but it wasn't the silence of before. This was soft and full…warm and hopeful.

"That's why I climbed in the truck with you and TJ," she added quietly. "I wasn't being kidnapped. I wasn't being forced anywhere. I wanted to go with you…I wanted to be with you. I've wanted to be with you since I was fifteen and thought you were my very own knight in tarnished armor."

Creases fanned from his eyes. The corners of his mouth tilted. "Tarnished armor, hmm?"

She could see him back as they were in high school. She

remembered how he'd avoided her all Fall of her freshman year, even though she knew he was aware of her. She knew he knew she was there. And she didn't know why he kept his distance, but as the weeks passed, September to October, and then October to November, she didn't want him to keep his distance. She wanted him close, talking to her, close, dancing with her, close, kissing her.

She just wanted him close.

She just wanted him. Not sexually—she wasn't that mature, or precocious—but she craved his company and wanted to look into his blue eyes and see if she could see more, see deeper. She wanted to look until she was full, look until her heart was overflowing.

"I chose you a long time ago," she added, voice dropping to a whisper. "And we've had some hard years. Now we just have to figure out how to make this work."

✺

THEY MADE LOVE in the four poster log bed in the master bedroom, beneath the heavy handmade quilts, with the snow stacked on the windowsill, blocking out much of the moon light.

They'd waited years to come together, years to be one, and the lovemaking was slow and hushed, breath catching, lips touching, hands skimming. Trey took his time kissing her, kissing everywhere, enjoying the satin and silk of her skin, the warmth of her body, the curves that were uniquely hers. He breathed her in, the heat, the taste, the scent and he loved her so much, so deeply, that in some ways he didn't know where he ended and she began.

She was that much a part of him and his heart.

For the first time in a long long time, McKenna felt completely safe. Completely at peace.

She was lying in the circle of Trey's arms, her cheek against his chest. She could hear his heart. She could feel his strength, his power deceptive when he was relaxed.

He shifted, rolling her over onto her back to look down into her face. "I want to marry you," he said. "I want TJ to have us, both of us together. A real family. He deserves that. We deserve that."

"Are you proposing, Sheenan?"

His lips curved but his expression was fierce, intense. "We were engaged the last time I saw you."

She swallowed, nodded. True. "I still have the ring. It's at the bank, in a safe. I didn't want anything to happen to it."

"Speaking of rings, where is Lawrence's? I haven't seen you wear it since we left White Sulphur Springs."

"It's tucked away to return it to him once I'm back in Marietta." She reached up to touch his cheek, her fingertips sliding over his cheekbone and then down along the hard chiseled jaw. "You know that I haven't done this since you left, four years ago. There's been no one but you. Ever."

He frowned. "You and Lawrence...?"

She shook her head. "We agreed to wait until we were married. I think he thought I was virtuous. I wasn't virtuous. I just wasn't...eager. It was easy to wait."

"How could you marry him then?"

"I was trying so hard to get over you. Trying so hard to build a life without you." She gulped a breath. "Thank God you arrived when you did. If you hadn't..." Her voice drifted away, her insides lurching. "It wouldn't have been good."

"Then we need to make this good. We need to be good." He turned his face into her hand, kissing her palm. "We can't be hotheads anymore. Can't be brash or impulsive."

"You're the impulsive one," she countered. "You're the one that leaps before looking."

His lips curved. "Maybe."

"Don't be brash anymore. Don't be stupid."

"Ouch." But he was smiling.

She smiled back, even as she wound her arms around his neck. "Be smart. Be safe. Be mine, forever."

"I am, babe. Forever and ever."

Chapter Fifteen

TJ WOKE FIRST. It was early, almost ungodly early as he shouted from the living room. "Santa came! Santa was here!"

McKenna quickly pulled her night shirt on and left the warm bed to shiver in the middle of the room. "Come on, Santa, you need to build a fire. I'll get the coffee brewing."

In the living room TJ was crouched by the Christmas tree studying the colorful packages that magically appeared in the night.

"Are any of these for me?" he asked, touching the gifts and trying to read names on the tags.

"I think most of them are for you," she answered, smiling as she buttoned up the oversized Salish knit cardigan she'd turned into her robe. "Santa must think you've been a very good boy."

"But someone wasn't good," TJ said, pointing to the row of stockings hanging from the stone fireplace. "One of them has black stuff in it."

"Coal."

TJ looked worried. "That's *bad*."

Yawning Trey entered the room and glanced up at the three

stockings hanging from the stone mantle. Two red and green and cream stockings, and one green and white one. "Which is mine?" he asked.

"I hope you didn't get the one with coal," TJ said.

Trey glanced from the stockings to McKenna, an eyebrow rising. "Bad, huh?"

She shrugged. "It's from Santa. He keeps the list, naughty and nice." Then she crossed to his side, and leaned down to whisper. "Although last night I think you were both naughty and nice."

His blue gaze warmed. "Very very nice."

"Or, very very bad…"

"Which can also be nice."

She blushed and kissed him before straightening. "I'm going to make coffee.

You guys build the fire and then we'll have to see what Santa brought everyone."

TJ LOVED HIS gifts, all of them, letting out delighted squeals every time he opened a new presents. He tore through the paper, destroying ribbons and careful wrap to crow with pleasure as he discovered the gift.

Boxes of Lego. The set of tin soldiers. A football. A Mine Craft backpack. Matchbox cars and a figure 8 track for the cars to race on.

TJ wanted to play with everything right away but then settled down with the tin soldiers, setting up two army camps on the floor by the tree.

McKenna went to make breakfast, eggs and hash brown and cinnamon coffee cake. She'd just slid the coffee cake into the oven when Trey came to the kitchen. "I have one more gift," he said, holding out a small box with an enormous red bow. "I found it in a little art and crafts gallery in Cherry Lake. It reminded me of you."

She put the pot holders down and took the little box with the huge crimson silk ribbon. It was so pretty. The ribbon itself was a work of art. "I don't have anything else for you," she said regretfully. "Just that Pendleton shirt I gave you earlier."

"I like my shirt. I haven't had a new shirt in a while."

"I would have shopped more but I was using your money. It didn't feel right buying you presents with your own money."

"Now that's not entirely true. You did give me something else. A very nice gift, full of tender loving thoughts." His dark head inclined. "Thank you for that wonderful sock full of coal."

She laughed, her expression mischievous. "I couldn't help it. The stocking *screamed* your name."

"I'm sure it did." His lips were still quirked and then his smile faded but his expression was infinitely warm. "And this one, Mac, screamed yours."

She tugged off the ribbon and removed the paper and lifted the lid. Inside the delicate tissue paper was a necklace. An angel hanging from a gold necklace.

And the angel looked like a miniature version of the angel ornaments she'd sold him all those years ago.

"You know what this looks like," she said.

"The dozen brass angels I bought from you."

"Yes." She lifted the angel, studying it more closely, the chain sliding through her fingers. "Is this a sapphire?"

"A Montana sapphire."

"I love it so much." She leaned forward and kissed him, and kissed him again. "I love you so much."

"I know you do."

"We're going to make this work, Trey. We're going to get it right this time."

"That's the plan."

"No craziness. Just family and work and love." She smiled into his eyes. "Lots and lots of love."

"Sounds perfect." He took the necklace from her, opened the clasp, waiting while she lifted her long hair and then fastened it around her neck.

She turned back around to face him. "How does it look?" she asked, touching the angel which hit just at her breastbone.

"Beautiful."

"Thank you."

"My pleasure." He hesitated. "Speaking of family and work and love...have you thought about where you want to live?"

She hesitated, her fingers rubbing across the angel and stone. "I would have thought you'd want to live on the Sheenan ranch."

"But I know the idea of living on the ranch makes you nervous," he said.

She said nothing, her gaze clinging to his.

"And yes, the ranch house is big enough. It has what? Five bedrooms? But it's not the space that has you worried. It's the fact that we're so remote."

"Yes."

"I think TJ would love living on the ranch. The horses, the dogs. All the space to play."

"I loved living on our ranch, until..." Her voice faded and she hung her head, rubbing the angel again, needing courage, and comfort. "But if it's what you wanted for TJ, if it's that important to you, we could try. I could...try."

"But you'd be scared."

She nodded.

"Even with me there," he added.

She nodded again. "I'm sorry."

He reached for her, drawing her against him, his hands looping low on her back. "Don't be sorry. I don't blame you for being frightened. If I were you, I'd be nervous, too."

She exhaled slowly. This had been a sticking point for them, years ago. Trey had wanted to live on the ranch. She had wanted to live in town. He couldn't run the ranch from town but she couldn't imagine living so isolated. What if something bad happened again? What if…?

She swallowed hard. "My fear is irrational, I know that. And Sheenans are ranchers, I know that, too. But I really really don't want to be way out there, especially if you're not at the house, and let's face it, you'll be out working on the ranch, taking care of the cattle and the property, not hanging around the kitchen."

"So we live in town."

"And the ranch?"

"We'll figure that out."

"What does that mean?"

"It means the ranch isn't half as important as you, and your peace of mind. Maybe Dillon will want to run it. Maybe I'll sell it—"

"Trey, no!"

"I've lived without the ranch for the past four years, and I was fine. But I wasn't fine living without you." His gaze was steady, his expression somber as he reached up to move a loose tendril of hair from her brow. His fingers were gentle, his touch sure. "A job is a job, but family is forever."

His tenderness made her chest ache. "And yet since I've met you, you've only wanted one thing—to run the Sheenan ranch one day."

"Two things," he corrected. "You and the ranch, but as I

said, I didn't burn and ache for the ranch at Deer Lodge, but honey, I burned and ached for you."

THEY HAD A leisurely breakfast and then Trey and TJ washed up the dishes so McKenna could take a bath and sample some of the bubbles and body wash and scented shampoo Trey had filled her stocking with.

McKenna sighed with pleasure as she soaked in the hot tub, the vanilla and nutmeg scented bubbles tickling her chin.

It had been a great day...a great few days. Christmas this year had been so joyous...an absolute miracle.

She reached up to touch the angel on her necklace, her fingers rubbing at the gold figure holding the sapphire hearth.

Just as Trey was her miracle.

And her angel.

AFTER MCKENNA'S BATH it was TJ's turn, and then he and Trey built one of his Lego sets and McKenna made an early lunch, serving the grilled cheese sandwiches and tomato soup with an apology for it not being more festive.

Neither of the boys seemed to mind but when Trey cleared the lunch dishes, bringing them into the kitchen, McKenna was already worrying about Christmas dinner. "What about tonight?" she asked. "I don't have a roast or turkey, nothing special for a proper Christmas dinner. Do you think there is anything open today...we could buy something, or make reservations somewhere?"

"We don't need anything fancy," Trey answered, scraping

the plates and rinsing the soup bowls. "TJ doesn't care about what we eat, and trust me, I'm not picky, either."

"But it's Christmas. Christmas should be extra special. Food, festivities, family."

He turned off the water, faced her. "We could go back to Marietta. If we leave in the next hour we'd be able to join everyone gathering at Brock and Harley's for Christmas dinner. They're hosting the family this year. Most of the Sheenans will be there...Troy and Taylor. Dillon. Possibly Cormac, but with Daisy he's not a given."

"Can we do that? Just show up uninvited?"

"I'm a Sheenan. I'm always invited, and there will be plenty to eat. Apparently Harley's from a big Dutch family and always cooks enough to feed an army." He reached for her, pulling her against him. "But we don't have to go. It's only if you want to. I don't want there to be any pressure or worries on Christmas Day."

She glanced behind her, over at TJ who'd returned to playing with his new Star Wars Lego figurines, delighted by the Storm Troopers. "Aren't they going to think it's strange, you showing up with us on Christmas when they know less than a week ago I was supposed to marry Lawrence?"

"I think they'd think it was strange if I didn't show up with you and TJ. I'm pretty sure they're rooting for us, hoping we can work it out."

"But they're not going to expect a big formal announcement, are they? I mean, you and I are still trying to figure it out."

He smiled and lightly rubbed at the worry line between her brows. "I can assure you there's no pressure in that direction. I think you know we Sheenans tend to operate under a Hope-for-the-best-but-prepare-for-the-worst scenario."

She made a face. "Or at least they do with you."

"As they should," he teased.

She glanced out the window at the blue sky and sparkling drifts of powdery white snow with the dark blue of the lake shimmering in the background before letting her gaze skim the interior of the cabin. "You think we can take down the tree and empty the cupboards and strip all the beds in an hour?" Her nose wrinkled. "It doesn't sound like a festive way to spend the morning."

"Let's just unplug the tree and toss out the perishables and then I'll just come back after New Year's with the new generator and get that installed and deal with everything else."

"That's a lot of work for one person."

Trey's laughter rumbled from his chest. "Darlin', I've just spent four years at Deer Lodge. Tidying up a cabin and taking a tree down is not hard work. Besides, I like it here, and I'd love to get that generator replaced so we can get all the Sheenans here and enjoy it as a family."

MCKENNA MOVED AS much of the food from the refrigerator to the freezer and tossed what wouldn't last a week or two and then turned her attention to making the beds since they weren't going to strip the sheets.

Trey unplugged the tree, put out the fire, and turned off the heater before crouching next to TJ to help him gather up the new toys and put them in TJ's new black and green Mine Craft backpack. McKenna smiled as TJ made decisions about which pockets would get which toys—some for the Legos, some for the miniature tin soldiers, and some for the Christmas taffy and treats.

"I wish we didn't have to go," he said mournfully, as the

new suitcase, filled with all their new clothes, was carried out to the truck.

"We'll be back," Trey said, rifling TJ's dark hair. "Not just this winter, but in the spring and summer. We'll get a boat and go out on the lake. We can fish and have camp fires and make s'mores. It'll be fun."

McKenna understood TJ's wistfulness. She had mixed feelings about leaving, too. These past few days had felt special…magical…and she wasn't sure she was ready to leave the safety and quiet of the cabin at Cherry Lake for 'real life' in Marietta.

Back in Marietta they'd get drawn into work and school and be subjected to everyone's opinions.

She didn't want everyone's opinion. She didn't want to be lectured or fussed over, or have well meaning family and friends give her 'advice'. She didn't want the gossip, either, and there would be plenty of gossip.

It wasn't that she couldn't handle the gossip—good grief, she'd been surrounded by it for most of her life—but she dreaded having TJ exposed to it. And she hated knowing that Trey would be at the center of it.

That bad Trey Sheenan was back…

Trey was home and already causing trouble…

He climbed the steps of the cabin and stood before her, arms crossed over his broad chest. "What's wrong?"

She managed a smile. "Nothing. Why?"

"Mac, I know you, babe. I know your face. I know your sighs. I know when something is on your mind. What is it? Don't want to do Christmas with my family? We don't have to—"

"This isn't about your family. I like your family, and I know they like me, and absolutely adore TJ…" She looked up into his face, searching his eyes, not wanting secrets between them but also unwilling to hurt him. "It's about you. I'm worried what people will say about you." She swallowed hard. "And me, us. But mostly, about you. They've never been kind to you—"

"Because I've never earned their respect," he interrupted flatly. "I'm not going back to Marietta expecting anyone to be a fan, or a friend. I don't need anyone's approval. But I hope their criticism doesn't extend to TJ. He might have my name, but he's not me. He's his own little person and a really good little person." His voice cracked and he looked away, jaw tightening and flexing as his gaze fell on TJ who was poking holes in the snow with a stick. "I don't mind if they hit me, and hate me. But they have to leave him alone."

McKenna fought tears as she wrapped her arms around Trey and hugged him, hard, harder. "He's a tough little boy. He's got the best of both of us, and a big family that will always have his back...the Sheenans and the Douglasses, two of the oldest, strongest families in Crawford County. You can't ask for more than that."

IN THE TRUCK as they pulled away, McKenna turned to get a last glance at the cabin. It was a true cabin, small and sturdy and simple, without luxurious bells and whistles, which was why it was so perfect.

They'd had no TV or computer games. Just Christmas carols on the radio, and the one NPR personality that read the stories on Christmas Eve.

It was an old fashioned Christmas, small and cozy with just the right amount of presents and surprises and holiday cheer.

It'd be easy to stay here and hide from life in Marietta, but their life was in Marietta and it had to be faced, sooner or later.

Maybe it was better it was happening sooner.

Maybe the best thing was just to face the haters and critics head on, and work their way through it.

Eventually the gossip would die down. Eventually the town would find someone new, or something else shocking, to whisper about.

She'd be glad when they did. Not that she wished trouble or small town gossip on anyone.

With the recent heavy snow fall Highway 83 would be too treacherous, if the mountain pass was even open, so Trey turned left onto 93, heading for Polson, and then they'd hit I-90 which would lead them straight to Bozeman and on to the junction of Highway 89.

But even the road along the lake was slick, and she was glad it was Trey at the wheel. He was far better with ice than she.

They were just a few miles from the cabin when they rounded a corner and deep tire marks sliced sideways through snow and ice, a diagonal slash across the road that stretched all the way to the embankment overlooking the lake. The skid of the tires looked perfectly fresh. The accident must have just happened.

"Oh no," McKenna said, leaning forward. "Look," she added, pointing to the group forming at the lake.

Trey pulled over, shifted into park and jumped out. McKenna told TJ to stay put and jumped out, too.

A small white car was parked haphazardly on the side of the road, and a motorcycle stood abandoned there as well.

People were on phones. Someone else was shouting for rope.

"The woman lost control and her car went into the lake," one of the female bystanders cried into her phone, almost hysterical. "Hurry! She had a baby in her car. They're under water."

People were shouting, cars continued to pull over. It was pure chaos. Trey glanced at McKenna for a split second—if that—but the Trey she knew was gone. The other Trey was here. The one who shut down emotions, the one who deadened feelings. The impulsive, reckless devil-take-all Trey.

Her heart fell. "Trey!"

But he was already gone, skidding down the icy embankment to the water's edge. A man stood next to the lake, his clothing soaked to his waist, dripping icy water onto the packed snow. "I couldn't get to her, man. I can't even see the car. The water is freezing and dark."

"How many people in the car?" Trey asked, stripping off his heavy jacket.

"Two, three. A lady and a baby. Don't know if there was more, but I saw the car seat. There was a car seat. I was right behind her when she swerved and went in."

Trey dove in.

THERE WERE MOMENTS engraved in one's memory, moments that became memories, both wonderful and horrifying.

The time Trey spent underwater was endless. The actual time could have been seconds, minutes, but it felt like a lifetime.

McKenna saw a lifetime of memories and moments with him. In high school. After school. Working. Loving. Fighting. Conceiving TJ. Struggling. Loving. Missing. Suffering.

Life with Trey could be difficult, but life without him was impossible.

Life without him wasn't like living at all.

And this—this thing he was doing—was exactly what she feared most. She hated the reckless dangerous Trey. Hated that he had so little regard for his own life. Hated that he could just abandon her and TJ without a second thought…second glance…

Hated that the one person she needed most, didn't need her the same way.

If he loved them, he wouldn't jeopardize his family…

But in the very same moment she knew that he did what he did, took these incredible risks, because he had heart.

His strength was a gift.

His courage set him apart.

He was brave and foolhardy, but weren't all protectors that way?

In that moment where she thought she'd lost him forever, swallowed by the icy cold lake, she understood him best, and what happened that day at the Wolf Den.

A man was putting his fist in a woman's face.

A girl disappeared in a fast-flowing river, and no one realized it was serious until too late.

A car went into a freezing lake with a mother and child inside.

Trey couldn't stand idly by. Trey couldn't look the other way. Trey was not a bystander, and he'd never do nothing if he could do *something*.

Even if it meant he lost everything he loved.

He risked all, because he knew what it was to love.

And then he was up, dragging a woman to the surface. People rushed forward to take the woman and then Trey was gone again, diving back under.

HELP CAME RUSHING in, in the form of a helicopter from

Kalispell Regional Medical Center, the helicopter landing on the closed highway, sheriffs and fire trucks now blocking the road to keep the area clear.

McKenna stood with TJ, shivering uncontrollably while the helicopter slowly rose, blades whirring, blowing snow as the helicopter airlifted the mother, the baby and Trey out together. The paramedics had told McKenna she'd have to follow in the truck as there was no room in the chopper, and she understood, but at the same time she was shaking so badly she couldn't drive quite yet.

Her emotions had run the gamut from fear to joy, and she felt worked...wrecked.

Trey surfacing the second time, with the toddler, had been beyond wonderful. The crowd lining the road had cheered. But then Trey lost consciousness and the local fire station medics rushed in and hauled him out of the water, and seeing Trey carried from the water, head hanging, body limp had been terrifying.

She'd thought they'd lost him.

She thought *she'd* lost him.

For a second, she couldn't breathe, couldn't get air. For a second, it felt like her heart had stopped.

"Do you want to use that phone now?" One of the ladies on the side of the road asked, holding her cell phone to McKenna.

McKenna stared at her blankly.

"You said you didn't have a phone, and you needed to make a call?" The woman's reminder was gentle. But then, people had been so kind, moved by Trey's actions, impressed by his courage and selflessness.

McKenna's hand shook as she punched in Paige's number. Thankfully Paige answered. "Merry Christmas, McKenna! Where are you? How are you? How's—"

"There's been an accident," McKenna choked, her throat constricting. "I'm over at Flathead Lake. I've been staying at the Sheenan family cabin outside Cherry Lake. Trey's hurt. He's being airlifted to the Kalispell hospital right now. Can you please alert his family? If Troy's not at the Graff, he'll probably be at Brock and Harley's."

"I'm on it."

"Thank you."

"Are you okay?"

McKenna reached up to touch the angel hanging from her neck. "Only if he is."

"He will be, McKenna. He's strong. He's Trey."

"I'm trying to remember that."

Chapter Sixteen

TREY WOKE UP slowly, thoughts thick and tangled, his body heavy and sore. Had he been drinking? Had he been fighting?

He glanced around. Everything was beige and bland. Sterile.

He tried to sit up but something tugged in his forearm. He reached over, fingers skimming the tape and tubing. His confusion increased.

Where was he, and what the hell was going on?

Where was McKenna? And TJ? Why weren't they here—where had he left them? Lost them?

And then pictures flashed, and it started to come back to him: the crowd at the lake, the tire marks that led from the road to the lake, and someone screaming about a lady and her kids.

He didn't remember pulling over. He didn't remember jumping out. He did remember looking at McKenna, briefly. He didn't remember what she said, or if she said anything, but he saw her eyes, saw her terror.

But he must have gone into the lake, because he remembered it was cold, shockingly cold, like a knife plunging into his lungs.

But he swam down. He swam for the submerged car and he dragged a lady up, and out. And then numb, he went down again.

It wasn't that dark down below, though, just terribly cold, and he shoved into the back of the car, wrestled with the buckles and harness on a car seat. The child wasn't moving. The child was still but Trey wouldn't think about that. He wouldn't think about anything but getting the child out, and then up.

Up.

Up.

Sunlight. Air.

"Hey, Baby." A quiet voice sounded at his side. Hands touched him, one hand on his arm, the other on his chest. "You're awake." And then McKenna was leaning over him, kissing his forehead and then his cheek. "Merry Christmas."

He struggled to focus on her face, and then she was clear, and beautiful, so very very beautiful. "Where's TJ?"

"With Troy."

"Troy's here?"

"Everybody's here. Well, everybody but Cormac, but Dillon said he might be coming."

"Why?"

"To spend Christmas together. As a family."

He was silent for awhile, processing, even as he felt the icy cold water all over again, remembered the bone chilling shock of it. "The baby in the car seat...is he...did he...?"

"She. She's a twenty-two month old girl, and she's been airlifted to Missoula, but from all reports, she's stable and the doctors are predicting a full recovery."

"Are you just saying that?"

"No. You can ask Brock or Troy. They've talked to the medical team at the Children's Hospital. You saved her. You saved both of them, the mother and the daughter." McKenna's eyes filled with tears. "You are a hero."

"Not a hero. Never been a hero—"

"You've always been my hero, even if you don't keep your armor all shiny and silver." She leaned over and kissed him carefully. "But you did scare me, babe. I thought I lost you."

He reached up and caught one of her tears. "Is that why you're crying?"

"I'm crying because I'm lucky. I'm blessed. You're a good man. You're tough and strong...absolutely fearless."

"Oh, Mac, not fearless. I was terrified."

"But you went after them anyway. There were others standing there. That man was standing there. They didn't go in. They were waiting for help to arrive."

"There was no time," Trey said. "I had to do it. Someone had to do it."

Her tears kept falling, and he couldn't stop them. His chest tightened, his heart hurting because he'd hurt her again. "I scared you," he whispered.

"You did," she agreed, drawing a rough breath. "And I could have lost you. For a while there, I wondered if we had. But I suddenly understood you, while you were down there, I suddenly understood why I love you. It's because you are a protector. And the world needs tough men, risk-taking men, men like you. And I hope and pray that when TJ grows up, he'll end up just like you. Flawed but perfect. Trey Sheenan, you have no idea how much I love you."

TREY WAS RELEASED late afternoon the next day from the Medical Center in Kalispell. McKenna was there to pick him up in Troy's big black SUV as Troy had insisted it was safer and more comfortable than Trey's old truck.

It was almost dark by the time they reached Cherry Lake and the drive up Cray Road still had lots of snow but the parking area by the cabin had been shoveled clear. "Who did this?" Trey asked.

"Your brothers," she answered, pulling into an empty spot and shifting into park.

"Why? Did they think I was coming home in a wheelchair?"

"I think they needed something to do." She turned off the engine and gave him a level look. "They were worried sick about you."

"Sounds like I did a good job of ruining Christmas."

"Hardly. Your brothers are like big kids. They've been having the time of their life, playing with the real kids." She saw his expression and added. "Mack and Molly are awesome with TJ, very sweet, incredibly patient. It's been good for everyone to be here as a family—"

"Where's everyone sleeping?"

"Dillon's on the couch. Brock, Harley and the twins are in the loft. Troy and Taylor have taken the guest room with the twin beds, and TJ and I are in the master bedroom, waiting for you to return."

"You sound pretty smug." But he was smiling as he said it, his expression gentle.

"Not smug, just happy." She leaned over and kissed him. "And it might sound corny, but I think your mom's here...at least, her spirit is here. There is so much love in that house...so much good will. I think she needed this, here, having all her boys on Cray land, in the Cray cabin."

"Not all. We're missing Cormac."

"He said he'd try to come. He was working on a flight."

"It's a long haul from Southern California—" he broke off as the sound of an engine pierced the quiet, and a big pewter colored SUV roared up the road and into the driveway.

Trey and McKenna looked at the driver and then looked at each other and smiled.

Cormac was here. He'd made it.

YOU WOULDN'T KNOW it was December 26th. It felt like Christmas Day.

Trey sat in the chair by the fire with TJ on his lap and McKenna on the floor at his feet, leaning back against his knee.

The Sheenans filled the small cabin, talking, laughing, sharing memories of Christmases past.

Trey enjoyed listening to his brothers tease and argue. They were as always—intense, competitive, boisterous, but ultimately loving.

It wasn't an easy family but it was his family, and he was grateful he had a son who would carry on the Sheenan name.

Just then Troy appeared with plastic red cups half filled with cold fizzy champagne. "Where did you get the champagne from?" Brock asked, wagging his finger at his twins, letting them know they wouldn't be drinking.

"Taylor and I picked up a couple bottles in town today, to celebrate Trey's return home, and our first Christmas together in years." Troy passed out the remaining cups so that all the adults had one. "If Trey hadn't played hero, this wouldn't have happened—"

"Not a hero," Trey protested gruffly.

"You are to us," Cormac said, from where he stood next to the tree with three year old Daisy in his arms.

"You are to *me*," Dillon added quietly.

"And me," TJ said, sitting up, looking around. "You saved a mom and a baby. That's like...well, being a superhero."

Brock smiled faintly. "Trey, our Superhero."

"Ha!" Trey protested, flushing and squirming a little, undone by the support. To have his family here, accepting him, including him, meant more than he could say.

"So I propose a toast," Troy said, lifting his red cup. "To Trey who helped bring us together this year. It's so good to have you home."

"To Trey!" they all cheered, and then drank.

The champagne was cold and crisp, and the bubbles fizzed, making Trey smile. The cabin might be small and rustic, and the champagne might be served in plastic cups, but this was one of the most festive Christmases he could remember.

Trey lifted his cup. "I have a toast, too." He glanced around the room, at his brothers, Harley, Taylor, the kids. His son. McKenna. And suddenly he wasn't sure he'd be able to make the toast. Suddenly he felt so much emotion he couldn't speak.

But then he felt a calm, and a peace, and he took a breath and tried to put his gratitude into words. "To Dad and Mom," he said, his deep voice cracking. "May we remember the best in them, and cherish the good, and may we forget the pain and hurts and forgive so that only the love remains."

The room was silent and for a moment Trey wondered if he'd said too much, maybe said the wrong thing. Then he felt McKenna squeeze his knee and Cormac raised his cup. "Beautifully said. To Mom and Dad."

"Mom and Dad," everyone echoed. "To the Sheenans and the Crays."

They stayed up late into the night talking and laughing and sharing stories as well as planning weddings. Troy and Taylor were still discussing a Valentine's wedding but it looked as if there would be a wedding much sooner.

Trey and McKenna wanted a barn wedding on the Sheenan property on New Year's Eve. McKenna joked that she'd take her wedding dress and cut it off at the knees and top it with the red flannel shirt tied at the waist.

"All you'd need would be some red cowboy boots," Troy said. "And I'm pretty sure you have a pair."

"No veil," Trey said. "You have to leave your hair down."

"And you, Trey, would have to come in all black," McKenna retorted. "Only appropriate if we're re-enacting the great wedding escape."

Harley glanced from Trey to TJ. "Are you two serious?"

Trey and McKenna's gazes locked and held. He was the first to smile. "I'd marry her today," he said slowly, blue eyes gleaming, "but we need a license."

"And the ring," she added, lips twitching. "It's in Marietta in a safe deposit box."

"But the barn will be cold," Harley said with mock sternness. "It's not an appropriate barn for weddings."

"And it'll smell," Taylor added. Maybe we can see if the Emerson Barn is free."

Harley nodded and reached for her smart phone, doing a quick search and then checking an online calendar. "I'm on their website events page now. The barn is booked for the 31st, for a large private New Year's Eve party, but it is open on the 30th and on the evening of New Year's Day."

She looked expectantly at Trey and McKenna. "Should we make a reservation request?"

"It's a huge barn and there's only a few of us," McKenna protested.

"You have to invite your brothers," Trey said. "And sweet

Aunt Karen."

McKenna rolled her eyes at the sweet Aunt Karen part, but Trey was right. She couldn't get married without her brothers and Aunt Karen there. They'd never forgive her. "Paige, too. And her kids. Plus Jenny and Colton Thorpe."

"Sage and Callan Carrigan," someone said.

"Well, Callan for sure," Dillon answered. "If you want all the family there."

The conversation abruptly died. Heads turned, eyes on Dillon.

Brock was the first to speak, his dark brows flat over intense dark eyes. "That was odd," he said carefully. "Want to repeat that?"

Dillon didn't immediately answer. Seconds passed and the tension grew. Finally he shrugged. "We have a lot to talk about."

More silence followed.

Trey and Troy exchanged swift glances.

Cormac frowned. "Does anybody know what's going on?"

"A little bit," Troy admitted. "But I think Dillon knows more than the rest of us."

"I do," Dillon agreed. "But I don't think this is the time, not with the kids here, not when we're supposed to be enjoying each other's company."

"It's that bad," Trey said flatly.

"Or…good…depending on how you look at it."

No one looked reassured.

"I think you're right about tonight not being the time or place," Troy said. "Not just because of the kids, but because this is the Cray cabin. This is Mom's place."

IT WAS WELL after midnight when everyone had turned in and the cabin lights turned off. In the master bedroom it was Trey and McKenna with TJ in the middle.

TJ had fallen asleep hours ago and Trey and McKenna held hands, their linked fingers resting on his hip.

"What do you think of your Christmas?" McKenna whispered in the dark.

"I think it was the best Christmas ever."

"Because everybody was here?"

"Because Christmas this year was a whole week long."

"How do you figure that?"

"Day 1, kidnapping you and TJ from the church."

"You can't celebrate that."

"Of course I can. Day 2, Explore Cherry Lake. Day 3, movie and Christmas shopping. Day 4, snow fun. Day 5, Christmas Eve. Day 6, Christmas. Day 7, everybody here with us."

She smiled in the dark. "That does sound like a lovely Christmas holiday."

"It was." He lifted her hand, kissed the back of her fingers. And then her wrist, and then leaned closed to kiss the inside of her elbow. "The most perfect Christmas ever. And I owe it all to you."

"Why to me?"

"Because you kept the family together when I couldn't. You took care of TJ when I wasn't there. You did the right thing for him and I will be forever grateful to you for that."

"I'm his mom. I'd always take care of him."

"You would, yes. Which is why I love you so much. You're my hero, McKenna. You're the one who gives me hope and strength—"

"Trey."

"And I might not be the man you always want me to be, but

I am your man, heart, mind, body and soul." He rose up on his elbow, and leaned over TJ to kiss her, and kiss her again. Maybe it was the Cray in him, but he loved her the way he loved water and air, wind and rain, the sun and moon. "I think we made a Christmas memory," he murmured.

She smiled against his mouth. "And if we're lucky, a Christmas baby."

"Then it's a good thing we're getting married this week," he growled.

THE WEDDING TOOK place on January 1ˢᵗ, in the big Emerson barn, even though there were only thirty-five guests attending.

But it was a beautiful wedding, even if somewhat unorthodox with the bride in a 'vintage' gown that had been chopped off at the knees, the beaded bodice covered with a red flannel shirt tied at the waist. She wore red boots to match the flannel topper and carried a bouquet of lilies, red roses, and hay.

The groom wore all black—black trousers, black shirt, black boots—and a wickedly handsome smile.

There was a ring bearer, but the five year old grew restless immediately and chased his friends around the barn and ignored the adults who told him to knock it off, be good, and stand still.

The Douglasses were there, and Aunt Karen who didn't call the groom Satan or a Convict, which pleased the bride to no end.

The Sheenans were all there, too, including Callan Carrigan who delivered the shocking news that the five Sheenan boys had two Carrigan half-sisters, thanks to Bill Sheenan's decade-long affair with Bev Carrigan. It wasn't easy to hear, and it stirred up the past, but no one could blame Callan, and they'd all known her for so long, since she was just a baby.

There were hugs and a few tears, and then dinner, music, dancing, and cake, too.

But most of all, there was love.

So much love.

Because after all, what God had brought together, no man could tear asunder.

The End

Come Home for Christmas, Cowboy

A Very Marietta Christmas Story

Megan Crane

Chapter One

O N DECEMBER 21st, the night of her thirtieth birthday, Christina Grey Cooper decided that it was finally time to stop lying to herself.

She was sitting in a very loud bar filled with people who made her feel deeply judgmental in a neighborhood she knew was filled with more of the same: trendy hipsters, as far as the eye could see, like the creeping vines that choked her mother's trellis in Marietta, Montana every summer. She was furthermore in Denver, Colorado, a city she never would have chosen for herself and yet had lived in for more than five years anyway.

And what did Christina have to show for the loyalty and love that had brought her here? To a bar bristling with ironic facial hair in a mile high city that still didn't feel like home? She cast a considering glance around at her surroundings, and tallied it all up in her head.

She didn't have the babies she'd always wanted and had expected to start having well before her thirties hit. She lived in a rented house she'd never liked much in a neighborhood that was convenient for Dare and his academic pursuits, but not so much for her and her daily commute to the other side of Denver—not that she'd ever bothered to complain, because how would that help anything? She had a journalism degree that she didn't use at her job as an office manager for a very small and boring commercial architectural firm, which she'd gotten purely to pay the bills Dare's doctoral program stipend and assorted grants couldn't cover. She wasn't chasing down important stories or writing much of anything at all, in fact, which was what she'd always thought she'd be doing with her life, with or without kids.

These days, she used her journalism degree purely to compose overtly jovial Facebook updates, the better to pretend her life was *awesome*. And online, it was. She made sure of it. Offline, she was addicted to all kinds of things. Angsty teen-oriented television shows. Erotically charged romance novels featuring often-paranormal men with control issues and ferocious, possibly life-threatening passions. Inappropriately fancy shoes from Zappos that she could wear around the house at night to feel like a queen with a glass of wine or three, then return for free come morning.

And, of course, she had Dare.

She eyed him then, sitting there across the table from her doing his best impression of a man all alone.

Dare, who she still loved with that roaring sort of fire inside of her that only hurt, these days. Dare, who she still wanted as much as she ever had, because she was a masochist, apparently. Dare, who didn't look like the microbiologist he was—whatever microbiologists were supposed to look like. He looked like a cowboy. Lanky and lean and darkly gorgeous, with that surprisingly lush mouth and distant dark blue gaze, like the far horizons were inside him, somehow. He looked like what and who he was, Darius James Cooper, the son of a coal miner from Gillette, Wyoming, who'd grown up hard and tough beneath wide open skies.

Dare, who also happened to have the quickest, sharpest, most impressive brain Christina had ever encountered.

She'd fallen in wild lust with Dare the moment she'd seen him sauntering across the University of Montana campus that early fall night in Missoula way back when, in his battered old jeans and an old grey t-shirt, that crooked smile of his that made his smoky blue eyes gleam poking out from beneath his dark brown hair.

She'd fallen in love with him shortly thereafter, sitting out beneath the dark canopy of a bright and breathless Montana night, while he talked to her in that deceptively lazy way of his about all the reasons he wanted to become a scientist.

And all that before he'd kissed her in that slow, patient, toe-curlingly *certain* way of his, which had made her so dizzy she'd almost fallen down. *Would have* fallen down, had Dare not caught her.

She'd believed—without question—that he always would.

Dare, who had married her in a ceremony that had made them both shake with giddy laughter one weekend in Vegas because they couldn't afford to do anything but elope in the cheapest "chapel" around. Dare, who had spent all of their money on a ring Christina didn't need, but treasured nonetheless throughout all the months of Ramen and rice they'd eaten to pay it off.

Dare, the husband who hadn't acted as if he liked her in a very, very long time, now that she was allowing herself to consider it.

The truth was that she hadn't *wanted* to consider it.

This, Christina understood tonight—with a flash of un-wanted clarity as she stared across the suspiciously sticky table at her surly and silent husband while he nursed his beer and kept his dark, brooding attention on anything and everything but her—was the story of her life. This *was* her life. This was what it had been for longer than she liked to admit, and what it would be for as long as she held on.

And she'd been holding on—if only by her fingernails—for ages now.

Happy birthday to me, she thought then, her gaze on Dare while his was on whatever it was he saw when he didn't want to see her.

Christina had spent the whole day convincing herself that everything was *fine.* That *of course* Dare hadn't forgotten her birthday the way he'd forgotten everything else lately. And by *lately,* she really meant the past year and a half. She'd told herself that the fact he'd come home so late the night before and left before she'd climbed out of the shower this morning—making certain he saw as little of her as possible, she'd finally concluded after months of this kind of behavior—meant that he had some or other exciting thirtieth birthday surprise in the works.

That had taken some pretty desperate mental contortions on her part, but by this point, Christina was so good at contorting that she was practically a yoga master.

Because she knew he hadn't planned anything. If she'd really thought otherwise, she wouldn't have called him at his lab that afternoon. Not on his direct line or his cell phone, both of which she knew he'd send straight to voicemail the minute he saw her name, but through the front desk so the call would be transferred to him and he wouldn't be able to use his Caller ID to avoid her.

Happy and healthy people, she couldn't help but think, didn't worry about Caller ID or plan their phone calls like black ops attacks. They probably called their husbands whenever they felt like it. Without having to *contort.*

Moreover, their husbands probably just answered their

goddamned phones—something, now that she was letting herself think about these things, Dare hadn't done in ages. She couldn't remember the last time they'd talked on the phone at all without her having to perform a whole choreographed series of her little yoga moves, in fact.

Happy and healthy, she thought now, *we certainly are not.*

"What are we doing tonight for my birthday?" Christina had asked him cheerfully when he'd answered the phone.

She was always cheerful when she spoke to Dare these days. The quieter and darker and surlier he got, the more she turned herself into Pollyanna—the psychotically perky Energizer Bunny version that made her feel crazy and didn't even work on him, but what was the alternative? Meeting his darkness with more darkness? They'd black out the entire Denver Metropolitan Area.

"My thirtieth birthday!" she'd said as if he'd said something or required more information, so happily it had given her an immediate piercing headache. "Hooray!"

Yes, she'd actually said *hooray*. Out loud, as if she was the embodiment of a teen girl's text message. That was how desperate things had become.

Dare had sighed, heavily.

That was how he communicated now. Deep sighs and rolled eyes. Muttered things Christina couldn't quite hear but suspected she didn't much *want* to hear. If she squinted and pretended hard enough, though, *everything was fine.* Like those photos she took on her phone with the filter that blurred out everything but the one small part she wanted to focus on, then posted to Facebook with a long wake of exclamation points and emoticons. That was how she held on to her marriage. She filtered. She posted. She chose to believe her own carefully curated version of her life.

He didn't *say* anything. They didn't *fight*. They were *fine*.

Yay!!!!!!!! :) :) :) :) :)

But tonight she seemed to have lost her filter.

"Fine, Christina," he'd said after one of those long pauses of his, during which she could practically *see* the way he rubbed a hand over his face as if he was right there in front of her, exasperated by her. This, too, was their new normal. "I'll be home around eight."

So really, it was Christina's own fault that she was sitting in this terrible bar that she suspected Dare knew perfectly well she hated. He might even have chosen it for that very purpose, as revenge for her temerity in demanding he spend a single evening with her out of the past five hundred. It was her fault that she'd dressed up for the great occasion. Not the occasion of her birthday, for which Dare had naturally bought her nothing but a too-sweet pink drink, but the fact that the two of them were out somewhere together. *Almost* like the real couple they'd been approximately nine million years ago. It was her own fault that she'd put on mascara and the perfume he'd once growled in her ear drove him so crazy he could hardly control himself.

He'd been in complete control, of course, when he'd looked at her with that blank expression on his face when he'd walked in the back door at eight-thirty, making Christina feel deeply pathetic for once again allowing hope to triumph over experience.

Christina didn't feel pathetic at the moment. Not any longer. She felt annoyed—at herself.

She could have been curled up on the couch right now, enjoying a birthday evening with her Kindle and a glass of wine and possibly a selection of cupcakes from her favorite bakery. That would have been a great deal more fun than sitting in a crowded bar listening to a bad cover band ruin "Rockin' Around the Christmas Tree" while her husband—still the most beautiful creature she'd ever seen, even surly and distant and refusing to meet her eyes—looked like he was made of impenetrable granite.

Dare looked like that a lot, lately. Maybe all the time, in fact—it was just that Christina saw so little of him, "all the time" was only a few sporadic moments here and there, collected over weeks.

This is my life, she thought again, harder. *This... sad little mess.*

A terrible rendition of an overplayed holiday song and a sticky table, in a city she'd never liked that much, doing things she didn't care about at all, with a man who hadn't seemed to like *her* in a long time, and was—if she was really going to look at it the way she'd been avoiding doing for a long time now, with no filter and no overly curated Facebook bullshit—almost certainly cheating on her.

She let that settle on her, that nasty truth she'd been working so hard to avoid.

That was what all of these things meant when she looked at them as a whole, didn't they? Dare had always been a distracted scientist, a dreamy academic type with his head a million miles away, trying to cure the incurable. But this wasn't *distracted*. This was disinterested, disengaged. Passive aggressive and annoyed. This spelled *another woman*. It had to, didn't it?

Christina had known that for a long time, too, somewhere deep inside where it hurt too much to bear.

But tonight she was thirty, and it was almost Christmas, and she couldn't seem to do anything else but face it. Face everything, in fact. All her filters were off. All her protective walls had finally fallen down.

And she felt... nothing.

Mildly annoyed. A little bit tired. Cranky about the loud, bad band and the sticky table. But other than that? Nothing at all.

Which was how Christina knew, finally, that this had to stop. That she had to let go before there was nothing left of her. Before she really was nothing more than a perky Facebook update surrounded by smiley faces, and utterly empty within.

She was done contorting herself to please a man who couldn't be pleased—who didn't *want* to be pleased. Not by her, anyway. It didn't matter how much weight she lost or gained, how often she went to Pilates class or baked him coffee cake she'd then eat herself, or how scrupulously neat and clean she kept the ugly little rental house he avoided like the plague. It didn't matter how often she cooked his favorite meals, how cheerfully she spoke to him, or how carefully she made sure to avoid any kind of fight or disagreement or *intensity* of any kind.

As if it could get any worse. As if *this* wasn't bad enough.

Christina had made herself into a walking, talking pretzel for this man, and to what end? He lounged there, that dark and haunted look on his face, his eyes smoky and far-away, as if being with her was like being a jail sentence he had to endure. When she knew perfectly well that if anyone was trapped in this marriage, it was her.

Dare was about five seconds away from a PhD and the life he'd always wanted and had worked so hard to achieve. Christina was just… his wife. Which she'd been perfectly fine with until he'd forgotten her and the fact they were supposed to be a team.

She felt more than mildly annoyed then—she felt like throwing her overpriced and overly sweet drink right at his heartbreakingly gorgeous face. But that would take energy. Passion. That wildness inside of her that Dare had once made sing, and had now gone silent like everything else. She felt nothing.

She felt flat. *Flattened.*

"I hate yoga," she informed him. "I hate *contorting.*"

Dare shot a look across the table as if he hadn't expected her to speak, and might even be a little bit startled that she had, but he only shook his head.

Christina didn't know what he saw when he looked at her now. She saw the past. *Their* past. She saw the night he'd held her face between his hands and whispered, so fiercely, that he'd never loved anything in his life until her and didn't expect he'd ever love anything else, ever. She could feel the way he'd touched her, as if she'd been created specifically for him and he couldn't get enough of her. She remembered the slow, heated way he'd looked at her when they'd returned to their hotel room in Vegas, husband and wife at last. And what had come after.

God, the ways he'd touched her, once upon a time.

Whatever he saw tonight, it didn't show on his face. Then again, Christina thought as she looked—really looked—at that closed-off, granite expression of his, maybe it did.

Dare indicated her drink with his chin, his gaze flinty in all the commotion of the bar around them, and her heart felt raw.

"Are you about ready to get out of here?"

And she was. She really was.

HE WAS GONE by the time Christina woke up the next morning.

As usual.

There wasn't even a dent in the sofa cushions in the den, so maybe he hadn't even slept in the house. This, too, seemed like more evidence, all of it pointing to the same conclusion.

Christina waited for that to hurt, but it didn't. Which was all the answer she needed, wasn't it?

So she packed up what little remained of herself into the tiny hatchback she'd bought with her own money that summer after college, she left a brief note telling him she wasn't coming back because she doubted he'd notice her absence otherwise, and she started driving north.

It took about ten hours, winter weather permitting, to drive to her hometown of Marietta, Montana, where her parents and sister and assorted other Grey family relatives lived. She drove out of Denver and into Wyoming on I-25, uninterrupted by any frantic phone calls from her husband. He probably didn't know she'd left him yet and was, she reminded herself harshly and repeatedly as she left her life with him behind her, highly unlikely to care if he did.

This was probably what he wanted. She should want it, too—and she thought she probably would, when she had a little more time to get used to the idea. When she was ready to accept that she'd finally given up on him.

When she was something other than numb.

Christina listened to the mixes she'd made while she and Dare were back in college together, all of which she'd loaded onto their computer a few years ago when she'd been trying to *feng shui* their life—another failed experiment in making Dare happy despite his clear preference to be anything but, which had been her primary occupation for most of their time in Denver.

Damn him.

She turned the music up loud and drove much too fast through the snow-covered grasslands of eastern Wyoming, not far from the place Dare came from and claimed he loathed deep unto his soul. She didn't want any of that in her head any-more—as if Dare's emotional history was stamped on the barren, winter-razed land itself. As if she had to look through him to see it.

Christina blocked out that unsettling notion and sang along

to the songs that had once filled her with so much emotion they'd actually *hurt* to hear. She listened to Landry Bell sing a quiet song about a hard, painful love he couldn't give up even though he knew he should. She heard Trisha Yearwood sing about hearts wrapped up in armor, Keith Urban apologize to his love for his terrible behavior, and Tim and Faith sing about ignoring each other after a bad break up.

Christina tried to cry. She *wanted* to cry. She waited for that tidal wave of emotion to wash through her, to make her pull over to the side of the cold, lonely highway and sob and shake and wail. To feel as if she couldn't breathe, the way she had when Dare had broken up with her after he'd graduated and was interning at a lab an hour south of Missoula in Hamilton, Montana.

Back then, she'd fallen to pieces. She'd been twenty-one. She'd thought losing him would *kill her.* She'd curled up on her bed and sobbed until the tears wouldn't come anymore, and then she'd stayed there in the fetal position. She hadn't felt right for the whole two days it had taken for them to get back together. And she'd known then that she'd never be whole unless she was with him. Never.

I love you, he'd said. *I'll never leave you again.*

See that you don't, she'd murmured against his neck.

And he'd kept that promise, hadn't he? *Jerk.*

But Christina didn't cry today, no matter what songs she played, and she felt whole and fairly hearty, too, all things considered. No matter how she tried to feel tragic. No matter how glum the weather was when she reached Billings, Montana, where her horn dog Uncle Billy lived with the woman he'd unapologetically stolen from his own son, Christina's cousin Jesse, and then married and impregnated. And maybe not in that order.

"I have my own map of emotional pain," she reminded herself out loud as she headed west on I-90 toward Livingston, following the great Yellowstone River as it wound its way toward Marietta and beyond to Bozeman. Slowly, surely, the Great Plains became the Rocky Mountains. *Her* Rocky Mountains— the Absaroka-Beartooths and the Crazies as the plains gave way—not the Colorado Rockies down in Denver that weren't quite the same and weren't quite right no matter how many years she'd lived there. And she'd been on the road for hours, so she kept right on talking to herself. "Everywhere I look in Montana, there's another part of me. Not *Dare and me.* Just me."

Her family had been in Montana for generations. Greys had come across these same plains in covered wagons in the 1800s, leaving far worse things behind in Boston than one surly husband who was probably—almost definitely—cheating on her with one of his fellow doctoral candidates. At least Christina had a heater in her old car and the ability to stop in gas stations to stock up on sugary, salty, highly-processed road food for her journey.

And the sad truth was, she felt fine, more or less. Better than she had in years, because this was the first day in a long, long time she hadn't lied to herself about a single thing. She might not feel entirely herself, but then she'd had a long time to get used to that, hadn't she? Maybe that was what growing up was. Maybe that's all this was, too: her childish infatuation with Dare finally running its inevitable course.

Maybe this had been coming from the start. Maybe they should have stayed broken up all those years ago. Maybe she was only just catching up.

She jammed her foot down on the gas pedal. Because it was December 23rd and dark outside already, and after all this time wasted, all these years lost, Christina just wanted to get home.

DARE SAT IN his truck outside the dark house, and knew.

She'd finally done it. She'd finally left him.

He didn't have to go inside the shitty little house she'd worked so hard to make a home. He didn't have to look for empty spaces where the signs of her had been. He already knew. He already felt it creeping through his body like frost, chilling him to the bone.

The house was dark. Cold. In all the years he'd known Christina, he'd never come home to a dark house. She'd always, always left the light burning for him, even on those nights he'd muttered not to expect him or had simply stayed away until dawn.

He supposed he'd started to imagine she always would. That she'd just… take it, all the crap he'd dumped on her, forever and ever.

Had he really thought that?

Dare's hands tightened around the wheel, and he couldn't seem to move. He couldn't climb out of the truck and go into the house, because that would make it real. Inside that house was the life he'd decided he needed to live, the one without her that he'd never cared for much when he'd experienced it before, and the worst part was, she had no idea that he was doing her a favor. That he was saving her.

She thought what he'd wanted her to think. That he was done with her. That he was no longer in love with her.

If she'd left him, she must finally hate him.

Or, even worse, he'd succeeded in taking all of that joy and heat and love away from her at last, the way he'd shoved it outside himself in order to do this, and left her with nothing inside for him—for them—but all of that darkness.

His darkness.

He was such an asshole, it made him ache. It made his whole body hurt, like the flashing onset of one of the viruses he studied. He wished he didn't know better. He wished it would just kill him, so he could escape his own head, the cold, dark finality of his own actions. His own terrible fate.

He couldn't bring himself to go inside. He didn't want to confirm his success, at last. He couldn't accept that after all of this, after all this time, she'd finally gone and done what he'd pushed her to do.

What he'd been so damned sure he wanted her to do.

Until now.

So instead, Dare backed the truck out of the driveway, pulled out into the street, tried to keep breathing though he could hardly see the point without Christina, and went after her.

Chapter Two

"**Y**OU LEFT."

Christina didn't have to turn around to identify that low, accusatory voice, burned as it was into her very bones, and so she didn't. She stood very still, scowling into the interior of her parents' refrigerator as if that might make a tube of cookie dough appear before her where there was only a half-eaten tuna casserole in Tupperware, and waited.

Because maybe she was still sound asleep upstairs in her childhood bedroom and this was but a dream. Maybe Dare wasn't really standing there in her parents' kitchen doorway in a cloud of December cold at six-thirty-three on the Tuesday morning the day after she'd left him, when she hadn't expected he would notice she'd left for at least a week. Maybe two weeks. Or maybe not at all, if he decided to "stay at the lab" indefinitely.

She certainly hadn't imagined he'd care enough about her absence to drive ten hours north to Marietta. This had to be a dream.

But he shouldered his way inside and closed the door behind him with an emphatic click that echoed in her head like a gunshot then scraped over her as if she'd narrowly missed the bullet. And she had to accept that yes, he was really there. *Right there.* He'd chased after her, apparently. She couldn't believe it. She didn't.

And to spite her, her heart lurched a little bit at the sight of him. That was why it took her a minute to process that tone of his. As if *he* was angry. At *her.*

Surely not.

"All your stuff seems to be packed in that car out in your parents' driveway," Dare continued when she didn't say anything or look at him directly. And he seemed so *big,* then—looming there out of the corner of her eye, lanky and dark and that smoky gaze of his fixed on her—that the familiar old kitchen seemed to shrink tight around him. Around her, too, much as she tried to pretend otherwise. "I could see it through the windows. Did you move out, Christina? Without bothering to tell me first?"

Old habits died hard, because her first, immediate reaction was panic.

She was *panicked,* not that he was apparently in the mood to be both talkative and confrontational, but that she was letting him see her like this. Her dark hair was in a scruffy bun on the top of her head. She was completely un-showered after a long, restless night. And she was wearing not just her ratty old yoga pants and a long-sleeved PBR championship t-shirt she'd bought at a bull riding event back in high school and had found stuffed in a drawer in the old bedroom she'd shared throughout her childhood with her older sister, Luce—but a pair of horrible, bright blue wool socks her mother had knitted during her "amateur knitwear as gifts" phase.

Her pulse raced with sheer, dizzying anxiety at the idea that presenting him with anything less than herself as perfect as humanly possible would *prove it*—prove that he was right to have stopped loving her. Her heart pounded so hard and so high she thought it might choke her.

Christina had to remind herself—sharply—that she'd left him at last. It was over. It didn't matter what she looked like. Or how beautiful he was, even when he was glaring at her like that, drilling holes in the side of her head. Or that this was the first time in ages that he'd actually looked at her, by choice, for more than two derisive seconds in a row.

"I'm sorry," she said, when the silence had dragged on a good, long stretch, and Dare was still there and still watching her in that way of his, dark and much too intense at once, which she could feel perfectly well even while she was pretending to be *consumed* by the contents of the fridge. "You haven't voluntarily spoken to me in so long. I'd forgotten what that sounded like."

"Here I am, Christina. You want to talk to me? Go for it."

Everything inside of her clenched tight and then *hurt*. Christina told herself it was anger, nothing more. Righteous indignation, in fact. But she didn't want to give him the satisfaction of seeing her upset. She didn't want to *contort*. Ever again.

She let the refrigerator door fall shut and pivoted, scowling at the full sight of him to cover the way her heart leaped even higher and pounded harder. Because peripheral vision couldn't possibly do him justice. Dare glared back at her, so tall and so beautiful, even with a rough night's beard on his jaw and that intense, shattering look in his gorgeous eyes. Even his jeans looked tired, and his dark hair was spiky, as if he'd been running his fingers through it all the way north, the way he did when he was agitated, though his big, hard hands were thrust in his pockets now.

All of this told her things she didn't want to know, and

didn't believe anyway.

Not anymore. Christina was done believing. She was done with faith. She was certainly done with parsing the many dark moods of one Darius James Cooper as if that was her primary job.

She was *done.*

"That sounded almost belligerent, Dare," she said, pleased she sounded so cool. So unbothered. "But I know that can't be true. Because what on earth do *you* have to be mad about?"

"You really want to ask me that after I drove ten hours in the middle of the night to get here?"

"No one asked you to do that. I stopped asking you for anything a long time ago, you might have noticed." She shrugged, a brittle jerk of one shoulder. "Or not."

She didn't recognize that glitter in his smoky eyes then, much less the leaping thing inside her that made her stomach clench tight.

"So let me make sure I understand what's happening here," he said softly, with an undercurrent of something darker in his low voice. "The last time I saw you, in Denver, where we live and which is over six hundred and fifty miles south of where we're standing right now, you were having a major attitude because you wanted a big birthday party."

"I did not want a big birthday party. I didn't want a party at all—I wanted my husband to acknowledge my birthday." *And by extension, me*, she thought, but did not say. She lifted her chin and tried to keep her teeth from grinding together. "They're not the same thing."

"You didn't like the place we went. Not that you said so or offered any suggestions about where else to go, mind you—I was supposed to pick that up by telepathy. You sat there like a pissed off princess, mad and quiet, like you've been doing for months now."

"I thought your doctorate was in microbiology, Dare, not creative writing," she seethed at him, losing her grip on remaining anything like cool. "And nice try, but you're not going to *argue* me into your version of the last couple of years. I was there. I remember what actually happened."

"And then I come home from a long day at the lab and you're gone. Just... gone. Boom. Without warning. Certainly without any conversation."

She crossed her arms over her chest. "I left a note."

"A note." His voice was incredulous and deeply pissed at once, and there was no reason at all that it should skid through her like that, like hunger. Like a kind of need she'd thought had died a long time ago. Christina had to pull in a breath before she shuddered. "We've been together for over a decade, married for more than half that time, and when you decided you were done you... left me a note."

"If you needed me to explain the contents of the note to you, you could have called," she pointed out. "Rather than leaping in your truck and chasing me here to make up some fantasy version of our life where I'm the spoiled drama queen and you're the bewildered, innocent party."

His gaze felt like a touch from all the way across the kitchen, and she hated how much she wanted to relent. To go to him, hold him—anything to stop this. But she couldn't do that. She couldn't let herself give in. Because she'd only end up right back here again. She knew it.

"And what would have happened if I'd called you?" Dare asked, into the rising tension in the room, sharper than the cold outside.

"You mean, other than me swerving into oncoming traffic on the interstate because I haven't heard your ring tone in so long?"

His smoky eyes narrowed, and that mouth of his was firm. "Would you have done that aggressively perky thing you've been doing lately? Like a morning talk show host?"

That smarted, she could admit it, because it was a direct hit. But it didn't change the facts.

"What do you want, Dare?" she asked, her voice clipped even to her own ears. "Why are you here?"

"You took your belongings and disappeared while I was at work," he said gruffly, and she had the impression he'd been repeating that to himself over and over again throughout his long drive. It had the sound of a catch phrase, more than a comment. "That's the way people leave abusive relationships, Christina. It's the way people *escape*. How exactly does that apply here?"

She didn't know what to do, suddenly. The impulse that had pushed her into her car and into that long, bleak, cold drive had deserted her somewhere around Casper, Wyoming. She felt hollow. Which wasn't at all the same thing as numb, it turned out. For one thing, hollow *hurt*. And it had never occurred to her that he would come after her. Or that he'd be pissed off at her if he did.

There was a part of her that desperately wanted that to *mean something*.

"What did you expect me to do?" Christina was furious that her voice came out like that then, nothing but a harsh little scrape into the early morning.

"I don't know." His voice was dark, but the look in his eyes was worse. Much worse. She felt something turn over inside of her, and was afraid it was too much like shame. "I might have tried *having a conversation* before I fled across state lines."

"Who is she?" she asked, because really, that was the crux of it, wasn't it? All the rest of this was sound and fury. And so what if she didn't really want to know the answer? She wanted to stand here and have him rail at her as if *she* was the problem in their marriage even less.

"What?"

"The woman. Whoever you're cheating with." Christina found that when she said it out loud, when she made it real, whatever emotional distance she'd thought she'd been maintaining exploded into something much more gristly and tight and close within her, making her chest constrict and her vision blur. "Whoever keeps you warm all those nights you sleep somewhere else. I'm assuming it's someone from the lab. Some smart PhD scientist type just like you, far more appropriate to your new station in life, presumably. You never struck me as into bimbos." She let out a sound far too painful to be a laugh. "Then again, I never thought you'd cheat on me, I'll admit."

For a moment, he looked as if she'd clubbed him over the head. Then he blinked, and he looked nothing so much as grim. And if possible, even more furious than before.

"I'm not cheating on you, Christina."

It was the way he said it that made her stop and blink that rush of emotion away so she could see him clearly again. That stark, harsh, appalled tone. That look on his face, as if she'd plunged a jagged knife deep into his chest and it hurt but he was too angry to notice.

She believed him.

And for one second, that felt like light, pouring in like summer from above. Relief, sweet and pure.

But then she thought about it and realized that if there was no other woman, if Dare had been behaving like this simply because he felt like behaving like this, that made it all significantly worse.

"I see," she said. She did not see. "So you just… hate me? Is that it?"

Dare let out one of those exasperated sighs of his, and he might as well have punched her. She thought she could live another three lives in rapid succession without hearing that sound again. It made her shrivel inside.

It made her want to punch him, and for real this time.

"I don't hate you," he said, sounding impatient, though his gaze looked a whole lot more like tortured. "I don't—" He shook his head, and then raked his hands through the fall of his thick, messy dark hair, and Christina would have given a great deal to know what he'd *almost* said just then. "You didn't have to run back home to your parents at a moment's notice because you didn't like how one night went."

"You can't possibly think that if you keep acting like this was all me, I'll start believing you, can you? Because it doesn't work that way." She pointed at him because it was the next best thing to walloping him. Better, because she didn't think touching him was a good idea. Touching him had never led to anything but trouble. More than ten years of trouble. "I'm not the one who's spent more time at the lab than at home. The one who stopped speaking. The one who hasn't touched his wife in months. The one who rolls his eyes every time I speak. I wasn't running back home to my parents, Dare. I was running away from you."

And Christina finally understood, in that moment, what that hollowness inside her meant. Because it was one thing to have a broken heart. At least the heart was still in there, if shattered, doing its job in pieces.

Dare had ripped hers out and stamped it into oblivion, and she didn't see how there was any coming back from that.

And the look he was giving her then made her want to cry.

He swallowed, hard.

"I wasn't cheating on you," he said then, his voice gruffer than she'd ever heard it. "I don't break my promises, especially to you. You know that."

She got it, then. In a big, nauseating sort of slide into clarity. It made the polished wood floor seem to rock beneath her feet.

"Is that what this was?" she threw at him, somewhere between *aghast* and simply *hurt*. "Were you deliberately pushing me away so I'd be the one to break the promises here?" She was so upset then she thought it must have been rolling off of her, like the heat from the radiator that hugged the floorboards around the edges of the room. "What's the matter, Dare? You got what you wanted. You should be thrilled."

"This is me," he growled at her. "Fucking ecstatic."

And the tension in the room seemed to ripple, then grow, demanding that one of them break it by any means necessary, just to relieve the terrible weight of it—

The back door flew open again with a great *woosh*, slamming against the far wall and making Christina jump. Actually jump into the air, then plaster herself back against the refrigerator when she hit ground.

And for a moment it was nothing but cold air and commotion. Her sister Luce charged inside like she was a heat-seeking missile. She shepherded her three boys in front of her while her two big dogs bounded all around the four of them, and was dispensing orders left and right like a drill sergeant as she went.

Christina's nephews were a blur of pure boy energy ranging in age from an irrepressible ten down to a Tasmanian Devil-like six, and they all shouted greetings to Dare and Christina and complaints to their mother at the same high volume as they careened inside, each dragging backpacks and what looked like camping supplies in their wake. The dogs, both of unknown mutt origin with sloppy grins and too much triumphant barking, ran circles in and around the wake of the rowdy trio like a kind of rough and tumble holiday parade.

And it was only a reprieve, Christina was well aware as she dispensed hugs to three sticky little bodies in motion. A small intermission, and she was perfectly happy not to look at Dare as it happened. Because she had no idea how to resist him. She'd finally come to terms with the quiet, distant husband she'd thought was cheating on her. She'd come to terms with it last night and she'd made the decision to leave him.

This Dare, she barely recognized, but he reminded her way too much of the man she'd fallen in love with all those years ago. And she knew exactly how dangerous that was. There was contorting—and then there was melting. And Dare had always been really, really talented at making her melt down into a puddle whether she wanted to or not.

"Into the den!" Luce was ordering as she kicked the door shut behind her, slinging a couple of overstuffed duffel bags on the floor of the kitchen, near their mother's prized wooden table where all the best meals of their childhood had been conducted. "You have five minutes, guys. *Five minutes* and then we head out!"

And then she pulled her hat off of her head, let her shining blonde hair—long the bane of Christina's existence, it was so effortlessly pretty no matter how little attention Luce paid to it, unlike Christina's own red-streaked dark hair that was best left to its own devices—tumble down around her shoulders like sunshine on a bitterly cold winter morning like this one, and blinked back and forth between Dare and Christina in the sudden silence.

"What are you guys doing here?" Luce asked finally, when it became painfully clear that no one else was going to speak. "I thought you said you couldn't do Christmas back home with the family this year."

"Nice to see you, too," Christina murmured, trying to pull herself together—or out of that heart-pounding tension, anyway. She didn't look at Dare, who'd always found family in general and Luce in particular a bit of a challenge at times. After all, he hadn't spoken to his own relatives since he'd left home at eighteen.

And Luce was Christina's best friend in the entire world, always had been and ever would be, but *challenging* was the least of what she was when she got going. It was a Grey family trait, Christina knew: hardheadedness to their own detriment and an utter lack of respect for the tough lessons of their own family history.

Luce frowned at them both. "You look like you're in the middle of divorce proceedings in Mom and Dad's kitchen, two days before Christmas."

"We're not getting divorced." Dare's voice was low and hard, and Christina felt the kick of it deep in her belly. And something much warmer that she didn't want to examine everywhere else.

But she still didn't look at him. "We're talking about it, in fact. Not that it's something we need to discuss as a group, if you don't mind, Luce. And where are Mom and Dad, anyway? Out on a trip?"

She hadn't thought it was particularly weird that her parents hadn't been here when she'd staggered in the night before, punchy from the long drive. Ryan and Gracie Grey had never locked their doors in all their lives here in Marietta just a ten minute walk from Main Street and they never would, so Christina had strolled in and made herself at home as if she was still sixteen and college and Dare had never happened.

And, if she was honest, she'd been relieved that she hadn't

had to explain what was going on to anyone just yet. It made it all that little bit less real. She'd assumed her parents were off on one of the outdoor adventure trips they conducted all year long as part of the Montana Wilds Adventure Company they owned and ran from a shop above the bookstore in downtown Marietta.

"Season's pretty much done," Luce said, pulling off her gloves and shoving them deep in her coat pockets. She'd know, given she ran the shop. "There's some New Year's dog sledding thing, but we're not sure yet if Dad or Marshall McKenzie will run it. Mom and Dad went out to Big Sky to help Gram and Grandpa get the Big House ready for Christmas." She eyed the two of them, her slender body visibly tense beneath her winter coat. "And I'd hug you both, but you can't get a divorce. Not right now. That's completely unacceptable, I'm sorry."

"Your support is terrifying, Luce," Dare murmured, from where he leaned against the kitchen counter, looking for all the world like a lazy cowboy, if Christina ignored that hard glint in his smoky gaze. "But appreciated."

Christina didn't bother glaring at him. She focused on her sister instead. "Are you really—What are you talking about?"

"It's Christmas," Luce said, as if that was all the explanation required. She held up a finger, then yelled toward the den. "Two minute warning, gentlemen! Start the countdown!" Then she faced Christina again. "You know how Mom gets if the magic of Christmas is threatened. You know it's a whole thing."

"I'm wearing the wool socks of doom right now." Christina stuck a foot out as evidence. "I'm *filled* with the Christmas spirit."

Luce shrugged, when normally she would have laughed. "So you see my point."

Christina couldn't keep herself from sneaking a look at Dare then, as if they were still a team. As if they ever had been. But his expression was carefully blank. Too carefully blank. Granite all the way through, again, and *that* felt like another, much harder kick, because he wasn't behaving the way she'd expected he would. The way she'd been so sure he would—and that was why she'd left him. She didn't have the slightest idea what to do about it.

But she couldn't punch him in front of her sister, as much as she might feel like it just then. Christina was the good daughter, the well-behaved sister, the child who had always done precisely what was expected of her, and happily. Luce was the belligerent loudmouth troublemaker of their little corner of the Grey family, a role she got away with because she was also willowy, slender, and shockingly beautiful. And well she knew it.

"Luce." Christina tried to exude a calm sort of authority she didn't feel. "Mom is a grown woman. I know she likes to get into the Christmas spirit with a vengeance, but she can handle a little bit of reality, even in December. I promise you."

Dare shifted audibly, but she refused to look at him. She refused.

"I kicked Hal's broke, cheating ass out," Luce announced with a kind of grim finality that made Christina feel the slightest little trickle of reluctant sympathy for the brother-in-law she hadn't been fond of since way back when they'd all been at Marietta High, when he'd been an overly-entitled member of the varsity football team and merely one of Luce's many boyfriends. But only a very little trickle, quickly gone. "Being the complete loser that he is, he'll probably spend Christmas drunk and cleaning out our house to see what he can sell to pay for more strippers. He likes strippers. And I'm pretty sure 'strippers' is a euphemism." She pulled in a breath that sounded far more ragged and painful than her harshly amused tone would suggest, but that was Luce. Hard like a rock on the outside despite how beautiful she was, and secretly breakable within. Far within. "I told him that if he's still there when we get back from Grandma and Grandpa's, I'll shoot him and save myself the trouble of arguing over the money he owes me in court. I'm kind of hoping he thinks I'm kidding."

She turned to yell at her sons again, and Christina couldn't help it. She looked over at Dare. He didn't *quite* widen those smoky eyes of his in return, and that felt too good. Much too good. As if they were communicating again—but a single glance didn't make up for all that silence. It couldn't. She recollected herself and jerked her treacherous gaze away. Then she tried to transmit the compassion she didn't entirely feel, not when she'd never wanted Hal for her sister in the first place, when Luce turned back again.

"So you understand," Luce said, as if they'd settled a critical point between them.

"I'm really sorry to hear that you and Hal broke up, if that's what you mean."

"No, you're not. You don't have to be so polite about it, Christina." Luce smoothed her hair back from her forehead and sighed. "You hated Hal ever since he snapped your bra in the ninth grade, and who can blame you?"

Christina tried to be diplomatic. "I always thought Hal had some impulse control issues, yes."

"That's what you call it when they're little shits in high school," Luce said then, and though she frowned Christina understood it wasn't directed at her. "Little shits who have three kids and no job? You begin to call it other things."

"Luce, I'm so sorry—"

"I'm not. I only married him because he knocked me up and my kids are worth putting up with anything, even their father." Luce stood straighter and her brown eyes burned, but she didn't crack. "Don't be sorry. Just don't be *this*." She waved her hand in the wide, cold, brutal space between Christina at the fridge and Dare by the counter. "I think one Grey family marriage on the rocks at a time is about all Mom is prepared to deal with, especially at this time of year. To say nothing of what Grandma will do if she find out *both* of us are about to be divorced."

Christina winced, which had no doubt been Luce's intention. Elly Grey was the fearsome matriarch of the Grey family and about as far from the stereotypical apple-cheeked, affectionate grandmother as it was possible to get. A whole lot more Calamity Jane than Mrs. Butterworth, Christina and her cousins had always joked—but never where Grandma might overhear.

And Grandma's two favorite topics of conversation, especially at holidays when she could gather the entire family together as her captive audience? One: the epic disappointment that was their Grandpa, renowned across the state of Montana and probably Idaho and Wyoming besides for his wandering eye. And two: the ways in which *most* of her four children, two of her three sons and her only daughter, had let her down with their terrible life choices. Luce and Christina's father Ryan was the only one of her children whose marriage *hadn't* fallen apart, and the only one Grandma ever spared her sharp tongue.

The favorite son, her uncles would mutter darkly at her father during the inevitable lecture on morals lost and promises kept at every single family gathering ever. *How sweet.*

Christina's mother Gracie would be heartbroken that both of her daughters' marriages had failed. Distraught all the way through, as if her own relationship was on the line. Grandma, on the other hand, would see it as nothing more than the validation she'd been waiting for that this next generation of Greys was as wretched as the one before it.

You're all cursed, she'd announced in her direst tones at last year's Thanksgiving meal. *You can thank your grandfather for that. Blood will tell.*

Thanks, Pop, her Uncle Jason had muttered in that dark, gruffly irritated way of his that kept the patrons of his bar, Grey's Saloon, under his control or swiftly back out on the streets of Marietta before they knew what hit them. *Have some potatoes. And the blame.*

Happy freaking holidays, indeed, Christina thought now. Grandma's bitterness was one of the reasons they hadn't driven up for Thanksgiving this year. That and the fact Dare had worked the entire holiday weekend and had suffered exactly fifteen minutes of Christina's makeshift attempt at a holiday meal before stalking off.

She'd eaten all the stuffing and gravy, gained five pounds in a day, and didn't regret a damned thing.

"Well," Christina said now, as briskly as she could. "Dare and I can't *pretend* to be happily married, Luce. Not even to avoid Grandma's wrath."

"Why not?" Luce pounced on that, her brown eyes gleaming in a way that Christina recognized from a thousand Luce-led 'adventures' in the past. She braced herself and sure enough, her sister kept talking. "Just until January. Who will it hurt? All you have to do is make it through the next few days. A week at most."

"What? No. Absolutely—"

"Sure." Dare sounded darkly amused and something else Christina didn't particularly want to identify. Certainly not right there in front of her sister, when so many things were happening inside of her she couldn't count them all. "We can do that."

She turned to look at him. Slowly, as if he'd transformed into an obstreperous elk while she'd been glaring at her sister. "Are you insane?"

Dare shrugged, his smoky gaze a challenge and his mouth in its little crook, and she still felt the wild *heat* of it. It still moved through her like a lick of pure flame.

It still felt like perfection.

The only difference was, she hated that it did. Her marriage had been nothing but a kamikaze death spiral for the last few years, it was destroying her, and she finally wanted it to stop.

Didn't she?

"Consider it a Christmas present to your whole family, Luce," Dare said, turning up the wattage on his smile and aiming it straight at Christina's poor, heartbroken sister, the jerk, when he hadn't smiled at *Christina* in ages. "It's the least Christina and I can do."

Chapter Three

D ARE HATED HOLIDAYS.

In his family, not getting his ass kicked or ending up in the ER after a family gathering was considered a major gift—if not a blessing—and that was rare enough. Pointed "family time" holidays had always been opportunities for high expectations that quickly fell apart and turned into entirely too much drunken brawling.

He'd opted out of that mess when he'd left. He'd opted out of all of it. The great, gnarled family tree made of alcoholics and violent lunatics, as far back as anyone had ever bothered to trace it. Not that his relatives spent a lot of time worried about their genealogy. It was pretty obvious. Go to Gillette, Wyoming, look around for the biggest wastes of human space involved in some or other depressingly public downward spiral, and that was likely to be a Cooper family gathering en route to another disaster.

He was sure it was why he'd started studying viruses as an undergraduate and become obsessed. Because he had the usual scientific fantasies of making the world a better place, sure. But also because his family was its own virus, for all intents and purposes, and he wanted the cure. His father had been made entirely of rage and paranoia and had been well-lubricated at all times by vast quantities of his beloved sour mash. Leroy Cooper had beaten the crap out of anything within his reach, with the family trademark of dark, sadistic glee. His own brothers. Random neighbors in their run-down trailer park. Anyone who looked at him funny, according to him. Dare's mother, who had never *not* looked at him funny, by Leroy's account. Dare himself, by virtue of existing.

Until Dare got big enough to challenge him back, that was—which was when Leroy had decided to enact his final cruelty. He'd taken himself out and had dragged Dare's brutalized mother with him one bullet after the next on a snowy March afternoon, right there in the living room of their trailer.

Fifteen year old Dare had been the one to find them, the one to call the police and report the tragedy. And as he'd stood there waiting for the cops to come and clean up yet another Cooper family mess, he'd stared down at what was left of the two people who should have loved him the most and he'd understood, deep down, that they hadn't been able to love anything. Not him. Not themselves. Just like everyone else in his world.

Just like him.

Because he was as infected as the rest of them. Dare knew that. Hell, he'd always known that, no matter the external differences between him and his down-and-out kin. They might still have been playing their desperate games back in Gillette while he'd lost himself in academics, but inside they were all the same. That awful truth had been stamped into his bones on a cold March afternoon more than fifteen years ago now, when his grandmother's response to his parents' murder/suicide had been to smack Dare in the face and complain about having to care for "another goddamned parasite." And he'd been as messed up as the rest of them, because he'd only laughed.

He'd only pretended he could ever be something other than a piece of shit no matter how many degrees he collected because Christina had always felt like an antidote to that poison in him. Like the cure he'd been looking for, if he was honest.

She still did. And it still rocked him all the way to that dark, dark hole where his soul should have been. But viruses didn't have cures, only antiviral remedies that never lasted long before the virus overcame them. Prevention was far better than any potential cure—and that meant Dare had been kidding himself. And he was standing here in her parents' house in Montana, so that meant he still was.

The day before Christmas Eve, no less.

Suffice it to say, he'd never really understood Christina and her family's fascination with Christmas, as if it was an annual miracle that could save souls when really, it was just a day. An overhyped day at that. Dare knew lost souls didn't happen back one day, no matter how many pine trees died for the cause.

This year was no different. Ryan and Gracie's house was already stuffed with enough holiday cheer to fell a battalion of elves. There were stockings over the fireplace. There had been reindeer with blinking lights out on the front lawn. There were evergreen garlands wrapped around the staircase railing leading up to the second floor and a fully decorated, gleaming tree in the living room, despite the fact no one would be here on the actual day of Christmas. Every Grey around packed up and headed out to Big Sky every year to spend Christmas Eve and Christmas Day with their intimidating grandparents and the rest of the extended family.

Dare would have said the Greys didn't exactly get along, but they didn't get into fistfights, either, so he supposed that was better than the so-called Christmases he'd suffered through as a kid. But he still didn't get it.

Now, standing here in his in laws' living room looking at all the handmade Christmas tree ornaments stitching together a patchwork of obviously happy family memories that made him feel itchy and restless by virtue of his proximity to them, it was even more baffling than usual.

Because he didn't want this. He knew better than this. Why was he here?

Why couldn't he let Christina go?

He never should have caved, years ago. He'd broken up with her when he'd graduated from college and he should have left things that way, because it had taken exactly one look at Christina Grey in Missoula to understand that she was forever. That she was every single one of the things he couldn't have, because he knew he'd destroy them. Home. Happiness. Family.

Love. Hope.

He'd known it that very first night. He'd known it when he'd kissed her. He'd certainly known it when that insane chemistry had erupted between them, blotting out everything but what they could do to each other in bed. He'd known it when he'd walked away from her and he'd known it when he'd given in to that howling thing inside of him and gotten back together with her, too.

He never should have stayed with her and he never should have married her, because he'd known from the start that this was where it would lead. She would want all the things he couldn't give her, he wouldn't have it in him to give them, and then what?

This, he told himself darkly. *This is what.*

He was a coward, just like his father before him. Christina was the warmest, brightest person he'd ever met. Her smile shifted the stars around in the sky above him without her even trying. He'd never laid a finger on her and he never would, but that didn't mean there weren't other ways of hurting people. He was a coward and a bastard besides, making her as lost and sad as he was. And here he was after she'd finally left him, lining up to do more damage. What the hell was wrong with him?

But he knew the answer to that. He always had.

He reached over and touched a big ornament made of orange construction paper and purple pipe cleaners that said her name in giant, loopy childish letters, as if it was some kind of magical talisman. She was his own personal bit of sunshine, his own magical spell, and she deserved to get every single thing she wanted.

And Dare couldn't give her any of them.

Not one.

But he still couldn't seem to leave her, either.

"I hope you're proud of yourself," Christina said from behind him, and she sounded neither warm nor bright then. He let go of the ornament and straightened, feeling as guilty as if she'd caught him at something truly illicit. "You've made a sad, painful situation into something far worse."

Luce had charged off into the cold morning with her pack of unruly creatures in tow, and Christina had stormed upstairs without another word to him. Dare had heard the shower go on and had let out a breath he hadn't known he'd been holding, because at least she hadn't kicked him back out the door when he'd walked in. He hadn't known how much he'd expected her to do exactly that until she hadn't.

"I'm looking at it as an opportunity," he said now, facing her.

He immediately wished he wasn't. She'd been cute enough in her pajamas, with her hair twisted back out of her way. But now she was dressed, and not in that strange, preppy-meets-plastic way she'd been dressing the last little while, all blow-dried hair and too much eye make up. Today she looked like his mountain girl again, in jeans, boots and a long-sleeved henley, her hair brushed but still wet at her shoulders, her face scrubbed clean of everything except her pretty eyes and that frown.

God, he loved this woman. He didn't know how to stop, no matter how destructive it was. No matter how little he knew what that word meant.

"An opportunity to do what?" she demanded. She stood at the bottom of the stairs, more in the foyer than in the living room, as if she didn't trust herself any closer to him. Or as if she didn't trust *him,* and he'd earned that, too. "Ruin every last thing I love?"

"Yes. That is my only goal."

There was a time she might have smiled at that, even in the middle of a fight. Not today.

"Congratulations," she said, her voice much too cold. "You've achieved it and then some."

"I accept that I deserve the gloves off."

"You said it, Dare," she snapped at him. "Not me."

"You want to hit me?" he asked softly. It was easier to be pissed than contrite—and he'd fed that part of himself all the way up from Denver. He let it move through him now, too. "Go right ahead. But you should know. If you put your hands on me, I won't necessarily keep mine off of you."

She blinked at him. "Oh, I'm sorry. Was that sexual? I can't remember what that's supposed to sound like. It's been nine hundred years."

He didn't mean to move toward her. But the truth was, he'd only been able to freeze her out when she'd let him. *This* version of his wife—spirited and bright even in the flare of her temper, the way he remembered her—he couldn't keep away from.

Then again, he didn't try that hard.

Christina stood her ground, but flushed when he came close and then even closer. He kept moving so she had to tip her chin up to keep looking him in the eye. And it had been so long. He felt as drunk as any one of his no-account uncles, wild with it and the spiraling sensation deep within him, telling him that if he didn't taste her right here, right now, he might never get the opportunity again.

"What are you doing?" she asked, and there was something solemn, nearly sacred, in the husky scrape of her voice in all the quiet. It lit him on fire.

He reached over and slid his hands over the perfect curves of her cheeks, feeling the way she fit so beautifully in his grip. She was little and delicate and made for him, and she still made him feel like he was the man he'd always wanted to become. It was why he'd stopped touching her. She made him *believe.*

And then, though it wasn't fair, he couldn't keep himself from asking the worst question. The one he didn't want to know the answer to. "Why did you let me do it?"

Christina sucked in a breath and he could feel the shock move through her, could see it in her dark eyes.

"*Let* you?" she hissed at him. "Are you crazy? *Let* you? I practically begged you to treat me like I was slightly more interesting to you than a piece of furniture!"

"No matter what I did or said, you never called me on it." He sounded furious. He could hear it. When inside he was nothing but cold. And he couldn't understand it. Or why he was still touching her like this, when he knew better. "I don't understand why. Why put up with it all this time? Why not tell me to go to hell?"

"Go to hell, Dare. Happy now?"

"You always used to fight me like you were three times your own size, Christina. Like you were larger than life. What changed?"

She sucked in a breath and he felt it as if she'd touched him. "You did."

"That's what you keep saying." His hands held her fast, but he noticed she didn't try to pull away. The heat of her skin seared through his palms, making it next to impossible to remember any reason in the world why he wouldn't do whatever it took to make sure he kept touching her. "But I didn't change that much. I got quiet, maybe. But you disappeared."

"I thought that was what you wanted." She didn't sound angry then, she sounded hurt, pure and simple. And here he'd thought he couldn't possibly hate himself more. "Something different. *Someone* different."

"The only thing I ever wanted was you," he whispered, as if it was a harsh condemnation of the both of them. "But I fucked that up, too."

And he couldn't handle the misery in her gaze then, slick and deep.

So he kissed her.

She tasted sweet and rich, the way she always had. She tasted like she was his, like she'd never been anything but his.

She tasted like home. The only one he'd ever known.

He kissed her again and again, and it was like the first time. Better. Promise and regret, apology and hope, and he didn't know what he wanted to get out of it. He only knew he couldn't seem to stop. He angled his head and took her deeper, tasting her and loving her and wishing this could be the beginning and the end of it. This kiss. This moment.

This.

He wished they could live right here, in this whirl of sensation, where everything made sense. His fingers sunk in the damp silk of her hair. Her hands pressed against his chest. That sweet little body of hers arched into his, fitting him perfectly, the way she always did.

He wished they could stay like this forever.

But that wasn't reality.

He pulled back, and saw an expression like agony move over her face, worse than that sheen of misery before. Harder to take.

"Why won't you tell me, Dare?" she whispered fiercely. "Why won't you tell me what's wrong?"

He didn't know what he'd say, there in that quiet foyer with a Christmas tree gleaming softly behind them, like the kind of blessing he refused to accept was real. He felt as if he was out on a terrifying precipice and the slightest little bit of wind could hurl him over the side, and the thing about that was, Dare didn't know which he wanted more: to keep up this balancing act or to let himself fall. He didn't know how to talk about this, or he would have. He didn't know what to say—only that he couldn't seem to do anything without hurting her worse.

"I'm not who you think I am," he told her instead. Gritty and dark. "I never have been."

"I think you're a pretty big jerk, actually."

He felt his mouth move, just slightly. "No, you don't. It would be a whole lot easier if you did."

Her face twisted. "Dare…"

But she never finished. Because the back door opened again, and Christina jumped back as if she'd been zapped with a cattle prod. Her parents' voices drifted in from the kitchen and he saw the yearning sort of look that was so foreign to him cross over her open features. He knew that Christina wanted nothing more than to run to her parents, tell them everything, let them help her through it. Through *him*. He'd never understood that kind of dependence on anyone. Even when his parents had still been alive, he'd spent most of his time hiding from them or perfecting the art of being invisible in plain sight. Christina's relationship with her family was yet one more thing about her that simultaneously intrigued him and baffled him. It made him feel like an alien creature set down on her planet from far, far away.

But today, he couldn't allow it. Whatever the hell it was.

"Not until after Christmas," he warned her, his voice low.

She frowned up at him, her mouth still soft from his. He could still taste her. He still wanted her, desperately. He was hard and angry and empty besides, and it was all her fault. And his, for allowing it. For perpetuating it.

"Since when do you care about Christmas? Much less protecting it?"

"I don't," he replied, that thing in him that felt like temper but he knew wasn't, not quite, sparking again and running deep. "But your mother sure does."

She mouthed something deeply unladylike with the same mouth that had just been lost in his, and he grinned despite himself as she stalked off down the hall toward the kitchen because *this* Christina didn't care if she pissed him off.

This Christina was the one he couldn't resist. At all.

This Christina was a Montana girl through and through, made of Rocky Mountain heights and long, cold winters, and she could take care of her own damned self. *This* Christina took after her mother, three parts ferocious and one part pure, humbling sweetness, and he couldn't seem to walk away from her.

No matter how hard he tried.

And not even if she walked away from him first.

CHRISTINA WAS IN hell.

There was no other explanation for it.

And kissing Dare certainly hadn't helped—if anything, it had made everything that much worse. She felt all the things she'd cycled through on the long drive to Marietta, from steely resolve to that hollow ache inside, but now she got to experience it all along with the crazy fire that was all Dare and that talented mouth of his roaring through her, too.

Making her feel as if she'd betrayed herself.

Making her want more.

Damn him.

She went out to greet her parents, playing the whole thing off as if this was a delightful Christmas surprise she and Dare had cooked up just for them.

"What a perfect Christmas gift!" her mother cried, wrapping her arms tight around Christina and making a whole lot of things feel instantly better. "And for your thirtieth birthday, too! I was so disappointed that we wouldn't get to celebrate with you!"

"We couldn't bear it," Christina said, which was true, at least. For her. And then she started in with the lying. "We had to come up."

"In two cars," her father murmured when it was his turn to hug her, and sling a welcoming arm around Dare's strong back. "One of which looks awfully over packed for a Christmas visit…"

But he subsided when Dare only smiled blandly at him in reply.

"Welcome home, sweetheart," her mother said, and Christina wiped the extra heat away from her eyes that *absolutely was not tears because she was a grown woman* when no one was looking.

Then the morning wore on, and life with it, even on December 23rd in her mother's tricked out North Pole of a house with Christmas carols blaring all the while. Her father went into the shop. Dare went to take a nap on the couch in the den after making his apologies for driving all night, as if he and Christina had planned it that way. And Christina and her mother baked the last of Gracie's usual Christmas cookies, packed them up into their tins the way Gracie did every year, and then took to the chilly roads to deliver the handmade gift baskets all around town.

Delivering Christmas cheer, Gracie had always called it.

This had always been one of Christina's favorite parts of Christmas, especially after she'd moved away from home, and today was no different. There was something about retracing the lines of this particular map of her childhood that she loved, deeply. It was like driving around inside her very own Christmas card. There were the actual streets of Marietta and the roads that led up into the hills and off to the ranches, and there was the Grey family's own geography superimposed on top of it. And then Christina's personal memories of her eighteen years here like one of the filters she used on Instagram, bringing everything into a particular focus. The idyllic, the funny, the bittersweet, the faded into dim memory. All of it jumbled together into baked goods left on front porches or delivered to smiling friends and neighbors who more often than not had a gift for Gracie in return.

This never happened in Denver and after a few years of trying to replicate it in her busy neighborhood filled with young professionals who went elsewhere for their holidays, Christina had stopped trying.

Here on Bramble Street was her mom's best friend since they'd been kids together, who sent them on their way with her homemade hot chocolate in travel mugs. This pretty ranch had been in the MacCreadie family forever. This stretch of land belonged to nice summer people, the land over there to snooty rich folks who hid behind their dramatic gates and only emerged in fleets of Range Rovers, and that road led up to fancy Crawford House that was being made into some kind of museum.

It took her a long while to realize that she was homesick. And not for Marietta itself, though she loved this place dearly. But for those versions of herself she'd never get back—those ghosts of Christmases past who rode along with her in this SUV today, herself at eleven, fourteen, seventeen, so thrilled about what her future might hold. She looked out over the whole great valley and felt more lost, more adrift, than she had in years— since those first heady, unnerving weeks before she'd found her feet away at college on the other side of the Rockies, in fact.

"You seem so many miles away that you might as well be back in Colorado," Gracie observed as they headed back down from Crawford House. They'd left a present on the front steps for Mrs. Collier, the last grand dame of the once marvelously wealthy Crawford family, as she had always been the first to remind anyone in earshot.

Slumped there in the front passenger seat of her mother's Explorer, her hot chocolate long gone, Christina kept her eyes on the view before her and told herself it was the cold, cold Montana air that was making her eyes sting again. Despite the fact her mother's heater was working just fine, blasting too-hot air against her cheeks. There was snow up on all the mountaintops in all directions, but it was a shatteringly clear day today. That meant that this far up in the hills, she could see everything laid out before her as the winter sun catapulted itself toward the horizon. Her hometown sat like a perfect painting down there in the distance with the frozen river lazing its way through it, like a snow globe sitting pretty on a shelf somewhere, waiting for someone to shake it up.

"I'm thinking about geography," she said after a moment or two.

"Are you really?" Her mother laughed. "Not that there's anything wrong with geography, of course. I don't mean to laugh."

"I just mean… the maps that we make out of our lives. Mine started here."

She could see all the way across the valley to the far hills. The evergreens bristled but the rest of the trees were bare, and she knew this view so well. So very well. She could have drawn it with her eyes closed. She knew every craggy dip and turn of every mountain, from great Copper Mountain looming at her back out to the Crazies and beyond. They were etched into her bones, her flesh, no matter how dislocated she felt just then.

And so was Dare, in much the same way, and she didn't have the slightest idea how to go about changing that. If it was even possible.

"Why didn't you and Dad go somewhere else? Why did you stay put?"

She felt more than saw her mother's considering glance. "We like it here."

"But how do you know that if you never lived somewhere else? How do you know what the right thing is if you never try anything but the thing you already know entirely too well?"

Gracie took a moment to answer, and Christina heard her own voice as it hung there in the quiet—a little too rough. A little too revealing.

Maybe a little more than *a little*.

"I think most folks are born with restless hearts of one variety or another," her mother said, sounding as if she was choosing her words carefully. "And they keep on feeling that restlessness until they find the thing that cures it. Sometimes it's a place. Sometimes it's a person. A career, maybe. The chance to travel where they like. It's different for everyone." She slowed to go around a tight curve in the old mountain road, and Christina breathed out as the sheer exhilaration of it—the mountain, the stark view, *Montana*—flowed over her. She'd forgotten that, too. "And your father was that thing for me, right from the start way back in high school. So *where* we were didn't matter as much, after that, as long as we were together. I always got the impression that Dare was that thing for you."

She didn't ask the obvious next question, and that alone almost brought Christina to tears. And this time, there was no pretending they were anything but tears.

"I don't know," Christina said quietly. "Maybe the thing changes. Maybe it was never *one* thing at all. Maybe both of us were kidding ourselves."

Gracie kept driving, but she reached over and put her hand on Christina's leg the way she'd done when Christina was a kid, and it was as good as a long, tight hug from someone else. It felt like pure, concentrated love in a single gesture, and she had to close her eyes against it, it was so sharp. So good.

But Gracie's words burrowed deep.

"Your heart has always been your compass, honey," she said quietly as she drove them back toward town. "And a good one. Let it show you the way home."

C HRISTINA LET HER internal compass, which she wasn't sure
could lead her down a straight path with illuminated
billboards lighting the way, no matter what her mother seemed
to think, take her out that night.

They'd all had dinner at her parents' house without men-
tioning the word "divorce" even once. Her nephews had charged
around screaming bloody murder and enjoying themselves
immensely. The dogs had maintained a canine chorus throughout, interspersed with begging. Luce and her father had argued
about some political issue as if their entire lives hinged on
beating the other into submission. And Dare had practically
flirted with her mother as if he'd downed a bottle of charm pills
after his nap.

It was the perfect dinner, really. Happy, silly, loud. Like a
scene out of a family-friendly holiday movie.

Too bad, Christina had thought as she'd nursed one of her
father's favorite artisanal beers from the new local microbrewery
and tried to keep her smile in place, *that it isn't entirely real. That
most of us are putting on an act.*

When the political arguments had waned, the dishes had

been done by committee, and the grandparents had taken charge of the kids, the three of them remaining had sat there around the kitchen table reliving the morning's *pretend you're happily married* conversation.

Or that was what Christina had been doing, as she'd scowled at the Christmas-themed centerpiece involving merry snowmen and dancing candles and had attempted to pretend she hadn't been *that aware* of Dare sitting *right there beside her*—

"Let's go out," Luce had said abruptly into the strained silence, as little boy feet pounded up and down the upstairs hallway overhead. "It will be like a Marietta High School reunion in every bar in town." She'd checked her watch. "Except the microbrewery in the old train depot, FlintWorks, which just closed. So, you know. The other two."

"Is the high school reunion aspect supposed to be a draw or a warning?" Dare had asked as he'd lounged there looking beautiful and out of reach, as usual—with the faintest hint of the drawl he pulled out from time to time. It had made Christina feel melty and weak, the way it always did.

It had also made her mad, because she'd been sitting in her usual seat at the kitchen table with a straight line of sight down the hall to the front foyer, where she'd kissed Dare earlier that morning as if she hadn't packed up and left him the day before. What had *that* been about? Was she really *that* weak?

But she hadn't really wanted to answer that question.

"Let's go to the inevitable family reunion at Grey's," Christina had said instead of succumbing to all the *melting*. She'd wanted to ignore Dare but instead, had fixed a glare on him. "You can be our designated driver. Thanks for offering."

"Planning to dance on the tables?" he'd asked, sounding lazy and delicious and something else that had wound around inside of her and hadn't felt anything at all like a *compass*. It had felt a great deal more like an engraved invitation. "Your uncle won't like that."

Christina was well aware that Uncle Jason's "no shenanigans" rule was practically law around Marietta. Historically, he hadn't restricted that rule to only his saloon, either.

"Yeah, but we're family," Luce had said impatiently. "He won't throw us out. That's our name on the sign too."

"You say that like Uncle Jason hasn't thrown out family before," Christina had pointed out dryly. "You, for example. More than once, if memory serves. Pretty much every single one of our cousins, especially Jesse that Christmas his own father hooked up with his girlfriend. Uncle Billy himself about a thousand times, come to that. Not to mention Uncle Jason's *own* kids, who actually worked there. The man is merciless."

"Oh," Luce had replied airily. "He's totally mellowed."

And that was how they all ended up in a crowded Grey's Saloon on Christmas Eve's Eve, with what appeared to be half the town of Marietta.

Luce, unsurprisingly, melted off into a sea of locals who Christina knew enough to smile at, but not enough to walk right up and talk to without a little fortification first. Fully aware that Dare was right behind her, she made her way toward the bar, prepared to catch her surly, obviously completely *unmellowed* Uncle Jason's eye and try to convince him to make her about twenty margaritas, STAT.

"You don't have to look for our troubles at the bottom of a glass, Christina," Dare said, entirely too close to the back of her neck. She fought to restrain a little shiver as her reaction to that stampeded through her, all fire and need.

"Because you're standing right here?" she asked him, perhaps a touch too sharply. "Maybe I just want to be blurry. Is that okay with you?"

She was being flippant and she spun back to gauge his reaction—and froze. If it weren't for the hand he shot out to steady her, she would have slammed right into the nearest good old boy.

And then, suddenly, she didn't know where the worst—*or best,* something whispered—of the wild sensation was coming from. His hand, wrapped over the curve of her hip in an easy sort of hold that spoke of an intimacy she'd almost forgotten had ever existed between them. Or that look in those smoky eyes of his, serious and direct, cutting straight through her.

"I'll take care of you," he told her, and it sounded a great deal like a vow. Chiseled in stone. Direct and real. "Whatever happens."

She jerked herself out of his grip, aware that her cheeks were blaring with heat, and equally aware this had nothing to do with the fact she hadn't taken her bright red, too warm winter coat off when they'd come inside. Oh, no. It was all Dare.

"I've heard that promise before," she reminded him, and she didn't care that they were standing in public. That she knew probably eighty-five percent of the people here, or their families. That the country version of the Christmas carols coming out of the jukebox wouldn't muffle her entirely. "Sickness, health. And so on. You're not a good bet."

And Christina hated herself when his gaze went dark. Something like tortured. And his beautiful mouth set into a solid line that made her chest ache.

He reached over and ran his knuckles over one too-hot cheek, and there was no containing that shiver, then. There was nothing she could do but respond to him, and she didn't know which one of them was more miserable. She only knew it hurt. It all hurt. And that shiver still ran deep, arrowing straight into the core of her.

His mouth shifted into something too painful to be a smile. "That's what I've been trying to tell you," he said quietly. "For years."

Then he dropped his hand, and there was no reason in the world that Christina should feel so lost again. So bereft.

"I'm going to get hideously, embarrassingly drunk," she announced, because it was better than marinating in that sense of loss. Because anything was better than that. And maybe there was a little too much challenge in the way she said it, but that, too, was better. "Margaritas will be tossed back with abandon. Shenanigans will be pulled despite the Jason Grey hard line on that. Reputations will lie in ruins at my feet."

"Or maybe you could try one drink," Dare suggested. "Two at the most."

Except really, it was more of an order, Christina thought as she eyed him, noting the faintly arrogant tilt to his head. The Dr. Know It All pose, as they'd called it when they'd still teased each other affectionately about such things. She hadn't seen it in a long while, and she didn't want to admit that it warmed her up even further to see it now. And when she raised her brows at him, he smiled. Just a little.

"You're the designated driver, not the designated Dad, thank you."

"I'll keep that in mind." Dare's voice was low and dark. His gaze was still much the same. And she didn't understand how she could be *this* angry with him and *this* sad and still want him so much it felt like a wildfire surged, dangerous and uncontainable, right beneath her skin. "I'm going to check out the pool table. And maybe while you're sacking reputations and doing a face dive into a tequila bottle you might remember that you're a noted lightweight, and if you drink more than about a margarita and a half, you'll fall asleep. Wherever you happen to be standing at the time."

That was possibly the most annoying thing he'd said all day, because it was true, as their entire history together had proved more than once. *Damn him.*

"I've developed a major tolerance while you've been off at the lab," she told him, which wasn't exactly true. But he didn't need to know that, so she embellished further. "I drink a case of wine a night. Two or three, for all you know."

"On the couch at home?" he asked mildly. "Where you then... fall asleep?"

Christina rolled her eyes, ignored the low sound he made that was far too much like the kind of laughter she didn't think he was capable of any longer, and headed for the bar again. She peeled off her incongruously cheerful winter coat as she went, determined to charm her constitutionally uncharmable uncle into letting her get sloppy and even a little bit crazy in his saloon. The way assorted historical Greys and the town's rowdier denizens had been doing since the Gold Rush era, when Marietta had been chock full of miners and the upstairs of the saloon had been the province of prostitutes and their clients—none of them exactly famous for their good behavior.

But the bartender standing closest to her when she snuck her way through the crowd was not her uncle—who would likely refuse to make margaritas at all on the principle that this was a saloon in rural Montana not the goddamned ritzy city, now that she thought about it, and she was fairly sure he'd actually said that to her before verbatim—but her cousin Rayanne, one of Jason's three daughters and only a couple of years older than Christina. Rayanne was remarkably pretty. She had been when they were kids and she was even more so now. Her golden blonde hair waved down to her shoulders and she had the kind of body that made a white tank top and old jeans look like a granted prayer. Rayanne had the biggest, widest smile in the state of Montana, and one of the best singing voices, and Christina still didn't understand why she wasn't a household name after all her years in Nashville.

Rayanne threw her hands up in delight, then rounded the bar to hug Christina tight.

"I didn't know you were coming!" she cried, and she pulled back to kiss Christina soundly on each cheek. Then Rayanne glanced down the length of the bar to where her father stood, his arms crossed over his solid chest and his usual scowl welded in place. Jason Grey and his lifelong bad mood were an institution here, and for some reason it made Christina smile to see it. She couldn't imagine the place without him. "Dad told me about sixty times that it was going to be a cold, lonely Christmas with no one to talk to but the wind. I should have realized he meant that was what he *hoped* would happen."

She moved back around to take her place behind the bar again, stowing Christina's coat and smiling away the overtly appreciative noises of some of the gathered gentlemen as she did—and who could blame them? Rayanne moved like she was dancing. She was lithe and lovely and had always been like this, always *that* pretty and fairly bursting with happiness besides. She was always on the near side of bubbly, always *this close* to bursting into song, and those were only a couple of the reasons she was everyone's favorite cousin.

"Tell me what you want," Rayanne said, and rolled her eyes when Christina reached for her wallet. "Don't insult me. Family discount always applies, silly."

"On all seventeen margaritas that I want right this minute?" Christina asked dryly. "And yes, they're all for me."

Rayanne eyed her for a moment, but didn't inquire. Maybe because it was the holidays, and no further explanation was required than that. It was perfectly possible to love the holiday season with every inch of one's soul and simultaneously want to take a little vacation in oblivion, after all. That was the peculiar magic of the season.

"Why don't we start with one and see what happens?"

"I'm trying to get drunk here, Rayanne. Very, very drunk."

"That's not hard, though, the way I remember it," Rayanne said with her easy grin. "Remember that New Year's Eve when you and Joey were thirteen and drank the leftover wine from your parents' dinner party?"

She laughed, which told Christina that Rayanne certainly remembered it. She did, too. Unfortunately. Christina and Joey, Rayanne's little sister, had heard this story almost every time they'd looked at an alcoholic beverage in the presence of a family member since. And it had happened more than half a lifetime ago. Literally.

"I'm so glad I have so much family," Christina said ruefully. "On the off chance I forget anything, ever, you'll all be hanging around to remind me."

"Only about the embarrassing stuff, Christina. No one cares if you were a good person, or a good student, or saved kittens every afternoon. Your family is here to mock you and humiliate you and remind you of all the things you'd like to forget, forever."

They both laughed at that, and Christina looked down the bar again. Uncle Jason was giving a familiar-looking cowboy the kind of glare that could easily escalate into someone getting tossed out the front door. Reese Kendrick, the man Jason had taken in as a kind of surrogate son way back when and who now operated as the saloon's manager, was setting up drinks with his usual stone-faced efficiency way down at the other end. There were a couple other bartenders Christina didn't know who seemed remarkably cheerful at the surliest bar in Montana, and two notable absences.

"Where are your sisters?" she asked Rayanne. "Have they fallen off the face of the planet? That's Luce's theory, you know. Has she run it by you yet? It involves the Northern Lights, a couple of grizzlies and a possible Sasquatch, and a lot of references to the early seasons of Supernatural."

"Luce is out of her mind."

"This is not news."

"Lorelai's still out in Los Angeles doing that Hollywood thing," Rayanne said, sliding the margarita she'd put together in front of Christina with dramatic flourish. "It would have been far more convenient for me if her dreams matched mine and we could do Nashville together, but that's Lorelai for you. Always doing exactly as she pleases. And Joey's still kicking ass and taking names in New York. I'm just happy she went with law school rather than the entertainment business. She can take care of the rest of us in our old age."

Christina grinned at the idea that sharp, focused, not-even-remotely maternal Joey might take care of anyone. Ever.

"I don't know," she said, and then something flipped over inside of her and pushed its way out whether she wanted it to or not, that grin of hers fading as it did. "The older I get, the more I think Grandma might be right after all. We're all cursed."

She could have pulled it off with a laugh, made a joke of it, maybe, but she didn't. And Rayanne had been leaning against the bar, easy and loose, but at that she straightened. Something uncharacteristically dark moved over her face.

But it was gone so quickly that Christina was almost convinced she'd imagined it.

"I refuse to give Grandma the satisfaction of being cursed," Rayanne said with a certain firmness that her troubled gaze didn't match at all. "We're all going live happily ever after, Christina, just to spite her. You heard it here first."

Rayanne went back to tending bar, leaving Christina no choice but to face her own not-so-happily ever after. She wove her way out of the crowd that was packed four deep around the bar itself. Once she was free of the crush, she could see Dare standing near the closest pool table, looking like the man she'd loved for so long now she couldn't imagine what her life had been like before she'd met him. She could hardly remember it. In her head, it was nothing but vague, dream-like impressions of her mostly happy teenage years and then Dare, sharp and in stark focus, as if he was the embodiment of clarity.

She took a pull from her drink and let the tequila do the thinking for her. And when she saw a group of folks she knew from high school, she pasted on a smile that was only a little bit forced and drove down a different memory lane altogether.

And for a little while, everything felt almost normal.

They'd been here before. They'd done this. The night before the night before Christmas, with all the rest of the town making merry all around them. Dare playing pool because he'd never been much of a socializer and Christina catching his eye every now and again as she went about the important business of catching up with her old classmates and friends.

Margaritas made it way too easy to pretend that they'd simply… slipped back over the rougher spots in their marriage to a kinder, gentler place that felt entirely too easy. Too natural. And fit much too well.

Christina laughed, and soon enough she wasn't forcing any of it. She caught up with the lives of old friends and heard all the gossip about everyone she'd known growing up. She saw her sister doing much the same, if more drunkenly and with a bit more emotion than was wise this close to Uncle Jason's temper, and figured what the hell. If Luce wanted to pour out her troubles in a public place, who was Christina to second guess her? She'd never understood the need for that kind of thing more than she did tonight. She danced a little bit with some of her old girlfriends when a fun song came on, teased and was teased in return by people she'd last spent serious quality time with when they were all still teenagers and now only saw once a year at most, and it was *fun*.

It was more than fun. She was feeling as close to happy as she had in years, light and buoyant, and maybe that was why she forgot herself. That and the margaritas. On one trip to the bathroom, she didn't see Dare at the pool tables. She assumed he was at the bar getting himself the appropriate pint of Coke for the driving he'd be doing later. And so when she ran into him in the little corridor that led to the private office and the bathroom only employees and family used, it was a surprise.

Except it didn't feel like a surprise. It felt… good.

On the jukebox, Bon Jovi begged someone to come home for Christmas. And Christina smiled at Dare as if he was still the husband he'd been all the other years they'd been right here in Marietta, in Grey's Saloon, on this very same night. As if he was still *her* husband, the one she'd loved so much for so long. As if they'd never lost each other along the way. It was a big and loopy smile, and yes, it was a little tequila-tinged, but it came straight from her heart all the same.

But Dare wasn't tipsy in any way, she noted immediately, much less lost on some nearly-Christmas trip down memory lane. He only gazed back at her, that dark thing in his smoky gaze and his mouth a firm, forbidding line she probably shouldn't find sexy.

That was the thing about tequila. It made everything feel like sunshine. Even this. Even Dare.

"You could smile," she told him. "It won't kill you."

"It might."

He didn't crack a smile, so she couldn't quite tell if that was meant to be a joke. But she was shot through with enough sunshine to not care about that the way she might have earlier.

"You're the one who wanted to pretend we were happy together," she reminded him, and there was no particular accusation in her voice. It was simply a fact. "This was your idea. You could have been sitting at home in Denver all by yourself if you wanted. You probably shouldn't have come all the way up here and agreed to lie about your feelings if it's this hard for you to crack a single freaking smile."

"It's never just a smile, though. Is it?"

It occurred to her that she wasn't necessarily thinking clearly—or at all—when her back came up against the wall of the hallway with a little *thwack*. She hadn't realized they'd moved. Or that Dare had moved and she'd moved with him without noticing, and there he was, leaning over her and getting much too close.

And the situation got out of hand, just like that.

"Dare…"

But she was whispering, and she had no idea if she was warding him off or begging him to come closer. Or to come home to her, just like the song.

"First it's the smile," he said, his voice a husky thing in the momentary privacy of the back hall. "Then all the things that come with it. You make me imagine I can be that man you smile at, Christina. You make me think that if I play him long enough, I'll turn into him one day. But what happens if I don't?"

"I have no idea what you're talking about."

She also didn't care. The hallway was dimly lit, his mouth was so close to hers as he stood there in front of her that it was the only thing she could think about. Then he flattened his palms on the wall on each side of her head and the world disappeared into that gaze of his, smoky and intent.

"You know where I come from," he said, his voice like a dark throb along the surface of her skin, then deep beneath it. "You know what that makes me. Why do I have to keep reminding you?"

"You were a kid who deserved better and a man who overcame a deeply crappy start," she said, not following him. But it was hard to follow anything just then that wasn't his mouth. "You were also an awesome husband for a while, but then you went deep freeze on me. That's on you, Dare."

"You're drunk."

"I'm tipsy. *Slightly* tipsy. And what does that have to do with anything?"

He leaned closer and Christina trembled, thinking he would put his mouth to hers again. But he didn't. He angled himself so his mouth was right next to her ear, so that when he spoke his voice shivered over her and into her as if his hands were running along her skin.

She wanted that more than she could bear.

"That's too bad."

"Why?" She hardly recognized her own voice. Tight and needy and breathless besides. "I thought you told me not to get drunk."

"But if you were, I might tell you all the ways I want you, because you wouldn't remember. You wouldn't hold me to it in the light of day." His breath fanned over her skin and she *wanted*. She'd wanted him forever. She thought she always would. God save her from the things she *wanted*. "You wouldn't know."

"I already know." She didn't mean to move, but then her

hands were at his hips, touching him as if she'd never lost that right. As if he'd never shut her out. As if his body was as much hers as her own had always been. She'd forgotten how good that felt. How *right*. "But that doesn't matter if you won't do it, does it?"

"Christina." Her name was like fire. It streaked through her, searing her to the bone. "I try so hard to keep you safe, especially from me, and yet all I seem to do is hurt you."

She wasn't drunk, but she wasn't thinking particularly clearly, either. And maybe that was a good thing. She wrapped her arms around that lean waist of his, luxuriating in the feel of the hard muscles she loved so much even through the long sleeved shirt he wore. The exquisite perfection of his finely-hewn back. He sucked in a breath and she tipped her head back, her face still caged between his hands on the wall on either side and her arms caging him in turn, and their gazes tangled. Held.

"Then stop it," she suggested, and then she lifted herself up the remaining distance, high up on her toes in her favorite old boots, and kissed him.

She meant it to be a sweet sort of kiss. A longtime kiss, heat banked, just to remind them both of all their history—

But Dare had a different idea. The kiss stayed sweet for three seconds, then he simply held her face fast, angled his jaw, and took it up a notch to pure sex.

Insane sex, like gas on an open flame.

Everything ignited.

Fire streaked through her. Carnal. Longing. *Hot*.

It was as if they'd never touched. As if this was new. Sex and desire, passion and need, swirled between them, illuminating them both like a whole block of houses wreathed in Christmas lights. She felt *bright*. She felt *electric*.

Dare shifted, stepping between her legs and making Christina wish she wasn't wearing jeans. That she could press herself against him right here. That he could be inside her *right now.*

And still, he kissed her. Again and again, slow and hot and perfect, as if he could do it forever and would. Drugging. Mesmerizing. Wild. It was dirty and beautiful. It was yearning made real. It was everything the past year or so hadn't been.

It made her broken heart feel strong and whole and mad for him. It was better than it had ever been before, and she had no idea how that could be. Only that it was. And that she couldn't imagine ever wanting anything more than she wanted this man. In all these years, she never had.

She slid her hands up beneath his shirt, reveling in the feel of his smooth, hot, muscled skin beneath her palms. She didn't remember when she'd last touched him and she didn't know when she'd get to do it again, so she had to make this count. She soaked him in. All that gorgeous male heat. That delicious tension in his beautiful body that made the ache deep in her belly pulse, then spread.

He was her addiction. And she'd wanted him for so long now, and had walked away from him thinking she'd never see him again. Thinking she'd never touch him again. Thinking this would never, ever happen again.

And it was almost Christmas. And he'd come after her. And she couldn't seem to take this as anything but a gift.

She pulled back, and that hurt. Dare's gaze was unfocused and hungry, and it made a deep, dark thrill course through her.

"Come on," she said.

She took his arm and pulled him back down the hallway, further away from the noise of the bar and the music. She passed the private bathroom and the office, and the second hallway that went on toward the kitchen. Before she made it to the exit, she found the small utility room and pushed Dare inside.

Christina was perfectly aware that she couldn't have dragged Dare here if he hadn't wanted to go. Maybe that was why she was trembling when she followed him in, locked the door behind her, and then leaned back against it.

"Christina," he said, his voice a low, sexy growl. She felt it everywhere. "You want to be real clear about what you're doing."

"No," she corrected him, and her own voice was barely more than a rasp. "I really don't."

And then she threw herself straight into his arms.

Chapter Five

A BETTER MAN might have thought twice.

But Dare was not that man. Not even a little.

He caught her, hauling her up against him and taking her mouth with his again, unable to stop himself. Unable to get enough of her. Unable to think of a single reason why he'd denied himself this—her—for so long.

A better man wouldn't have pushed her away in the first place, he reasoned, so he stopped worrying about all those dark and lonely things and lost himself in Christina instead.

At last.

He poured the tangled things he felt into every slick slide of his mouth over hers, because he knew he'd never say any of it out loud. How he loved her. How he needed her. How he was barely a man at all without her, and nothing like a good one.

He maneuvered them to an old chair that sat in the corner of the small room, then pulled her down to straddle him as he sat. She wrapped her arms around his head and kissed him, again and again, until he thought he'd never see straight again.

God help him, but he was tired of seeing straight if it meant going without her.

And Dare couldn't hold himself back. His hands re-learned her, streaking down the delectable line of her spine to hold her against the place he ached the most with his hands hard against the curve of her lush little bottom.

And then he groaned into her mouth when she moved against him.

She was so hot, so sexy, so perfect in every possible way, it hurt. And most of all, she was his.

Christina laughed, a low, delicious sound that made everything inside of him go taut. Then she shifted back and slid to her feet, standing between his widespread knees, her pretty brown eyes locking with his as she tugged down the zipper of her jeans.

He watched her as if she was a meal and he was very, very hungry. He was.

She was the sexiest thing he'd ever seen. She shimmied the jeans down over her hips, then shoved them down her thighs along with a bright scrap he knew were her panties, and then she let out a small laugh.

"I haven't done this in a long time," she said, breathlessly. "I forgot about my boots."

"I know exactly when you last did this," he reminded her, because she'd done it with him. Only and ever him. She laughed again, and then let out a higher-pitched sound when he grabbed her and pulled her back to him. He used his foot to shove the tangle of her jeans and panties down further, then thrust his legs through the opening between hers.

And when he stood up, holding her, she slid into place against him and they both sighed. He turned, propping her against the wall behind them, and held her there for a minute as she crossed her legs around his hips.

But Christina didn't want to wait. Her hands were busy between them, on his belt and then at the button of his jeans, and he bit out a curse when she reached inside and pulled him out.

"You're killing me," he told her.

But she didn't seem to mind that much. She laughed against his mouth, shifted against him, and then he was thrusting deep inside of her.

Finally.

For a moment they stared at each other, as if they'd both forgotten, somehow, the sheer perfection of this. The slick beauty. The *rightness* of it. Of *them.*

Then Dare began to move.

And it wasn't a seduction. It wasn't graceful or elegant or any of the things she deserved from him. But it was honest and it was frenetic and it was *them.*

It was *them* again. Finally.

Christina shook against him, sobbing out her pleasure into the crook of his neck, and when he followed her over into all that glory only she had ever showed him, he told himself he'd never let her go again.

That he'd die first.

Because living without her was the same damned thing.

CHRISTINA WOKE UP in the middle of her favorite dream.

Curled up in a warm bed with Dare wrapped around her, his chest hot against her back, letting herself drift as she reveled in the way they fit together so well. As if they'd been made for precisely that.

It took her a moment to realize that if her eyes and mouth felt *that* dry and her head ached the tiniest little bit, she wasn't dreaming at all. And then another moment—or maybe more like ten—to actually open up her eyes and assess the situation.

She recognized the set of shelves directly in her line of sight, with all her father's favorite dark mysteries stacked up with more enthusiasm than organizational prowess, and it all came back to her. Leaving Denver. Being back home in Marietta. Grey's Saloon. The utility room in Grey's Saloon, more importantly. Then the rest of last night, which had involved another unwise drink slid at her by her unsmiling uncle. She'd only had a few sips of it before she and Dare had to tend to a rowdier-by-the-minute Luce—before Uncle Jason took care of her himself, still without cracking a smile, no doubt.

They'd wrestled Luce into Dare's truck as she'd speculated about Hal's parentage with all of Main Street and the frigid night, then led her into Mom and Dad's house, snickering as if they were all teenagers again as they'd snuck up to the girls' old bedroom. Luce's boys were already there, sleeping piled up in their sleeping bags on the floor like a heap of puppies. Luce had stepped over them in the careful manner of one who had done so many times before, then done a header on the twin bed she'd slept in throughout their childhood and had been out, just like that.

And it had been the earliest hours of Christmas Eve by then and the house was cool and still. Outside the windows, the stars were distant and cold, and still felt like great songs welling up inside her every time she looked up at them. The way they were supposed to, Christina had thought as she drew a comforter up over her sister. The way they always did back home in Montana on a winter's night.

Christina and Dare had made their way back downstairs to the den, where her parents had set up the pullout couch for them. They'd still been laughing a little bit as they'd undressed and gotten ready for bed, with a kind of easy intimacy that had made it almost seem as if they'd shared a bed recently. As if everything between them was as it ought to have been. If Christina hadn't known better, she'd have believed it herself. And when things looked as if they might veer back toward their usual painful conversation and strained silence, Christina had made the command decision to head that mess off at the pass.

Which was why both of them were naked this morning, she realized, after another handful of moments passed.

Not just any morning, she remembered then, as she inhaled deeply and smelled cinnamon and bacon in the air, but Christmas Eve.

Dare stirred behind her, then sat up with a big, lazy stretch, and then there they were, suddenly. Staring at each other on a crisp, cold Montana morning, with that sharp winter light bleeding in through the windows. No margaritas or tequila sunshine. No dark night with all those winter stars shining down, making her feel dizzy. No blurriness and no excuses.

He looked shut down again, more by the second as they gazed at each other. There was something she couldn't identify in those smoky eyes of his, and that mouth of his—that clever and beautiful mouth she could still taste on hers, and all over her body—was a resolute line. Christina wanted to cry. Scream, maybe. Anything to keep them in that happy, bright sunshine sort of place they'd found in the saloon hallway last night. Or the quiet, reverent place they'd fallen asleep in, wrapped around each other in a sweet tangle of heat.

Anything to keep them from sliding back into all that bitterness she still didn't understand.

"We didn't use anything," she blurted out.

That was certainly not any kind of going to the sun road for them, she was aware as she heard those words fly out of her mouth, but there it was. Sitting out there between them. She could have detonated a bomb in the center of the brightly colored comforter that stretched across the pull out bed and it would have been less destructive.

Christina had no idea why she'd said that. No matter that it was true. It would also have been true several weeks from now, when she would know if it was actually an issue.

Dare blinked. That was not a good sign. "When?"

"Last night. You didn't use a condom. Either time."

He blinked again, but otherwise did not move. At all. That was a worse sign. "And that's an issue because…?"

Why had she mentioned this? But she had. So she pushed on.

"Because we haven't had sex in such a long time that I went off the pill," she told him bluntly. "I thought maybe it was manipulating my hormones and that was why I *thought* you were shutting me out when maybe you weren't." She smiled, faintly. "It turned out, you really were just shutting me out, with or without hormones."

He'd gone very, very still. Alarmingly still. No wonder she couldn't seem to stop talking. It was self-defense. It was warding off his inevitable reaction.

"Then I thought that it would be great to lose those five pounds I could never shift while I was on the pill, because surely you'd notice and then maybe that would spark your interest. Or something." He was worse than granite then. He looked carved from ice, and she felt it creep through her, too, freezing everything as it went until she felt like the frozen river that wound through the town. "But then I got a little overzealous and lost almost ten and, no. You still didn't notice."

"You're not going to get pregnant, Christina. You can't."

Flat. Harsh.

And she wanted to sink back into the warmth of the bed,

pile the covers over her head, and hide. Or start this morning over again, anyway.

But she wasn't the wife he'd ignored all this time, not anymore. She was the wife who'd left him. She was the woman who'd claimed him because she'd wanted him last night in that hallway. She was the one who'd crawled over him in this very bed because she missed him—and she hadn't missed this.

She was done putting up with his shit.

"You don't know whether I will or won't," she pointed out, her voice as cool as his was harsh. "You're a scientist. You're not God."

"You can't have a baby. *I* can't have a baby. You know that. And that's the end of the discussion."

He flipped back the covers and got out of the bed, because for him it really was the end of the discussion. The way it had been every single time he'd shut down the baby conversation for years now.

Years upon years.

The Christina who'd *contorted* had taken that, mostly. She'd told herself that he'd come around. If she was good enough, patient enough, caring enough, *something*. If she could figure out how to reach him. If she could make him feel safe, or trusting, or whatever it was he didn't feel. But she was done with that, too.

"Fine," she said, perhaps a little bit flippantly. "So if I do get pregnant, should I assume that means you don't want me to text you down in Denver to let you know? That seems a bit much, even for you, but if that's what you want, that's what I'll do."

He looked something like incredulous, except much darker and far more furious, and it took everything she had to keep her expression bland.

"What the hell are you talking about?"

"I've always wanted babies, Dare. Yet you've refused to talk about it for years and I let you, because I thought you'd get over whatever your problem is." She shrugged. Also flippantly, as if she was wearing something more than the comforter and too many memories. "But we're splitting up. I don't care what your problem is. And I can love a baby whether you're in my life or not."

He paused in the act of dressing, his jeans at his hips but still unfastened, and she thought it was deeply unfair that even when he was doing this stonewalling thing he did so much lately, she couldn't keep herself from noticing all those fine, masculine lines of that body of his.

All of which she'd reacquainted herself with last night.

Not that thinking about that was particularly helpful, just then.

"You can't have my baby without my permission," he told her, in a very low and very harsh way.

And despite the fact that she would normally agree with a sentiment like that, if not the tone in which it was delivered, because she thought men and women should make these decisions together and that all babies should be wanted by everyone involved, surely, today she only sniffed dismissively.

"Then maybe you should have been more careful."

"You knew you weren't on birth control and you didn't say a word. *Twice.*"

"You didn't ask."

His jaw worked as if he was biting something back, and she couldn't help the near-masochistic thrill that moved through her as she imagined what that might have been. What other, terrible depths they could sink to. If this whole thing didn't hurt so much, it would be fascinating.

"Is this what this was all about?" he asked, his voice as grim as that look on his cold, shuttered face. "You lured me up here so you could impregnate yourself against my will?"

"Oh, go to hell," she snapped at him then, and she realized she was shaking. That however masochistic the thrill of this on some level, the reality of it just left scars.

"I grew up in hell," he gritted out at her. "And now I carry it with me wherever I go. Why don't you get that? Why don't you understand?" His hand moved to his chest, as if he was showing her whatever lurked inside it. Warning her. "I would never inflict this on an innocent child. *Never.*"

He sounded furious. As if he was holding himself back from exploding with sheer force of will. As if he could shatter things with his voice alone.

But it dawned on Christina that actually, this was fear. All of this.

And that made the fury drain out of her, as suddenly as it had come. It made the shaking stop. Change into something else as she gazed up at him.

"You're not your father," she told him, her voice soft.

The effect on Dare was electric. He jolted back a step. He even paled. Then he scowled at her, and the fury was back again and darker than before.

"You have no idea what you're talking about."

"I do know. I know you."

"You don't know anything about me," he threw at her, and she thought that was panic, not temper. "Because if you did, you would have run a long time ago. You would have escaped."

"But I didn't."

"You didn't, and now look where we are. You packed up your car and left me without a word. We had sex in a god-damned supply closet in the back of a bar."

"It's the utility room in a saloon. Far less tacky."

"This isn't a joke, Christina."

She had never felt less like joking in her whole life.

"You," she said, holding his gaze, her own deadly serious, "are not your father, Dare. Not in any way. You never have been and you never will be, no matter how you punish yourself. Or me."

She saw that wash over him. And then she saw him reject it. He straightened, his expression going darker and grimmer than she'd ever seen it, and he pulled on the rest of the clothes he'd left in a pile on the floor last night. He shrugged into his coat and grabbed his keys, and he didn't look at her when he walked out the door.

But he didn't slam it on his way out, either.

Christina sat there for a long while, not the least bit sure how she felt about anything. Not sure if she'd fallen apart already, or was about to, or was entirely too wrecked to fall any further.

Eventually, the prospect—and tantalizing scent—of a home cooked breakfast won out over all considerations, so she pulled herself out of the bed. Her parents had brought her duffel bag downstairs while she'd been out the night before, and so, when she stood there for a moment without shattering into a million pieces, she rummaged around until she found a pair of decent yoga pants and a sweatshirt. Plus her mother's awful bright blue wool socks, of course. She yanked off the sheets and the comforter, then reassembled the couch. She tied her hair in a serviceable knot at the back of her neck, made herself smile, and then went out to join her family.

Or the part of her family that wasn't Dare, anyway. Because she might not have heard his truck drive off but she knew that there was no way he was lounging at the kitchen table making small talk with her parents while Christmas carols played on the radio and everything was calm and bright. Or the Grey family version thereof.

Her nephews greeted her with shouts of glee that made her feel like she'd won a lottery or two when she walked into the warm, bright kitchen, then shot past her in their own wild stampede, complete with barking dogs at their heels.

"They want the television," Luce told her from her place at the table, where she was gripping a giant mug of coffee like it was a life-preserver, all her gorgeous hair wound into a messy braid that fell over one shoulder. Only Luce could look *glamorously hung over* without even trying. "Though I'm sure they're excited to see you, too. Deep down beneath the prospect of unrestricted cartoons."

"I felt the excitement, definitely," Christina assured her. "No matter how deep down."

"That was nice of Dare," her mother piped in from her own seat at the table with the local paper, the Bozeman Daily Chronicle, and the Livingston Enterprise spread out before her and her feet propped up on the empty chair beside her. "He said he had a few things to pick up, but was happy to take my last minute marketing list, too. Saves me that one last trip to the supermarket. It's always a madhouse on Christmas Eve."

"He's a sweetheart," Christina managed to say, and she didn't flinch when Luce's gaze swung to hers with all those questions she couldn't answer.

And still, somehow, she didn't shatter. She had no idea how.

She skirted around her father at the stove, where he was frying up bacon and wielding the pair of tongs that were his favorite brunch weapon, to pour herself a mug of coffee as big as her sister's and with twice the creamer. And to give herself a moment to breathe through the unexpected swell of emotion that almost took her down to her knees—bright and sharp and full besides.

But still, not a shattering.

Because she'd thought Dare had left for good. She'd thought that had been the end of them, that awful little conversation on a pull out sofa bed on a cold morning after such a warm night. She hadn't known how she would explain it, what she would say. Much less how she would survive it.

And it told her all kinds of things she wasn't sure she wanted to know that the news he hadn't left her for good licked through her like the sweetest kind of relief. Vast. Enveloping. Something like life-altering, if she let herself think about it. She didn't.

"Big night last night?" her father asked, sounding amused as he glanced at her, then turned his attention back to the sizzling strips of bacon in the cast iron skillet before him that was older than Christina.

"Yes," Luce said from the table in her dry, husky-voiced way. "Because partying under the watchful eye of your angry older brother is always the *most* fun."

"Fun fact about your uncle Jason," their father replied cheerfully. "He's soft as a marshmallow underneath. Cuddly, really."

There was a small pause. The only sound was a chorale version of "God Rest Ye Merry Gentlemen" from the radio and beyond that, the zany, animated voices of whatever cartoon the boys were watching in the den.

Then everyone laughed.

Louder than necessary, and maybe a little sharper than usual with all the treacherous things waiting there beneath, but honest and gut-deep all the same.

The way they had more often than not, growing up. The way, Christina thought then, they always would. No matter what happened to each of them individually. That was the point.

And finally, it felt like Christmas Eve.

MARIETTA WAS LIKE a goddamned Christmas card, another tradition Dare hated.

It was like some ridiculous, picture perfect rendition of all the things he'd never had and never would, and Dare couldn't figure out for the life of him why it wasn't in his rearview mirror.

What was he still doing here? Why did he have his mother in law's marketing list in his back pocket? What was the matter with him?

He didn't have an answer to that.

All this time and he still didn't have an answer to anything.

And Marietta was like a taunt all around him, daring him to figure it out before he lost this, too.

He'd picked up a change of clothes or two in one of the are-we-quaint-or-are-we-fancy boutiques in town. Then he'd headed to the supermarket, where the Christmas carols were on an endless loop and it took him almost twenty minutes to locate all the things Gracie wanted.

But the worst part were the families, he thought. Crying kids. Stressed out parents. Threats and breakdowns everywhere he looked. Santa Claus wielded like a battering ram—and he remembered this part. The only difference between his family and the rest of the world, Dare thought as he waited in a too-long line behind an exhausted-looking father and two caterwauling toddlers the man had clearly given up on trying to soothe, was that the Coopers didn't *pretend.* No one had used Santa Claus to modify Dare's behavior when he'd been little, they'd just smacked him until he'd shut up.

He told himself that it was honest. That it was *better,* really. That there was nothing the matter with him, it was the world that had lost its mind and Christina right along with it if she really wanted to participate in this massive *delusion*.

But that didn't explain why his chest ached the way it did on the short drive back to the Grey's house.

He told himself he'd drop off the groceries and then get the hell out of here. Because it might feel like he was dead anyway without her, but that was better than the alternative. He needed to let her go before he forgot himself all over again and woke up another ten years down the line, after he'd well and truly ruined Christina and made certain neither one of them had any way out of the mess he'd made of their lives.

Dare already knew how that ended. He'd seen the inevitable conclusion of this kind of madness once the Cooper family virus had run its course on a cold March afternoon when he was fifteen. He still couldn't block it out of his head, no matter how Christina smiled at him or how she claimed she knew him—or worse, how desperately he wanted to believe her.

He'd never be free of his past, his parents, his blood. He knew it. It was the lens through which he saw the world. It separated him—and that was what made him a great scientist, he liked to think. He could observe from a distance, research without emotion.

But the things that made him an excellent scientist made him a piss-poor husband. How many more ways did he need to prove that to himself? To Christina?

You should have let her go.

Dare parked his truck in the Greys' wide driveway and wasn't surprised when the back door opened as he was slamming the driver's door shut. He braced himself, but it was his father-in-law who jogged out into the cold, his usual affable, welcoming smile on his face.

"Thought I'd give you a hand," Ryan said as he approached, sounding perfectly friendly. There was no reason that should put

Dare on edge. It was his usual holiday phobia, he told himself, rearing its ugly head again. "We really are thrilled that it worked out for you and Christina to make it up this year."

Dare made a noncommittal noise he hoped sounded at least as friendly, and hefted up some grocery bags. Ryan did the same.

"I know you're not much for the holidays," Ryan continued in that same easy way of his. "I can't say I blame you. Between my mother and Gracie, I never had a chance to do much but surrender."

He smiled when Dare met his gaze, and Dare had a sudden flashback to when he was still just a kid, really, and Christina had brought him home to meet her family for the first time. Ryan had smiled at him exactly like this. Friendly, certainly, but with a certain measuring distance in his gaze that reminded Dare, now he knew the family better, of ex-Marine Uncle Jason.

"Anything I should know about?" Ryan asked then, as Dare had known he would. He indicated Christina's still-packed car with his chin, his smile still in place.

And Dare didn't have the slightest idea what to say. He shouldn't have come back here. He should have escaped while he could and left Christina to pick up the pieces any way she chose. *Christina and a baby, possibly*—but he definitely couldn't think about that.

But he certainly didn't want to stand here with this man, who was the closest thing Dare had ever had to a real father, and talk about the thousands of different ways he'd let Christina down. Especially not when Ryan had told him all those years ago, in the nicest way possible, that he'd tear Dare's limbs off if that ever happened.

"Not much you don't know, I think," Dare said eventually, his voice as even as he could make it.

"More than I should and less than I'd like to, I imagine,"

Ryan agreed, in much the same way.

He shifted, and Dare braced himself for the hit. But Ryan only reached over with his free hand and clapped Dare on the shoulder, the way he had that first day. The way he always did. And just like every other time, Dare… didn't get it. His own father had never touched anything or anyone like that. With that affectionate ease that felt to Dare like peering over the side of a great, howling abyss, it was so foreign to him.

Still.

And he was still tense, waiting for a blow. The fact it wasn't on its way came a little too close to choking him up.

"I think you're a lost soul, Dare," Ryan said then, very quietly. "And your curse is that you've always been smarter than any man should be, so you know that about yourself. So I'm not surprised that you took one look at my daughter and held on tight. I'd think you were a fool if you hadn't done exactly that. I did the same thing with her mother."

They'd shifted position, and Ryan wasn't looking at him straight on or touching him any longer. His eyes were on that beat up old hatchback Christina had always insisted they keep with its University of Montana Grizzlies sticker in the back window. And that ache in Dare's chest worsened.

"Is this where you tell me I'm not good enough for your daughter, Ryan?" he asked, not doing anything to alter that harsh note in his voice. He should have known the blow would come—just not from Ryan's fists. Ryan was far more subtle than that. *But there was always a hit.* Dare knew that better than most. "You're a little late. But I know. Believe me, I know."

Chapter Six

RYAN TURNED TOWARD him then, frowning, and Dare understood he'd said far too much, standing out there in the driveway in all the December cold with too much Christmas in the air, like a scent. And far too loudly besides.

But it was as if everything inside of him was that damned ache, and it was cracking him wide open from within and knocking down all the barriers he usually kept inside him along with it.

He couldn't seem to do a single thing to stop it.

"I was going to say I'm sorry to see you look this lost again, after all this time," Ryan said after a long, considering moment, when there was nothing but the cold air between them. "I'd thought that life with Christina agreed with you. Made you happier."

Dare felt as if there was a hand at his throat, choking him, and maybe it would have been easier if there had been. He felt out of control. Crazed. Not separated from things the way he usually was. The way he preferred. But tangled up in too many *feelings* he couldn't begin to understand.

"It does," he gritted out. And then, because he really must

be lost, or at least insane, "that's the problem."

"Ah."

They stood there in silence for a moment, and that was just one more madness to put next to all the rest. It was another bright, cold winter day. The mountains scraped up into the chilly blue above with their great snowy peaks, all the plump little houses on this comfortable street had smoke coming from their chimneys to dance sinuously in the stark branches of the barren trees, and lights twinkled from the windows in anticipation of the winter nights that came too soon, here.

Yet his lunatic father-in-law stood there in nothing but his usual flannel shirt, looking as comfortable as if he was inside next to the old woodstove. And the overtly cheerful world filled with *normal people* around them should have felt like a slap. Like a kick in the head, because living Christmas cards like this one weren't for monsters like him. He knew that.

But today, Dare felt it all like grief. Dark and profound, not a slap at all, but a weight. He didn't understand that, either.

"Christina has a heart as big as the Montana sky," Ryan said after a long while, when only his breath against the cold had indicated he was something other than turned to stone where he stood. "But you know this. She will love you until the day she dies, whether you love her back or not. That's how she's made, and the father in me wants to punch you in the nose for not worshiping her like the goddess I firmly believe she is."

Dare let out a sound that wasn't quite a laugh. It hurt too much. "Who says I don't?"

Ryan smiled. "Fair enough. No nose punching necessary, then, which is a good thing. That's more my brother's department."

He faced Dare then, his hazel gaze direct. Not unkind, but unflinching all the same. Man to man. The way Dare imagined fathers might look at their grown sons, not that he'd know such things from experience.

Dare found himself standing a bit straighter all the same.

"A man isn't necessarily put on this earth to be happy," Ryan told him. "But that doesn't have much to do with whether or not he's a good man. It's a choice. You make it every day."

"Some people are predisposed to darkness," Dare managed to say past that pressure in his throat. "They infect everything they touch."

Ryan's gaze was so kind then it made Dare think of Christina's this morning. *You are not your father.* And he couldn't handle it any better now.

"No," Ryan said, his voice quiet but bigger, somehow, than the cold or the sky or the mountains all around them. "It's a choice. And no one, living or dead, can make it for you. But the trick is, you must live with the choice you make."

He headed inside after another moment, still looking supernaturally unaffected by the bitter temperature. And this was Dare's chance. This was it. He could leave the groceries at the door, turn his back on this house and everyone inside it, and go. All he needed to do was get in his truck and drive. He could put miles and mountains and whole states between him and these people who kept tearing him apart, bit by bit, with all this wretched, undeserved kindness he still couldn't quite process. Much less believe.

And he could leave this grief—this terrible darkness that burned in him like the inverse of all the happy candles in all the shining windows on this quietly happy little street—behind at last.

But instead, he pulled in a jagged breath and he followed his father-in-law inside.

BIG SKY CHRISTMASES were the same every year and normally, Christina loved them.

Her extended family started gathering together as the day edged over into darkness. The elder Greys' spread was out near the ski resort in Big Sky, about an hour and a half from Marietta, on about ten woodsy acres that backed up into National Forest land with achingly lovely views back down over the Gallatin River and on to the Gallatin Range.

A Grey ancestor had laid claim to the land generations back. For decades there had only been a small log cabin on the property, which assorted Greys had used to access all the skiing and outdoor recreation in the area. But when Richard Grey had finally retired from running Grey's Saloon and handed it over to Jason, his eldest son, as tradition dictated, he and Elly had started building the house they'd always wanted. The original cabin remained because there was nothing Greys liked more than their own history, unless it was arguing about that history. The cabin was used as a guest house or family overflow location these days, and the Big House that stood higher on the hill with more of a commanding view was a sprawling thing, made of log and timber that managed to be airy and open yet cozy all at once.

Truly, it was a beautiful house. And at Christmas it was nothing short of perfect.

It sparkled with Christmas trees in all the soaring windows, with decorations carefully chosen by Grandma, who liked just the right amount of fuss—no more and no less. Every room was quietly resplendent in her favorite fashion, surrounded by the warmth of the log walls and the heat of the fireplaces. Dare had once remarked that the house felt more like an upscale ski lodge than a house, with the wings that rambled off from the great room in three directions, but that was precisely what Christina liked about it. It was deliciously comfortable, yet big enough that all the prickly members of her family could interact with each other and also, crucially, avoid each other when necessary without either action being obvious.

Uncle Jason usually left the bar in Reese Kendrick's capable hands on Christmas Eve and came rolling in around dark, like the surly dark cloud of gloom he was. Rayanne was like his own, personal sunlamp every year, a smiling shot of vitamin D so bright it almost made up for Jason's… *Jason-ness.* That and the fact her two sisters hadn't come home to Marietta in years, much like Aunt Annabel, their mother, who'd left when the three girls were teenagers and had never returned. Not that anyone dared mention her in Jason's hearing. At least, not while entirely sober.

Uncle Billy, the second Grey son, and his third wife, Angelique—who had first met the family while home for a different Christmas with Billy's son, Jesse—had come in the night before from Billings with their twin toddlers. Billy's other children, especially Jesse, tended to spend Christmas with their embittered mother on the other side of the Bitterroots in Idaho, where they no doubt discussed the fact that Angelique was just about the same age as Billy's own daughters. Another topic no one mentioned directly in Billy or Angelique's presence—because the only person who might get a pass on that topic, Jesse, had steadfastly refused to speak to either one of them since Angelique's defection.

Aunt Melody, the baby of Grandma and Grandpa's nuclear family, usually swept in sometime during the day in her hippie-dippy way that drove every other member of her family insane which was, she'd once suggested to Christina, why she enjoyed it so much. She was pretty in the way many of the Grey women were, willowy and blonde and effortless. These days she was living in Jackson Hole, with a selection of men she liked to refer to as her *lovers* in front of her horrified parents and brothers. Her two daughters were a few years younger than Christina and usually turned up themselves at some or other point on Christmas Eve after flying into Bozeman, where the fact they were the product of different fathers—one of whom Melody hadn't bothered to marry, because, as she liked to tell everyone, he was an outlaw biker who wore no such chains—was usually brought up in conversation by Grandma within the first five minutes.

"As if," Devyn, the oldest of Melody's girls and the closest in age to Christina, had complained last year, if quietly, "Grandma wants to make sure I haven't transformed into the biker bitch within since she saw me at Thanksgiving."

It was already the sort of controlled chaos that Christina loved when they arrived in the late afternoon, and Luce's boys immediately ratcheted that up to crazy as they whooped and hollered and ran around. Luce's dogs and Grandpa's dogs howled their greetings at each other. Glorious smells wafted out of the kitchen, meats and pies and sweets galore. Carols played from the sound system, Christmas movies were on in the TV room, and there were plates of food to nibble at on almost every table the dogs couldn't reach.

And everyone hugged and shrugged out of their coats and schlepped their things to the various bedrooms that had been allocated for their use, while Grandpa prepared drinks and in the middle of the great open central room Rayanne told marvelous stories of her fancy Nashville life that were really more like mini-performances, and probably not very true. When she was finished dispensing her brand of sunshine, all the assembled cousins gravitated to one side of the room while their parents—and Angelique—clustered on the other.

Christina smiled and laughed. She caught up with her cousins. She played with the newest and littlest as they charged around on their wobbly toddler feet and tried to get their chubby little hands into Aunt Melody's famous crab dip. She chatted about absolutely nothing important with her grandparents and avoided her parents. She watched Dare do the same on the next couch over, his smoky gaze almost sweet as he did the family thing she knew would never come easy for him.

But this year, it all felt like ashes and empty gestures. That miraculous sense she'd had at breakfast that everything would be all right, somehow, was there still—but stretched thin. It was something to do with the stiff way Dare was holding himself. With the way he'd managed to avoid speaking to her alone all day, which was quite a feat, when she thought about it.

She tried not to think about it. And she tried not to drink too much of her grandfather's wicked egg nog, either, because she already knew how little *that* would solve. If anything, she hurt worse today than she had before she'd had the bright, tequila-infused idea to have sex with Dare last night.

Sex had never been their problem. It was everything else around the sex that had messed them up. Why hadn't she kept that in mind? Why hadn't she thought a little bit more about what today would feel like in the wake of more sex with Dare that *felt* life-altering but was, in fact, just… sex.

Christina understood that he acted the way he did because he was afraid. She even felt for him. But that revelation, like everything else, changed nothing, did it? They were still sitting here in the middle of all this light and laughter, alone. Apart. Maybe it was time to accept that this was how it would always be. That Dare had been right all along. That this could never, ever be anything else.

She drained her egg nog in a single gulp and told herself she felt *free,* not *depressed.*

Grandma announced that dinner would be in about thirty minutes, which meant everyone peeled off to their respective rooms for a little breather before the rest of the evening. Dare was nowhere to be found when Christina pushed her way into the cozy little room on the far side of the house, down on the ground floor with its own little deck looking out toward the mountains. She told herself it didn't matter. That she didn't care where he was. That they had only one more day to get through and then they'd be free of each other anyway.

Just like she told herself that the surging emotion inside of her then was *joy,* damn it, at the prospect.

She changed into a slightly dressier sweater, brushed her hair, and was considering applying make up for the sole purpose of making herself feel less frumpy next to all her naturally gorgeous blonde relatives when she heard the door open.

"Careful," she said from inside the bathroom when she saw Dare appear in the mirror. "We're all alone in here. You might actually have to talk to me. And then who knows what might happen? The world could end."

He came up behind her and stood much too close, pressing his chest into her back. And Christina knew she should push him away. She knew she should tell him exactly what she thought of his crap this morning, of his position on a possible pregnancy, and the fact she'd thought he'd bailed on her.

But she didn't say a word.

She only stood there, her eyes fixed on his in the mirror. On the two of them. He was so beautiful, still so damned beautiful, and when his arms came up to sneak around her, she felt beautiful too. She felt his heat and his strength, blasting deep beneath her skin. In the mirror, they looked like they fit each other perfectly. In the mirror, they looked connected and breathless and *alive.*

In the mirror, they looked like they were still in love.

And it was Christmas Eve. And she missed him. And she was losing him, more and more, with every breath they took, and she honestly didn't know how she was going to survive this. Him. The end of *them.*

"You don't have to pretend when we're alone," she whispered. Because she had to protect herself—something she always seemed to fail to do around this man. Again and again and again.

His lips grazed the side of her neck. His arms tightened around her.

"That's the trouble," he whispered back. "I stopped pretending. And it doesn't make it any better."

She shut her eyes against that, and then, after a deep breath, pulled away from him. He didn't fight it, but he also didn't go anywhere. He looked hot and a little bit dangerous as he lounged there against the bathroom counter and watched her much too intently, in a dark button down shirt she'd never seen before.

"I like your shirt," she heard herself say. Absurdly.

His mouth kicked up in one corner. "It's from a Marietta boutique. Just for you."

"It's like Christmas came early."

"I'm not sure Christmas Eve actually counts as early. Not really."

Did she actually laugh then? She couldn't believe that was possible, but his smoky gaze gleamed as he looked at her, telling her she must have. Christina stopped playing with her hair and let it fall down around her shoulders, the red streaks looking brighter under the bathroom lights. And even though she knew it was a defensive gesture he would read too much—or just enough—into, she crossed her arms over her chest when she pivoted and faced him.

"I forgot about Christmas," he said.

Of all the things he might have said, she hadn't expected that. "Really? Despite all the trees and decorations and stockings and family and, I don't know, the fact we're standing here in Big Sky pretending to be happy?"

His gaze managed to be lazy and amused and much too dark all at once, and her cheeks felt hot. Almost instantly, and then her stomach flipped a little, too.

"I mean, the gift giving part."

Christina didn't want flushed cheeks. She wanted her stomach to stay put. She wanted him, yes, like a mindless addict with no will of her own, apparently—but if she couldn't have him she wanted this to be over. Didn't she?

She cleared her throat and concentrated on her temper, not the emotion kicking at her just beneath it. "You 'forget' that every year."

The air between them seemed charged, then. Taut and fierce.

"Are you suggesting that I'm a liar? Just say it, Christina."

She'd wanted to say it every year, in fact, but hadn't because she'd wanted to preserve his feelings. That didn't apply tonight.

"I'm suggesting that Christmas is December 25th of every single year. It never changes. It never hides from you in February or makes you look for it in October. Always December. Always the 25th." She lifted a shoulder and then dropped it. "I think it's interesting that a man of science, whose entire life is about tracking tiny little details, manages to miss that. Annually."

His voice was gruff. "I don't like Christmas."

"This I know. Guess how?"

"Because I keep telling you I don't like Christmas?"

"Because every single Christmas Eve you have a panic attack about how you didn't remember what day it was—despite the fact that you've usually had six Christmas parties with various friends and colleagues by then—and then you download all your family issues all over me, so I can feel bad about the fact I bought you a bunch of stuff and wrapped it and put it under the tree I decorated all by my goddamned self because you claimed you were studying. Again."

Her cheeks were more than a little flushed then, and her voice was too loud for the confines of the bathroom, and Dare's gaze had narrowed dangerously with every word.

"I'm a terrible person, clearly," he said in that low, edgy way of his. "And yet you think we should have babies together. Maybe I'm not the crazy one here."

She released her arms before she cut off her own circulation and turned to head back out into the bedroom before she could do something worse than say things she'd held back for a decade. Like reach out to him. Soothe him. Apologize.

"It's fine," she muttered. "I took care of Christmas."

"I don't know what that means."

"What do you think it means? It means that while you developed a sudden deep and abiding interest in watching animated movies with my nephews, Luce and I went into town and I did all the Christmas shopping." She shot a glance at him over her shoulder, and her whole body pulled tight to see he'd moved to the bathroom doorway and was leaning there, looking rangy and dangerous and entirely too edible. *Stop that,* she snapped at herself. "But you can go ahead and give me a divorce, Dare. And look at that. Best Christmas ever."

She didn't know what she expected. Maybe for Dare to turn a cartwheel of joy? Produce papers for her to sign on the spot?

But instead, he watched her for a long, long moment that bled into another, then hung there between them. Something like sweet.

"If you're pissed at me, you should probably just say so."

"I assumed that was clear."

When he looked at her like that, her temper ebbed away. It left her feeling weak and wobbly. Too needy. Too precarious.

"That's the trouble, Christina," he said quietly. "None of this is clear. I don't know how to be the man you want me to be. I don't think I'm capable of it."

"I know you are." She didn't recognize her own voice. Fierce and sure. "But you have to try."

"How can you possibly know that?" he asked, and he didn't sound cold then. He sounded as lost as she felt. "I saw all these families in town today. And I felt *thankful* that I'd never have to put up with that again. The lie of it. The fighting and the stress and the *ruin* of all that pressure to *pretend*."

"Not all families are like your family."

"Is it better to be like yours?" he threw at her. He raked a hand through his hair, leaving it in spiky disarray. "Every year they all come back here and poke at each other and eat too much and drink too much. They throw salt in old wounds and lie about history everyone else remembers the other way. They fight a little bit, they pretend they're all closer than they are and they pretend they mean it when they hug each other, and then every year they vow they'll never do it again. But they do. It's like Stockholm Syndrome, with pie."

His voice had risen during the course of that outburst, and Christina thought her heart had come to a halt. She couldn't breathe. And she couldn't summon up even the faintest hint of that temper any longer.

She understood, then. Temper protected her. When that ebbed away, all she felt was hurt. For Dare. For what he'd suffered. For the way it was still wrecking him now, and her too.

"Of course it's not Stockholm Syndrome," she managed to

say.

"Then what would you call it?" he demanded, his face darker than the night outside. "There's no other reasonable explanation for anyone to participate in this kind of wholesale delusion!"

She opened up her hands as if she could hold the two of them between her palms and heal them both somehow. She wished she could. "Love."

He pulled in a ragged breath, staring back at her across the polished blonde wood floor and the cheery expanse of the sleigh bed with its patchwork quilts piled high. As if that hadn't been her voice, but the ringing of a bell, loud and insistent.

"What?"

"It's called love, Dare," she said, simply. Quietly. With everything she was, everything she felt, because she understood, then. How lost he really was. How she must have failed him, all these years, if he still didn't understand. And how tough he was to have suffered this, all this time, thinking it was something so twisted. So wrong. "This is what love looks like. It's complicated. Sometimes it drinks too much and steals its son's girlfriend. Sometimes it picks fights. Sometimes it's ugly and scared and shitty. But it's still love. It comes back home. It believes its own promises and it keeps them, too, in its own way. Because it's love. And it matters." She wanted to hold him but she knew, somehow, he wouldn't let her close. She knew. So she put it in her voice, tried to hold it her eyes. "And so do you."

"Love shouldn't hurt," he gritted out.

And she didn't know when she'd started crying. Big, slow tears that made tracks down her cheeks, overflowing from deep inside of her, where all she wanted was to love this man the way he deserved, and be loved by him in return in the same way. She wiped them aside and focused on him.

On this. On them.

"Everything that matters hurts from time to time," she told him. "Love shouldn't cause damage. It should heal it. But that's the thing, Dare. Healing hurts, too. It all hurts. *Life* hurts. In the end, that's how you know you're alive. Isn't it?"

But she wasn't surprised when he didn't answer.

As if he still didn't know.

Chapter Seven

MUCH LATER THAT night, Dare stood awake in the great room while the house slept all around him.

The Christmas lights still twinkled in the trees that stood in the windows, so he could see his own reflection. And then the shadow behind him that was first nothing more than a darkness on one of the far couches, but which gradually became a surly Jason, walking toward him.

The older man didn't say anything as he came to stand beside Dare. And for a while, they stared out into the woods together. The night wore on. Outside, it was so cold it seemed to shimmer off the glass of the window, and the snow flurries that had been coming down on and off all night took a little break in deference to the wind.

"There aren't any answers out there," Jason said, long after Dare had given up on him speaking at all. "I've looked."

"Maybe I'm looking for different answers."

Jason didn't laugh. Dare wasn't sure he'd ever laughed or even could. But still, he managed to give the impression of laughter with only a faint tilt of his head.

"I doubt that."

"Do you have the answers, too?" Dare asked.

"I've been a bartender for thirty years. I have nothing but answers."

The older man took a pull of the beer dangling from his fingers and it occurred to Dare, suddenly, that Jason wasn't simply bad-tempered. That he was broken. *Sad*, even, and all the way through.

He blinked, not sure what to do with that revelation.

"Okay," he said instead, when he was certain none of that would show in his voice. He doubted Jason would seek or appreciate any kind of sympathy. "Tell me why marriage is hard, bartender. From your thirty years of experience in giving advice."

Jason grunted, then glared out at the night. "Marriage is hard because it's a bait and switch."

"Because…what? Women are evil?"

"First of all, my niece is not evil. Let's be clear."

Jason, Dare realized then, wasn't merely sad. He was a little bit drunk. Another thing Dare didn't think he did. Ever. Then again, no one was awake but the two of them, this long after Grandma had called it a night and closed down the kitchen.

"Agreed," Dare muttered. Because Christina was a whole lot more complicated and dangerous than simply *evil*.

"And second, you go into it thinking it's about the fun stuff. Sex. Love." Jason shifted, but still glared out at the darkness. Or maybe his own reflection. Dare couldn't tell. "But it's not. It's about intimacy. And intimacy is the hardest thing there is. Most people suck at it."

"Maybe marriage is what sucks."

"Marriage is an abyss. Two separate people go into it together."

"And only one comes out?"

"That's if you're lucky, dumbass," Jason gritted at him,

shifting that glare from the night to Dare's reflection. And it felt like a punch. "If you're *lucky*, you figure out how to make two separate people come together into one couple. But most people are too busy clinging to their own shit to ever make that happen. Believe me. I know."

Because of his own doomed marriage, Dare thought. Because his own wife had run out on him years ago and had left her daughters behind, too, as if she couldn't bear the sight of any of them any longer. He couldn't imagine that—but then, wasn't he standing here trying to gear himself up to do the same thing, more or less?

He met Jason's harsh glare in the window's reflection.

"Because you're a bartender, right?" he asked quietly. "That's how you know."

Jason didn't say anything for a long moment. Then his mouth moved into the closest thing to a smile Dare had ever seen on his hard face.

"Because I'm an object lesson, asshole," he said gruffly. "And if you're as smart as everyone says you are, I suggest you learn fast."

He gulped back the rest of his beer and then, without another glance, he walked away and left Dare where he stood.

Alone.

No matter how much he hated it. No matter how much he wished he could be different—be that man Christina still seemed to see when she looked at him.

While outside, where it was already technically Christmas morning no matter how far away it was from dawn, it began to snow again in earnest.

THIS TIME WHEN Christina woke, it was to find Dare stretched out beside her in the cozy little sleigh bed.

She shifted, making sure that she wasn't naked again—that the egg nog hadn't led her down the same dangerous road as the tequila had—and found that she was indeed wearing the pajamas she'd climbed into last night. When, if memory served, she'd crawled into the soft bed alone because Dare had been engaged in a card game with her entirely too smart—and correspondingly smartass—younger cousin Sydney, who spent her life doing top secret things in Washington, DC, or so she claimed.

Christina rolled onto her side, propping herself up on one elbow, and looked down at him. She had no memory of him crawling into bed beside her, but the fact he had meant she could take a moment to study him while he slept. Her beautiful, smart, broken husband. She wanted to trace those dark brows of his with her fingers. She wanted to burrow into the hot hollow where his neck met his shoulder. She wanted to kiss her way across the lean expanse of his chest and follow that dusting of dark hair all the way down. But any of those things would wake him and she didn't want that. Not just yet. She wanted to bask for a moment. Catch her breath.

She didn't understand how she could love him so much, even when it hurt.

But then, that was what she'd told him last night. This, right here, as painful as it was beautiful, was the point.

She had to look away from him before she forgot herself and when she did, she gazed out the windows across the room and couldn't help smiling at the world outside, drenched entirely in white.

It had snowed in the night. A whole lot, apparently. Great drifts piled up against the house and as far as the eye could see the world was pristine.

And it was Christmas. And it was perfect.

Even if it was supposed to be the last day of her marriage.

Christina climbed out of bed and dressed as quickly and as quietly as she could, freezing every time she thought she heard Dare shift beneath the quilts. Then she snuck out of the room and pulled on the boots and coat she'd left down here near the back entrance.

She still didn't want to wake Dare. Not yet. She wanted to pretend just a little while longer.

It was what she'd done all last night, she thought as she snuck out into the breathtaking morning. The rush of the cold swept over her, through her. She pulled the hood of her red coat up over her head and wiggled her fingers deeper into her gloves before she stuck them deep into her pockets, and then she set off through the deep powder, her breath loud and hot against the inside of her scarf in the still morning.

She kept going until she hit the edge of the field her grandparents had cleared, up high on the hill that offered her sweeping views over the valley below. The Gallatin River was a shimmering band in the early morning light, the trees looked soft and perfect all covered in snow, and the evergreens looked fully dressed at last in their brand new winter wardrobe.

In the distance, chimneys breathed into the chilly air from the scattered houses, and clouds over the hills hinted at more snow to come. There'd be no getting out of Big Sky any time soon, she thought, and it made her stomach drop.

Because the truth was, she didn't have this in her. This game. This *pretending*. She loved Dare. That was the beginning and the end of everything, and she didn't know how to live in this in-between place. She didn't want to leave him, not really, and not only because they'd failed to use any protection. But she couldn't stay. Not when it was all so awful and he still didn't trust her at all. Could she?

She still didn't know.

The traditional Grey family Christmas Eve celebration went on long into the night. There'd been card games and board games. A long, loud dinner and an even longer dessert experience featuring enough pies and berry crumbles to feed the entire state of Montana. Definitely too much egg nog, as had become clear when Grandpa and Uncle Billy had started singing Johnny Cash songs from the piano, which always marked the tipping point in any Grey family gathering. Before Johnny Cash? A controlled, if occasionally boisterous affair. After Johnny Cash? Mayhem.

Christina had left the shouting—over proper song lyrics, of course, which no amount of Googling could solve to anyone's satisfaction—behind and had padded into the den, where Luce had been sitting by herself with *Love, Actually* playing on the big TV screen in front of her. Christina had plopped herself down next to her sister, made her share her cozy throw, and tried to lose herself in her favorite Christmas movie. Quite as if she wasn't sitting in the same house as her soon-to-be ex-husband who she suspected loved her *at least* as much as she loved him, little though he might know how to identify it. Much less act on it.

Watching Hugh Grant's British Prime Minister find love seemed like an excellent way to avoid thinking about any of that too closely.

"Don't do it," Luce had said during a quiet moment in the film, without looking over at Christina.

"Eat more crumble?" Christina had asked lightly. "I can't help myself. I think Grandma's secret ingredient is heroin. That's how addictive it is."

Luce had turned to look at her, their heads almost touching on the back of the leather sofa.

"Hal never looked at me the way Dare looks at you," she'd said quietly. "Not even way back in high school when he thought getting in my pants was a religious experience." She'd smiled faintly. "No one's ever looked at me like that."

"Luce…" She hadn't known what to say. "The only person Hal ever really loved was himself. You know that."

"I don't think you want to divorce, Christina. Not really. Neither one of you."

Christina had looked away. Back to the TV screen, which blurred in front of her, making it impossible to see what the actor who had once played Darcy in *Pride & Prejudice* was doing. Good thing she knew it by heart, all the risks people madly in love were prepared to take. When had she lost that? Where had it gone?

"He pulled away from me," she said after a moment. "But the thing is, Luce, I let him. Or I didn't do anything to stop him. What do you have if no one fights to save it when it disappears? Isn't that a divorce already, without bothering to say the words?"

"A divorce is when there's nothing left to save," Luce murmured. "And that's me, Christina. It was me about five years ago, if I'm honest. But it's not you."

"I don't think it matters," she'd said softly. "I think our marriage needs a miracle, and I can't seem to conjure one out of thin air."

Luce had slung an arm around Christina then, pulling her close, and they'd sat like that for a long time, tucked up under the throw blanket together the way they'd done when they were little girls.

"It's Christmas," Luce had said when the movie was over. She'd stood and stretched, and smiled slightly as she'd looked down at Christina. "It's like that song—miracles will happen while we dream. Believe in Santa and he will come. You know how this goes."

"What if they don't happen no matter what we dream?"

"This is your life, not a Christmas movie. You can fix the things you break." Luce had grinned. "Make them happen."

This morning, out in all the unspoiled winter snow, Christina still wasn't sure. She knew they'd both played a part in breaking their marriage apart, no matter what she'd told herself. She stood out there on the edge of the field, staring out at this land she loved so much it felt as if it was a part of her. She let that ache in her spread out and settle in, and she accepted that it would stay that way. That it wouldn't change. That Dare was the love of her life—but that didn't mean she got to keep him.

She shut her eyes and felt her tears freeze against her cheeks. And when she opened her eyes again and wiped at her cold, cold face, she couldn't say she was *happy,* exactly, but for the first time since she'd looked at Dare across that bar table in Denver and decided to leave him, she felt okay.

She'd get through this, in whatever form it took. She'd survive. With or without the baby they might have made. With or without him, no matter how much that tore at her. Because some broken things needed two people to fix them, not one. And she was standing out here alone.

She'd told him that love hurt. That life hurt. Christina had never believed that more than she did just then. And sometimes, the hurt was all you had.

I can live with that, too, she assured herself. *I will.*

But when she turned back around to start toward the house and face this strange, make-believe last Christmas with Dare, he was there. Just standing there a few feet away near one of the bare-branched trees, watching her as if he'd been doing exactly that for some time.

Waiting, something inside her whispered, but she ignored the little leap her heart gave at the notion.

"It's okay," she said, her voice sounding brash and harsh against the pristine winter morning, as if the snow itself took exception to her tone. "I'm not going to ask anything of you that you can't give."

Dare looked almost haunted then. She let her gaze move over him, taking in every detail of him and hoarding it as if this was the last time she'd ever see him.

Because what if it was?

She couldn't let herself think about that, so instead she traced his features. Those marvelous eyes. That mouth. The jaw he hadn't bothered to shave since he'd left Denver and the beard that was growing in there, making him look as surly as one of her uncles. And as rogueish as one of the heroes from her beloved romance novels. She sucked in a breath and tried to hold on to that sense of acceptance she'd felt only moments before.

"Maybe you should," he said, his voice a dark scrape against the snow. "It's the 'not asking anything of me' that got us here, don't you think?"

She didn't know why that seemed to snake through her like an earthquake, when it was such a simple question. When, she told herself, she didn't even know what it meant.

But that was a lie. She knew.

"This isn't anyone's fault," she said, and her voice was a fierce thing to hide the constriction in her throat.

"I figured out how to be married to you," he told her then. A gust of wind blew the powder against them, but he didn't flinch. Or stop. "It was like dating you, really. It was easy. I know how to love you. I know how to have sex with you. I'm good at it."

She frowned at him. "Were we having a research project or a

relationship?"

"I don't know the difference, do I?" he demanded, and she'd never heard that tone in his voice before. Not angry. Not lost. But ferocious all the same, and her heart kicked at her, as if it recognized what it meant when she didn't. When she didn't dare. "Research *is* a relationship, as far as I'm concerned. And I thought I was doing pretty well. But you wanted kids. And the closer you got to thirty, the more you wanted them."

"Dare. You don't have to do this. We don't need a postmortem. What's the point?"

He shoved his hands deep in the pockets of his winter coat, but didn't otherwise move. He didn't close the distance between them. He didn't walk away. And it seemed as if the complicated blue sheen of those eyes of his took over the whole of the world.

"The point is that I've always been a bad bet. And you've always been the one person in the whole world who didn't think so." He laughed, though it wasn't exactly a happy, mirthful sound. "And I've never been able to figure out why. No matter what I told you. No matter what I *showed* you. No matter if I was hot, cold, mean, sweet. You loved me anyway."

"That's what love *is*, Dare—"

"Until you stopped."

Christina thought her heart quit. Her mouth actually fell open. There was nothing but Dare, and what he'd said, and the intense quiet of the snow-covered world surrounding them.

"I *never* stopped loving you," she managed to say, though it was barely a thread of sound, swallowed up by the wind.

"How would I know?" he asked her, his gaze intent on hers. "We both fight dirty and quiet. We're both good at it."

She blinked, then shook her head as if she was trying to clear it, the past year and a half whirling around inside her head like too much tequila. She felt dizzy.

"I'm not blaming you for anything," he said gruffly. "That's not what I'm trying to do here. But you should know that I think every single minute that you think you're in love with me is a miracle, Christina. And every minute that you're not? I want to make sure you can get the hell away from me and find someone better. You deserve that. God, do you deserve that."

"Do you want me to find someone better, Dare?" she asked, and she didn't know where her equilibrium came from, suddenly. How she suddenly stood taller. How she was calmer, somehow, when nothing was solved. "Is that what you came out here to tell me on Christmas morning?"

"I would rather die than lose you," he gritted back at her. "Obviously, or I wouldn't be here. And yes. I'm aware that I was the one who pushed you away."

"I let you," Christina said softly, because it was true and it was long past time she said it to him. "I posted pictures of the meals I made you to Facebook and then I ate them alone, and some part of me liked that at least I could say I was trying. I had proof. But you shut me out." She was whispering. "You disappeared, right in front of me, and I let you."

He let out a breath, as if he'd been running hard.

"I'm never going to think you made the right call, Christina. I'm always going to think you could do better than me. Than this... *mess*." He shook his head. "I *know* you could."

"And that's why you think we can't have children. I get it," she pushed out, aware that her hands had curled into fists inside her gloves. Because she did get it—she just hated that he thought he was anything like the people he'd left behind. "Because you think the only truth that matters about you is what happened to you in the family you left when you were eighteen. Despite the fact *I know* you'd be an excellent father. And how do I know that? Because most of the time, you're an excellent man."

"I think the Cooper family is a wasting disease that creeps into the bones and ruins everything." His expression was so cold then it made the deep snow on Christmas morning seem warm in comparison. "Or kills."

"Except it's been over ten years and you still haven't hit me. You've never hurt me at all. Your version of fighting is a year of silence or the occasional loud word, or sex we both like. I left you and I'm still alive. I'm still right here. Completely unharmed."

She shook her head at him, exasperated and emotional at once. Yet deep inside, there was something warm and bright doing its best to make itself a flame. Because he was here. Because they were talking.

Because she believed in hope, especially today.

"You're the scientist, Dare. You know about exposure risks and incubation periods. I'm going to go out on a limb and suggest that maybe, just maybe, you developed a natural immunity."

He let out another long breath she could see as well as hear, and there was absolutely no reason at all she should feel it like light, dancing over her face and all through her body. Making her feel buoyant. Different, in that single breath, as if they'd both been waiting for him to let it go.

A little bit like happy, even, though she hardly dared complete the thought.

"I have a radical suggestion," Dare said then, when moments had passed, or maybe whole eras. "Maybe it's the Christmas spirit. I don't know. It's not like I would recognize it either way."

"You'd recognize it." She didn't look away from him. She couldn't. "It feels like love."

He smiled then, and it roared through her, because it was a

real smile. And it had been so long. It was more than light, more than the holiday spirit as it swelled over her and through her and inside of her. It was more than a miracle.

Or maybe it was all of those things at once.

"Why don't we stay together?" Dare asked.

And everything disappeared. The Big House in the distance, bright and gleaming against the backdrop of pure white. The snow bending down the tree branches. The cold all around them.

There was only Dare. There was only this.

There was only the *trying*, or what else did they have?

"Why don't you find a job you like?" he continued. "Why don't we live where you want, for a change? Why don't we go completely crazy and have a kid? Why don't we work it out and live happily ever after?" His gaze moved over her face and felt like a caress. "These are only suggestions."

"What happens the next time you get scared?" she asked, though she didn't want to. She wanted to throw herself at him the way she had in that saloon. She wanted to declare them healed and make it so. "Will I have to leave you to get your attention again? Is this what we do now?"

"Well," he said, and that smile turned crooked. "It looks like it worked."

She tried to frown at him, but her features weren't obeying her. Her heart was a kettle drum and there was something singing inside of her, deep and true.

"I promise you this," Dare said, in that way of his that felt like words carved into towering stones. Like vows pressed into her heart. "Every time you leave me, no matter why you leave me, I'll follow you. And then we'll find our way back together. I don't think it matters how we fall apart, Christina. What matters is that we keep coming back together. Forever."

"Forever," she whispered.

And she would never know which one of them moved. She only knew that one moment they stood apart, separated by a few feet of snowy ground and all those things that had seemed insurmountable scant seconds before—and then the next Dare was taking her into his arms and pressing his mouth to hers.

And this kiss was a vow. A promise. This kiss was forever.

It was coming home. At last.

"I love you," he said against her mouth, holding her against him. Then he said it again. And again.

"I love you, too," she told him, and then she smiled.

She reached up and took his beautiful face between her hands, so she could fall into those gorgeous eyes of his again and again and again.

"See?" she teased him. "This is Christmas. It's about love, Dare. Messy and complicated and exactly what we make of it."

"It's perfect," he said gruffly. "We can make it perfect."

And then they walked back up to the sprawling log house beneath that huge Montana sky while the Christmas snow began to fall again, like a blessing.

Like a miracle, after all.

CHRISTINA WASN'T PREGNANT, and the weirdest part of that was how much it bugged him.

"I didn't think you wanted a baby right now," she said, because something must have showed on his face when she told him.

"I didn't," he told her. "Right now."

And Christina smiled that little smile of hers that suggested she knew the darkest things in him by name, and loved them all. He was defenseless against it. Against her.

He hitched her hatchback up to the back of his truck and drove them both back down south to Denver, and he didn't stop off in Gillette on the way.

"Why don't we?" she asked as they neared it on the highway "We can put a few ghosts to rest."

"There aren't any ghosts in Gillette," Dare said. "There are only sad people living sad lives who probably don't remember me anyway." He took the hand she'd had resting on his thigh and carried it to his heart. "The ghosts are in me, Christina. I'm the only one who's haunted."

Her hand clasped his, hard, and he pressed it against his lips, his eyes on the road and her warmth inside of him like a song.

"Ghosts are only frightening when you let them scare you," she told him. "Otherwise, they're nothing but memories."

Dare wanted new ones. He wanted the memories they made together to be stronger than the past. Brighter than the darkness.

They took it slowly, as the winter melted into a brand new spring. Christina never went back to that job she'd hated, and they were both a whole lot happier for it. She took a class on freelance writing at the university and went for it, with Dare's full support. They reverted back to a Ramen and rice existence, but when she got paid for her first article, the picture she posted to Facebook was of the two of them dancing in their tiny kitchen, and it was real. Not a fake meal no one ate.

What came afterward, of course, was far better and unpostable, but she didn't seem to mind.

Life was pretty good by the time Dare finally graduated from his PhD program, and he was more moved than he knew how to express when a whole slew of Greys showed up to cheer him on.

"You all didn't have to make the trip," he managed to get out to Ryan at the celebratory dinner they had later.

"You're family," Ryan said, in that affable, matter-of-fact way of his that made Dare feel like a kid again. Or the kid he'd never been. "We love you."

And if he got a little choked up at that, Dare would never admit it.

They left Denver in the middle of June, headed back up north to a post-doctoral fellowship position in the same research facility in Hamilton where Dare had worked before. And Montana suited them both, so much and so well that it took all of a couple of weeks for Denver to seem like a long, strange dream.

The summer was a cascade of soaring, hot days and nights

that stayed bright until almost ten o'clock. The dizzy joy of a short, sweet summer in a place where winter reigned. They took full advantage of it.

They laughed. They talked. And when they fought, this time, they didn't let the silence draw out and become more powerful than it ought to be. They didn't let it become who they were. They found ways to get back to each other.

And when fall came again and the temperatures dropped, they were tucked up in a house they both loved in the beautiful Bitterroot Valley, nestled in the foothills of the Sapphires with the Bitterroots right there to greet them in all their glory every time they walked out their front door. Dare was enjoying his work at Rocky Mountain Labs and hopeful he'd be offered a full-time position when his post-doc was up, and Christina had found a job at the local paper to go along with the articles she'd started selling with happy regularity to national magazines.

And when her birthday rolled around, Dare knew exactly how to celebrate it.

She came home that evening to find that he'd turned the entire house—which they hadn't decorated at all because, Dare had argued while knowing he had this planned, they were going to Big Sky for Christmas anyway and what was the point—into his own, personal version of the North Pole.

He'd wrapped evergreen garlands everywhere they could be wrapped. There wasn't a single doorway without a sprig of mistletoe or two. There was a Christmas tree in the living room window, fully lighted, if without the kind of handmade ornaments he knew she loved. He'd bought those weird, lighted reindeer and set them up on their front porch, and he'd even gotten one of her mom's Christmas cookie recipes so the whole house smelled like home. Sweet, sugary home.

He started the Christmas carols when he saw her headlights in the driveway, and he was standing there at the door when she came inside, so he saw it. That look of pure wonder on her pretty face, as if Santa Claus really had appeared out of nowhere and just for her. As if this was magic.

And that was the thing, Dare realized. It *felt* like magic. Maybe Christmas was less about his own ghosts and more about the happiness he gave to others. To Christina. Maybe that was the point.

"I can't believe this," she whispered, standing in their living room with the lights from the tree dancing over her face and the bright red coat she still hadn't taken off. "Am I dreaming? Did I have a stroke?"

"Hold that thought," Dare suggested.

He went to meet her in the center of the room and dropped to his knees, and her eyes filled with tears. Instantly.

"Why are you crying?" He was laughing as he looked up at her. "You don't know what I'm going to say yet."

"You already proposed, Dare," she told him, her pretty eyes still too bright and that wonder in her voice, making it husky. "I said yes and everything. Did you forget?"

"I haven't forgotten a thing." He took her hands in his, and gazed up at her. His wife. His world. "Happy birthday, Christina."

"You got me a whole Christmas," she whispered. "I love it."

"Yes. And I want a baby," he told her, and watched the tears spill over and splash down her pretty face to hit that big smile of hers. "I want our baby. Our family. I want to love the way you do, all in and forever."

She pulled in a breath that sounded like a sigh and then she sank to her knees with him, wrapping her arms around his neck and pressing wild kisses to his face, his neck.

And they got a little bit lost in that, for a while.

But eventually, they were stretched out on the floor in varying degrees of undress, both breathing a little too heavily.

"If having a family is even half as much fun as making one," Christina murmured, grinning down at him from where she sprawled there across his chest, "I think we've got the whole thing figured out."

He smiled, brushing her hair back from her face, and understanding that this was home. She was. And he had no intention of forgetting that ever again.

"I want a family with you," he told her, like a vow. "I want the chaos. I want the complicated love and all that laughter. I want handmade Christmas tree ornaments and Johnny Cash duels over spiked egg nog. I want the Stockholm Syndrome."

She wrinkled up her nose at him, her eyes shining. "As long as it comes with pie, you mean."

"Of course. The pie is the whole point."

Christina laughed. "I love you. I love this birthday. I love this life."

She was light and love and she'd showed him a way out of the darkness. She did it every day. She was the cure. *His* cure.

So Dare told her so, softly and with great care and until she begged him to stop—or not—all over that sweet body of hers. All over again.

And when they threw themselves straight on toward their future family at the most wonderful time of the year, right there beneath their own, shining Christmas tree, Dare got it. They made their own miracles, and they always would.

Because the greatest miracle of all was that they loved each other.

And that was forever.

The End

A Sweet Montana Christmas

A This Old House Story

Roxanne Snopek

For Heather,
cousin + friend!
with love,
Roxanne

Chapter One

T HWACK!

Splinters of bark and wood exploded onto the snow as the last log split apart at his feet.

Austin Sweet yanked the axe head out of the stump, straightened up and stretched his back. A cord and a half of dry lodgepole pine, split and stacked neatly next to the honey shed. Would it be enough to heat the 150-year old pile of ugly he now called home, through to spring?

He took off his work glove and wiped the sweat off his face, surprised again by the beard. He hadn't intended to grow it exactly, but a month without shaving will do that.

The temperature dropped dramatically in December after dark and suddenly he felt it. Time to go in. He looked across the yard at the house, the sagging wrap-around porch, the weathered shingles, the shutters falling drunkenly away from the windows, like his grandfather's eyes after the stroke that finally killed him.

Maybe, thought Austin, if he closed off the parts of the house he wasn't using, the firewood would last long enough. "Come on, Speedy Gonzales, let's go scrounge up some food."

The ancient Malamute or husky or wolf or whatever he was

began the process of getting to his feet. His actual name was Jackson. According to the neighbor who'd handed him the keys, the dog came with the farm. From the way he moved, you'd think he'd been there from the beginning.

"I feel like you look, buddy."

Jackson's tail swayed politely, too busy putting one foot in front of the other for any more enthusiasm. Could also be he was deaf.

Austin shrugged his jacket back on and hiked up his jeans, reminding himself to punch another hole in his belt. And to go to town for some groceries.

Bring home the bacon, son. That's what a man does. A husband provides.

He shook his head, trying to erase the thoughts but they were on replay. The best he could hope for was a shuffle.

He hated going to town. Shopping meant people. And people always had questions.

Are you reopening Sweet Montana Farms?

How are you handling the adjustment from Chicago?

Aren't you lonely, out there all by yourself?

And the worse one of all.

So what brought you to little old Marietta, Montana?

The answers were yes, badly, yes and don't ask.

Austin helped the dog up the rickety steps to the porch and through the front door.

"Yeah, yeah," he muttered, at a particularly loud creak. He told himself yet again that he'd fix it. The whole thing. Tomorrow.

Or, he'd let it fall off and put a milk crate under the front door. Who cared? What did it matter?

Inside the kitchen, he opened a can of dog food for Jackson and a can of human food for himself. The dog ate from his dish on the floor. Austin stood at the sink and didn't bother with a plate. They finished at the same time.

"So," he said to the dog. "That's dinner. Now what?"

With no cable or Wi-Fi, no city or nightlife, what did a single guy do?

He looked down at the wedding band still on his finger. Was he single? He wasn't divorced. They weren't even formally separated yet. But if a man moves to the forest, and his wife isn't there to share his spaghetti-os, are they still married?

Austin yanked the door of the wood stove open and shoved in some more firewood.

The same slug hit his chest the way it always did when he thought about her.

The fire was mostly dead, the edges of the wood inside black and ashy, the only sign of life a faint red glow underneath. The fresh log lay on top, smothering the dying embers, the cold fuel impenetrable and useless in the fragile heat.

Was she happy now, without him? Had she found someone new? Had there already been someone in the wings, just waiting for the right moment to swoop in?

He deserved it, if there was. She deserved to be happy.

He reached in and took out the log, then replaced it with the smaller sticks and kindling that could bring the fire back to life. His wrist brushed against the edge of the stove and he jumped. He kept forgetting how long that heavy cast iron held heat.

Melinda hadn't betrayed him; he knew better than that. He hadn't betrayed her either but he'd still given her more than enough reason to leave him.

A husband provides.

It ran faster now, like a ticker-tape at the bottom of a CNN telecast, reporting up-to-the-minute news on the latest disaster.

A husband provides for his wife. And beneath that:

Sweet and Morgan Financial Services' Doors Closing. Investors Furious.

Deposed Financial Wizard's Wife Stands By Him. But For How Long?

Sweet Golden Son Tarnished By Failure in Business and Marriage. As predicted.

The red mark on his wrist was already forming a bubble. Like a scientist observing an experiment, Austin noted that it hurt. He should probably put something on it.

But that was Mel's purview, one of the perks of being married to a nurse. He didn't have so much as a band-aid.

Jackson, stretched out on a blanket in front of the stove, gave a long, low groan.

Austin thought, why not?

He shucked off his T-shirt and jeans and pulled on his Montana State sweatpants, the ones Mel kept trying to throw away. He wrapped himself in a blanket, lay down on the couch and went to sleep.

THE EIGHT-YEAR-OLD HONDA Civic bounced over the cracked and ridged asphalt with enough bone-rattling enthusiasm that, had there been room, the packing boxes behind her would have gone flying.

Melinda Sweet hit clutch and brake, fish-tailed briefly, then pulled over to the side of the road where she killed the engine and sat, hugging her belly, willing her pulse to return to normal, aware of the perspiration running like ice between her shoulder blades.

She squeezed her eyes tightly, then opened them. It felt like peeling the shrink-wrap off a jello mold at a church social.

"Pull it together, Mel," she muttered.

She forced herself to look at the scenery outside her window. The brilliance of the snow pierced her retinas like an ice pick. No wonder she'd let her eyelids droop. All this jagged, unrelenting white, with the mountains looming in the background like a hawk, lazily biding its time while the rabbits played below.

I'll sleep when I get there, she'd assured her mother.

She'd left her mom's home in Billings before dawn, after pacing the floor for most of the night. She couldn't sleep in the king-sized guest bed, but she drifted off while driving stick?

Her circadian rhythm was still monumentally messed up. As long as you stayed doing night shifts, you were okay. It was the days off in between, the attempt at normalcy that caused the problems.

She shifted in her seat, tugging the track suit jacket tighter around herself. She felt like the broken Christmas ornament she'd kept for so long, a gift from her grandmother, brittle, sharp, wrapped in cotton wool and taken out year after year only to be set aside, useless.

She rubbed her eyes, wondering if it was possible to rip your corneas off, then restarted the car.

Within a few minutes, she saw it: *Sweet Montana Farms, 4 mi.*

The faded wooden sign listed sideways and had what looked to be a bullet hole through one corner. Nice. Might as well say Sweet Montana Farms. Help Us, We're Dying.

She turned down the side road and thump-thumped over a little bridge beneath which a trickle of water flowed over multiple layers of ice.

Another turn, another frozen field. A bunch of goats popped their heads up as she passed by.

There it was: *Welcome to Sweet Montana Farms.* This sign

made the one at the road look good.

Instead of turning in, she drove past, getting a sense of their new home.

Austin's new home, she corrected.

Her welcome wasn't guaranteed. He didn't even know she was coming.

She made an awkward turn at the end of the road, to take a second pass from the other side, preparing herself.

The house was straight off one of those calendar shots of picturesque, falling-down farms. Lovely to look at but to live in?

No.

The barns or sheds looked like barns and sheds. A three-line barbed-wire fence bisected the snow-covered field on one side. Dead weeds poked up through some of the snow clumps and random pieces of equipment acted like props for ice sculptures.

Melinda rubbed her neck. Her hands were freezing.

She guided the car over the rutted driveway. One good snowfall and the Civic would be shut in for the duration.

For a second, panic fluttered up like a hummingbird inside a garage window. Shut in for the winter in a place like *this*.

Her mom's words came back to her:

You can't give up now. You and Austin have what it takes.

Love can conquer anything, huh Mom? An unlikely motto for her to have, since the only clue to Delores's love life was a photograph of her with Melinda's father, before Melinda was born.

Mel hoped she was right.

She'd also told Mel that Austin deserved the truth and if he didn't hear it from his wife, he'd hear it from his mother-in-law.

Delores might be a romantic, but she was no pushover.

The car shuddered to a stop and silence fell. So much silence. She stepped out, feeling like the Tin Man in need of a good oiling and let the door slam shut behind her, the noise a gunshot over the vast yard.

She tucked her bag tightly against herself and forced her feet toward the listing front porch. But before she got there, the door flew open and a figure stepped out, blinking and shading his eyes against the bright morning sun.

Melinda stopped, unable to feel her feet. The figure was Austin. Rationally, she understood that. But it wasn't the Austin she knew, gym-fit, clean-cut, Boss suits, sparkling smile.

This was Austin as she'd never seen him, stripped down, bathed in testosterone and unleashed to hunt bear.

"Ah-roooo," said the raggedy-looking creature beside him. "Who's there?"

Even his voice was rougher. He lifted his arms to drag a T-shirt over his head. Muscles in his chest and torso flexed and rippled. Her eyes fell to narrow hips, to which those wretched sweats of his were barely clinging.

"Um," she said, hearing the quaver in her voice. "It's me."

AUSTIN FROZE.

Melinda?

He shoved his head through the neck of the shirt, hearing something rip. His mind was foggy with sleep. His eyes smarted, still adjusting to the vicious light, but they worked well enough to know that yes, that was his wife standing in his yard.

"Mel?" he said, anyway.

"It's really early," she said, glancing back at her car. "I can go and come back, if-"

"Mel." He stepped out into the light. "What are you doing here?"

Her hair was pulled back into a messy ponytail. The circles under her eyes were, if possible, darker than they'd been a month ago. She was wearing shapeless fleece track pants – what was it with women and track pants? – And a matching hoodie.

Yet she'd never, in all the years he'd known her, looked more beautiful.

Anger tightened his belly. She'd asked for the separation. To come out here and surprise him like this, to dangle herself, their marriage, their life together, in front of him without warning was nothing short of cruel.

"I'd have c-called," she said, tightening her hoodie around her neck, "but your ph-phone wasn't working."

It wasn't working because he'd turned it off and tossed it in a corner. He kept the plan alive because there was no land line to the house and who knows, maybe one day he'd need it for an emergency.

The cold finally bit through his thoughts. He was shivering but worse, he could hear Melinda's teeth chattering.

He leaped down the porch steps, heedless of his bare feet. He wanted to catch her up in his arms, to hold her, to bury his face in her neck, but he settled for hoisting her luggage from the back seat.

"You're freezing," he said. "Come on in. I've got a fire."

Chapter Two

S EEING HER HUSBAND again had shaken Melinda far more than she expected and when she entered the old house, the sense of unreality got worse.

The smell of damp wood and smoke assaulted her and her stomach lurched. She pressed a knuckle hard under her nose and breathed through her mouth.

Better.

The entry and main room were spacious, with rough-hewn beams and a vaulted ceiling between which cobwebs hung like torn bridal veils.

On the wall between the main room and the kitchen stood a big, black, pot-bellied stove from whence came the smokey smell. On the flat top were four round holes, like the burners on an electric stove. Each hole was covered with a notched disc flush with the surface. She could see a handprint in the dust where someone had lifted one of them.

It was an impressive beast. The gas cooktop in their old house had been retro-styled, but this was the real thing, cast iron and meant to last.

A large moss-colored couch sat in front of it. From the

balled-up quilt and pillow, it appeared that Austin had been sleeping here when she arrived. The intimacy of being so near where he'd been sleeping felt familiar and foreign at the same time.

She thought of their butter-colored Italian leather couch and love seat, now yard sale prizes in the home of strangers. Beautiful. Stylish. Expensive.

But never intimate.

Austin grabbed the jeans lying over the back of the couch and before she knew it, he'd stripped off his sweat pants, revealing that a) his lower body had been chiseled just as lean as his upper body, b) he wasn't wearing underwear and c) he didn't care that she was watching.

She whirled around, feeling her face heat up.

"Relax," he said. "Nothing new here."

Wrong.

She attempted a carefree laugh. Failed.

"Okay if I look around?" she said.

He chuckled low in his throat. "You want me to slow down? Put on some music?"

Her mouth went dry, her head empty. She was acutely aware of the zipping and slipping sounds as he did or did not finish dressing.

Bathed in testosterone wasn't even close to describing this new Austin. He was *simmering* in it, dripping with it, sizzling and juicy, calling to her like a perfect steak to a starving woman.

"I meant," she said, hoping she didn't sound as carnivorous as she felt, "at the house."

"Whatever," he said.

She moved away to check out the rest of the room, forcing herself away from her husband as he tucked and buttoned. But the hunger didn't turn off immediately.

"Didn't know that bare wall was so interesting."

His amusement had an edge to it. He wasn't interested in making this easy for her.

She struggled to focus, to recover her equilibrium. He was hurt, she reminded herself.

"What's that?"

In the center of the room a group of items, furniture probably, sat clustered together and draped with sheets. Austin's parents had said the place would be "partially furnished;" he hadn't asked for specifics and she, not thinking it mattered, hadn't pushed him.

"Furniture. Junk, mostly."

Her fingers itched to pull off those tarps. She'd always been drawn to old things, places with history, things with stories behind them, and memories. But these weren't her memories and it wasn't her place to pry.

Austin was dressed so she allowed herself to look freely around the room.

"Like what I've done with the place?"

Austin stood by the fire, finger-combing his hair.

Every wall had spots where the plaster had been punched out or chewed out or been the victim of someone with a picture to hang and no stud finder.

The fly-spotted windows were covered with shabby floral curtains, several of which had slipped off their rods to puddle on the floor.

Now that had potential. Made of irregular planks, it was probably beautiful in its day but buckled and warped now, with some boards the perfect height to stub an unsuspecting toe and cause a stumble. She wondered if it could be restored.

"You mean it was worse?"

"Kidding." He went into what appeared to be the kitchen.

"Want some, uh, tea? Or something?"

She followed him, feeling like she was walking through a dream. She felt a little wobbly; either the sleep deprivation was finally catching up to her or she needed to eat.

Or maybe this was the sort of situation not improved with full consciousness and her body was protecting her from the full impact of where she was. And why.

It wasn't an option for her, but the best way to tour this place was probably drunk. Or stoned.

Immediately the image flew in: sea-green tile, gleaming chrome, the rusty smell of blood, a screaming, wild-haired woman on stained white sheets, writhing out of the stirrups as her drug-addled newborn entered the world.

She shuddered. The deep purple bruises on her thigh had long ago faded to sickly yellow and disappeared but she rubbed the spot absently, from habit.

"Still sore?"

He frowned, the lines on his face disappearing beneath the thick stubble on his jaw.

"I'm fine." She clasped her hands together and squeezed, until the memory receded. "So, this is the kitchen?"

It was hideous. A deep, rust-spotted sink stood beneath a wide window that overlooked the yard. Cupboards hung off the wall, probably built at the same time, and with the same skill, as the saggy porch.

Austin filled the kettle from the gooseneck faucet and set it on the electric stove.

"Fridge and stove work," he said. "I'll fix the cupboards."

"It's, um, rustic."

"Really, Mel? You want to talk about the decor?" He blinked once, slowly, then crossed his arms, his expression unreadable. "Say what you're here to say."

All words she'd planned so carefully during the long night and practiced on the drive, all the explanations and rationalizations and excuses and yes, apologies, fled from her mind.

She sucked in a deep breath and opened her mouth.

"Austin," she said. "I was wrong. I think we should try again."

"TRY AGAIN." IT was like the words didn't compute.

The kettle squealed, an auditory cattle prod. Austin jumped and grabbed the kettle, pulling it off the stove. Hot water bubbled from the spout and he leaped back, hoping to avoid another burn.

Success.

A scorched smell rose from the stove.

Melinda paled visibly and lowered herself into a chair.

"Sorry," he said. He poured the water into a mug, then looked around him. Surely he had tea. Didn't he?

"No problem," said Melinda. She took the mug from him and wrapped her fingers around it, like she was more desperate for the prop than the beverage.

Actually, their problems were legion. And Austin had been sorry for months, felt it bleeding out of him every time he opened his mouth, and all he wanted was for Mel to blame him, yell at him, scream, anything. But she never did.

So they kept on having the same conversation.

Sorry. No problem.

Until they stopped talking altogether.

Try. Again.

She hadn't come running to him in tears, holding out her arms. She hadn't said she wanted to start over, she'd missed him desperately, he was the love of her life, she couldn't live without him.

I think we should try again.

"You *think*," he said. "You're not sure."

She winced.

"*Should*." He stared hard at her. "*Try*. Gee, Mel, I'm tearing up here."

He'd lost his business, he'd lost their house, his car, their furniture, the place at the lake. His dignity.

And what had she done? She'd ripped his heart out of his chest and tossed it aside, leaving him an empty shell, yet still aching so much from her absence that if she turned around right now, he'd throw himself at her feet, beg her to stay, tie her up to keep her from leaving.

He was powerless and it infuriated him.

Austin braced his arms on the sink, unable to look at her for fear he'd break down.

"My mom convinced me," she said in a small voice.

Better yet.

"You mean, she kicked you out."

The comment was beneath him. Delores would never, ever kick her out. She'd never interfere in something like this. She loved Melinda.

But it boosted him a bit that his mother-in-law had pushed Mel toward him. At least she believed in him.

"Austin." Melinda kept her eyes on her mug, watching the swirling steam as it danced into the air. "A month ago, I couldn't imagine any way we could possibly recover from everything we'd been through. We tried so hard, for so long."

Shame twisted inside him again, and he gripped the edge of the sink so hard he felt it bite into his skin. She'd worked herself to the bone, working nights, picking up extra shifts, delivering crack-babies and getting beaten up by their wigged-out junkie mothers, all so that he could salvage what was left of his reputation.

Sweet and Morgan Financial had folded, but they'd avoided personal bankruptcy, because she'd supported them, night after night until she made a mistake and they sent her home.

Except there was no home so she'd gone to her mom's instead.

A husband provides.

"You shouldn't have come, Mel." The words came up from a deep, dark pit, where he could still hear echoes of the man who'd been worthy of her love. "You deserve more than… this."

"Austin."

He heard the chair legs scrape across the floor as she stood up.

He heard her take a hitching breath, like a sob and he turned around, just in time to catch her as her legs buckled and her eyes rolled back in her head.

MELINDA FELT AUSTIN'S strong arms beneath her. Her eyes felt like they were weighted down with rocks and when he set her on the couch in front of the fire, it was all she could do to open them.

He crouched on the floor beside her and smoothed a lock of hair out of her face.

"Hey, there," he said softly. "Welcome back."

Her throat tightened. This was the voice she remembered. Not his big public voice, the firm tones that cut through the chaos, all smiles and control. Not the tight, terse voice that was all he had left afterward, when he didn't have to pretend anymore because it was only her.

She reached up and pressed his hand, holding it to her face, feeling the tears well up inside and trying to push them back. There was the kind face, the gentle touch she'd missed so much.

"Weren't satisfied with the shock factor of just showing up, huh?" He smiled. "Had to up the ante by fainting, too?"

"Mmm," she said.

"Okay, I'm shocked. Satisfied? No need to fall off a roof or anything. Hear me?"

"Mmm-hmm."

His familiar just-rolled-out-of-bed muskiness sent a wash of bittersweet comfort over her. They'd been on opposite schedules for so long, she'd forgotten how warm he was in the morning, his unique scent, how the rumble of his laugh went straight to her sternum.

"When's the last time you ate, Mel?" He ran his finger down her jaw, touching her collarbones. "You're too skinny."

"Flatterer."

"Seriously. I can make eggs and bacon and toast and, well, not tea as it turns out. There might be some orange juice."

Her stomach clenched.

"Toast, maybe," she said.

"Promise me you're not going to die here if I leave you?"

He lifted an eyebrow at the less than ideal choice of words.

"I won't die," she said. "Can't promise I'll stay awake though."

"Go ahead. If you sleep, I'll eat the food and make more when you wake up."

She heard the lulling domestic clatter of dishes and utensils, a refrigerator door opening and shutting, bacon sizzling in a hot pan.

She meant to tell him. That's why she'd stood up. The

words were on her lips. And for some reason, her body said no.

Melinda curled up tighter on the couch, tugging the Austin-scented quilt over top of her, and touched the small mound in her belly.

I'll tell him when I wake up, she thought as she tumbled down, finally, into a real sleep.

Chapter Three

MELINDA WAS SNORING gently by the time Austin had a plate ready for her, so he covered it with a towel and set it on old Bessie, the cast-iron wood stove. Bessie would keep it warm.

"Come on, boy," he said to the dog as he pulled on his heavy winter jacket. Mel's collapse had jolted him out of his self-pity. She was here now, he couldn't worry about the details. He had work to do.

Jackson got to his feet, then turned around in a tight circle and lay down on a fresh spot in the blanket.

"You sure about that?" He pointed at Mel. "She's your responsibility then, okay? She needs anything, you let me know."

The dog's tail flopped against the floor.

He went outside, careful to close the door softly. No wonder Mel was crashing now. Daylight was her trigger to sleep. She could be out for hours.

He tried not to think of what it meant, her sudden reappearance. He didn't want to get his hopes up. If he'd learned anything in the past year or so, it's that a woman's heart was a place of mystery and even when you're as close as two people can be, there are things going on in her that you'd never dream of.

Best not to speculate. She'd talk to him when she was ready.

He went first to the goat barn, to distribute their daily allowance of hay and pelleted food and fresh water. The little beasts had stolen his heart way too easily, just as the next-door neighbor, Chad Anders, had warned him.

As the fill-in caretaker for Sweet Montana Farms, Chad had given Austin a crash course in both beekeeping and goat husbandry those first few weeks. He'd helped winterize the hives, pointed out which vegetable and flower gardens needed a last tilling before frost, mentioned bulbs and tubers and cold storage and compost piles and the merits of goat manure.

Goat manure as an asset. You had to laugh.

He quickly cleaned the pens, forking the soiled straw into a wheelbarrow, to be dumped on the steaming compost heap. By the time spring rolled around, Chad told him, all that straw and manure would be broken down into great fertilizer. The gardens would grow wildly, as would the fields of clover, blue thistle, milkweed and heather all of which were necessary for the end result: the famed Sweet honey.

Austin had to give his great-great-whatever-grandfather credit for putting the family name to work. He also gave thanks that he wasn't Austin Butcher. Or Austin Crematorium-Operator. Or Austin Crash-Test-Dummy.

Though the last one was fairly fitting, given the spectacular nature of Sweet and Morgan's demise.

Financial advisor to farmer. Why not?

The white Alpine doe nudged him in the leg. She looked like she'd be dropping her kid soon. It seemed to Austin that spring would be a kinder time for new babies to be born, but farmers had their reasons and he figured he'd learn. At any rate, the shed was solid and tight and with all the animals inside, it stayed plenty warm. Barring a blizzard, they'd be fine.

Another nudge, more forceful this time. Austin reached into his pocket for the alfalfa chunks they loved.

"Once," said Austin, handing them around. "I give you treats one day and now that's all you care about."

The Nubians, with their aquiline noses and pendulous ears, pushed their way in, eager for their share, as did the cashmeres, with their big woolly coats.

The cashmeres, he'd been told, were the earners. The fleecy undercoat, Chad explained, made beautiful, highly-prized yarn. Cashmere was a big hit at farmers' markets.

Austin would be happy if he could manage to sell the honey, let alone make goat-hair yarn.

He'd be happy if he could get them all through the winter, alive.

He glanced over at the house, wondering if Mel had woken up. Not likely, if she'd crashed the way he suspected she needed to.

By that last horrible week, both of them had been under so much stress, withdrawal had been a means of self-preservation. Mel was still black and blue from the assault and even quieter than usual. When his father had offered to let Austin take over the farm, he could hardly turn it down. Once spring came, they'd sell and Austin would get a percentage and he and Mel could take it and start their lives over again.

"Win-win, right my boy?" Bill had said in his too-loud voice.

Mel had been suspicious. If it sounds too good to be true…

"Hey neighbor!"

It was Chad, waving from his snowmobile. He hopped off, walked through the gate and closed it behind himself.

"I see you've got a guest," said Chad, striding up to him.

They did the handshake-backslap thing that seemed to be the custom around here.

"My wife," said Austin, not feeling much like explaining himself.

"Your wife!" Chad's eyebrows went up. He nodded. "Kept that one tucked up your sleeve, didn't you? When will I meet her?"

"She's sleeping. Rough night. You'll meet her eventually."

Chad didn't question further, but went to the honey shed, gesturing for Austin to follow.

"Meant to tell you," he said. "There's not enough honey jarred for the Christmas open house."

"Open house?" Austin followed him into the honey shed. "What's that?"

Chad stopped and faced him. "You don't know about the open house? It's a touristy thing. Your granddad loved doing them. Sleigh rides – I'll help with that. A feed-the-goats pen for the kids and the display hive, so they can see the bees. Cider and treats in the house, where you'll sell the honey. And that shed over there? It's full of decorations and lights, ready to use. Of course, no one's done it since he's been gone."

When Austin didn't respond, he tipped his head and frowned. "You weren't expecting this?"

Austin felt sick. "Communication's not our strong point in our family."

They began moving toward the honey hut.

"I'm getting that," said Chad.

Granddad Sweet had leased forty acres to the neighbor, for his rescued mustangs. Chad helped with the honey production and generally looked after the old man. He knew the farm as well as his own and certainly made himself at home.

Maybe Chad hoped to buy it, come spring.

Or maybe the cowboy could stick to his side of the fence for two minutes and give Austin a chance to figure things out on his own.

"It'll be a lot of work, given the state of things here. But you should go ahead with it, if at all possible. It's your last earning opportunity before spring."

Earning opportunity? Why was he learning all this from a stranger? Austin felt a flash of irritation that his dad hadn't mentioned any of this to him.

Of course he'd put on the open house. As strapped as he was, he couldn't turn down any chance to make some money. Of course he'd look after the bees and the goats and the surprise herd of wildebeests or whatever else Bill might have forgotten to tell him about.

Fix up the house a little, his dad said. Keep the bees alive. Tidy it up for spring, that nebulous, faraway spring, when they'd put a For Sale sign at the gate and ride off into the sunset.

Bill and Ducky hadn't even bothered to adjust their schedule, so they could meet him here. No, their annual winter trek to Arizona took priority.

Austin should have known there'd be more than "a little home renovation" involved. He hadn't signed up to be a farmer, but it wasn't the work itself that bothered him. It's that he'd been blindsided. Played.

Melinda had seen it coming; she'd suspected it was a classic Bill Sweet over-sell, under-deliver situation. Question was, now that she was proven right, would she stay and help him through it?

That's when he heard her scream.

MELINDA AWOKE REFRESHED and feeling better than she had in days. She found the plate of food sitting on an oven-warmed towel and picked at it, forcing herself to eat the scrambled eggs. She needed the protein. The toast felt good in her stomach and the honey she drizzled on top was delicious, better than any grocery store product.

She gave the bacon to the dog, who took it politely and then followed her every movement from then on.

She needed to get busy, do something, figure out what this place was about and how she might possibly fit in here. Either that or implode, which she was hoping to avoid.

Male voices rose and fell across the crisp winter air, and she looked out to see Austin with a neighbor, another big man with boots and a hat. Squaring off against each other? No. She heard her husband laugh, and it brought a smile to her lips. Unlike her, his need for social contact meant that he made friends easily and this neighbor appeared to be a useful friend to have. She didn't feel much like meeting a stranger, so she was glad to see them disappear into one of the barns.

Melinda began the task of unloading her car.

First thing, bedding. Napping on a couch, under a quilt was one thing. Sleeping there every night surrounded by furniture under sheets was edging into a crazy place where eventually you were on the six o'clock news, in a feature on hermit hoarders.

She carried the first box of linens to the porch, which creaked suspiciously under her weight, as it had done earlier, but held firm. She set it in front of the front door, to prop it open, then quickly made trip after trip, with box after box, until the car was empty and everything was piled in the main room.

Then she pulled the door closed. Despite the bright sunlight, the temperature was frigid. As long as she was moving, she didn't feel the cold, but now standing still, it was way too chilly inside.

Surely there was a furnace control somewhere. But for now, she hunkered down to the big black stove, from which the most delightful dry heat radiated. Should she feed it more wood?

Melinda tugged on the door. It opened with a screech and she could see the bright coals inside. With two fingers, she picked up a small log and tossed it inside. Sparks flew up and ash drifted out onto her arms. She closed the door and hoped for the best.

In the back of the main room was a narrow staircase, which she expected led to a closed-in loft where she'd find bedrooms. She made her way up the steps to find she was right. Three rooms, all smaller than her mom's guest room.

But it appeared that each room contained a bed, disassembled and propped against a wall. She plunked the box of linens on the floor of the largest room and went to peek under the sheeting.

A new-looking boxspring and mattress and a metal bed frame. Austin hadn't even bothered to put it together.

She pulled off the covering, hoping she wasn't about to find a nest of mice, and was pleased to find the items still factory-sealed in plastic. No chew marks, no scat.

Quickly she assembled the metal bed frame and maneuvered the mattresses on top, then stood back to evaluate her work.

"Hope I've got some sheets that will fit," she muttered, wiping her brow.

This bed wasn't a king. It wasn't even a queen. What did that make it? Double? Standard? Too-Bad-For-You? The Little-People Bed?

She sat on the mattress and ran her hand over the quilted surface. Funny, people put such pretty designs on mattresses, yet who ever saw them? You brought your mattress home and then covered it with layers upon layers, sheets and pads and duvets and coverlets, spent a third of your life on it, but probably wouldn't recognize it in a line-up.

She bounced lightly. Firm. Good. Austin liked a firm mattress. His feet would hang over the end and they'd be elbowing each other all night, but at least it was firm.

It was ironic. She and Austin had been on opposite schedules for so long, barely seeing each other, let alone sleeping together, that their king bed was always half-empty. Now that they'd be together all day and all night, they'd be crammed together in this little bed like sardines.

The spot on her thigh throbbed suddenly and she got to her feet to shake it out. She needed to make up at least one other bed too. She wasn't sure she was ready to sleep next to a man who was part stranger, yet part of her heart at the same time.

Fresh fatigue washed over her but she ignored it. No time to wallow, there were miles to go before she slept anywhere.

A quick survey of the kitchen revealed it was as bad as her first impression. Through the window over the sink she could see the two men, hands deep in pockets, shoulders hunched against the cold, kibitzing like old friends. If there'd been a sniffing and circling part, it was long over.

She bit her lip, a shard of worry shifting inside.

He was getting attached, already. She could tell.

Her hands were dry and dusty, so she turned the hot water faucet to wash them. An explosion of brown water spluttered and farted all over her hands. She leaped back in disgust, automatically keeping her hands over the sink, so as not to befoul the floor, while leaning as far back as possible.

The smell was hellacious, and she'd once been recruited to treat an ER full of German tourists with food poisoning.

All pipes flow to the sea? It seemed some of them detoured to Sweet Montana Farms, just to be ironic.

How long could she go without breathing? Would she be trapped in this position forever? Is this what hysteria felt like?

A laugh rose, and she turned her face toward her sleeve and let it out. She laughed until she had to squat down and cross her legs because, oh man, she had to pee and she hadn't yet discovered the bathroom and if the water was bad here, what would it be like in there and if it was worse than this, they'd have to bomb the place and sometimes, what else is there to do but laugh?

She laughed and laughed until finally, still hooting, she stretched her arms even more and opened the cold water too. This appeared to run clear and was, like the rest, freezing cold.

Probably a blessing, given the smell. Thank you, Lord, we've got no hot water!

If this was hysteria, she'd have to do it more often.

Eventually the episode of plumbing-diarrhea resolved itself and the water ran clear. She rinsed the inside of the sink, scooping the water in her hands, shuddering as she did so. That odor would be in her nose for days, in her hair, on her skin.

How naive she'd been, she realized. In a house this old, indoor plumbing of any kind could not be assumed. Nor electricity, though that seemed fine, so far. The avocado green electric oven and harvest gold refrigerator lurking in the corners of the room had already been proven functional according to Austin, though she'd reserve judgement on that until she'd used them herself.

She turned off the water, shook her icy hands dry and went to find the bathroom.

The bathroom, or water closet as it might have been called originally, was located under the staircase. The only one in the house, it was a quarter of the size of a typical modern bathroom and it had no window. She could barely see in.

She patted the wall, searching for the switch and as she reached in further, something cold and thin stroked her cheek, making a faint clicky noise before it slipped away.

She whirled, running from the room shrieking and slapping at her face, not stopping until she was standing outside on the porch, shuddering into the truly frigid early evening air.

Being a good sport was one thing. But this was awful, all of it.

AUSTIN TOOK OFF for the house, Chad hot on his heels.

Melinda was on the porch, laughing or crying, he couldn't tell.

"Mel, honey!" Austin grabbed her arms and peered into her face. "What's wrong? Are you okay?"

Chad hung back at the bottom of the steps, a real-life cowboy, not a poseur like himself.

"I'm fine," she gasped, between breaths. "Enjoying a little hysteria, that's all. It's quite therapeutic."

He could have shaken her, for giving him such a scare. But the wildness in her eyes suggested that the few hours she'd slept on the couch were too little for healing, but plenty enough for taking inventory.

"You don't say." He stroked a hand over her hair, as if she was a child. "Why don't you tell me what's going on, huh?"

She waited a long moment, then heaved an enormous sigh and sort of wilted against him.

"Ahem," said Chad, looking acutely uncomfortable. "Is there anything I can do to help?"

"Chad Anders," said Austin, "my wife, Melinda. Melinda, our neighbor Chad."

"Forgive me," said Mel, the crazy still right under the surface, "if I don't offer tea and crumpets. It's like a refrigerator in there, the plumbing has raging dysentery and there's a long-tailed creature living in the bathroom ceiling. Can you fix those things? Also, I have to pee and if you tell me to go to the outhouse, I'll, I'll…"

"Come on inside." Austin couldn't tell if she was shivering or shuddering but he knew it was too cold to be standing outside.

"May I?" Chad stepped past them. "I might know where your granddad hid the space heaters."

Of course he might.

"G-g-good," said Mel, her teeth chattering loudly.

He'd never seen her this emotionally fragile. Not that he wanted the separation to leave her resplendent with happiness, but he didn't wish this kind of misery on her.

He let her go to spare her this kind of misery.

"I think I found your long-tailed monster," called Chad. "The facilities are now safe for use."

"Wh-what was it?" said Mel, cautiously approaching the bathroom.

Chad fingered the chain-pull from the ceiling light in the tiny room. He tugged on it, turning the light on and off, then draped it over his face. "If you didn't know what it was, it could feel pretty freaky."

Melinda took another step forward, then touched the chain. It put her much closer to Chad than Austin would have liked. Also, he was a bit ripped off that he hadn't been the one to slay the dragon for the damsel. He could use a hero moment right about now.

"You're sure there's nothing living in there?" asked Mel, frowning at the toilet. "No alligator or snake or sewer rat?"

"Check it out." Chad lifted the lid and seat, then hit the flush handle on the toilet. "Could use a cleaning, and that, ahem, cracked seat could be unpleasant. But I can safely say it's uninhabited."

"In that case," she stared at them, "if you'll excuse me."

"Oh, right!"

Chad backed out of the room, crashing into the doorframe in his haste. He ran to the pot-bellied stove and stood in front as if preparing to interview it for a job.

"Thanks for your help," said Austin.

"Hey, it's nothing. You getting along with Bessie okay? I saw your cordwood outside. Nice job."

"I'm managing."

Austin waited.

"Okay." Chad put up his hands. "Well, I'll take off then. Let me know when you want to talk about the open house details. We need to get that going as soon as possible."

"Sure," said Austin. He opened the front door. "See you around."

Chapter Four

S HE WAS GOING to need more hand sanitizer, thought Mel as she watched the water swirl around the stained sink. It looked clear enough, but how could she trust it after what she'd seen in the kitchen?

She rubbed the back of her thigh where the crack in the toilet seat had pinched. Should she ask Austin to fix it? If the situations were reversed, she probably wouldn't appreciate him waltzing in and pointing out all the defects.

She exited the bathroom, self-conscious about her earlier meltdown. Especially in front of the neighbor. Last thing she needed was a reputation as Austin Sweet's crazy wife.

"Feeling better?" Austin came through the door with an armload of firewood. "Are you gladder now that your bladder's flatter?"

His tone was light but he busily avoided eye contact.

"Don't tell me you haven't been caught by the Crack of Doom," she countered.

"Guess I'm more of a hard-ass than you thought."

Nice.

"Any chance that could be fixed?"

"Depends." He dropped the logs into a battered aluminum washtub, turned and looked straight at her. "How long you planning to be here?"

Before she could respond, something darted out from the logs and scuttled under the stove.

"What was that?" she yelled. "Did you see it? It was huge! Get it, get it!"

Austin laughed. "And we have lift-off."

She was taking giant, jumping steps, the way people always do when safety is up and away. There may have been hand flapping as well.

Mel hopped onto the moss-green couch. "Was that a mouse?"

"Yeah," he said. "Don't tell me that freaks you out. Surely Nurse Mel's dealt with much scarier things than that little guy. Besides, he's gone now."

"He is not!" She grabbed a flashlight from a box and leaned down to shine it under the big stove. The flash from a teeny-tiny set of eyes stared back at her. "There it is! It's a mouse!"

"Like I said." Austin swept bits of bark and sawdust from the floor. "I probably brought it in with the wood."

She gaped at him in amazement. "Is that supposed to make me feel better? Get it out of here!"

With a deep sigh, he poked the broom into the creature's hiding place.

"There it is, there it is!" yelled Melinda as the mouse scrambled back into the wood-box.

Austin carried the box to the porch, where he carefully took out each log. Mel followed, peering over his shoulder as the box emptied.

"Hey there, little fella," said Austin. A drab little thing with enormous grey ears sat huddled and twitching in the corner.

"Oh," said Mel. "It's so small." And not threatening in the least.

"I'll be right back," said Austin. He walked the box over to the shed closest to the house and tipped it, letting the animal go back to wherever it had come from.

He squatted there for a moment, as if making sure the mouse was all right.

"I'll get some live traps tomorrow," he said when he returned. "In case he's a mob boss and I just triggered a turf war."

"Thank you."

Melinda pulled two chairs out from the furniture collection and sat them in front of the stove, watching her husband feed the fire.

"You know you're probably bringing all sorts of vermin in with the wood."

"Probably."

"So, why use the stove then?"

He crouched down and pulled open the handle. "Furnace is crap. Bessie works just fine."

"Bessie?" The cast-iron stove had a name?

He stirred the coals and added a larger log, sending a small shower of sparks popping inside the iron belly.

"She's a good old gal." He jammed another log inside. "She keeps me warm at night."

Ah, thought Mel, hearing the subtle emphasis on *she*. The easy-going facade slips. Good. Not everyone would pick it up, but she heard the thread of anger.

It was about time he faced it.

They'd been struggling long before the final break but it's not like she'd deliberately withdrawn from him and she certainly hadn't been withholding sex as a punishment. She wasn't that kind of person. And it wasn't like Austin had made overtures;

they'd barely seen each other, barely spoken at all those last few weeks. They didn't sleep together because she worked nights.

And it just so happened that made it easier for her.

For so long, all she wanted was to yell, to cry, to shake him until he screamed at her and ranted and railed at the monumental dump the universe had taken on his head. Then she could scream with him and they could finally, finally get rid of the poison that was destroying them.

But he refused. Austin dealt with things properly. Reasonably. Rationally.

And if he couldn't be mad, well neither could she, because it wasn't *her* business that had gone belly-up. If she let out her anger, it would look like she blamed Austin. Which she didn't.

At the time, it seemed he barely noticed her distance. Now she realized it must have hurt.

"Wood stoves have risks, Oz," said Melinda, unable to take the silence. "Carbon monoxide, sparks, smoke inhalation, it's not safe to have an active fire in the house."

"I've been here a month. Hasn't killed me yet."

Austin's optimistic glass-half-full resilience was what she loved, and hated, most about him. He was one of those guys people liked on sight, all friendly, hardworking sunshine and buttercups. Even when Sean Morgan confessed to the risky trade that brought down their company, Austin didn't throw blame. They were partners.

And Sean had lost as much as they had, more if you counted his fiancee.

Well. Melinda had balanced that out, hadn't she?

Austin took the other chair, set it across from hers and straddled it, resting his arms on the back. He looked at her, his expression blank, waiting, his blue eyes hooded and deep, as unreadable as those of a stranger.

Melinda's throat felt dry and she was aware of her increased heart rate.

His civilized good cheer, the quick smile and easy laugh that went along with their frenzied old life had been chiseled away, replaced with a kind of stillness, as if he'd become attuned to the slow quiet rhythms of this new life.

Not peaceful, exactly, but watchful. Patient.

Like a hunter.

AUSTIN RESTED HIS chin on his hands, just looking at her, grateful and terrified at the same time.

She was here. He tried not to think further than that.

Melinda chewed on a corner of her lip, unable to sit still.

He remembered that feeling. The stress, the pressure, always needing to run faster, faster, to do more, and still more.

For what? To earn still more money? So they could qualify for an even bigger mortgage? To buy another car? More furniture to sit in their beautiful home, unused because they were always out, running, doing, earning.

Always apart.

What's the deal, Mel? He wanted to shout. *Are you really back?*

Part of him wanted to throw down the words and demand an answer, find out the truth. It was simple. Yes. Or no.

They were married. He still loved her. Did she still love him?

A bigger part of him was afraid that she wasn't ready for a yes or no. She was dancing around something, preparing herself, evaluating him maybe, unable to commit fully again, but unwilling to give up completely too.

That was good. Wasn't it?

So much for not thinking about it.

Melinda got to her feet. "Not to be critical but what have you been doing for the past month?"

He tightened his lips over his teeth. Through the whole S&M debacle, as he now referred to it in his mind, she hadn't criticized him, hadn't complained. It seemed that phase was over.

In fact, he'd been working his ass off outside, but he'd let her have this one.

"Not a fan of my decorating style, I take it."

"Not a fan of your third-world camping amenities."

Good, he thought. Definitely an edge there.

"Okay if I explore the 'junk'?"

"Your funeral."

She took hold of the tarp and hauled it to the ground. A cloud of dust billowed up and she turned away, coughing, holding her gut and waving him away.

"Make yourself at home," he said. "I've got work outside."

He'd already checked the hives and fed the goats but he needed to plan for this open house he was throwing. In less than two weeks.

Jackson joined him this time at the door, jauntier than Austin had seen him yet.

"You like her, huh?" said Austin, once he was out of earshot of the house.

The dog wagged his tail.

"Yeah." He looked back at the house. Knowing she was inside changed everything. "Me, too."

He bent down, picked up a handful of snow and tossed it into the air, watching the icy particles catch the light, little diamonds floating to the soft earth.

"Ah-ROO," said Jackson.

As THE CHOKING cloud settled, Melinda made out a sight that kicked all other thoughts from her head.

Partially furnished?

For once, an understatement that ended in a good surprise. She took a step forward, drinking in the jumbled beauty before her.

Their house in Chicago had been furnished by the decorator they'd hired when they moved in. Minimalist, clean lines, stylish and practical. Perfect for entertaining, which given her schedule, they never did. Perfect for raising a family, ditto. Perfect for relaxing together with a cup of coffee on a Sunday morning or a glass of wine in the evening. Ditto, ditto and ditto.

Elegant, tasteful, expensive – and soulless.

All those sleepless hours she'd spent surrounded by a triumph of design and decorating, watching trash-to-treasure, do-it-yourself and home-and-garden shows on cable, and she'd never so much as set foot in an antique store.

But she knew enough to recognize the wealth before her.

She ran her hand along the deep, dark wood of an ancient dining room table, with elaborately tooled legs, built by an expert craftsman long gone from this world.

Behind the table was a matching buffet and hutch and a curio cabinet at the back that needed a glass pane replaced but was otherwise lovely. There were coffee tables and corner tables and a rugged, scarred butcher-block table that made her want to bake bread. With a worktable like that, she thought, maybe even that wretched kitchen could be redeemed.

Beneath the second sheet she found a huge deep armchair made for cuddling, and a rich purple floral… fainting couch?

She left the heavy items in place, of course, but pulled the other things out into the open, where she could look at them more closely. By the time Austin came inside, she was actually bubbly with excitement.

"That's a lot of junk," said Austin, rubbing his hands together in front of Bessie. "I'll ask Dad what he wants to do with it. Donate it to Goodwill, if anything's still usable."

"Oh no, Austin." She ran her hand over the purple half-couch. "These are treasures. Some of these items might even be valuable."

"What's that, a chaise?" asked Austin. "It's kind of ugly."

"It's not ugly!" Melinda sat down and spread her arms protectively over the small back. "It's beautiful! My grandmother had a couch just like this."

"The stuffing's coming out."

"I don't care." She examined the spot he indicated. Yeah, the fabric was torn and the upholstery was flat in places. "I might be able to fix it."

He lifted his eyebrows, but said nothing.

"I could learn to sew."

I'm not working, after all.

Loss struck, like a hawk diving out of the air to snatch away her peace of mind before it had fully emerged from its burrow, leaving her breathless with sorrow.

She loved nursing. She loved delivering babies. She was good at it, and even though it was back-breaking, and heart-breaking sometimes, she missed it. Her patients were some of the poorest of the poor, marginalized, underserved, forgotten, but on her floor, they and their babies got the best care possible.

"It's not ours, Mel," said Austin. "None of this is ours."

"Nice of you to say *ours*."

Austin's face darkened. "It's ours until you say otherwise."

"Tell that to your dad."

The farm and everything on it belonged to Bill Sweet. The deal was, come spring, when he sold the farm, Austin would get a percentage of the sale, as payment for the renovation work.

Except he had that tendency of bombastic people to gild the story as he wished it to be, rather than as it actually was. Melinda would bet her sweet patootie that her father-in-law didn't intend to sell.

In Bill and Ducky Sweet's opinion, the ten years she and Austin had spent in Chicago were nothing more than a glitch, a hiccup, a derailment that never would have happened if not for her dragging their son away from his home while she followed her dream job.

Forget that Austin himself wanted to go.

Forget that his cousin, Sean Morgan, was already there, ready and waiting to set up Sweet and Morgan Financial.

"Dad doesn't mean anything by that," said Austin. "It's just how he talks."

Yeah. As if she wasn't there at all.

However, beggars can't be choosers and regardless of their motives, it was kind of them to offer up the farm.

"Would your dad mind," she asked, "if I worked on it? If, like you said, it's junk or headed for Goodwill anyway?"

"Actually," said Austin, "we've got an event to plan for. An open house. Two weeks of inviting the public in to buy our honey and play with our goats and have hay rides. But mostly, buy honey."

Mel looked around her. "An open house? Here?"

"It's gonna be a lot of work but Chad says we could sell most of our inventory." He looked out the window. "We need the money, Mel."

Of course they did. But inviting people into this hovel?

He walked to the window and leaned against it, looking out.

She could see tendons in his neck standing out like cords.

"So what do you think now, Mel? Still think we should 'try again'?"

AUSTIN AWOKE ALONE and freezing in the little bed his wife had made up for him upstairs. Frankly, he'd been more comfortable on the couch. Sometime during the night, the room had gotten too warm and he'd unplugged the space heater.

Instead of plugging it back in and trying to go back to sleep, he pulled on his jeans and T-shirt, a fresh pair of thick socks and a sweat shirt. Not surprisingly, Melinda had stayed up, claiming that her earlier nap had ruined her bedtime.

He shouldn't be disappointed. She'd assured him she was staying, but an ocean of unsaid words still lay between them and he knew only one way to bridge the gap.

The smell of coffee drew him to the kitchen, where he found her standing in front of the sink, watching the mist starting to burn off in the morning sun. She was wearing a thick fleece sweat suit with the hood up.

He came up behind her, moved the hood aside and kissed her neck. She jumped, but didn't immediately draw away. That was something.

"Good morning," he murmured, his lips lingering on her warm skin. "You smell good."

"Hey, you scared me. Good morning. You're letting the cold air in. Coffee's ready. I'll get you a cup. I did some organizing last night so I'm the only one in the known universe who knows where things are now."

She ducked out from beneath his arm but not before he saw the circles beneath her eyes. Last night he'd dragged the scarred butcher-block table from the main room into the kitchen for her, and now it was neatly stacked with their dishes, silverware and the non-perishable food items he'd brought with him but hadn't bothered unpacking.

"I've made toast, too. And Chad was right about the honey. It's amazing."

One touch and he was desperate to hold her again. And she was as elusive as a wild bird.

"Did you get any sleep?"

"Oh, you know," she said airily, adding cream and sugar to his brew. The ancient refrigerator had a wide pull-up handle and a tiny icebox tucked inside, and from the look of it, she'd cleaned it.

She pushed the mug at him, then edged out of the room.

"So what's the deal with the hot water?" She pointed to the small bathroom under the stairs. "I'm dying for a shower but I'm not desperate enough for a cold one."

He was about ready for a cold one. He thought of her nipples, pink and peaked, and had to grit his teeth.

"See those pots of water sitting on top of Bessie? That's our hot water."

She glanced between the sink and the big black stove, as if by looking enough times, she could change the truth of the matter.

"People don't live like this, Oz." She spread her hands helplessly. "You have to get that fixed."

"Fine. I'm going to town today. I'll talk to someone about it."

"I'm going outside for a walk, now that the sun's up," she said. "There's milk in the fridge and the honey's on the counter. Holler good-bye before you leave for town, okay?"

But once he'd dressed and eaten, she was at the far end of the property, so all he could do was lift an arm. She didn't see him.

Chapter Five

MELINDA PICKED HER way around the snow-covered garden, enjoying the occasional freeze-dried seed-head that popped through. Amazing how snow lightened and brightened everything, softening the edges, smoothing over rough spots.

She chunked over a ridge of frozen dirt, feeling the satisfying squashing sensation beneath the low block heel of her boot. They were her favorites, these boots. Comfortable, durable, with just a kick of sexy.

She hadn't worn them in ages.

Austin's lips on her neck had triggered a long-forgotten desire inside her. The closeness of being inside the same house, no rushing off to work, no TV or internet to distract them, it made it difficult to pretend she wasn't aware of him.

She squatted down to finger a stiff dried dahlia stalk. One of them, she could tell by the crunchy petals still clinging, was a lovely deep crimson. Her favorite color.

Used to be her favorite color, she amended.

That moment in the kitchen when she'd found herself actually responding to Austin's touch, she ached for their former closeness, but it also scared her. The honesty and intimacy of sex was beyond what she could handle right now. The great conundrum: sex makes men feel loved; communication makes women feel loved. Austin didn't know what she needed and as bad as she felt about it, she refused to go to bed with him until she could be fully honest.

The longer these situations went on, the worse they got. Small issues turned into bitter resentment and pain. She didn't want that. But she wasn't ready, not yet.

"Hey neighbor," called a voice from the fence.

She'd been so lost in thought she hadn't heard his ATV.

She straightened, brushed at her jeans and swept her hair away from her face, then realized what she was doing and stopped.

"Chad Anders," he said. "You were having a rough day, not sure you remember."

His long legs ate up the ground between them until he was standing next to her in his Levis and checked shirt and open jacket, all howdy-ma'am and fresh air.

"I remember."

Sweet Mustang Sally. How tired had she been?

Chad Anders was, objectively speaking, a delicious bit of cowboy. Mel suspected that women everywhere did double and triple takes every time he walked into a room. And that he was well aware of it.

But after the shock of seeing Austin's bare chest and legs and... well. Seeing her husband naked again after a long dry spell, all rough-cut and rangy, made Chad seem like a catalog offering.

An exceptional sample of a handsome man. Two-dimensional and flat.

Whereas Austin – she shivered – he was live, in the flesh,

and hers.

Maybe. Probably. Technically.

Warmth flooded into places long cold, deep inside. She wanted to get back to the house.

"Austin's gone to town. He's looking for a contractor."

"Logan Stafford's the guy to get. He's got vision, when it comes to these old treasures."

"He's going to need it." She allowed herself a quick once over behind her sunglasses.

Chad tilted his head and narrowed his eyes. "Not such a treasure to you, huh?"

"I'm more of a city gal." She forced a smile. "Shouldn't you be bringing a pie or something to welcome us to the neighborhood?"

He tilted his hat further back onto his head and looked away. "I'm not much good in the kitchen."

She stuffed her fists deep into the pockets of her jacket and took a step away.

"Was there something you needed?" she asked politely.

"We should talk honey."

Ah, the importance of a comma. Or rather, the lack thereof. Flirting was probably as natural to him as breathing and it amused her, observing her own lack of response.

"I harvested in August," continued Chad, "so there's about one hundred twenty-five pounds of product to process and jar. I told Austin he'd want to sell it during the Christmas open house and it's just around the corner."

"Yeah. He mentioned." She frowned. "Did you say hundred and twenty-five pounds? Of honey?"

He gestured to the shed closest to the house. "Sitting right there, waiting. All the equipment is there but you'll still need to do the jarring and labelling by hand. It's a tedious job; might want to find some help. Too bad there was no one to make jams this year. With a variety of products, you can make gift baskets."

"I can make jam," she said, her mood leapfrogging upward. The summer she was fourteen, she'd gone to stay with her grandmother. They'd made preserves of all sorts, jams and jellies, but chutney too, and salsa and apple butter.

Chad lifted his eyebrows. "You can?"

She could intubate a flat baby and bring it back to life in five seconds, but home preserving, that's what impressed people.

"It's been a while, but yeah. I can. But where would I find the fruit?"

"I can tell you who to contact for frozen berries and whatnot."

"That would be great," she said. In the back of her favorite cookbook, that also once belonged to her Gram, were numerous handwritten recipes for all the concoctions she loved best.

She remembered the pride she'd felt to line up those sparkling jars filled with preserves that they'd enjoy throughout the winter. She hadn't understood until years later that her Gram's creativity and thrift had been born of necessity.

Austin didn't believe she was prepared to pitch in; this would be the perfect way to show him.

HE PULLED HIS truck into the parking lot of Big Z Hardware, pleasantly surprised by the size of it. But Marietta had changed so much since he'd been a kid. He wondered if the town had attracted some decent restaurants. Maybe if he took his wife out on a date, she'd warm up to him again.

"Welcome to Big Z's." A friendly-looking man with a pencil behind his ear waved at him from across the customer service desk. "Can I help you find something?"

Austin glanced around him. "Yeah, everything."

The man set aside his tablet and came around the front of the desk. "Paul Zabrinski, owner. I'm guessing you're a little out of your depth, if you don't mind me saying so."

"Austin Sweet." They shook hands. "If you're throwing me a life preserver, I don't mind at all."

Paul laughed, then cocked his head. "Sweet. Wait. Hey, are you connected to the honey farm north of town? Sweet Montana?"

"Guilty. I just moved in. We. We just moved in. And I think you and I went to middle school together."

He'd switched to Livingston for high school, but he remembered Paul. Zabrinski wasn't a name you forgot easily.

Paul swatted a glove against his leg in delight. "That place is a legend. We'd just about given up anyone ever reviving it. Do you own it? You must have gotten a hell of a deal. Chad's maintained the garden and the bees, but the house needs some serious love. You've met Chad, haven't you?"

"Yeah, he's great. But we're just looking after it for my parents, and only until spring," said Austin, feeling that twist of shame again. They were transient, no fixed address. Unemployed, unsettled. On a derelict farm. Gratefully accepting a family handout because it was their only option.

"We," said Paul. "I heard you were on your own."

Yeah, thought Austin. Probably everyone had.

"My wife was delayed," he said.

Paul nodded, as if the comment was nothing important. "The market isn't moving. Why commit until you've had a season or two to see how you like it. So I'm guessing you want to do a bit of renovating?"

"Something like that. Problem is, I'm not exactly handy."

"Where do you want to start?"

"Let's see," said Austin, prioritizing Mel's complaints on his fingers. "There's no heat, the kitchen sink is almost rusted through, the kitchen pipes are full of e coli – her words, not mine – the plank floor is buckling, there's a cracked window frame upstairs letting in cold air and something smells when I turn on the light in the furnace room. But the biggest problem, the one I've been given strict instructions to not come home unless I can fix it, today, is the toilet seat. It's cracked. And hideous. And it's the only one in the house. There was a situation."

Paul winced sympathetically. "A woman can put up with a lot, but a deficient bathroom is a deal breaker. Don't worry, my friend. You're in good hands."

By the time he was through the checkout line, he had a new toilet seat, complete with instructions on how to install it, plus a bucket of instant spackle, a hand planer, an array of sandpaper, and more importantly, an appointment to meet with a local contractor. Not to mention the names of several people Paul had introduced him to as they walked the store. Including a young pregnant woman who was thrilled to hear his wife was a nurse.

"Don't forget," called Paul. "Consider the furnace out of commission until we get the wiring checked out. Stick with the wood stove."

Yeah. He couldn't wait to tell Mel.

"HEY, MEL," CALLED Austin from the porch. "I'm back."

"Good," she answered, getting to her feet. She'd spent the morning while he was out scrubbing the entire surface area of the kitchen, including the floor. Now that it was clean it was… still horrible.

She shuddered. She was reasonably satisfied that they weren't going to die of hanta virus or mold or bat guano or ebola but if you could die of ugly, they were still in big trouble.

"I've got a good news, bad news situation here."

"There was the chance of good news?" She walked to the porch and began taking items from him. "Just tell me."

"I'll have the toilet seat fixed in an hour."

"Okay." She eyed him cautiously. "That's not good news. That just gets one bit of bad news up to neutral."

He leaned forward and kissed her cheek, a deliberate move.

She felt her face light up with warmth, and remembered what she'd been thinking about outside, while she talked to Chad.

"The local hardware store owner, Paul, is a guy I went to school with as a boy. Great guy. He put me in touch with a local contractor. He's coming out tomorrow."

She sighed with relief. Austin did know how to work the schmooze factor. "That *is* good news!"

"Paul introduced me to a bunch of people including a girl who really wants to meet you."

He lifted his eyebrows like he was about to give her a prize.

"She's about, I don't know, twelve months pregnant and getting, and I quote, a 'little squirrelly.'"

A pregnant girl. Blood on the floor. Pain. Fingers scrabbling, so close, so close.

She took the groceries to the kitchen, pushing back the memories, not sure which were which or whether they were even real and not some bleak footage conjured by her mind to fill the holes. The incident report had been straightforward.

The hospital board had been very understanding. Too understanding, in fact.

She put the jug of milk in the refrigerator.

"Austin, I don't think I'm ready to get back on that horse."

He plunked a bag of canned goods on the butcher block table, and made a face. "She's not a headhunter. She's a girl who wants to talk. Has anyone banned you from talking? Making new friends? Sharing your vast knowledge of the feminine mystique?"

She couldn't help but smile. "I'll be happy to chat with her if I get the opportunity."

It would probably be good for her. She didn't want to lose her nerve entirely. Some nurses switched departments after a mistake, or left practice entirely, unable to trust themselves ever again. Unable to forgive themselves.

"And, the bad news." Austin wrinkled his nose. "It'll take at least six weeks for a new hot water tank."

"Six weeks!" She touched her hair. "I'll have to go to town to get shampooed."

It was the longest conversation they'd had in ages and suddenly silence hung in the air, as if he'd recognized it the same time she did.

It felt normal, the way they used to talk. Before everything went wrong.

Their eyes met and held. She recognized the yearning in his gaze and knew that he saw the same in hers.

She saw his chest rise and fall and then, without taking his eyes off hers, he took off his jacket.

"Maybe I can help with that," he said.

Chapter Six

AUSTIN SET THE aluminum tub on the butcher-block table in the kitchen.

"Come here," he said.

Melinda looked at him with caution, but he could feel excitement, thrumming around her like a field.

Fear and temptation.

She stepped up to him and he handed her a towel.

He wanted to unzip that thick hoodie and pull it off. To lift up the shirt beneath, little by little, revealing her creamy torso by inches, until he could see the lower swelling of her breasts.

"Eyes up, big guy."

He jumped. "Sorry." He laughed shakily. "Habit."

He gestured to the chair. "Sit. Put this around your neck. I'd ask you to take off your top, but…"

To his surprise, she slipped out of her hoodie. Underneath, she wore a tank top and it was fantastically obvious that she was braless.

Her breasts looked larger, the nipples pink and straining through the thin fabric.

He adjusted his pants. This was going to be harder than he

thought, pun intended.

"Are you going to wash my hair, Austin?"

She asked it in a smokey voice that might have come straight out of an old western saloon. Low and slow and smooth as honey.

"I am." He helped her lean back and draped her hair into the small tub. "Comfortable?"

"I'm okay."

He scooped a bowlful of water and poured it over her head, being careful not to get any in her eyes.

She groaned, deep in her throat, a sound that sent more blood rushing southward, a sound he'd only heard when she was in his arms, sweaty, sated and limp with pleasure.

He stroked her hair, lifting it and continuing to pour, getting every bit saturated.

Then he squirted a handful of shampoo and began massaging it into her head. He'd never done this before and water splashed onto the table.

A bit of foam dripped onto her throat, then slid slowly toward the neckline of her tank top. She lifted her hand and caught it, without looking. The sight of her fingers, caressing her skin, so close to those rosy nipples...

"Ow!"

The towel beneath her neck slipped, allowing the sharp edge of the tub to bite into her skin.

"Damn, sorry, baby," he said. He tried to tug it up but his soapy hands slipped. He bumped the tub with his elbow and suds splashed onto the table.

Way harder than he expected. In every way.

Suddenly he was aware of Mel, giggling. She put her hand to her mouth, trying to hide it, to let him carry on.

Then she grasped the back of her head and sat up, dragging

the towel with it, laughing freely.

He felt like an idiot. Washing a woman's hair was supposed to be a sensual thing, not a comedy show.

She leaned forward, laughing with her whole body now, and he felt the humor tickle him, too.

"That," she said, between gasps, "was the single best shampoo... I've ever had."

"Liar," he said. But her joy unlocked something inside him and before he knew it, the two of them were bracing themselves against each other, bent over at the waist, howling, while water dripped onto the floor and Mel's still-soapy hair sagged onto her shoulders.

"We're going to have to heat more water," said Mel, when she got her voice back. "I need a rinse."

Her face was flushed and her now mostly-transparent tank top had slipped off one shoulder. Dark hair, red lips, those pink nipples. She looked like a strawberry sundae, with chocolate drizzle and whipped cream on top and yeah, he wanted to eat her up.

"There's enough hot water," he said, taking her hand, "to do this properly."

MEL'S LAUGHTER FADED away as the intensity in Austin's eyes grew. He'd attempted something so sweet, so sensual, so not a guy-thing, and it touched her deeply.

The hilarity at the end lifted the weight of whatever came next and instead, reestablished the friendship.

He was safe now.

He was her Austin again.

"Give me two minutes," he said. "Then meet me in the

bathroom." His eyes drifted down to her chest again and she saw the effort it took for him to turn away.

She ran upstairs and stripped off her damp clothing, nearly tripping in her haste. Whatever he had planned, she was ready for it. They were going to get through this nightmare after all, and come out of it stronger. She wrapped herself in her robe, smoothing over the small rise in her belly.

You were right, Mom. It's time.

Austin met her at the base of the stairs, downstairs again, with his sleeves rolled up, his face shiny with steam.

"Come with me, my lady."

"What are we doing?"

"You'll see."

His voice was harsh but she knew it wasn't anger. He wanted her, and was holding himself back, waiting for a sign from her that it was safe to proceed.

Her throat tightened with gratitude. He understood her better than she thought.

He led her to the little bathroom under the stairs, from which a wonderful smell flowed.

"Austin," she said, and then stopped, looking about her in wonder. "How long was I upstairs?"

"You like?"

She hadn't noticed when she came down that all the pots of water sitting warm on the stove were gone. The old-fashioned clawfoot bathtub was filled to the brim with steaming water, thick with foamy eucalyptus-scented bubbles.

Candles sat on every surface available, and the overhead light was off, its offensive chain pull looped onto a c-hook on the wall.

He pushed the door shut so that they were enclosed in the small candle-lit room together, steam rising around them.

"I thought… you were."

She shivered. He said it lazily, as if thgoing to rinse my hair."

"I will." They had many pleasures to explore and all the time in the world to do it.

"May I take your robe?"

"I'm… not wearing anything underneath."

"I was counting on that."

She let him pull it off her shoulders, suddenly self-conscious. He'd seen her naked a million times before. She shouldn't feel strange about it.

But would he notice?

"Mel," breathed Austin. "You're so beautiful."

She held her arms tightly against her body. In the candlelight, his blue eyes were black and glittery.

"Here." He took her hand and steadied her as she put one foot, then the other into the billowing foam.

"Oh," she moaned, despite herself.

"Good?"

"Amazing."

She gripped the edges and lowered herself gently into the water, letting it flow over her, around her, loosening tight muscles and easing guarded flesh.

He put his head closer to her face. "Lie back. Rinse first in the tub, then, when you're all done, I'll get fresh water for a final rinse."

She let herself slip back under the water, swishing her hair back and forth behind her, like she was a mermaid, like she was floating on the waves and nothing, nothing could take away the pleasure of the moment.

She sat up and waved the water over her chest, washing away the bubbles that covered her, revealing her breasts, shining and dotted with bits of foam. They were tingling, sensitive even to the suds.

"May I," said Austin, his voice hoarse. "May I wash your back?"

"Okay," she said, sitting up.

He scooped a water jug of bathwater and poured it over her head, again keeping it away from her eyes.

She was vividly aware of her nakedness, everything from the waist up clearly visible, slippery and shiny and each breath she took only emphasized the view.

"Mind if I take my shirt off?" asked Austin. "It's hot in here."

"Go ahead."

He peeled it off and there they were, those raw, chiseled muscles.

"Wow," she said, softly.

He dropped the cloth and put his bare hands on her and she let him, revelling in his touch as he ran the warm soap over her back, down to her hips, up her rib cage and then to her breasts, lingering on them, holding them in his palms, fingering her nipples, so exquisitely sensitive she nearly cried out.

She closed her eyes as another jugful of bathwater slid over her body, rinsing away the soap and any remaining shampoo. Then Austin moved her until she was sitting on the edge of the tub, her back to him, her feet still in the water. He dried her off, then wrapped a towel over the front of her, her bare back against his chest, her wet hair on his shoulder.

She shivered again.

"Cold?" he asked.

"No."

He chuckled silently, the movement rumbling from his chest into her.

He took a jar of cold cream and rubbed it into his hands and from there, her arms. He applied it with long, soft strokes, her arms, then her chest above the towel, then her neck. Then more cream, and beneath the towel, over her hips, her thighs, the rough skin on her knees, then up her thighs again and then higher, where she was hot and wet and aching.

Melinda gasped.

"Shh," said Austin.

He touched her, dipping and slipping his fingers, then settling into a rhythm that had her rocking against him, little mewing sounds coming from her throat.

"That's my girl," he whispered in her ear. "That's my sweet wife."

The orgasm burst over her like a firestorm, wilder, higher and more sudden than she'd ever experienced. He held her with one arm as the sensations rocked through her, only releasing her down into the water when her trembling turned to shivering.

She let herself slip beneath the water, her now-chilled and over sensitized skin still rippling with pleasure. She had not been expecting that.

She lifted her hand. "Join me?"

Austin's eyes widened, the hope in them making her heart clutch in her chest. "Really?"

In a flash, he was naked, sliding into the water in front of her. She held him against her chest, hugging him with her knees as she took him in her hands and kissed the back of his neck and murmured her love, the love that had never died, but had only been waiting for the spark that would bring it blazing back to life.

MELINDA STOOD BESIDE the stove, rubbing her hair dry with a towel, the robe slipping off her shoulder, revealing the sweet curve of her breast.

She turned and smiled at him over that bare shoulder.

"Let's go upstairs," she said.

The image of her backlit by the fire, offering that most basic of intimacies, while shadow and light danced around them was the most beautiful thing he'd ever seen.

But her face was shrouded, impossible to read.

Step by step, she led him to their bedroom. At the bedside she turned, letting the silvery moonlight from the window fall over her, making her skin gleam. Her chest rose and fell quickly. A muscle twitched in her jaw and there was a tiny line between her eyebrows.

Was she nervous? Afraid? Of *him*?

He slipped under the covers and waited for her to join him. But she sat on the edge, instead.

"Mel?"

She touched his lips, unsmiling.

"I have to tell you something."

He got up on his elbow and touched her cheek with his palm. "What is it?"

"It's good news."

She smiled, but her lips twisted as if she wasn't certain.

This time she let him pull her under the covers. He held her tight against his chest.

"Is it about work?"

She hadn't said much about the incident that happened in her last week at Jackson Park.

What if she'd found a better position in a newer hospital or a nicer city?

His heart felt like a stone in his chest.

"It's not my job."

But now, having considered the worst, he found himself

clutching her to him even tighter, afraid that he'd misread everything about this past evening.

"Austin," she said, holding his hand over her belly. "Look."

He glanced down. Had she put on weight? She'd always been slender. So her belly wasn't as flat as it had been. He didn't care.

He looked up. "You look great, Mel."

Her lips still trembled, but this time her smile lit up the room.

"Austin," she said. "I'm pregnant."

It was so far from his fears and expectations that he didn't understand the word. It didn't make sense.

That was her job, working with pregnant women.

They couldn't have a baby. They'd tried and tried. They'd had their hopes up twice, only to have them dashed.

"Did you hear me?"

"Pregnant," he said.

By the time they stopped hoping, sex had become an assignment governed by calendars and clocks.

No fun. No joy. Mel was a generous woman, but Austin knew that in the last year, sex had been a chore, an obligation, a task to cross off her list.

"It's not like I was keeping it from you," she said, holding his hand as if she expected him to push her away. Her words tumbled out too quickly, he was having trouble processing them.

"I didn't even know, not until the night of the… incident. I mean, I'd been feeling lousy, but with all the stress and not sleeping, it never occurred to me."

"Pregnant?" he said, as the cogs started to fit.

He threw back the covers and got to his feet, suddenly hot. He stood at the window, relishing the chill that came off the pane. Wind whipped outside, casting icy shards against the glass.

Was he happy? He was supposed to be happy, wasn't he?

Was Melinda happy?

She looked nervous. Desperate, almost. He wanted to give her the right response, but he had no idea what it was.

"Remember that night when you came home and told me you couldn't save Sweet and Morgan? It was damage control only and you said we stood to lose everything?"

"I remember." He didn't want to talk about that. They'd made love that night, if you could call it that. He'd been so angry and humiliated he feared after that he might have hurt her. She assured him that he hadn't, but he was still ashamed of using her body as a refuge, without giving anything in return.

"It must have been that night. It was the only time." She took a shaky breath. "Things got worse for you, crazy with lawyers and the banks and your clients, then selling the house, then your parents offered you the farm, then it was packing, and I was working so much, opposite shifts, we hardly saw each other-"

"I remember, Mel," he repeated. "I was there."

She was sniffing back tears and he knew he should go to her, offer comfort, but he couldn't.

"That night at the hospital." The words were almost inaudible.

A husband provides.

The whole thing was the epitome of failure, culminating in…he forced himself to say it.

"When you called me and I didn't answer." He shoved off the window and turned to face her. "God, Mel, why are we doing this? Why are you torturing yourself? And me? Can't we just let it go?"

She's pregnant, he reminded himself. That's the point here.

"I have to tell you everything. That night at the hospital, it was… worse than I told you."

"I saw the bruises."

He'd seen her name come up on his phone, but he couldn't bear to answer. He'd just handed the house keys over to the agent and he'd been sitting in his truck, the trade-in he'd gotten for his BMW 7 series.

"I hit my head when I fell. I thought I was fine. But that's the reason I… dropped… that baby. I passed out in the delivery room, just as the shoulders emerged."

He'd had, literally, nowhere to go and it was late and his wife had just gone on shift. So he sat in his truck while his wife was on a gurney, semi-conscious.

Austin knew it was cold in the room, but he felt like he was burning from the inside out, like he might explode. With everything he had, he forced himself to stand still.

"They did a pregnancy test in the ER. That's how I found out."

Melinda's voice was steady now. Like she was reporting facts for an article.

"You should have told me."

"You should have answered your phone."

"Instead, you came to the motel the next morning, pretended everything was okay and somehow forgot to mention that you were carrying my child."

"You weren't even at the motel when I got there, Oz. Should I have texted you with the news?"

"You were in the shower when I got in, Mel. I saw the bruises. I saw how upset you were."

"That's right!"

She got on her knees on the bed, right up in his face. "And you felt so horrible about it, you could hardly look at me! We'd drifted so far apart, you and I. Our life was being torn away from us while you ran around putting out fires, telling everyone it was a minor setback. I know you were suffering, but you had to put on a brave face, keep spinning those plates in the air, even as they crashed around you. That's why I went to my mom's. I couldn't do it any longer."

Austin walked naked to the window.

Then, without turning, he spoke.

"Is that what you thought of me, Melinda? That I wouldn't be able to handle the news that my wife, who was already carrying me financially, was also carrying our child? That I had to be protected from the news? That I wouldn't celebrate a child, no matter the circumstances?"

He lowered his hand into his face and to his horror, he heard a sob escape his throat.

Melinda leaped off the bed and stood next to him, holding him, stroking him.

"I was wrong, Oz, I'm so sorry."

He opened his arms and she wrapped herself in them, and their tears mingled as finally, finally, the barriers came down.

Chapter Seven

MELINDA AWOKE TO a strange sensation. Even after several nights together, it still took her a moment to realize that she was in bed, with her husband, and he had his hand on her belly.

After the emotional catharsis, Austin had become incredibly tender toward her. She sensed it would be some time before he got over the pain of her not telling him, not going with him to the farm, and taking refuge with her mom.

His hand moved and she felt her body light up. She nudged her pelvis toward him and instantly he responded, dipping his fingers beneath the lace of her panties.

They were making up for lost time, she thought, as his big body covered hers and they came together again in a flurry of passion.

"Stay here," said Austin, once he'd gotten his breath back. "I'm bringing you breakfast in bed."

"Oz," she complained. "You don't have to do that."

But she knew he would anyway and secretly, she was delighted.

He was solicitous to the point of irritation, not letting her pick up anything heavier than a spoon, wrapping her up like a mummy before she so much as stepped out on the porch and feeding her constantly.

She knew now that part of her misery and malaise during their last chaotic weeks in Chicago were normal first trimester ailments. With that behind them, and their future looking, if not prosperous then at least secure, her spirits were higher than they'd been in months.

She threw back the covers and went downstairs to eat with her husband in the kitchen. They had lots to do and she'd wasted enough time.

THEY STOOD IN line at the ticket booth of Marietta's only theater. It was date night, and his girl had requested dinner and a movie.

Actually, Mel had changed her mind about the dinner, opting for fast food instead, probably for the sake of their budget.

"Two for the sappy romance," he said to the girl at the ticket counter.

If a Nicholas Sparks movie is what she wanted, that's what she'd get. With her hormones all over the map, he was willing to do what he could to keep them on the up-side.

Actually, the transformation in Melinda since telling him of her pregnancy was astounding.

Cliche or not, she was actually glowing. Her energy was back, her eyes sparkled again, she smiled easily and often.

Though he still struggled with the fact that she hadn't trusted him, that she had almost given up on them, he understood better how she'd arrived at that place.

It hadn't been about the house or the cars or everything they'd lost. It's that he'd stopped talking to her. Without even knowing it, he'd shut her out. No wonder she'd lost faith.

It was only fair that he shoulder the blame.

And he wasn't really complaining. They were together again, emotionally and physically. And the sex? It was out of this world. She was a wild thing, insatiable, responding quickly to his touch, uninhibited and generous with him.

Even thinking about it now had him aroused.

"Do I know how to show a girl a good time, or what?"

He put his arm over his wife's shoulders as the lights went out in the theater.

"You always did," said Melinda. "You still do."

They passed the snack counter where the line-up had trickled to a few people.

"Popcorn?" she said.

"You just downed a cheeseburger, a milkshake, all your fries and half of mine. How do you still have room for popcorn?"

She shrugged. "I'm eating for two."

"Hey!" said the clerk, "you're the guy from the hardware store."

"Hey, Leda," he said, recognizing her as the pregnant girl he'd mentioned to Melinda. "You work here."

She made a gun with her forefinger and thumb. "Nothing gets past you. Is this your wife?"

"Hi, I'm Melinda." She extended her hand over the counter and Austin saw the light he associated with baby talk come into her eyes.

"You really are pretty!"

Mel blushed and shot him a quick glance. "Aw, he says that about all his wives. Should you be on your feet this late in your pregnancy?"

Leda snorted. "In a perfect world. What can I get you?"

They ordered their snacks and after they paid, Mel surprised him by hanging back. "Leda," she said, "would you like to come out to the farm one of these days? I'm jarring honey for the open house and I could use a hand. Payment is in honey only, I'm afraid." She paused and he saw her gather her courage. "If you want, you can pick my brain. Labor and delivery is my thing, after all."

"Deal!" said Leda. "I can use all the advice I can get!"

Mel's face widened into a smile.

"Good," she said.

THE OPEN HOUSE was quickly approaching. Snow piled up in big, fluffy layers and the temperatures continued to drop. Austin pulled his boots on, happy to discover that they were warm and dry, thanks to Bessie.

The furnace was working now – thankfully, it hadn't required extensive work and nothing was living in the ducts – but Melinda had made peace with the big black stove, and they'd grown accustomed to the warmth of the fire, using the forced air only as a back-up.

They'd been less fortunate with the hot water tank and there were potentially more plumbing problems associated with that, so they continued heating water on top of the wood stove.

Sharing a bath to conserve water was a hardship Austin was happy to endure, he thought as he tromped out through the snow to the honey hut.

They were finally, he hoped, adjusting. The dissolution of Sweet and Morgan still stung, badly, and he still hadn't come up with a good answer to the inevitable questions when he met the local people. What brought you to Marietta? Are you rebuilding the honey farm? How does your wife like country living?

He couldn't quite get a bead on that last question. Melinda had taken on her projects with a vengeance. She'd set aside repairing that purple couch until later. Preparing the honey for the open house was her main priority. But cooking and canning vast quantities of fruit preserves was the biggest surprise. He had no idea this was in her arsenal of skills. The fact that she enjoyed it was the best part.

He pulled the door open and kicked it gently to knock off some ice.

She was still restless at night though. He worried that she missed the bustle of the city, though she insisted she didn't. The other day, he'd been shocked to see her releasing a mouse outside, into the woodpile. She didn't know he was there, and he was about to comment but when she stood up, he saw that she was crying. He let her go back into the house without seeing him and didn't mention it, but his heart ached that he'd brought his pregnant wife to a strange place with so few basic comforts.

Austin shook the fresh snow off his jacket and went inside, focusing on his current task of re-insulating the hive that would be used in the open house. He should have done it days ago; without protection from the cold and wind, the bees might not make it through the winter. But with everything else going on, he'd forgotten.

He loosened his hood around his face. It was freezing. He couldn't wait to get back to the house and warm his hands by the fire.

The display hive box was attached to the outside of the structure, the entrance tube running up to the roof, well out of human reach. But the wall where it attached had been cut open and replaced with a glass panel, so that on the inside, viewers could watch the colony work and even identify the queen, all from within the shed, without disturbing the bees.

They weren't very active in winter, but it was still interesting to the uninitiated.

Chad had impressed how important this was as part of their open house tour. Fun and educational, that's what got parents out in droves.

Austin found it fascinating, himself. Since they wouldn't be actively working with the hives until spring, it gave him a chance to observe a working colony from close up, without risk.

The humming sound was quieter than it had been. The bees were moving sluggishly and he could see frost at the edges of the glass.

Crap. They were too cold.

Quickly he ran to the equipment shed and grabbed the roll of tar paper that Chad had shown him. They were still alive, that was something. He cut the pieces to size, then stapled them over each exposed side of the box, making sure to keep the entrance free. The black paper would not only protect the colony from cold winds, but it would absorb enough heat from the sun to keep them alive through to spring.

He went back inside the shed to take a closer look at the queen. He found her, closely guarded by her subjects, fanning the air around her. She looked okay, but would he know if she was suffering? Or would he miss the signs?

She was the life of the hive, the raison d'être for every single drop of honey, every drone, every worker.

It was all about keeping the queen alive.

Winter, he thought. We're all just trying to make it through the winter.

"I'm sorry," he whispered to the queen. "Give me another chance."

AUSTIN WAS STILL outside doing chores when a truck bounced onto the yard. It was the contractor. The back of his truck was loaded with what, she couldn't tell, since it was covered by tarp.

She waved from the porch, noting that he wasn't alone.

"I brought my fiancee," said Logan, striding toward her. "Melinda Sweet, meet Samara Davis. Sam, Melinda. Austin said you might be ready for some company."

"Mama," said the little girl who followed Samara out of the truck, "I wanna go with Mr. S."

"That's my daughter, Jade," said Samara. "And her dog. Bob's a girl and no, I don't know why. Jade named her."

"Mama!"

Mel noticed that she spoke without making eye contact.

"Logan?" said Samara.

"It's fine with me." He swung the little girl up onto his shoulders. "Come on, Chipmunk. Come on, Bob."

"What a lovely family," said Melinda, watching them trudge through the snow. The dog pranced around and wagged her tail madly, but kept looking up at the girl.

"We're not-" began Samara. Then she shook her head and started over. "Thank you. I think we will be. I'm still getting used to it. We haven't set a date or anything. And apparently I babble when I'm nervous."

Mel laughed and opened the door wider. "Please, come in where it's warm."

"Sorry to drop by unannounced," said Samara, shedding her coat and boots, "but when Logan told me you were transplants from Chicago, I knew I had to meet you. I came from New York City in September. It's a big adjustment but trust me, if I can do it, anyone can."

Melinda put the kettle on for tea.

"We're only here until spring," she told Samara.

Samara and her daughter had beautiful olive skin and dark hair, but Jade had an Asian cast to her features that her mother didn't. Was she adopted?

She and Austin had discussed adoption, but his family put a lot of value on blood relations. And now of course, they didn't need to.

She hugged her belly, holding her precious secret close.

"Oh. Well, too bad for us then," said Samara. "Logan didn't mention that."

"Austin might not have told him," Mel explained, surprised at the disappointment on Samara's face. "His family owns the property and they'd rather we stayed. We're here to fix the place up for resale."

Samara looked around her. "Really? You don't want to stay? It's so pretty out here. I love these old homes. That's what drew me to the area, a great real estate deal on a refurbished heritage house. Yours is just as nice as mine, or will be, once you're finished with it."

Suddenly Melinda envied the air of settledness that Samara wore about her. She'd moved here, deliberately, and she was staying put. Finding a home and new love, building a life here, raising her daughter here.

Maybe Mel would feel differently about Sweet Montana if it hadn't been thrust upon them. If they hadn't been so desperate that they had to accept it.

"What did you do in Chicago?" asked Samara.

Melinda opened her mouth to give a vague non-answer, but she was tired of dancing around the truth. It was what it was.

"My husband was a financial planner."

"Oh," said Samara. It was the sound of sympathy. Everyone

knew someone who'd lost all their investments when the economy tanked.

"Yeah." She sighed heavily. "His company crashed. We lost our house, everything. I'm not sure where we would have gone, if Austin's parents hadn't offered us this place."

She poured tea into the cups and handed one to her guest, surprised to see that her hands were rock steady.

"And you?"

Surprisingly, Melinda found she welcomed Samara's gentle probing. She hadn't spoken about her job to anyone since their arrival. Hadn't really spoken to anyone, period.

"Senior charge nurse at Jackson Park, maternity," she said. "It's an inner city hospital. Lots of high-risk births."

"How exciting."

But Mel caught the slight shudder that ran through the woman.

"Not a fan of hospitals, I take it?"

"It shows, huh?" Samara grimaced. "I've got some, um, negative associations I'm working through. Are you going to work at the Marietta hospital while you're here?"

"No job openings," said Melinda. Small community hospitals didn't have much turnover, certainly not in maternity. And certainly not for someone at her level.

She went to the counter where a sheet of rosemary shortbread was cooling, and slid some onto a plate.

"Do you miss it?"

"Of course," she said, automatically. But something about the candid way Samara asked the question caught Mel off guard. *Did* she miss it? She'd worked her tail off earning that position. She loved her job. Lived for it. It defined her.

And she was good at it.

Usually.

Mel took her time arranging the cookies. "I was pretty burned out at the end, though. There was… an incident…"

She cut herself off then, shocked at saying so much to someone she'd just met. And now that she was going to have a child of her own, did she even want such a high-pressure job?

Samara made another soft sound, as if she understood what Mel couldn't bring herself to say, in essence, if not in fact. It made Mel's chest hurt. It made her want to spill everything, pour all her feelings onto the table so she could pull them apart and order them and then put them away, finally.

But she also knew that this was not the time or place. Or the person.

"You don't have to say anything more," said Samara, taking a piece of shortbread. "It's okay. You're holding back from making friends, so it won't hurt when you have to leave."

Melinda raised her eyebrows at the frank statement.

"Let me just say this." Samara leaned forward, her dark hair falling off her shoulder. "However you got here, or when you're leaving, you're here now. This place can change your life, but you have to let it. I didn't want to let anyone in but I couldn't resist. I was a little… crazy, actually. Long story. Long, ugly story."

Couldn't be any longer or uglier than her own, thought Mel.

"But everyone was so warm and welcoming. I wasn't allowed to wallow. Now I'm paying it forward. For however long you're here, I hope we can be friends. Okay?"

Melinda sensed that, if she'd had a sister, she might be someone like Samara.

"What the heck," she told Samara. "At the risk of overshare…"

Samara leaned closer, her expression serious. "I wasn't trying to pressure you."

"I know. But I think it might do me some good."

"Then I'm listening."

Melinda held the warm mug with both hands, but it didn't penetrate the chill.

"It was my last week of work. A patient came in, high on PCP, and in labor. I was getting her admitted when she flipped out and assaulted me."

She let go of the mug and rubbed her thigh. She could still feel the gouge of the metal gurney. "We got her under control and in restraints but she was crowning before we knew it. I was all ready to catch that baby…"

She trailed off. Funny how talking to a complete stranger was sometimes easier than talking to those who knew you intimately.

"I almost got him. I felt him, the slippery heat of a newborn on my gloved hands. Then I passed out."

"Oh, Melinda."

No need for details. Not now.

"Thank goodness my co-worker caught the kid. It could have been a tragedy."

Samara reached across the table and put her hand on Mel's arm. "I'm so sorry. That sounds horrific. Are you okay now?"

Another good question. She and Austin were recovering, she thought, getting their marriage back on track. But she was worried about Austin, about the upcoming open house, about what would happen in spring. This was more than she'd spoken about the incident to anyone since it had happened.

She got up, suddenly embarrassed. She wasn't used to being listened to like that. It was dangerous. She should find something else besides cookies.

"Wow. Sorry about that," she said, rummaging through the one functional cupboard. "I got carried away."

"Not at all." Samara took a sip of tea. "Everyone has a history. I consider it an honor that you trusted me with it. Now, let's change the subject. Tell me what you're cooking in that pot that smells so heavenly."

They exchanged a glance, and Mel took the lifeline Samara offered. For the next hour, she showed off the jellies she'd made for the open house. Though she hadn't done it since her grandmother had passed away, and she was delighted to find that her hands easily recalled the various tasks. And thrilled with Samara's response.

"You'll have to give me the recipe," said Samara, just as the sound of stomping interrupted them.

The men were dumping equipment and supplies onto the porch and within minutes, they heard the sounds of sawing and hammering.

The door opened and Jade came in, holding her ears.

"Mama!"

"I know, honey." Samara jumped up to help her shed her outdoor clothes, and wiped down the dog.

"Don't worry about the floor," said Mel with a laugh. "I think that goes without saying."

Samara grabbed the towel by the door and mopped up anyway.

"Logan can't work on this if it's wet. You won't believe what this will look like once he's done with it. You should see mine."

She set her daughter onto the moss-green sofa and gave her a box of cards.

"Bob is my dog," said the girl suddenly, to no one in particular. "She's a girl dog. She's part Labrador retriever, part Border collie and part luck of the draw. Bob is my dog."

Ah, thought Mel. The deliberate cadence of Jade's speech, plus the subtle behavioral tics suggested a spot on the autism spectrum. Her opinion of Samara went up another notch.

"I'm pleased to meet you both." She didn't approach Jade, but gestured to Bob, the dog. "She's welcome to sit on the couch with you, if you'd like."

The dog leaped up before the words were barely out, curled up next to Jade and put her head in the girl's lap.

By the time the men were finished for the day, Mel felt as if she and Samara had known each other forever. And as she waved goodbye from the porch, with Austin's arm around her, she wondered, is this really what it could be like?

AUSTIN SMASHED HIS hammer against the rusted nails holding the pathetic metal sign on the gate. But the whole thing was fused onto the wood like a skin graft.

He had a new sign ready and waiting, but this darn thing had to come off first.

He gave it another vicious blow, then stood back and wiped his brow with the back of his gloved hand.

Mel had enjoyed her visit with Samara. Her posture had softened and the tightness around her mouth had relaxed. But he sensed it had been a reminder of her newness here. Her strangeness.

She was working hard to do what needed to be done, but not for an instant did she forget about her true goal: to return to her Real Life and the job she loved.

For his part, he didn't miss Sweet and Morgan. He missed Sean, but not the work, the constant hand-holding of worried clients. He was more relaxed than he'd been in years. The physical work agreed with him. True, he'd almost killed one colony of bees already, but he was learning. He was determined to do a good job.

And Mel was cooking and baking like a fiend, to have inventory to sell at the open house. She seemed to enjoy it, but was it real?

And the real question on his mind: what if, even come spring, they still couldn't afford to leave? They couldn't list the farm until it was ready to show, and even once they'd listed, it could take months to find a buyer.

If they found one at all at the price they needed.

What if they had to stay? Would she?

He gave the sign one last kick and to his surprise, it popped free, both nails breaking off at the head, leaving the spikes buried in the wood.

If Melinda found a good job, somewhere they could afford to live, they might be able to swing it. But she was due in May and surely she wanted some time with the baby?

He looked at the rickety, rusted sign, lying on the frozen soil, and wondered if his grandfather might want it. He was a sentimental old man.

Quickly, he drilled holes and fixed the new welcome sign to the gate. While it stayed true to the original in spirit, Austin had updated the font and brightened the colors. He stood back to admire his work.

Perfect. This was the welcome he wanted to give visitors to Sweet Montana Farms.

As he stooped to gather his tools, movement by the goat barn caught his eye. Melinda was outside by herself again, her dark hair contrasting with the brilliance of the fresh snow. She was carrying a pan. He saw her crouch down, and to his surprise, a cat slunk out from behind the shed. A moth-eaten tabby with notched ears. Then another one joined them, this one grey and fluffy like a dust mop.

He didn't even know there were cats out there.

While he watched, the cats approached the pan, then settled themselves at the edge, keeping an eye on her but not too worried. She reached out to the grey one. It flinched away, but then allowed her to stroke it.

Such a big heart she had. Some nurses became hardened after years of witnessing so much hardship and pain, but not her.

When the pan was empty, she picked it up and went back into the house, her head down, her shoulders hunched.

He picked up his tools and tromped back through the snow. If she wanted to go back to work after the baby came, they'd go wherever her job led.

And what would that mean for him?

Chapter Eight

THE CHRISTMAS SCENES were set up in various spots around the yard and Austin wanted her opinion. Melinda walked ahead of him, letting the bright sunshine pour over her face, filling her lungs with the fresh, cold air.

She didn't know cold had a smell.

"Tacky, huh?"

Santa had rust spots on his bowlful of jelly. The nativity scene was a ragtag affair with characters and props thrown together from several incomplete sets, as evidenced by the lamb being larger than the donkey.

Electrical cords ran up and down the sheds, criss-crossing the yard like scars from a flogging.

"It will be lovely at night," she said.

"So ugly it's charming?"

She turned to him, grinning. "You should put that on the flyers!"

It felt so good to be joking with him again. She linked her arm through his as they surveyed the property.

"Amazing, isn't it?" Austin lifted his face to the sky. "How long has it been since you smelled air like this? It's so fresh, it crackles. It's good for you. Good for the baby."

A lot better than all those nights under fluorescents.

"It's been awhile."

He took her hand. "Come on. Let's see what's what."

Melinda let the country air in her lungs and felt the muscles in her chest let go a little, as if she'd opened the top button of a too-tight shirt. She imagined the air slipping into the alveoli of her lungs, the way a drop of blue food coloring swirls into a glass of clear water, first a shock of contrast, then gradual fading, the change subtle but irreversible.

"Look," said Austin, pointing to the sky.

A group of Canada geese, black and white against the grey sky, way late in their journey. As they watched, their pattern shifted, then settled back into the typical vee pattern.

"Did you see that?" he said. "They just changed leaders."

They took turns battling the wind resistance, then falling back to rest in the wake of the other birds, calling out to each other as they flew, to ensure they stayed together, mile after endless mile.

"Smart birds," she said.

"It would make a great painting," said Austin, examining the house from the perspective of the yard. He tapped his mouth with his gloved fingers. "We could stand in front of it, all pinched and stern. Our American Gothic winter."

"Our American Horror Story winter, you mean."

He bumped against her as they walked, the kind of casual nudge couples did without thinking about it.

"Or," he thought for a moment, "How the West was Won?"

She sniffed. "A Million Ways to Die in the West."

"Girl, that's just mean. I know: Mel and Oz's Excellent Adventure."

At the end of the fence line she turned and spread her arms.

"Nope. I've got it. Dumb and Dumber on the farm!"

With an elaborate bow, he conceded. "I grant you the win. However, let us not speak such words outside the sanctity of our twosome."

He lifted his face to the sky and bellowed. "Beware, the first man who dares speak such ignominious words against my beloved. I shall not suffer him to live!"

"Oz, stop it!" Laughing, she balled her fist for a gentle punch, but he evaded her easily.

"Do you fear for the good name of Sweet in this, our new land?"

"I think your countrymen will put you on a watch list, if that's what you mean. Let's keep our crazy to a minimum, okay?"

"As you wish, my queen."

She fell silent, the game over. He had such high hopes for this open house. It was Austin's gift, finding the good in any situation, lifting the spirits of those around him, bringing out the best in them. But it made it all that much worse then to see his rugged, ever-so-handsome face slack with sorrow and disappointment.

They were tromping across the frosty grass from the furthest shed when the sound of an engine broke the silence between them.

Chad's snowmobile was coming their way, rumbling and tumbling over the rough pasture on the other side of the barbed-wire fence, the rider's leg muscles visible through his jeans as he stood up for the worst bumps.

"Hey, neighbors," he called. "I heard you yelling. Everything okay?"

"I told you." Melinda aimed another punch at Austin and this time he caught her arm and twirled her so she was tucked up against him.

"We're fine," called Austin. "Just admiring our work."

The neighbor dismounted his machine and instead of using the gate, spread the barbed wires and stepped through, like this was his farm instead of Austin's.

As if they were the visitors.

He lifted his hat at Melinda and flashed a dazzling smile. "Ma'am."

A bell may as well have tinkled. The man could do toothpaste commercials, if he didn't already. Again, she saw what every woman saw and was untouched.

Aside from the hat, her husband was every bit as tall and gorgeous as the cowboy, thought Melinda. If she wasn't mistaken, Austin's chest and shoulders were a little higher than they were a moment ago and she sensed the men exchanging measure, a subtle test of where the power lay.

"Need anything?"

Austin's arms tightened. "We're good."

Melinda's heart went out to him. No matter how he hid it, his pride was still deeply damaged from the failure of Sweet and Morgan Financial Services.

"Turns out we're more than house sitters with hammers," said Mel. "Especially Austin. You should see what he's done in the house. The goats adore him. And you should hear him talk about bees."

Chad let out a rolling laugh.

Austin put his arm around her shoulders and gave her a kiss on the cheek. "Thanks, honey."

Her husband's gestures were the modern equivalent of hair-dragging her to his cave, and stopping to pee on the corner once there. While the feminist in her cried foul, she couldn't deny the primal pleasure of being claimed. Chad straightened up and put his gloves back on.

"Beekeeping is all about the queen," said Chad. He winked at Austin. "No wonder you're a natural."

MELINDA SHOVED THE scraper against the stubborn paint. The built-in shelves in the sunroom weren't ugly structurally but mud-brown paint?

Given what it was covering though, perhaps it had been. She could count the layers, like tree rings. There was a yellow phase, a white phase, an unfortunate peach phase and finally, a sweet blue, the kind you'd put in a baby's room.

Maybe this had been a playroom.

She imagined a jabbering toddler, slapping away at his blocks, while his mother watched from the kitchen as she worked.

Maybe it would be again.

The scraper dug in hard and a huge, satisfying peel came off. This was barely a house, let alone a home. The stipend from Austin's parents was enough to live on, and the renovation budget gave them leeway with the house, but it was hardly a long-term plan.

Hardly the way to start family life.

"Hey," said Austin, poking his head through the doorway.

She jumped, nearly dropping the scraper. "You nearly gave me a heart attack."

His cheeks were red from the cold but his eyes were sparkling.

"Found a surprise in the goat pen. Thought you might want to come see."

She gestured to the shelves. "Maybe later. I want to finish

this."

"I thought you might say that."

He came fully into the room. In his arms was a tiny brown and white creature with long, flicking ears and hooves so fresh and clean they looked like they were made of wax.

"Maa-aaa," it said.

Her heart melted and she reached for it.

"He's pretty new," said Austin. "Seems like the wrong time of year. But you know babies."

"They come when they come," she murmured.

Babies might come as a surprise, she always said. But never an accident.

She stroked the tiny nose. It was the cutest thing she'd ever seen in her life.

Or maybe that was the hormones speaking.

Anticipation washed over her. They were having a baby. Her chest spasmed. She'd started crying yesterday when she heard the baby's heartbeat through her stethoscope, while Austin was outside. She hadn't even known how worried she'd been.

Then she cried because their child would be delivered here, in Marietta's little hospital and would be coming home to… this.

"He needs a name."

"Oh, I couldn't." Mel put her finger to the kid's mouth and immediately it latched on, suckling enthusiastically, bumping her hand with his bony little head. "How about Mocha?"

"Mocha it is," said Austin.

He'd reluctantly agreed not to tell his parents about the baby yet. They were desperate for a grandchild. Once they knew, the pressure to fall in with Bill Sweet's plans would intensify.

Plus, it bothered her that they only seemed to care about her as their son's accessory. Austin's wife, vessel for the coveted next generation. Like anyone with a functioning uterus would do.

She pulled her finger free. "Mocha is hungry and I'll bet his mama is none too pleased that you took him away."

"He's got a twin, so I think mama's fine. You should come out and see them."

He wanted so badly for her to share in his enjoyment but she held back. They weren't staying. Getting attached would only make it hurt when they left.

And they were still leaving, right?

"I don't have time." She pointed to the area that would be their retail showcase at the open house. "See that grain? Once I get it sanded and varnished, those little jars will glow against that background."

Austin smiled. "Well, look who's gotten the refinishing bug."

"Blame Logan. Or rather, blame Samara."

"I thought you might hit it off." The same eagerness bloomed all over Austin's face again, making her wary.

"She's lovely."

"Logan said she had a rough landing here, too. Lost her husband not long before moving."

So that was the long, ugly story Samara had alluded to. She'd certainly gotten an idyllic ending, hadn't she? A nice widow who moved to a small town to restart her life, found her soulmate and was now living happily ever after.

She began scraping at a fresh spot.

"They seem very happy," she said.

"How about us?"

Melinda lifted her head in surprise. A full frontal, that wasn't like him. He nuzzled the baby goat while awaiting her response.

"You've worked so hard to make it easier for me here, and I

appreciate it." She stood up and wiped her hands, wincing at the pinch in her low back. "We're good now, Oz. Aren't we?"

He didn't respond.

"Aren't we?"

A chunk of hair fell over her eye. She shoved it back. She'd been working non-stop, they both had. They were tired and irritable. The honey was ready for sale. She'd cooked up so many pots of jam, jelly, chutney, relish and salsa she ran out of jars. She'd baked batch after batch of cookies, despite the temperamental kitchen oven. She'd decorated the inside of the house to match the outside.

What more did he want from her.

"I'm good," he said quietly. "I'm asking about *you*."

"Oh." She looked down at the floor, covered with debris, and started sweeping it up. What was there to say? She was eating again, sleeping beside him at night, mostly. She'd learned to work with Bessie, to burn whatever trash they could and bury kitchen scraps in the compost heap.

He was such a good sport, her Oz. He rolled with things. It's who he was.

But they couldn't live like this forever. Even if they wanted to stay, the little hospital in Marietta had no openings for a maternity nurse.

Each day, time and money slipped by and the pressure to find a job, a decent one that could support them – and a baby – ratcheted higher.

And always, underneath that thought trailed the memory of her hands clutching and missing that slippery little body.

She shook off the thought and set the broom carefully in the corner.

"Say what you mean, Melinda."

The challenge lay there between them, pulsing, as the words

tumbled inside of her. Come spring, they'd be gone. To where, or with what money, or what job, she didn't know.

It would be up to her to support them, to pay back Austin's parents and she wasn't even sure she could do it anymore.

Again Melinda pushed at the hair escaping from her ponytail. She took a deep breath and looked him hard in the eye. "I'm worried, Oz. I think you'd like to stay here permanently. I'm not sure I can do that."

AUSTIN LOOKED AROUND the honey shed at the posters he'd put up, the visual aids, the cute stuffed bees that would go home with some lucky kids when it was all over.

As long as people actually came out. Chad assured him it would be well-attended, but what if all this work was for nothing?

So much uncertainty in their lives. Until their talk, he hadn't realized how much anxiety Mel carried. It killed him to hear it. She didn't need the stress now, not in her condition.

He kicked at a bale of straw. Of course his dad hoped the Sweet heritage would be carried on for another generation. Austin had explained, again, that as soon as they found new jobs, somewhere they could afford the rent, they were gone.

His dad had sputtered with outrage at the news – though it wasn't news – and Austin had felt again that twist of humiliation. Mel would be the deciding factor. She still had a viable career.

Or did she want to stay home with the baby?

He snorted. Stay home where? Here? While they lived on handouts from his parents?

No wonder she was stressed.

He took a deep breath and forced his mind to calm. Whatever lay ahead, this was their present. The past was painful, the future unknown; only now was certain and he intended to grab whatever joy he could from it.

What was Christmas for, if not joy?

And they had the most special gift of all to celebrate.

But first, the open house.

On that note, he took a moment to review the prep work they'd done.

The shed with the decorations stood empty now; everything inside had found a place, the lights, the blinking candy canes, the multitude of colored balls that hung from every tree within sight.

A metal Santa complete with sleigh and eight reindeer pranced next to the level driveway with its fresh load of gravel.

A large frame in the shape of a star stood on the roof, a nativity scene was set up in front of the goat barn and the front of the honey shed was covered with twinkling icicle lights. They left the back side dark, so as not to disturb the bees.

In the harsh light of day and all the white, it still looked cluttered and even trashy. But when night fell and the only backdrop was the starlit sky, it was magical.

"Hey," called Chad, waving from the fence. They'd installed a gate between the two farms, big enough for the tractor that would be hauling the sleigh to pass. He'd made a nice hard track over the snow with his ATV.

He pulled the gate shut behind him. "Ready for your crash course in apiary lore?"

Chad was in charge of sleigh rides; Mel would be in the house, serving cider and selling her fancy jars; the pregnant girl, Leda, had begged to help, so she was in charge of watching the goat pen, to make sure the kids weren't too rough on the animals, and vice versa.

Austin's job was talking about bees. And, more importantly, answering questions.

"I still think I should do the sleigh rides," he responded.

"And you've driven a tractor how often?" asked Chad.

"That hurts, man." He thumped himself in the chest. "Right here."

He followed Chad through the door of the honey shed, to the display box and stopped at the workbench.

"A craft accident?"

It was the broken tree ornament that Mel treasured, the one that had belonged to her grandmother. He'd found it amongst their own Christmas decorations.

"I thought I'd try to fix it. I haven't told her. In case I can't."

"Good luck with that," said Chad. Then he turned to the buzzing pane of glass. "Now, when it comes to bee talks, these guys will do most of your work for you."

Austin covered the pieces of the ornament and sent up a silent prayer of thanks that the hive hadn't died of exposure at his hands.

Chad proceeded to explain how to point out the distinguishing characteristics of the different bees, how to help kids count egg cells, and what parasites and illness the bees were prone to. How to identify the queen, her unique role in the colony, and their constant, ongoing drive to make honey.

Most kids barely knew where honey came from, let alone that the colony needed it to survive. Honey farmers had to know how much they could harvest. If they took too much, the bees would have to be fed to keep them from starving before spring.

That was a concept Austin knew all too well.

He and Sean had built up a great thing with Sweet and Morgan. Then, in hopes of increasing their returns, they'd overreached, chosen the wrong mutual fund. Put too many eggs in one basket.

"There's gonna be a quiz, you know." Chad propped a foot up on an old paint can.

"I'm listening. The queen. You were telling me about how the colony cares for her."

"That's right. She's the heart and soul of the colony.

He scrambled to remember what else Chad had told him.

"Every year the queen gets replaced."

"Might get two years, with a mild winter."

"What about the rest of them? Do I have to replace them, too?"

"Nah. It's a continuously renewing thing, a colony. The queen lays eggs, that's her only job, to make more bees. When one dies, it gets wrapped up and taken out."

"Like trash. Rough life."

"Bees are very meticulous creatures. Death and decay is counterproductive to their purpose, so they deal with it. Very efficiently, I might add."

Austin thought about spring, how their child would be born just as the colony came alive again. Mocha would be joined by other baby goats; the garden would be sprouting with all manner of things. The barn cats would have kittens. Birds and bees and flowers and trees, all a wild mess of procreation.

Every living thing wants to survive, to thrive, to create more life, to move on, keeping their tiny part in the wheel of life moving.

Mel was right. He would be sorry to say goodbye to it all.

THEY COULDN'T HAVE asked for more perfect weather for their grand opening of A Sweet Montana Christmas Open House.

The air was filled with the scent of pine and fir sap, from the boughs they'd trimmed and put up over the doorways.

The full moon had passed, leaving the night sky a black counterpane dotted with stars. Melinda couldn't remember ever seeing stars like this in Chicago. Too much light pollution. Plus, she was usually going on shift, or coming off shift, neither situation conducive to star-gazing.

"Nice, huh?" said Austin, coming up to stand behind her on the porch. He put his arms around her, hugging her tightly against him and resting his hands on the little mound in her belly.

"Do you think anyone will show up?"

"Are you kidding? The place is going to be crawling with Christmas spirit."

"But do you really think it'll be worthwhile? Money-wise?"

She'd sealed, labeled and tagged so many jars of honey, turned the windfall apples into sauce, pickled, spiced and preserved everything edible from the cold cellar. She'd even, after a fortuitous farmers' market score on frozen red currants, made her grandma's famous jelly.

She felt Austin shrug, his big body moving against hers.

"Even if it doesn't, it's good promotion."

She stiffened.

Promotion. As if they'd be staying.

"Aw, Mel, stop thinking so much. Look at us." He turned her to face him. "We're alive, we're healthy, we're together. We've got little Gumball in there to look forward to. It's not a bad way to spend the winter. Let's not worry about what comes after."

He touched her chin then and his gaze dropped to her mouth. Her breath quickened at the passion in his eyes.

He lowered his face and touched his lips to hers. For a moment, she couldn't breathe.

She slipped her arms up around his neck.

"Mel," he murmured against her cheek, "everything I need in the world is right here, in my arms."

She pressed her mouth against his to keep him from talking. All she wanted was for their life to go back to normal.

Except she didn't know what that was anymore.

A crunching sound rode across the crisp air, followed by a swath of light from a car pulling into their driveway.

They pushed apart, their breath surrounding them in clouds of white mist.

"Hello," called a voice. "Not to interrupt you lovebirds, but I'm here for some honey. You got some?"

Austin pressed his forehead against her hair, chuckling silently, then stepped forward to meet their first guest.

THEY'D HAD AN even better turnout than he'd hoped for, thought Austin, as the last car turned off the yard and headed out into the night.

He began the long walk to the far end of the yard, to shut off lights, unplug cords, put the goats to bed and secure doors against intruders, human or animal.

Chad was busy with sleigh rides all night, for which they charged a nominal fee. Leda sat, surrounded by kids and goats, like a smart-mouthed Madonna in a nativity scene gone wrong. And he'd done okay with his first round of bee questions.

But when one of the kids had pointed out that the queen wasn't moving as much as the others, he'd found himself stumbling over the answer.

It was natural, he told them. The rest of the bees work to

take care of her. She's the center of the hive; everything revolves around her. In winter, their job is to keep her warm and fed because the health of a colony depended on a strong queen."

But in truth, she was weak, probably hurt by the cold snap during which they hadn't been properly insulated. He'd neglected the hive and this was the price.

He'd neglected Melinda during the demise of Sweet and Morgan, thinking that they'd have time after the crisis to sort out everything between them. He'd been frantic, she was always working, they hardly saw each other and when they did, it was for exchanges of information, debates, decisions to be made.

Never blame. He bowed his head. She'd never blamed him, never.

He promised he'd make it up to her, but it wasn't working out that way, was it?

He found her resting in the kitchen, her arms folded on the table. To keep with the old-fashioned Christmas theme, they'd gone with safety-candles and a wood fire, which threw a soft, flickering glow over the main room.

"Hey," she said, lifting her head. She smiled and it seemed to him that the candles grew brighter.

"Tired?" he asked. He stood behind her and began massaging her shoulders.

"How did you know?"

"I'm more than just a pretty face."

"Who knew that a farmer could have such a pretty face," she murmured, so beautiful he ached.

"Ditto, sweet Melinda Sweet."

"Ever wonder why you hear people talk about farmers and farmers' wives?" She sounded half-asleep already. "I mean, what's that about? Farm women work just as hard as their husbands."

"If what I saw tonight was any indication, this place has a

farmer and a farmer's husband."

"Two farmers. That's all I'm saying. Why can't they be equal?"

Her voice was loose and lispy. He put his hands on her shoulders and lifted her up.

"Come with me."

"I need to blow out all the candles first," she said, her voice clearer now.

"Not yet." He led her to the half-couch she'd refinished and loved so much. How she'd patched it with the same purple fabric, he didn't know. "Sit."

She sat, watching him.

"It's time for a little pampering," he continued. "I'm going to get some fresh firewood."

Austin dumped the split logs into the box beside the stove while his wife sat on the couch cross-legged, watching. She'd taken off the flannel checked overshirt she'd worn as part of her Sweet Montana Farmwife outfit; the black yoga top and tights showed off the strength in her arms. He could see her nipples clearly through the thin fabric, and the small round belly.

"You'd have made a great boy scout," she said, as he stirred the embers.

Carefully, he reached inside and placed the kindling and small branches. There was no rushing a fire, he'd learned, especially when you'd let it die down too far.

Melinda rubbed her hands over her exposed upper arms.

"Chilly?"

He wanted her naked and rosy with passion.

"Not really," she answered.

"Then what?"

The embers rushed up, strong and ready to catch, just waiting for fuel.

"Let's call it anticipation," she said.

He braced two bigger bark-covered logs at an angle on top, to give the blaze stamina, then sat down next to his wife and began warming her up.

Chapter Nine

I T WAS A day full of surprises, thought Melinda, looking through her lashes at the fire.

She hadn't expected to get so caught up in the excitement and promise of Christmas but with the soft flickering lights and the sparkling tree in the corner, she couldn't help it. The laughter of children, dashing through the snow in their parkas and boots, was the perfect accompaniment to the carols playing in the background, too.

It really was magical.

Austin lifted the hair away from the nape of her neck and planted a soft kiss, then another and another.

She felt the sensation down to her toes and suddenly she had to fight back tears at the sheer joy at his touch, of connecting with him in this way again, after coming so close to losing it entirely.

He slipped the spaghetti strap down over her arm and let his lips wander further. The slight moisture from his warm mouth left cool spots on her skin as he moved on, and the contrast made her shiver.

"Here," he said, trading spots with her so she faced the fire.

"You're cold."

"I'm not." She was trembling for some reason, though.

"Scoot onto the floor," he instructed. "I'll rub your shoulders."

With the fire warming her front side and Austin behind her, his strong denim-clad legs sheltering her on either side, she felt warm and secure just how, she imagined, an infant feels before its final journey into the world.

He lifted her hair again and spread his fingers against her scalp, massaging firmly. The sensation was breathtaking and she must have moaned because Austin chuckled.

"You like, my queen?"

"Mmm," was all she could manage.

Gently, he dug his thumbs into the hard muscles at the tops of her shoulders, working them until she felt them soften. His long fingers crept down the front of her chest as he worked, close to her breasts but not close enough.

She pulled away long enough to strip off the top, then leaned back.

"Keep going," she said.

She dropped her head back, against his thigh, to give him access to her breasts, but he didn't take it, focusing instead on her throat, trailing whisper-light touches from her jaw to her collarbone and back.

With a quick shift, she was on her knees in front of him, reaching for his belt, but he grabbed her hands.

"Uh, uh." He lifted her to her feet and set her bottom on the couch again. "You warming up?"

She nodded.

"Good. Then you won't be needing these."

She helped him slide her tights and underwear off until she stood naked and shivering before him.

"It's not fair," she whispered, looking him up and down.

Austin, her Austin, the man she'd been with for over a decade, was gone and in his place was this, this…

"Life's not fair," he said, pushing her to lie down.

Between the warmth from the fire beside her and her husband's touch, Mel felt as if all her nerve endings were reaching up through her skin, like buds surfacing through winter-cold soil, following the life force of the sun.

She quivered as he rubbed the stubble of his jaw against her instep, then moved upward, against her ankle, then her knee, then her thigh, then down the other side, ignoring the one place she wanted him most.

She'd heard pregnancy sex was good, but this new-old Austin had her quaking with desire, crawling out of her skin.

He ran his fingers over her torso, bringing fresh chill-bumps. He cupped her breasts, then leaned down and put his mouth over one hard bud and suckled.

Nerves sizzled from her nipple down, down her body, the normal hormonal reaction exquisite and excruciating all at once.

She grabbed Austin's shirt with both hands and tore it off him, pulled him until he was lying next to her on the couch, her hands working frantically on his jeans. It was too much, too much sensation, too much intensity.

Too much love.

Too much to lose.

"Hey," said Austin, catching hold of her hands. "What's going on? Mel? Are you crying?"

"No! Don't stop," she said, closing her eyes and turning her face away. "I need you. I need this! Please, just keep going. Ignore me."

He quickly stripped off the rest of his clothing and fit himself between her and the half-back of the fainting couch.

"I can't ignore you, Melinda," he murmured into her ear. "You're my life. Understand?"

His hand trailed down her belly, making circles around her navel. The heat and desire was back and this time, she allowed herself to be carried away, to a place of wholeness and joy and forgiveness and the pleasure of being loved.

CHRISTMAS EVE AT the farm was like a page from a children's book, thought Melinda, standing in the shadows of the porch. Lights twinkling across rooflines, the star shining in the darkness, pointing visitors to the nativity scene.

A couple of kids, barely school-age, danced up and down, their tongues out, racing to catch the fat, lazy flakes of snow drifting softly over them.

She hugged her middle, feeling as light as one of those flakes, herself. The last month had brought a new well of gentleness between them. His smile was bright with their shared secret. They touched each other more now and when she caught his eye, it felt as if everything inside her connected briefly with everything inside him.

They were one again. A unit. Pulling together.

And look at what they'd accomplished.

The biggest rush of open house was over and it was perfect, thanks to Austin. She'd never seen him so focused and purposeful and yes, happy.

She was happy too. Despite the worries always lingering in the background, the past weeks had been fun for her too, much more than she'd expected. She had a small turkey prepared for tomorrow, but they'd agreed not to spend money on gifts. Now she wished she had something to tuck under the tree for him tonight, something that might show how much she loved him.

They'd keep the lights and decorations up for another week, as many families enjoyed outings on the days between Christmas and New Year. It would be sad to take all this apart. But to everything a season. She thought of her grandmother's ornament, lost in the move, after all those years. She'd have to find a new one to remember her by.

Leda came trudging up from the goat barn. "It's completely, totally awesome out here, isn't it?"

She was beautiful in an innocent schoolgirl kind of way, like she might be a high school cheerleader, all legs and hair and bright white teeth. Except for the puffy cheeks and the enormous belly.

Melinda couldn't wait to waddle proudly like that.

"No arguments," she said. "You taking a break from goat-herding?"

"I gotta pee. Aren't those goat babies the cutest darn things you ever saw in your life?" She stroked her belly, following Austin with her eyes as he chatted with another group. "You're so lucky."

Melinda laughed. She *was* lucky.

"Despite our sad story?" The tale of losing their home had grown easier with the telling, though she kept it superficial. The saddest part was a burden for her and Austin alone.

"I mean, to have a guy like that. He loves you a lot, you know."

She said it with the melancholy of a woman whose luck had yet to land in such a spot.

"Leda, how old are you?"

"Twenty." Leda wrinkled her nose. "At least I escaped teen pregnancy, right?"

"No baby daddy, then?"

Leda shook her head. "I followed my stupid boyfriend to Marietta, but guess who found a better job the second I got here? He didn't want a baby. Didn't want me, either, I guess."

"I'm so sorry. That's a rough start." She touched the woman's shoulder with her gloved hand. "But don't give up on love, okay?"

Leda tucked her chin and wrinkled her nose. "I swear, I don't normally indulge in pity parties."

"You're tired, it's Christmas and you're awash in hormones. I'd say you're entitled. Just this once. Go in and take a break. You must be freezing."

She thought for a moment about the health care team who would assist her. She'd attended normal, low-risk births at Jackson Park. But the moms usually had partners or coaches with them and honestly, there wasn't much for the team to do. They were the "boring" cases and she thrived on the adrenaline.

But now she wondered. No tox-screens, no restraints, no social workers waiting in the wings. Just a strong, young mother and her normal, healthy newborn.

Had she been so hooked on the rush that she'd lost sight of the slow-blooming miracle that was also childbirth?

"What are you still doing out there in the cold," said Leda, coming back out to the porch.

"Got distracted, I guess," said Mel, joining her inside. "Feeling better?"

Leda shrugged. "It's all relative, isn't it. I dreamed last night I tried to blow a softball out of my nose and my face exploded. Kind of freaked me out."

The laugh grabbed Melinda by surprise. "Now there's one I haven't heard. Believe me, honey, nothing's going to explode. Now, it's time for you to put your feet up."

AUSTIN WATCHED HIS wife go inside the house with Leda. Her laughter rang out over the cold air and he smiled in response. She was back, Melinda, the woman he loved.

He wondered how they'd cope once they rejoined the rat-race, how they'd keep from getting sucked back into a life that had given them so much stuff, but so little value.

Another laugh, and then the door slammed shut against the cold. It was good for Mel to have people like Leda around again. She thought she could hold herself apart because this wasn't their 'real' life, but she was wrong.

"Mr. Sweet?" said a little girl. "Is there really a bee that's a queen?"

He let the child take his hand and draw him into the honey shed.

"There most certainly is, young lady," he said. "Would you like to meet her?"

An hour or two later, when he'd answered the last question from the last child, he actually felt as if he was an expert. He waved goodbye and glanced around the yard, checking for stragglers.

But as the families left, he realized that they were left with a different group, the people who had nowhere else to be on Christmas Eve and were loath to exchange the warmth and good cheer for whatever awaited them at home.

He couldn't blame them, he thought, as he made for the house himself. A chill wind was picking up and the forecast was for heavy snow overnight.

He quickened his pace, eager to see if Mel had enjoyed herself as much as he had.

But as he approached the porch, he saw two familiar figures

approaching the house.

His parents?

Here?

On Christmas Eve? He and Mel were looking forward to a visit with Delores, following the holidays. But Austin's parents celebrated with their snowbird friends.

He went to meet them, mentally preparing himself.

"Mom, Dad. Merry Christmas. I thought you were in Arizona!"

"Merry Christmas, sweetheart," said his mom. She reached forward and drew him into a hug. "We were. Some friends invited us to go skiing at Big Sky. We thought we'd surprise you!"

"Mission accomplished, Mom." He kissed her cheek soundly. No suggestion that they spend the holiday together, but it was good to see them, at least.

"Son," said his dad. "Merry Christmas. It's quite something, what you've done here. I'd forgotten all about the open house."

Austin took the outstretched hand and returned the greeting. His dad's smile looked as if it might crack with the cold.

"Can I take you on the Christmas tour?" he asked, taking his mom's elbow. Her long white coat and high-heeled boots weren't the best for trouncing around a farmyard.

"Oh, that's not necessary," she said. "But I'd love to see the house. I so admire these old estates, so much history."

"We can't stay long," said Bill, ignoring his wife.

"Come in, have a mug of cider." He put an arm around each of them and propelled them toward the door. "Say hi to Mel."

They walked up the porch steps, where sparkling lights and glittering tinsel set off the new wood and fresh paint. As he ushered them through the door, pride nudged his cold lips into a smile.

Three slow-cookers simmered, the rich scent of apples and cinnamon adding to the fresh smell of pine from the enormous tree in the corner. All that junky old furniture had been polished and arranged in what Mel called 'conversation hubs' or something. Between the candles and old Bessie, the entire room had a cozy, time-gone-by Yuletide atmosphere.

It was perfect.

And there, in the sunroom stood Mel, his everything, his anchor, the missing piece to the puzzle of his life, deep in conversation with the pregnant girl.

Instantly, his nerves calmed.

He got his parents set up with a mug of cider each and a plate of Mel's shortbread cookies.

"Sit here and enjoy the fire. I'll get Melinda," he said, wishing his mom would stop brushing imaginary things off her coat. Wishing he'd put vodka in his dad's mug.

"Hey, honey," he said. "Hi, Leda. I hate to interrupt, but my parents are here."

Melinda's face dropped into confusion, followed by wariness.

"Your parents? Came here?"

They didn't know about the separation, which could probably stay a secret, or about the pregnancy, which would be shared, only when Mel was ready.

He took her by the arm but addressed the girl. "I promise to bring her right back, as long as you promise not to give us a live nativity scene here tonight."

Leda made a face. "I'll do my best! Go ahead, Mel. I'll watch the inventory while I enjoy my drink. The last thing I need is to pee more, but your cider is so delicious, I can't resist."

"That's nice of them to come all the way out here," said Mel. He watched her put on a welcoming smile, an armored faceplate he wished she didn't need. Then she walked ahead of him, shoulders straight, head high.

He was so proud of her, it hurt.

"Bill, Ducky," she said. She leaned in to hug them in turn, kissing Bill on the cheek. "Merry Christmas. Welcome to Sweet Montana Farms. What a wonderful surprise!"

"We had to see what our son has gotten up to out here in the sticks," boomed Bill.

"It's lovely, just lovely," said Ducky. "It's like a wonderland. And so many people! That's one thing about our Austin, he makes friends wherever he goes, doesn't he?"

"Mom and Dad are going skiing at Big Sky with some friends," said Austin. "They stopped by to surprise us."

"I'm so glad," said Mel. "You'll stay with us, I hope?"

Her grace never failed to amaze him.

"Goodness, dear," said Ducky. "Aren't you kind. But we're staying in town."

Of course they were. His mother didn't sleep on anything less than 700-thread-count sheets.

"We've got a gift for you," said Melinda.

She came back from the sunroom with an enormous wicker basket containing preserves, jars of honey with little wooden twirlers attached, biscotti and shortbread and all sorts of goodies. She handed it to Ducky with a warm smile, knowing full well that her mother-in-law wasn't a made-with-love sort of person.

"Well, isn't this darling," said his mother. She fingered the packaging, as if unsure what to do with it. "All homemade, too, you clever thing. Bless your heart."

Austin sucked in his breath, but Mel caught his eye. *Don't.*

Bill took the basket from Ducky and put it on the floor without looking at it.

"I hope whatever your friend has is catching," he said, gesturing toward Leda.

Leda smiled and gave a little wave, which Bill ignored.

Ducky leaned forward, her eyes bright. "Now that's the Christmas gift we really want, dear!"

"Mom!"

He understood why Mel insisted they announce it the way they wanted, when they wanted. His parents had a way of co-opting things.

"It's okay," said Melinda, putting her hand on his arm. "I'm just giving advice, Ducky. Helps me not miss my job."

Ducky's face fell. "Oh."

"Why would you miss handing out bedpans," said Bill, "when you could be a mother?"

"Dad!" He had the sensitivity of a chainsaw. "Mel's career is far more than that and you know it. Her choices are none of your business."

"But it's the perfect time and place, Austin!" said Ducky. "She's not getting any younger-"

"She's right here," interrupted Mel. Twin spots of color sparked her cheeks. "And she's had enough. You know nothing about me, what I want, what Austin and I have been through-"

Her voice shook and she stopped. Austin watched her pull herself together. "I'm sorry, I have to go. There are people waiting. Merry Christmas, Happy New Year and enjoy your skiing."

Her jaw was set in a hard line and he felt waves of heat rippling off her. She returned to Leda without looking at him.

A log hissed and shifted inside the wood stove. Deliberately Austin turned his gaze to a pair of young women admiring the various gift bags Mel had made, smaller versions of the one at Bill's feet.

Telling his parents about the baby would thrill them to no

end, but doing it now would be like rewarding bad behavior. Maybe they'd invite them to the kid's first birthday, tell them then.

Or maybe later. Like high school graduation.

The first time she'd miscarried, it happened before anyone knew about the pregnancy, and they'd been grateful to be spared the questions and explanations. They'd made it longer the second time, again keeping their excitement and then their grief, to themselves.

Even now, he knew his wife was afraid of jinxing things.

"You're both way out of line," he said, when he could speak.

"We just want you to be happy, Austin." Ducky put her hand on his knee. "It's hard to see you with someone who doesn't understand how important family is to you. I'm sorry, honey, but it seems selfish."

"Coming from you two? That's rich. You weren't even planning to see us until it happened to align with your ski trip."

"Now, now," said Bill. He flicked his hand as if the whole interaction was a mere annoyance. "We came here for a reason. I'll make this quick. I'm giving you the deed to the farm."

"Very funny."

But his father wasn't smiling. He pushed a thick envelope across the table. "Merry Christmas."

Austin stared at the envelope.

"You can't be serious."

"It's what your grandfather wanted."

It was exactly what Melinda predicted, that his parents would find a way to manipulate them into staying, fulfilling an inconvenient familial obligation that no one else would touch.

"It's such a small farm," said Ducky. "But your father's attached to it."

She took a sip of her apple cider and raised her eyebrows, as if surprised to find it delicious and Austin was suddenly reminded of her blue-blood, ultra-wealthy background.

Was that part of the problem? Bill had married above his station and Ducky's land-baron father had never let him forget it.

But this, Sweet Montana Farms, was Bill's property, his father's before him, and his father's father before that. It might not be much, but it was independent of Ducky's family or their money.

A husband provides for his wife.

Unless his in-laws get there first.

He felt a pang of sympathy for Bill Sweet, farmer's son-turned-accountant, never quite good enough for the debutante he fell for.

"It's very generous, Dad," he said, calmer now. "But Melinda and I will have to talk about it."

"What's to talk about?" said Bill. "It's a home. And after all…"

Beggars can't be choosers.

The unspoken message hung in the air between them.

And it was a generous gift, of course. Too generous.

"It's getting late, dear," said Ducky, glancing at her watch.

"I've already had my lawyers draw up the paperwork," continued Bill. "Come up to Big Sky, do a little skiing. We'll talk the details over then."

Mel didn't ski, as he'd explained to them both, several times.

"Dad, I'll discuss it with my wife, but we're more than happy to take our percentage of the proceeds when the farm sells."

"When it sells?" His father laughed. "In this market? I'm giving it to you, Austin, because I know you'll take care of it."

"But Dad, this isn't where we want to live. Melinda's looking forward to getting back to civilization. I'm sure you can understand."

Bill's eyes narrowed. "I'm giving it to *you*, Austin."

Whatever sympathy he'd felt disappeared. He clenched and unclenched his fists.

"That was not the deal, Dad." He forced himself to speak slowly and evenly. "And the offer is to me and Melinda together. That's how we make our decisions. As a team."

He stood up abruptly, feeling his face twist.

"Until that offer has both our names on it, it's meaningless. And even then, unless Mel convinces me she wants it, one hundred and ten percent, we'll be respectfully declining. Now." He took a deep breath. "I'm sorry *we* won't have time to join you for skiing, but *we'll* be busy all week."

Chapter Ten

"THAT LOOKED INTENSE," said Leda.

They'd sold several baskets within a few minutes but now there was a lull. Mel sat down with a fresh mug of cider, wishing she had better ability to hide her emotions.

"In-laws." She attempted a light tone. Failed.

It looked like Austin was having the same problem. That spot at the back of her neck was aching again. Part of her wished he'd tell them off properly. The other part admired the respect he showed them.

Didn't understand it, exactly. But it wasn't her journey.

"Ooh." The girl's eyes sparkled with interest. "Don't hate me, but it makes me feel better to hear that. You and Austin are so perfect-"

A bark of laughter escaped Mel's mouth and she pressed a finger against her lips.

"Are you kidding? You're so pretty, he's so handsome, you're so in love it's sickening…Nice to see you've got the same problems as the rest of us."

Mel tried not to see Leda's frayed scarf and nails bitten down to the quick. Her clothes looked second-hand and there wasn't a spec of make-up on that flawless skin.

"Schadenfreude, honey. Believe me, if you knew the extent of our misfortunes, you'd be delighted to no end."

But who was she to make a claim on misery? Hardship was hardship. Everyone has their share and no one can take the measure of someone else's Hell.

They were lucky to have each other. Despite everything.

"I should get going," said Leda, easing herself up. "Give Mocha a juicy Christmas kiss for me."

She frowned and put a hand to her belly.

An older gentleman at the door waved goodbye and Mel waved back. Leda's hand didn't move.

"Braxton Hicks?"

Leda made a face, still waiting for it to pass. "My OB told me they'd get stronger as my date arrived."

Melinda let herself slip back into professional mode, braced for whatever bleakness might come with it. But to her surprise, all she felt was excitement.

"That's right. Your uterus is warming up for the main event. How does baby react?"

"Still punching," said Leda stroking her belly. "But would you mind copping a feel? Or is that too much like work? Or against regulations or something?"

"Too much like work?" Melinda laughed again. "Take off your coat."

She glanced around the room quickly. There were still several people perusing the honey selection. The purple couch was behind a table laden with poinsettias; she rearranged them for a bit more privacy and pointed at Leda to lie down.

Looked like Austin's parents were gone.

Thank goodness.

Leda's frame was so slight, the pregnancy could have been a

basketball shoved under her top. Melinda wondered if she was eating properly.

She pressed her hands onto the girl's belly through her top, and a wave of what she could only describe as homesickness washed over her. How she missed this.

Mel thought about all the things that could go wrong, how fragile that tentative hold on life was and how incredible it was to hear that first cry.

She pressed gently against a hard knob and felt an answering bump. *Hi, baby.*

Exquisite sweetness tightened her throat, making it impossible to speak. She'd be feeling her own child move soon.

Please. Please.

"You felt that, right?" said Leda. "It's not as hard as it used to be. It's like instead of kickboxing, she's doing Tai Chi now."

Leda's good cheer pushed away the fear. "That sounds about right. There's no room in there for kickboxing anymore."

The head had dropped, good anterior presentation, baby was probably about six pounds. Reluctantly, she took her hands off and stepped back.

"Everything seems normal. But it's good to keep an eye on those kicks. We still want some movement, even if it's only Tai Chi."

"Got it."

"Leda?"

"Feels good to lie down, that's all." She took a deep breath, then opened her eyes and got to her feet. "I wish you worked in the Marietta hospital."

Maybe, thought Mel. Maybe.

They hugged awkwardly with the baby between them, and Melinda felt her tense up again.

"Another one? So soon?"

"Yeah. Why? Is that bad?"

"You probably just need to get off your feet." But Leda heard the hesitation in her voice.

She clutched at Mel's arm, her eyes wide. "It's too early! I don't even have a crib yet. My sister's not here until tomorrow."

Melinda eased out of her grip and walked to the porch to check the weather. Their visitors were hurrying to their cars and she could see why. The picturesque puffy flakes of earlier had grown heavier.

She took Leda's cold hands and squatted down beside her. "There's no one at home with you?"

"I thought I had time," said Leda in a small voice.

Good chance Leda's sister wouldn't be on the roads tomorrow.

"You probably do. But you can't drive yourself home, not that distance, not on snowy roads and certainly – am I making myself clear? – certainly not alone."

She looked around her at the disheveled room, wondering how she'd ended up responsible for a pregnant girl on Christmas Eve.

"I'll tell you what. You lie down in the spare room upstairs, see if things settle down. I'll finish up here. If you feel fine, I'll escort you home. If not, I'm driving you to the hospital."

Leda gave in reluctantly and trudged up the narrow stairs.

Melinda straightened her Sweet Montana apron and went back to her jams and jellies, where another lineup had formed.

"We need to get going," said the woman first in line, beckoning her over. "It's past the kids' bedtime."

"And the wind has really picked up, too," said the man behind her. "Everyone needs to get home, and stay home."

With their customers all eager to take their purchases and hit the road, it didn't take long for the farmhouse to empty out.

Through the kitchen window, she thought she saw the lights on the sheds blink out. Austin was closing up too. He was walking quickly, his shoulders hunched against the flurries.

Melinda turned on the overhead lights and quickly gathered up the cash; she'd sort through it tomorrow. She swiped a mop over their wooden floor to get rid of the snow melting into it, then went from room to room, blowing out candles.

Just as she hung up her apron, a pop sounded and everything went dark. No clock on the microwave, no humming from the refrigerator, the iPod speaker dock stopped singing Christmas carols and the only sound was the hiss and crackle of logs inside the cast-iron stove.

And one other sound. A faint moaning. Coming from upstairs.

Melinda ran.

AUSTIN SAW THE lights go out in the house. Instantly, it felt colder outside. He glanced behind him, the hairs on the back of his neck prickling. The world was a collage of black-on-black, deep and dark, the stars above the only break.

His father's 'gift' weighed on him like an anvil. He needed to tell Mel about it. He knew already what she would say, and he didn't blame her.

Maybe they should consider it, though. The numbers Chad had given him on previous years' performance told him that the farm could produce a decent living. Nothing like they'd had before, of course, when they had two incomes.

But look at how much better they were doing. He felt as if somehow this whole last year had been leading up to this. They'd drifted so far apart. Could that drift have grown into two separate paths?

Would she have come back to him, if she hadn't been pregnant?

He plodded through the snow, his chest and throat seared by the icy air and tight with emotion.

He'd nearly lost her. He realized that now. His Mel, his heart. His life.

How could he have not seen how unhappy she was? Or more likely, how had he convinced himself that it wasn't real? He hadn't wanted to face the truth and so, he hadn't. It was that simple.

No way he would let that happen again.

He reached the porch and thumped the snow off his boots, eager to get her into his arms again.

They'd evaluate the information, make an informed decision, together, regardless of his parents' desires. As long as he had his wife, he could face the future.

So, whatever she wanted, that's what they'd do.

"MY WATER BROKE," gasped Leda, her eyes enormous in the flashlight beam. The light also picked up a shiny patch on the floor, dripping from the sheets.

"So I see. I have to examine you. Here. Hold the flashlight." Her hands shook and they were freezing. It felt like the temperature in the house was dropping by the second.

Leda's hands gripped the sheets, but she relaxed one enough to take the light. There was no chance of getting her anywhere tonight. It was lucky, in fact, that she hadn't begun the drive home.

Mel shuddered, snapping on her latex gloves, glad that she

always kept her medical kit stocked.

"Three centimeters dilated. We've got time. Don't know how much, though."

"I'm scared," said Leda.

Melinda heard the door slam downstairs. Austin was in.

"Up here, Oz," she called.

His footsteps pounded up the stairs, but when he reached the doorway, he skidded to a stop.

"Surprise." Leda shone the light over his face. "You know that nativity scene you mentioned earlier? This is your fault."

"We can't... you can't... have you called the ambulance?"

"Phone's dead. Way the snow's coming, the road will be shut anyway."

Leda cried out as another pain hit.

It was time to be a nurse again. She let her mind click into place, then began giving orders.

"We need to get her downstairs, Oz. It's going to be freezing up here soon. We need blankets, we need lots of firewood, we need every candle and storm lantern you can find."

It was a nerve-wracking trip down the staircase in the dark and Mel didn't think she took a full breath until Leda was safely on the fainting couch, propped up with pillows.

"What else do you need?" he asked.

"Warm water, to clean off the baby. Towels."

"No problem."

"How are you doing, honey?" she said, wiping a strand of damp hair off Leda's brow.

"Sorry to do this to you, Melinda." She sounded near tears and gruff with embarrassment. "This isn't how it was supposed to be."

"Babies come when they come," said Mel.

"At least we're in good hands." She gave a quavering laugh.

"That's my girl. I'm going to take a listen to this little gal, okay?"

Mel put the stethoscope in her ears.

She was used to a well-equipped unit, full of sterile drapes and instruments, drugs galore, monitors, bright lights and stirrups. Nurses, aides, obstetricians, paediatricians.

A team.

How could she do this alone?

She thought of the fist-sized bump in her own belly. So much was depending on her.

The rush of Leda's pulse filled her ears, as well as the fainter, faster heartbeat whooshing beneath it. For a moment she let the sounds surround her, blocking out the thoughts scrambling in her head.

Just breathe. You've got this.

In and out. Just like you're going to coach Leda, shortly. In and out.

She forced her chest open, sucking in air, the only thing that would quell the panic.

And the fear receded.

"How's it going?" called Austin, cradling another load of firewood. The room glowed and flickered once more from the light of candles and fire. They had warmth. They had shelter. She knew what she was doing.

"Good," she said, smiling at Leda. "We're all good."

She was going to do this. And it was going to be fine.

She had Austin.

*

HOUR AFTER HOUR, Austin's admiration for his wife grew. He always thought he understood her occupation. Nurses take your temperature, they give you pills in those little paper cups, they write stuff in charts, that sort of thing. They help the doctors, who make the real decisions.

But watching Melinda work now was a revelation.

She was calm, in charge, thinking, aware of her patient's emotions and working constantly to ease the woman's anxiety.

It was like she'd donned her favorite coat, after setting it aside for a season, to find it was still the perfect size.

He'd enjoyed his work with Sweet and Morgan, no question. And he'd been good at it. But it had never been to him what this was to Melinda.

It was her passion.

She couldn't give that up. He couldn't ask that of her.

"You can come closer," said Leda, from the couch. "I haven't turned into a toad or anything."

"Oh," said Austin. He looked at Mel.

"Grab a seat," she said.

"Things are about to get juicy," added Leda.

He winced. "Not what I wanted to hear. At all."

So far, he'd kept himself busy with the fire, making cups of tea and honey and checking on the animals as the snow got deeper and deeper.

He sat gingerly on the chair positioned at Leda's head. "Should I do anything?"

"You could massage my shoulders." Leda grimaced. "Oh, here comes another one."

She grabbed his hand and squeezed hard.

"Youch!" he yelped.

"Don't be... a baby," said Leda, between breaths.

"You've got a grip like a lumberjack."

He repositioned the cushions behind her back. He could feel her shaking.

"I'm tougher… than I look."

"Oh yeah?" he said. "Next contraction, let's see who blinks first, okay?"

"You got it, city boy." She fell back against the cushions, her eyes closed.

"That's good, Oz," whispered Mel. "I'm going to be busy here. She needs someone to talk to, someone to hold onto."

"You're amazing," he said. "I hope you know that."

"Thanks," gasped Leda. "You're a man, so I hate you. Aaahh!"

LEDA'S LABOR PROGRESSED much faster than Melinda anticipated, especially for a first baby. She kept checking the baby's heart rate with her stethoscope. A few late decelerations, but nothing too worrisome yet.

"You're at eight centimeters," she said. "Show time's coming up."

"I think I'm going to be sick," said Leda.

Austin held a bowl under her face, rubbed her back and cleaned her face with a warm, wet towel.

"Easy, girl," he murmured, "you're going to be okay."

Mel's beautiful husband had gathered every bath towel, every washcloth, every dishcloth and tea towel in the house and stacked them in a basket beside the fire. The rest of the house had gotten chilly enough to see your breath, but where they were, huddled together, it was toasty warm.

There was hot water on the stove, to give the baby a quick clean up, when she arrived. They were as ready as they could be.

Melinda had often imagined the kind of father Austin would be. He'd be the guy who'd swing them by their heels to make them squeal. He'd carry them on his shoulders and push them on the swings, toss them into the pool, roll down grassy hills with them.

He would do the fun stuff, because that's who Oz was.

It was harder to see him changing diapers or walking a colicky infant hour after hour or cleaning spit-up off his tie.

But here he sat, wiping the brow of a woman he barely knew, holding her while she retched, joking and teasing to keep her mind off the pain, as the wind howled around them and the night stretched toward dawn.

"It hurts," moaned Leda. "It hurts so much. I can't do this anymore. Make it stop."

Her voice rose as another contraction rolled over her and there it was, the first glimpse of the baby's head.

Mel slid closer, spreading her towel-draped knees, holding her hands, ready, so ready.

But what if…? Her arms shook. It was all down to her.

"You're doing great, sweetheart." Austin's voice penetrated, and for a moment, it seemed that he was talking to her. "Hang in there. You can do this. You're almost done. Come on, it's time to meet this baby, okay?"

He was talking to Leda, but then he looked over the mound of blankets, straight into Mel's eyes.

"You got this, baby," he murmured, with such a smile of confidence, her fears disappeared.

"Thank you," she mouthed, her throat tight with gratitude.

"Something's happening," cried Leda. She sat up and a deep groan came from her throat.

"She's crowning," said Mel. "It's time to push."

"No shit," roared the tiny mother-to-be.

She cursed wildly, hollering out in vivid detail the suffering she wished upon the absentee father of her child.

Mel was glad for the noise. It kept her from thinking about catching the child.

She looked at the thick layer of towels beneath Leda, the flannel sheets folded on her lap, the pile beside her, all ready to enfold the slippery little bundle as she emerged.

"She's got brown hair," she called.

"I don't care!" yelled Leda. "Get that… sucker out of me…before I split apart… like a tomato!"

Melinda cradled the baby's head securely, wiping her little face, clearing her airway. She checked for the cord – not noosed around her neck, thank goodness.

She heard Austin crooning words of encouragement and it didn't matter if they were for Leda or her or himself.

With a whoosh of fluid and a final howl from Leda, the infant slipped free, directly into Mel's waiting arms and the protection of the thick, fire-warmed towel.

"Is that it?" said Leda, lying back against Austin's arms. "Is it over? Is she here?"

"She's here," said Mel softly. "She's here and she's perfect."

She tucked the mewling child under the blanket, right next to Leda's heart. "Time to meet your mama, little one."

Chapter Eleven

B Y THE TIME the power returned on Christmas morning, the sun was bright-white and bone cold. Sun-dogs stood sentry on either side. Chad had come over by snowmobile to check on them and, after he got over the shock of Leda's baby, he got out his plow and cleared their driveway so they could get out.

Melinda packed mother and child into Leda's SUV and drove them to the hospital. Austin had to do a quick check on the animals, then he'd follow them in his truck.

He stopped by the kitchen to get his keys and saw the envelope still lying on the table. In the chaos of the night, he'd forgotten all about it. He picked it up. The papers inside were bunched awkwardly, as if they'd been folded hastily.

Had Melinda seen it? She'd been busy with Leda all night. And even if she had, she knew Austin wouldn't accept something like that. Not without discussing it with her.

He stuffed it into his jacket pocket and headed out to feed the goats.

He and his wife would make that decision together and together, they would tell his parents.

Melinda knew that, right?

"MY CHRISTMAS BABY," said Leda. "My little Christmas miracle."

Melinda glanced at the rear-view window, watching the duo coo at each other.

She should be exhausted, but instead, she was exhilarated.

"Merry Christmas," she said to Leda.

"Got that right. You, Melinda Sweet, are officially my hero."

Mel laughed. "Endorphins are great, aren't they?"

Behind them, Sweet Montana Farms grew smaller and smaller.

Was it just the brilliance of the day, or the hormones, or was it a lot prettier now than it had been when they arrived?

Did she really want to return to the crazed life they'd led before? She and Austin were closer now than they'd been in months. Maybe years.

They had their own baby on the way.

That's what mattered.

She thought of the hurt he tried to hide all those nights when she'd slept on the couch instead of going to him. Intentionally or not, she'd made him suffer along with her.

She never stopped loving him, even when they were apart, but did he know that?

Through everything, she'd never doubted Austin's love. It was there in every word he said, every gesture he made. She thought of the envelope she'd seen on the table. He hadn't told her about it, but there hadn't exactly been time.

But what if he didn't intend to mention it? Sweet Montana Farms was not what she wanted; it never had been. He knew that. It would be just like Austin to refuse the gift without a second thought, to sacrifice his own happiness, without even telling her, to spare her the guilt.

They pulled into the emergency room drop off bay and she set aside her thoughts.

"Here we go, baby girl," said Leda in the back seat.

Their arrival caused something of an uproar, with the general opinion being that Leda's baby was a miracle. Mel hung back as caregivers surrounded them, acutely aware that she had no role here.

The camaraderie underlying their brisk actions made her ache.

"Okay, we're good to go." The young man in green scrubs touched Mel's shoulder. Dex, according to his name tag. "Sorry, family only while we check her out. But I'll show you where to wait."

"Oh," she said, stepping back further. "Of course."

"You dunce," said Leda. "She's my sister. Cousin! She's my cousin."

She reached out and grabbed Mel's sleeve, causing the gurney to wobble. White coats flurried to settle it.

"My mistake, ladies." Dex looked from blonde-and-blue to olive-and-brown. "The resemblance is uncanny."

Mel's eyes filled. What a night. What a place.

"Sorry, honey." She hugged the new mom, kissed the baby's fragrant head. "I'll be back soon, I promise."

"You're the worst cousin in the world."

"Tell Austin to meet me at the hotel."

She sprinted to her car. There were things to do and no time to lose.

Chapter Twelve

I T TOOK AUSTIN some serious sweet-talking before he was allowed in to see Leda and her baby and when he got there, Melinda was nowhere to be seen.

"Everything okay?" he asked, once he found them.

"We're perfect, both of us." She beamed up at him. "Melinda did such a great job, my OB said I don't even need stitches!"

"Whoa," he said, backing away. "I'm here to get her. Where is she?"

"Oh, yeah. She said to meet her at the hotel. Why?"

"The Graff?"

"Yeah." The baby started grizzling and Leda tugged at her top.

"Breastfeeding is trickier than you'd think," she said. "Fortunately, I've got small nipples-"

"I've gotta go." He whirled around and dashed for the elevators.

"What's the matter? Austin?" she called behind him, but he didn't bother answering.

What could Melinda possibly want with his parents?

He drove as fast as he dared, grateful that the streets of Marietta were empty and it wasn't far. Grateful that the snow removers had been out early.

The cheerful decorations adorning the lamp standards waved to him as he rushed past. When he got to the hotel, he left his truck in guest parking and ran inside.

He skidded to a stop, nearly slipping on the wet tile.

"Hey," said Mel.

She was sitting on an elegantly tooled metal bench, her hands folded in her lap. He couldn't tell what was going through her mind.

He sat beside her and covered her hands with his.

"Mel," he said. "I have to tell you something."

She dipped her head at him, smiling gently. "It's okay, Oz. I saw the envelope. I know your dad's giving you the farm."

"Aw, Mel." His heart dropped. "I meant to tell you. They only told me last night and then the power went out and we were busy with Leda and-"

"I know."

When Melinda went to stay with her mother instead of following him to Sweet Montana Farms, he hadn't seen it coming. He should have, but he chose to ignore the signs. When she called to say that it would be best if they had some time apart, he didn't believe it. That she'd been trying to tell him how unhappy she was, but he refused to listen.

He wouldn't let that happen again.

"Mel, I won't let them decide our future for us. It's you and me. Okay? Together?"

His eyes felt hot.

"I'm not worried about that, Austin. Not anymore." She shifted on the bench so she could face him. "But family is family. I've been polite to your parents but I've always kept them at arms' length. I've been glad that we don't see much of them and that's wrong of me."

"No! If anyone's in the wrong, it's Mom and Dad. And me."

She leaned forward and this time, she was smiling, tearfully. "I'm into my second trimester now. I think we should tell them about the baby. It will make them so happy. My mom knows, so it's only fair."

"But what if-"

Mel looked down at her hands.

"Even then, we shouldn't bear it alone. I love you so much, Austin Sweet. I'm not afraid of what life has in store for us. And it's time I started showing it."

AUSTIN BRUSHED PAST the tastefully decorated tree, but the hostess – who had she pissed off to get put on Christmas? – caught up to them.

"Happy Holidays, sir. May I help you?"

"We're looking for someone."

The few people who were left lingering over their coffee and dessert looked up. Bill and Ducky were at a corner table, oblivious.

"Found them. Thanks."

"Austin," said Ducky, looking up in surprise.

"Hello, Mother."

"Merry Christmas, Ducky," said Melinda. "Merry Christmas, Bill. Where are your friends?"

The table, noted Austin, had been set for only two.

Color rose in Ducky's carefully powdered cheeks.

"They, uh," said Bill, pushing his plate aside. "Turns out their kids are at Big Sky."

"We didn't want to intrude," said Ducky. She was blinking too fast. Neither of them seemed to know where to put their hands.

"May we sit?" asked Mel.

Before they had a chance to object, she pulled a chair closer to Ducky and sat down.

"I wanted to apologize," she said.

"Don't Mel," he interrupted. "They're the ones who should apologize."

His mother's eyes were like saucers, the color in her cheeks now gone, leaving them ashen.

Bill pointed to a chair. "Sit down, son. Don't make a scene."

"We don't hold anything against Melinda." Ducky's voice was a little too high, her words a little too fast. "We understand the stress she's been under. There's no need to dwell on it."

"It's you, Mother," said Austin, "who needs to make amends. You've been rude and thoughtless to Melinda as long as I can remember and I've had enough."

"Oz," said Melinda. "Not like this."

An alarming shade of purple rose in Bill's already-ruddy cheeks. He half-rose to his feet and poked a fat finger at Austin's face. "Listen to your wife, boy."

Time slowed then, as something unfamiliar, dangerous, yet strangely irresistible rose within him, like heavy clouds over parched hills. You know the rain will bring lightning strikes, but you welcome it anyway. Better the snap of fire than another endless day of drought.

Austin grabbed the finger, hearing the rumble of thunder in his ears. The arc ran through him, razor-sharp and furnace-hot.

"I love you, Dad. But I swear to God, if you say another word, I'll snap that finger clean off."

"Austin!"

Melinda touched his face, made him look at her. The calm in her eyes pulled him back, just enough to peel his fist off Bill's hand.

The man dropped back heavily into his chair, breathing hard.

Conversations around them had grown silent and he was dimly aware that management was gathering. He'd probably be thrown out soon.

He braced his hands on the chair arms, leaning over his father, staring into his eyes and for the first time, Austin saw fear in them.

"You offered us a soft landing when we needed one and I'm grateful for that. But you lied to me from the start and Melinda knew it."

"It doesn't matter anymore," said Melinda.

"Neither of you have ever treated Melinda right and bad on me for allowing it. A husband takes care of his wife. That's what love is."

He pulled back then, feeling the heat thrumming in his ears. His arms were shaking.

"And," said Melinda, her eyes shining on him, "a wife takes care of her husband."

Ducky was crying silently, her hands pressed to her mouth. His father was breathing heavily, cowering into the chair.

The anger was gone and melancholy took its place. He'd made his mother cry. On Christmas.

"Mom, try to understand. Melinda is my life. If you make me choose between you or her, you'll see my dust before the words are out of your mouth. She is my family."

"We're all family." Mel reached across to clasp both his parents' hands in hers. "We can do better. I'm willing to try. Regardless of where we end up, or what we do, we appreciate your support. Bill, your offer of the farm means a lot to Austin. Ducky, I know it's a little rustic for you, but would you have Christmas dinner with us tonight?"

Ducky's eyes flew to her husband's. "I don't know... the Thompsons..."

"Oh, give it up, Ducky." Bill kept his hands safely under the table.

Ducky noticed. She observed her husband thoughtfully for a moment before coming to a conclusion.

She took a breath, collected herself, and addressed her daughter-in-law.

"I'm so sorry, Melinda. Dropping by unannounced last night was terribly rude. It's just... well." Her chin quivered and she looked down as she fought for control. "We didn't want to spend the holidays alone. We miss our son."

Austin's jaw tightened.

Ducky lifted her head and smiled softly into Melinda's eyes. "And it's time I got to know my daughter."

"Oh," squeaked a woman at a neighboring table. Then she immediately flushed red and put her hand over her mouth.

Austin was dumbstruck. He stared at his mother, then his wife, then blinked and shook his head.

"I'd like that," said Melinda.

She and Austin stood up.

"Come anytime," said Melinda. "We're roasting a honey-brined turkey. And, oh!"

She turned to Austin as if she'd just thought of it.

"We have a surprise for you. Don't be late!"

Chapter Thirteen

T HEY BUMPED OVER the little bridge that led to their turnoff. The wind of the night before was gone. Enough snow had fallen since then that every tree limb and fence post glittered with a fluffy layer.

"It's Beginning to Look a Lot Like Christmas," said Mel.

Austin reached over the console and took her hand.

"You're amazing, you know that?"

"Hm," she said. "Don't think I've heard that one. Or maybe it's a movie? Or a book?"

"Ah-amazing Mel," he sang. "How Sweet her love."

They pulled into the yard and he turned off the car.

"Sweetheart," he said, taking her hands in his. "You are the bravest, kindest, smartest woman I've ever known. I'm so lucky to have you."

She shrugged playfully but her eyes were full of tears. "I'm a crabby, tired pregnant woman who's about to start cooking a turkey. Let's see how you feel about me in an hour."

"What you said to my parents, Mel." He stopped, as if he couldn't find the right words. "You're first in my life. Do you understand?"

"I do."

"But letting them in like that, on your terms, Mel-"

She pressed her finger against his lips. "I should have done it years ago."

He pulled away. "About the farm-"

Again, she stopped him. "There's no rush. Whether we live here or we go somewhere else doesn't matter. As long as we're together. As long as we're a family."

"Aaa-rooo." Jackson stepped slowly off the porch where he'd been waiting.

"But you know," she added, "moving is a lot of stress on an old dog. It wouldn't be fair to him."

Austin's whole face twinkled like a Christmas wreath. "Now you're talking crazy. Come on, girl. Let's go inside. I want to give you your present before my parents get here."

Mel gasped. "We agreed!"

"I lied."

She stepped out, the cold air refreshing on her hot cheeks.

Once inside the house, he busied himself lighting candles and getting the Christmas carols playing on the iPod again.

She waited with her arms crossed, knowing that there was nothing he could give her that could make her happier than she already was.

Finally, he turned to her with that grin she so loved and handed her a small box.

"I hope you didn't spend too much."

She thought of the surprise she had for him, later.

"Even better. I didn't pay a cent for it."

She undid the ribbon and peeled off the paper taped around it and lifted the lid.

Her breath caught in her throat. Inside, nestled on a square of white cotton batting was a Christmas tree ornament, a silver star, glittery lines of glue showing where the cracks had been.

"Is this… oh, Oz… this is my grandmother's ornament."

He nodded.

"But how did you… what made you think of fixing it for me?"

He shrugged. "I saw it when I got out the decorations. You've had it forever. Each year you take it out, open the lid and look at it. Then you cover it up and put it away."

She lifted it out, very carefully, by the metal hanger by which it would hang from the tree. She ran her finger over the delicate silver swirls, the sparkling lines, the glittery edges.

Her throat was tight and the back of her eyes stung. She knew her grandmother was smiling down on her with approval.

"It's beautiful, Austin," she whispered. "But how did you do it? I don't even know if all the pieces were there."

Again, he shrugged it off, as if it was no big deal. "Contrary to popular opinion, guys can use glue guns. It wasn't as badly broken as you thought it was. I spread it all out on the table one night in the honey shed, where I knew you wouldn't see it and it just worked."

He took the star from her hand and gently replaced it in the box.

"It was something precious to you," he said. His eyes were glistening. "And you saved it. You didn't know how to fix it, but you refused to let it go. It took some work, on my part and it'll always have some scars. But I think it's more precious than ever. What about you?"

"I think I love you." She cleared her throat. "There's another thing I kept."

His eyes darkened. "Do tell."

She pulled him close. "Do you happen to remember that little black teddy you bought me, way back when?

"And they say hoarding is a bad thing." He nuzzled her neck. "You gonna model it for me?"

"Might look a little funny, with Junior and all."

"You'll be even more beautiful."

He tugged her toward the stairs but she held back.

"Patience. Your parents will be here any time. We've got a lot to do."

"PB & J sandwiches don't take long. They're traditional too, right?"

Go Tell It On The Mountain began playing on the iPod.

She pulled him away from the stairs and began swaying with him to the music.

So much to be thankful for.

"You know what this is?" said Melinda, sweeping an arm around them. "It's A Wonderful Life, a Miracle on 34th Street and The Gift of the Magi, all rolled into one."

Austin twirled her into a dip, then kissed her until she couldn't breathe.

"This," he said, "is a Sweet Montana Christmas."

"I THINK IT'S great if the woman is older," called Leda, lying on her stomach on the grass. Five-month old Hera lolled drunkenly against a pillow, and kicked at Jackson. The old dog – who looked much younger these days – lay on the picnic blanket, gazing adoringly at the baby.

"I'm definitely looking for someone younger than me," the girl added.

It would be too hot outside for the babies once summer hit, thought Melinda, but now, in spring, it was perfect.

"She's never allowed to babysit our son again," said Austin. He sat on the porch beside Melinda's rocking chair, whittling. Very badly. He had this idea that whittling would be a good thing to teach his son.

"I'll get a restraining order if I have to," he added.

As would she if he got any closer to their precious boy with that knife.

Melinda looked down at Abel, gurgling at her breast. "She's talking about the kids."

Scrape, scrape.

"Arranged marriage, huh?"

"Go for it," called a voice from the kitchen. "Regular marriage isn't tracking so hot."

Mel smiled. Turns out new motherhood was a pretty sweet deal. Her mom, Delores the love-sceptic, was inside chopping vegetables for supper.

"Your experience with Melinda's father has made you cynical, Delores."

Ducky came out to the porch with a bowl of cut-up celery and carrots. A regular store-bought miracle, what becoming a grandmother had done for Austin's pressed and polished mom. And instead of becoming rivals, she and Delores had become friends. Baby-sharing, soup-making, dish-washing friends.

The mind boggled.

"You're rocking the apron look, Granny," said Austin, taking the plate. "We need a picture."

Ducky lifted her chin. "Thank you, son."

Scrape, scrape, chunk.

The knife slipped and Austin almost dropped it. "I'm fine! See? No blood."

"You never, ever, try to catch a knife," Mel said. "How many times do I have to patch you up?"

"See?" said Leda. "He doesn't listen. He's older than you, isn't he?"

"When's Dad getting here?" asked Austin.

"Oh, in good time, I'm sure," said Ducky, somewhat mysteriously.

Austin and Bill were coming to terms about Sweet Montana Farms, starting off with Austin's insistence that any paperwork had both his and Melinda's name on it. That was non-negotiable.

It could be the hormones, but Mel still got teary, thinking about it.

The ownership details hadn't been decided yet. She and Austin had agreed that they needed more time, that they should have a full year on the farm before they could fully judge it. But she'd already decided that she'd never part with the goats, especially little Mocha, and there weren't a lot of goat-friendly rentals out there.

Being in business with family was always a risk, they knew that. But staying away from family carried a cost as well.

Melinda looked around her, at Leda babbling with her daughter, at her handsome husband valiantly attempting something new, never afraid to fail. At the mothers chattering over the sink.

At her father-in-law as he drove onto the yard, his fancy car splashed with mud.

At the delivery truck that followed him onto the yard and then out to the honey shed.

"What's that, Dad?" asked Austin.

"Equipment delivery," said Bill, waving to the driver. "If we're going to get the production really going, we need to replace those old hive boxes. Your extractor is old too. All sort of things."

"Didn't exactly need a big truck for that," commented Leda.

The driver turned the truck around, then backed it up to the kitchen door.

Melinda looked at Ducky, who was trying to hide a smile. Delores looked innocent.

The delivery men brought out a big square item and crab-walked it to the door.

"Need a proper kitchen stove to cook all those jams, right, Melinda?" said Bill.

"Your shortbread was marvelous already," said Ducky. "Imagine how good it will be with a reliable oven."

"Even if you don't stay permanently," added Bill, hastily, seeing Austin's face. "Whoever takes over needs proper equipment. I'm investing in the business. Nothing more."

Then Melinda saw the last item.

"That's not a business expense," she said. She stood up and carefully handed Abel to Ducky.

She looked into the main room, then stepped off the porch. She hadn't even noticed it was gone, with all the activity.

"We hope you like it," said Ducky, brushing her lips against Abel's downy head. "We tried to match everything to the original."

"No strings attached," said Bill, gruffly.

He lifted a corner of the protective packaging. It was the purple fainting couch. Reupholstered, refinished, solid, fresh, beautiful.

"Hera and I kind of messed up the original fabric," said Leda, cheerfully.

Mel touched it. The wood was warm, as if it was alive.

"For me?" she said.

"We asked Austin what we could do that would be special," said Ducky.

"Do you like it?" asked Austin. "I know you talked about refinishing it yourself."

Melinda laughed, and tears filled her eyes.

"I love it! This is so thoughtful. I can't believe it!"

"Then let's get it inside where it belongs." Bill gestured to the workmen and within moments it was sitting in pride of place.

Melinda sat down. Then she beckoned Austin. Ducky put Abel into her arms.

"There's your picture," she said, nodding with satisfaction.

She aimed her phone at them and snapped several quick

shots.

"Hey, wait," called Melinda to the delivery driver. She gave him Austin's phone. "We need another picture."

She stood Bill, Ducky and Delores behind the couch. With Austin on one side of her, Leda and Hera on the other, and her darling Abel in her arms, it was the perfect picture.

"Now," said Melinda. "No one smile."

"What?" said Delores.

"No smiling!" said Melinda. "Look stern, everyone."

"Got it," said the driver.

Austin looked at the shot. "Perfect. Okay, everyone can smile again."

He kissed her. "Our American Gothic."

"Sweet Montana Farms style." And she kissed him back.

The End

About the Authors

USA Today, and New York Times bestselling author
Jane Porter has been a finalist for the prestigious RITA award
five times, has over 12 million copies in print. Jane's novel,
Flirting With Forty, picked by Redbook as its Red Hot Summer
Read, went back for seven printings in six weeks before being
made into a Lifetime movie starring Heather Locklear.
September 2012 brought the release of *The Good Woman*, the
first of her Brennan Sisters trilogy, followed in February 2013 by
The Good Daughter, and book three in the series, *The Good Wife*,
released in September. A mother of three sons, Jane holds an MA
in Writing from the University of San Francisco and makes her
home in sunny San Clemente, CA with her surfer husband.

For more on Jane's books, visit her website at JanePorter.com

USA Today bestselling author **Megan Crane** writes women's fiction, chick lit, work-for-hire YA, and a lot of Harlequin Presents as Caitlin Crews. She also teaches creative writing classes both online at mediabistro.com and at UCLA Extension's prestigious Writers' Program, where she finally utilizes the MA and PhD in English Literature she received from the University of York in York, England. She currently lives in California, with her animator/comic-book artist husband and their menagerie of ridiculous animals.

For more on Megan's books, visit her at MeganCrane.com or CaitlinCrews.com

Born under a Scorpio moon, raised in a little house on the prairie, **Roxanne Snopek** said "as you wish" to her Alpha Farm Boy and followed him to the mountain air and ocean breezes of British Columbia. There, while healing creatures great and small and raising three warrior-princesses, they found their real-life happily-ever-after. After also establishing a successful freelance and non-fiction career, Roxanne began writing what she most loved to read: romance. Her small-town stories quickly became fan favorites; print editions of her latest series were recently launched in France.

Roxanne's personal heroine's journey contains many on-going but basic lessons: introversion isn't fatal; creativity is essential; and you always get lost coming out of the Vancouver airport. Accept it. Oh, and never, ever leave home without a book.

For more on Roxanne's books, visit her at RoxanneSnopek.ca

Thank you for reading

A Very Marietta Christmas

If you enjoyed this book, you can find more from all our great authors at TulePublishing.com, or from your favorite online retailer.

TULE
PUBLISHING

36653023R00255

Made in the USA
Charleston, SC
09 December 2014